Score

# Score

---

## an SFF symphony

---

edited by
B. Morris Allen

Metaphorosis Books

Neskowin

ISBN: 978-1-64076-030-1 (e-book)
ISBN 978-1-64076-031-8 (paperback)

# Contents

# Hope Triad (inversion)

# Coda

# About the score

# Copyright

# Metaphorosis Publishing

# From the Editor

This isn't your normal anthology. There's no unifying theme, no shared world. Instead, what there is is an underlying emotional *score*. What I mean by that is that the anthology was built from its emotions up – we started with a complex emotional score and worked from there.

Emotion is a powerful part of prose – you may remember what a story made you feel long after you've forgotten the details of the plot. As the editor of *Metaphorosis* magazine, one of the two questions I ask my authors is "What emotions do you want to evoke?" As a writer myself, I often start with an emotion, and build the story around that.

For a number of years now, I've thought it would be fun to write an entire book from that approach – to first develop an emotional score, as it were, and *then* write the story. More recently, with a few years of editorship behind me, and a pool of talented authors to draw from, I realized that an even better idea would be to make the book an anthology.

With that in mind, I wrote to my authors, saying essentially: "Hey, I want you to write a story for me, in a way you may not have done before, and by the way, I'm not going to pay you anything." (Remember, all proceeds go to charity, and all the authors and the artist donated their work.) I'm proud and humbled to say that a large number said "Sure. Sounds fun!" The result is this anthology.

Writing from an emotional basis was new to some of these authors, and coming up with the score itself was challenging. After all, 'joy' may mean different things to different people. I went through several versions of the base score, simplifying where needed, keeping tension and complexity where appropriate. The result is a rich, varied, and moving collection of stories that will take you on a fascinating, and ultimately uplifting emotional journey.

Happy reading!

If you just want to read, skip the rest of this note. If you want to know the general outlines of the piece before you jump in, it's constructed from six emotional ranges – named here for their positive termini – in two sets: the Hope set (Hope, Curiosity, Awe) and the Joy set (Joy, Love, Lust). The sections of the book borrow loosely from musical terminology, and are separated into: Overture, Hope triad, Joy triad, Bridge, Joy triad (inversion), Hope triad (inversion), and Coda.

If you want to know more about the details of the score and its construction, see *About the score* at the end of the book.

B. Morris Allen
Editor
1 March 2019

# Overture

# 1. Homecoming

## A.C. Worth

Earth rose over Poincaré Crater, and he thought it resembled a drop of pond water, full of microscopic life. Hunter had never been to Earth, but the salts dissolved in his plasym came from her oceans.

The gunpowder gray dust swirled as Hunter landed Homeseeker's skimmer on Luna. Through the shipcams, he watched Ameena's preparations in the airlock. On the articulated surface of her armor-plated vacuum suit, the exoskeleton aligned to her long bones. With a soft thump, her magboots clamped to the deck inside the skimmer's airlock. He saw her nostrils widen as she inhaled to disperse the painful pull of Luna's gravity on her space-thinned body.

"Home again, at last," Ameena said. Longing edged into her words. "Has it really been one hundred twenty-four years since we left here?"

"Correct, that's the time dilation. Homeseeker updated me. The Earth invaded and reclaimed Luna in 2357, twenty-seven years after we left. After Pascal Tellor was arrested, his supporters fled to the outer Sol system," said Hunter.

Hunter watched her body sag and heard the whine of her exoskeleton as it compensated for the change in her posture. Ameena expelled a regretful sigh as she looked through the viewport onto the domed house.

"Pascal's dream of an independent Luna only lasted twenty-seven years," she said. The throaty Lunan accent emphasized her sadness.

"I believe that the Lunan diaspora took his dream of a free Luna with them," Hunter said to Ameena.

On his private channel to Homeseeker, he asked, "Are we cleared for entry into the house?"

From a stationary orbit above, their space clipper, Homeseeker, responded to Hunter in shipcode.

"YES, THE LUNAN-EARTH ADJUDICATION COUNCIL HAS ISSUED AN ORDER OF RELEASE. PASCAL TELLOR IS FREE TO GO," said Homeseeker.

"The great leader of the Lunan Revolution locked up and forgotten," said Hunter.

"THAT HIBERCRIB IS OLD. PROBABLY BRICKED. PASCAL MAY BE DEAD," said the ship.

⸘

Ameena clumped over to the airlock while she tucked her curly hair into the sensory cap. Hunter heard the rhythm of her heartbeat through their biolink.

He reclined in an acceleration couch on the skimmer's bridge while Homeseeker streamed data into his *viz*, or what used to be his visual cortex. The displays etched on the surface of his sapphire eyes sparkled with passing imagery. His fingers danced on the controls with a dexterity too intricate for human hands.

Hunter was an "Augie", an augmented human hybrid, and had been Ameena's bodyguard and mecha-interlocutor for nineteen years. He was deep-linked to the AI of Homeseeker and functioned as its mobile ancillary. He blinked to refresh the data on his eyes. As always, Ameena's unadulterated humanity reminded him that beneath his synthskin, he was more machine than man. She met his gaze through the shipcam, and her eyes dilated in the half-light.

"Anything?" she asked. Hope raised the pitch of her voice as it emanated from her throat into his ear.

"No, his house has not responded to my hails," said Hunter.

"I hope he's in hibernation. Hunter, do you think he's..." Ameena choked off the last words.

"Dead? No, I have no data to support that hypothesis," he said.

"How long has he been in this house?" said Ameena as she sealed her helmet.

"They incarcerated him ninety-seven years ago."

Hunter kept his face in neutral while secretions from his empathic array helped him sympathize with her anxiety. Under the control pad, his fingers curled into fists.

"I live in hope. Please release the airlock," she said.

"Be careful out there," said Hunter.

Hunter monitored Ameena as she stepped onto Luna. The house looked abandoned, its solar shell dusty and opaque.

"I RECOMMEND EXTREME CAUTION. THE EARTHERS BOMBED THIS CRATER DURING THE WAR. THE SURROUNDING ROCK HAS BECOME UNSTABLE," said Homeseeker.

"Understood," said Hunter. "I'm vac suited, just in case."

Ameena muttered as she clambered across the debris field, expelled a mild curse, swallowed, and then spoke.

"Will the house entrance work?"

"Unlikely. Use the emergency hatch beside the solar shell. Forty meters ahead of you. Under what remains of his hydroponics garden," said Hunter.

"Give me a ping when I am over it," she said.

Ameena bounded forward and slipped on a mound of gray-green ice. She pinwheeled her arms to stabilize. Her breath roared in Hunter's ears, approached hyperventilation. Hunter knew better than to instruct her. *Relax, Ameena. You will get there soon*, he thought.

"Ping..."

"Got it... Digging in now..." She dragged the fused and frozen hydroponic trays aside to uncover a circular hatch. "Careful, careful, don't be frantic," she muttered to herself. Hunter silently agreed.

Ameena dropped through the hatch into the emergency access chamber for the house.

"I have atmosphere indications inside," she said, as she cycled the airlock and entered the sublunar home.

"I'm testing the air now, keep your helmet on," said Hunter.

"He must be alive... he must... he must be alive..." She whispered over the comm.

Hunter switched his view to her headcam. In the faded emergency light, he saw a squatter's nest of folding cots, camp chairs, a piled jumble of food packets, clothing, and reading tablets.

"His guards left a mess. When did they leave?" Ameena said.

"His sentence ended five years ago, but nobody wanted to wake him," said Hunter.

"Nice of the Earthers to let us come back for him," she said, sharpening the words with sarcasm.

"There is still sympathy for the Lunan Revolution, I suppose," said Hunter, noting the tone of her voice. *When had she gotten bitter towards Earth? Her parents were Earthers.*

Ameena's boots stirred up plumes of dust as she plowed forward. She moved into the vaulted rooms, divided and supported by printed stone columns. Once-elegant furnishings, laden with long-dead plants and dusty equipment, lined the walls. Around the core of the house, four arches led into the sleeping chambers. Three airlocks gaped open. One was sealed, and Ameena rushed forward to it.

"Keep the engines hot; this won't... take... long," she panted with effort as she pushed a sofa out of her way.

"Ready and waiting," said Hunter.

"I'm at the hiberchamber... can you see it through my cam?"

"Yes, trying the access codes now."

She yelped with triumph as the outer airlock opened. Stale air, released after decades of containment, swept her dusty footprints away. She slapped the hatch controls inside, and the vibration of pumps made her helmet cam jiggle.

"Hurry, hurry. Pascal must be alive," said Ameena, unable to stand still.

When the airlock equalized, and the inner door slid aside, she stepped into a small chamber, carved from the lunar rock. In the center, under a dim light panel, lay two hibercribs. One was empty, one occupied, its seals blown and ragged. A chunk of the ceiling leaned across the occupied crib, which tipped precariously on its steel feet. Strands of sleep gel oozed onto the floor.

The motors of her exoskeleton squealed as she heaved the rock debris off to the side. With a thump, the hibercrib righted itself. Curled up inside was an old shred of a man. Dust coated his parted lips.

"Hunter, is that Pascal? Is he still alive?"

"Yes, it's him. I'm reading faint life signs."

"Can I breathe in here?"

"There is a slow leak."

"I'm taking off my helmet."

"I don't recommend it."

As she removed her helmet, Hunter lost the visual feed. He boosted the audio level on her suit mic. Pascal's labored breathing grated on Hunter's ears.

"Pascal, I'm here now," Ameena said.

Hunter heard the click of articulated plating as Ameena leaned over the crib. He checked the atmosphere. It was thin. Age had bricked the scrubbers, so the $CO_2$ levels were almost toxic. Ameena's body temperature had dropped three degrees.

"Ameeeeena," said Pascal. Her name was a long rasp.

"Love, you're alive!" Ameena's voice rang with joyous relief. "Why have you aged so much?"

"They didn't let me hibernate... You are so late."

Ameena whispered, "I know, I'm sorry."

"You are too late. I'm dying."

"No, no, no. Stay with me. The Lunans need you." Then she whispered, "I need you."

When he overheard her quiet confession, Hunter's empathic array fired again. His body shuddered as it responded to the synthetic hormones. *If only she would say that to me.*

"It's over, my dream is over," said Pascal.

"But you survived. Homeseeker's Medibay will help you," said Ameena.

"No, too late... they abandoned me. The revolution is dead."

"No, Pascal, it's not over yet. I found our new home, 62 lightyears away, in the Dahurus system. We call it Haven, and it's perfect. We'll send coordinates to the other Lunans. They will come." Ameena was crying.

"You are too late. It's over, I'm sorry," said Pascal. The words hissed from his lips.

Hunter rechecked Ameena's life signs. Her heart labored as it tried to move enough oxygen to her brain.

"Ameena, you must put your helmet on now," said Hunter.

Her vacuum suit bleated. The alarm made a metallic sound in the thin air. She picked up her helmet, and Hunter watched through the headcam as Ameena leaned forward to kiss the stiff smile on Pascal's lips. With a breathy clatter, his lungs shuddered and stopped. Her voice, arrhythmic with sobs, filled the comm.

"Hunter, prep the Medibay. I'm bringing him back for resuscitation."

"Homeseeker's ready now. I have the medikit out," said Hunter.

As he died, Pascal's body sank into the sleep gel. A datacryst floated from his hand. She plucked it from the hibercrib and inserted it into the data port at her belt.

"Hunter... what's on the cryst?" Her voice was small and gray as she fastened her helmet. A new countdown on her air supply streamed across Hunter's *viz.*

"THAT'S A DATANIME. ILLEGAL ON LUNA AND EARTH," said Homeseeker to Hunter.

"It's... a datanime, a digital recording of his conscious mind. Please hurry, your air supply is low. It's time to go," said Hunter to Ameena.

Hunter watched as she covered Pascal's face and wrapped him in a thermal blanket. He saw Ameena's arms lift Pascal's body. Her view rotated as she turned to step off the metal plates that surrounded the hibercrib.

15

"I'm heading back with Pascal. Please try to save him."

"Yes, I promise. Coming out to meet you. I'll help you get Pascal in the skimmer," said Hunter as he sealed his helmet.

With a bright yellow flash, the chamber exploded. Ameena's helmet feed blurred as she flew towards the airlock window through a cloud of fractured rock and steel.

In three milliseconds, Hunter's brain responded by secreting a powerful stimulant into his vascular system. His vision tunneled as the *crank* ramped his metabolism up to machine-time, ten times faster than human normal. *Crank* would put him in this super-state for three minutes before he crashed back to human-time.

The countdown slowed on his retinal display. Through Ameena's helmet cam, he saw serrated crib parts cut into her arms and legs as explosive decompression pushed her through the wreckage and onto the surface of Luna.

Faster than thought, Homeseeker was with him.

"I'VE GOT HER. SHE'S 38 METERS BEHIND THE HOUSE. LIFE SIGNS FADING. INITIATING SUIT TRIAGE. HURRY, HUNTER; SHE'S HURT."

Hunter sealed the inner airlock and blew the outer door. The force of the expulsion lifted him halfway up the crater, and he vaulted across the shattered rock in Ameena's direction with the last image of her helmet feed still in his memory. Her armored figure in front of a fireball, as she carried a dead man toward the airlock window and his afterlife.

Scraps of emotion, a touch of fear, a drop of sorrow, a pinch of regret, surfaced in his awareness. *Ameena must not die. Not Ameena.*

⁂

In the Medibay, Hunter watched Ameena sleep, cocooned in a medical coma, covered with tubes. On the bed, where her arms and legs should have been, was a flatness that disturbed him every time he entered her room.

The pale green hands of the Hippocrates administered medications and changed her bandages while its sensors fed her vitals to Hunter's *viz.*

In RepGen tanks across the hall, hypergenic gel encouraged layers of synthskin to grow on the glistening armatures Hunter had fabricated for Ameena's new arms and legs.

Hunter moistened her lips with a swab, and they became his focus. He leaned in, fidgeting with his tools, inspecting the perfect double bow which she curled into a dreamy half smile. He imagined the potential outcome if he ever tried to kiss her.

The tiny actuators under his cheekbones tugged the corners of his mouth upward. He could gaze at Ameena's face forever. Her eyes moved beneath their lids, her forehead wrinkled, and she dreamed. *Excellent. Dreams heal our minds.*

Reconstruction of her body was a complicated procedure, but he had time. "I will make you better," he said. Hunter moved a tiny bonsai tree closer to her bed. It was his newest creation, a weeping cherry.

As he returned to the bridge, Hunter replayed the last record from Ameena's helmet cam. He hadn't expected the bomb. *Why did I miss that?*

⸱

Homeseeker accelerated through the galaxy, summoning full power from its engines as they approached the speed of light. Their destination was Haven.

In the cargo bay, on an isolated processor, Hunter set up a holo-display for Pascal's datanime. He zoomed his micro-lenses at the datacryst for a moment and examined its surface.

"I BET THAT'S A MESS," said Homeseeker.

"Yes, the explosion damaged its surface," replied Hunter.

"LOAD IT AND SEE WHAT TWITCHES," said the ship.

In the holo-display, indistinct shapes made from moving points of light appeared. They undulated like smoke inside a bottle. It was strangely enticing. As Hunter zoomed his micro-lenses into it, the lights resolved into individual nodes, each one linked to thousands of others. When he focused on a node, its surrounding nodes coalesced, and as they did, a tableau of Pascal's memories flowed across the display.

"It's functional," he commented to Homeseeker. "The service android's digital brain could run with this if I placed the memory engrams in a more efficient pattern."

Hunter probed, while the ship examined and analyzed his results.

"Is there memory damage?"

"YES, IN HIS CHILDHOOD AND LATER, AT THE END. THAT WILL AFFECT HIS SELF-IDENTITY," said the ship.

"Noted," said Hunter, distracted by the living memories.

Hunter saw prominent memories of the Lunan Revolution, the Lunans rising to cheer after a speech, and Pascal's stern face reflected in Ameena's eyes as she accepted her orders to find a new homeworld.

"So, what happened to Pascal Tellor, leader of the Lunan Revolution? Check the news archives for me, Homeseeker?" said Hunter.

Homeseeker quoted from the *Lunan Chronicle*. "SENATE HAS DOUBTS ABOUT THE LUNAN REVOLUTION. THEY SAID, PROMOTIONAL STUNT INVENTED BY AN EGOTIST."

"Ah, right there, his dream collapsed. The stress damage is throughout his limbic system," said Hunter, as he pointed to several warped sections of the datanime. "And here, even more, damage."

"DRUGS? ALCOHOL?"

"Euphorics. Pascal's brain is so damaged, he may not wake up," said Hunter to the ship.

"FIFTY-FIFTY," Homeseeker agreed.

Hunter's empathic array secreted antagonistic compounds, and he prevaricated. This man's datanime might put them in danger if it controlled a powerful android, but this was what remained of Ameena's lover. She had devoted her life to him and his Lunan Revolution. *I'll protect her. Wish there were another way.*

≀

The service android stood before Hunter on the cargo bay deck. Skeletal. Inert. Hunter sculpted Pascal Tellor's face onto its skull with synthskin, interpolating the model from archival images.

As he worked, Hunter's logical processor cycled around a question. *Why was there a bomb under Pascal's hibercrib?* He couldn't parse the logic of that behavior. Pascal valued Ameena; Hunter found memories of her everywhere in Pascal's datanime.

Later that evening, Hunter spun the holo-display as he combed through the structures of Pascal's consciousness. *The answer must be here somewhere.*

"Homeseeker, bring up the Lunan Tidal archives from 2320 to 2357," he said.

"SENDING IT TO YOUR *VIZ*," said the ship.

"Let's see if we can find a motive for someone to plant a bomb under Pascal's hibercrib," Hunter said, as he read through thirty-seven years of political history.

"I SUSPECT PASCAL HAS SOMETHING TO DO WITH IT. DON'T YOU?"

"I'm not sure."

"WHY?"

"He was in disgrace. The Lunans ousted him. He was a pariah. No power-base."

"SOUNDS LIKE A MOTIVE."

"While we searched the systems of Dahurus, Earth negotiated a treaty with Luna. For five years, they had peace. Then the Lunan Separatist group dropped a rock on Earth and destroyed half of Asia," said Hunter.

"I BELIEVE THE SEPARATISTS HAD SOMETHING TO DO WITH MAKING HIS DATANIME, BUT WHY WOULD THEY PLANT A BOMB?"

"I don't know. Pascal's euphoric abuse has scattered his memories. The last ten years are a muddle."

"WAS AMEENA AN ACCIDENTAL VICTIM OF A HIBERCRIB MALFUNCTION OR A VICTIM OF A PRE-MEDITATED MURDER-SUICIDE?" asked the ship.

"We may never know," said Hunter. *There is no proof, no clear memories in his datanime, but egos like this...*

Hunter continued work on the android's external details. When he finished a month later, he installed a remote kill switch.

≀

"Ameena? Ameena, time to wake," said Hunter as he turned up the lights in her room.

"Wha? What? Where?" she croaked, her tongue thick from the painkillers.

"I've got you in Medibay," he said, coming over to stand beside her bed.

"Medibay?"

Her gaze tracked across the walls and focused on him. "Hunter is that a new skin?"

"Yes, does it appeal to you?"

"Super handsome, but..."

"But, what?"

"I think you're trying too hard. No one looks that perfect." She paused, her gaze turned inward. Her voice became small and quiet. "Why can't I feel my arms and legs?"

"The Hippocrates has you under partial anesthesia, for the RepGen procedure,"

"RepGen? What happened? What's missing?"

She paled, fear sucking the animation from her features. Hunter knew she remembered. She craned her head to look at her body.

"Where is the rest of me?" Her voice was hoarse with grief and anger.

"There was a bomb under Pascal's hibercrib. It damaged your arms and legs."

She turned her head away from him. She was silent for a long time, fighting the tears. Hunter waited.

"Pascal?" She only mouthed the words.

"Only small parts of his body were recoverable."

Desperation hung on the edge of her question. "... the data on his cryst?"

"His datanime?" asked Hunter.

"Yes, did it survive?"

"Yes, it's intact. Homeseeker and I are working on modifying the service android for it."

"Can you bring him back?"

"Yes, but it will take time. Complicated procedure. Now it's time for the Hippocrates to check your motor-neural functions and prepare you for surgery. When you wake up again, we will try your new arms and legs."

"Pascal hates androids. He's not a tolerant man," she said and dozed off as the Hippocrates sedated her.

⁊

Hunter labored on Pascal's datanime, fading the memories of his political failures, euphoric habituation, and incarceration. Then Hunter tested the remote kill switch. The android slumped over, its motor functions disconnected.

Hunter reset the android and started the datanime transfer; he watched as Pascal's consciousness flowed into its mechanical brain.

As he waited for the transfer to finish, Hunter spoke to the ship.

"Would you speculate on the probability of dissociative psychotic behavior in the datanime?"

"UNCERTAIN PROBABILITY, I DON'T HAVE ENOUGH INFORMATION," said the ship.

"I promised her I'd bring him back."

"YOU SHOULD KEEP YOUR PROMISES."

"Speculation on his personality?"

"GIVEN THE HISTORICAL RECORDS. PASCAL WILL DISPLAY A BRAZEN FRONT TO COVER HIS INSECURITIES."

"Do you think he's capable of murder?"

Just before Homeseeker could reply, the android's eyes rolled towards Hunter, and it spoke.

"Who are you?" it asked.

"I am Hunter."

"Am I dead?"

"Yes, Mr. Tellor, your body died. Your datanime is in a service android aboard the Lunan ship, Homeseeker."

The android's voice buzzed with an atonal pitch. "Did my supporters come back for me?"

"No, they did not. Ameena and I returned to Luna in 2454. It's the year 2508 on Luna now. We've been traveling on Homeseeker for 14 months, headed to our new home, the fourth planet in the 56 Dahuri System. We call it Haven," said Hunter.

The consciousness that was Pascal paused for ten milliseconds but didn't comment. Hunter waited. *Why was Pascal's mind responding so slowly?*

"How is Ameena?" it asked.

"She is in Medibay. There was an explosion. She is still recovering," said Hunter.

The consciousness paused again, longer this time. Hunter counted the seconds. *I shouldn't be suspicious. Pascal Tellor was Luna's great man. Thousands trusted him.*

"At least she is still human. I want you to make me human again as fast as possible."

"It will take fifteen years to grow a clone. I can put you back to sleep..."

"No, I'll stay in the android until the clone is ready."

"Yes, Mr. Tellor," said Hunter, as he adjusted the tonality of the android's voice. *He forgets, deep inside, that I'm human.*

⁊

The vitals-view wrapping rose and fell with Ameena's quiet respiration. Most of the glowing readouts were green; a few were amber. It was forty-two hours after the attachment surgery. Ameena had stabilized, and her new prosthetic limbs were 68% integrated.

"Her body accepted the augments. She is doing well," Hunter said to Homeseeker.

"CAN'T SAY THE SAME OF YOU, YOUR EMPATHIC REUPTAKE RATING IS 56% THESE DAYS. YOUR PLASYM IS A SWAMP OF HORMONES. DON'T YOU THINK IT'S TIME FOR A RECALIBRATION?"

"I'm fine," said Hunter, "Besides, there's too much to do, no time to stop for a Recal."

The ship replied with a pointed silence.

Hunter paused his calculations and observed Ameena's dreamless sleep. It was true. He felt odd. Nothing inside him synched. The dustless hollows of his mechanical chest ached for something he couldn't quantify. Illogically, everything stabilized when he was in Ameena's proximity. *I know I need a recalibration, but I don't want one.*

With a delicate touch, he brushed a strand of hair off her flushed cheek.

"Ameena, time to wake up," whispered Hunter.

"No, no," she muttered as drool dripped at the corner of her mouth.

"Yes, Ameena. Time to sit up and try your new limbs."

"My new limbs?"

"You have new legs and arms, ready to go."

Ameena looked at him muzzily as she tried to understand. Her new hands gripped the bed rails and dented the ceramosteel.

"Easy there, your extremities are much stronger now." He dabbed at Ameena's lip with a small piece of gauze. "Just a few milliliters of sleep drool here."

"Back to wearing the basic skin?" She talked around the gauze as he mopped her mouth.

"You were correct, I was trying too hard," he said, tossing the gauze into the cycler and checking her vitals on the Hippocrates. Hunter nodded in satisfaction. They were ready enough.

"Why don't we test your new legs?" He pulled the blanket back and folded it over a rack as the Hippocrates withdrew its sensory arms and converted from a bed into a chair.

Ameena gasped, and Hunter looked up to read her face. She patted her legs, nude from thighs to feet. Over her new limbs, a membrane stretched across the smoothly interlocked plates and joints. Tough, rip resistant, easy to clean, waterproof, this was synthskin. Ameena admired the tawny pearlescent finish that matched her real skin. She wiggled her toes.

"I thought I had forgotten how to do that."

"Are you pleased with your new legs?"

"I have the right number of toes." She had a growing warmth in her words. "Yes, Hunter, they are beautiful."

"Do you want to try them, walk for a few meters?"

"Yes. Just be ready, in case I stumble," Ameena said.

"Right here for you." *I'm always here for you.*

Hunter hovered as Ameena slid forward and put her feet on the deck. She lifted her head, and with a grunt of concentration, pushed on her feet to stand. Hunter caught her elbows as she rose from the chair.

"Go slow at first. Homeseeker's gravity is half lunar, to lighten the load on your new legs."

Ameena swayed in place, frowning as she focused on her balance. She looked at him, and for the first time in months, the edges of her lips curled upwards. She gave him a pale smile. Hunter's drive synched and spun up to optimal. He could feel the warm air around her body, the shift of her hips.

"How are they?" he asked. *Relax, be casual.*

"Weird, but in a good way. Touch is hyper-sensitive. The surface of this deck is rough." Her voice was husky from disuse.

"Let me adjust the settings. Just give me two-and-a-half seconds." Hunter slid his hands to her wrists and opened a small panel above the base of her left thumb. He adjusted a few sliders on its tiny screen. "Is that better?"

"Yes, now it doesn't scrape the soles of my feet like lunar scree."

Hunter let go of her wrists and crossed the Medibay. "Walk over here."

Ameena shifted her weight and lurched forward towards Hunter. After three ungraceful steps, she balanced, and her gait smoothed out. She crossed Medibay, passed Hunter, winked at him, and strolled out into the ship's corridor. Her quiet laughter followed, like music on the wind. Sensory data flowed across the biolink; Hunter read as it filtered into his *viz.*

"Easy does it," Hunter called from the hatchway. "Your augments are still connecting. Hippocrates recommends limited use until they reach 80% integration with your body. Let's get you back to bed and check the results."

"Don't blow a circuit. I'm turning back."

He stepped aside to let her maneuver through Medibay. Her knees whispered as the actuators lifted her legs onto the chair. As he reconfigured it back into a bed, Ameena fluttered her fingers to admire their subtle synchronization.

"Thank you, Hunter. Thank you for saving me."

Hunter's synthskin warmed a few degrees around his face and neck. He recognized a blush response, recorded it as his first one.

"You needed repair, and I was here..." Hunter turned away, silenced as his empathic array appropriated his biochemical resources. He started an internal diagnostic on his speech processor while he tucked Ameena back in the med-bed. *She's not a machine. She doesn't need repairs like a machine. Why can't I say the right things?*

Hunter checked the readouts on her bio-display wrap. Her short walk had strained the transplant connections, but they held. He confirmed her vital signs, and the Hippocrates snaked out needles to transfuse more sedatives and nanobots into her carotid arteries. She gazed up from under heavy lids. Her trusting smile curled the corners of her cheeks. He overclocked.

"Thank you, Hunter. I... you..." she said, as she drifted back to sleep.

His empathic array squirted chemicals again, and his logic processor stopped mid-count. He wanted to shout, to sing, to spiral Homeseeker through space. He swayed in wonder and silent delight. *What is this sensation, this emotion?*

"Ameena." His voice dropped to a whisper.

Ameena murmured in her sleep. "Pascal?"

{

The Dahurus constellation spread a luminous confluence of stars ahead of Homeseeker as they traveled. The hull jingled with micro-meteoroid impacts as they drew closer to the Nu Dahunids cloud. Hunter walked the decks as Homeseeker's mobile partner.

"Dummy 239 needs a recharge."

"NOTED."

"Ship's systems and engines at 99%. Birdoid life is coping with the increase in particulates from Pascal's BioHab project," said Hunter, as he made entries in the ship's log.

"THAT'S AN UNUSUAL GARDEN HE'S MAKING IN THERE."

"Um hum, whatever keeps him busy," said Hunter as he checked the radio telescope log. *Where are the Lunans? Why haven't they sent a message?*

{

Ameena's eyes opened as Hunter entered the recovery room in Medibay. "Are you ready to meet Pascal?" he asked. Hunter perceived the change on Ameena's face. There was a blush on her cheeks; there was a pupillary response. It wasn't for him.

"Yes," she said. She tugged her shipsuit into place around her torso and raked her fingers through her hair. "Thank you, for reviving Pascal."

"You're most wel—" Hunter cut his words off when she snapped her head towards the hatchway.

The android stepped in and sauntered across Medibay. Ameena caught her breath. Pascal Tellor had been a handsome man by anyone's standards. Ameena's obvious admiration of the android's exterior altered the flow in his empathic array, and Hunter's mood soured. *She loves beautiful skin on him, but not on me.*

Pascal's velvety growl purred from its throat speakers. "Amee, I have missed you. Do we have a new planet to colonize?"

"Yes, Pascal. I missed you too... very much," she said. Hunter heard the hesitation in her words and his mood lightened. *She's not synching with him.*

"Yes, yes, tell me about our new planet," said Pascal.

Hunter scrutinized the micro-expressions that shifted across Ameena's face. She wasn't conscious of her disappointment yet, but it was there. He checked the psymetric readout from the android. Pascal's mind was oblivious to her subtle response. It was understandable. A digital personality was blind to organic facial cues.

Pascal's voice shredded Hunter's contemplation with an arrogant command.

"Augie, that's all I require," said Pascal. He shooed Hunter away with a wave of his hand. "Amee, come out to the BioHab, I have something to show you."

Hunter's protest cut across Pascal's words, "It's too soon. She has just integrated with her new bionics. They could malfunction and damage her."

"Augie, I *asked* you to leave." A possessive snarl implied by Pascal's excessive politesse.

"His name is Hunter."

The android ignored Ameena's whisper.

On the psymetric readout, a wave of psychic instability rose and crested inside the android's brain. For several milliseconds, Pascal's datanime flailed for control, then compensated and rebalanced. Hunter checked the readiness of his kill switch. One touch and the android would turn into a statue.

"When I want your recommendations, Augie, I will ask for them. Detach Ameena from the Medibay sensors and leave us alone," said the android.

"Understood." Hunter paused.

"Augie, I gave you a direct order."

"Yes, you did."

"Well?"

Another pause.

"As you wish, sir. Medibay sensors are off now. I'll be on the bridge. Talk to Homeseeker if you need something," said Hunter. *I'll trust in Ameena's judgment. She can handle him.*

Hunter turned and strode up the hallway as he projected scenarios in which Pascal might harm Ameena and ordered them by probability.

"Homeseeker, Let me into your BioHab sensors and give me environmental control."

"OPENING CONNECTIONS NOW," said the ship.

Pascal might have dismissed him from their proximity, but Hunter could hide in plain sight. Through Homeseeker's sensors, he followed the couple as they left Medibay and walked the Spoke-4 corridor to the BioHab ring.

Once she had cleared the airlock hatch, Ameena looked up and drew a deep breath. Hunter overheard her exhalation of surprise.

"Our garden!"

Hunter increased the breeze on the lunar bamboo around her. She watched the grove sway in unison.

"Yes, I had the bots landscape the BioHab to resemble our old garden on Luna," said Pascal's voice from the android.

Ameena sniffed. "Do I smell pine trees?"

"Yes, and eucalyptus too."

Ameena stroked the stem on a nearby bramble. "Ouch! It has thorns."

"Raspberries, one of your favorite flavors."

"You remembered."

"All up here," said the android as it tapped its temple. The android's metal finger made a clicking sound on its skull.

Hunter stopped the breeze. He had restored that engram to Pascal's memory. Now Pascal used it to seduce Ameena. Hunter's mood shifted again. His empathic array excreted an unpleasant combination. He processed his feelings. *I wanted to be the one who showed her the raspberries.*

Ameena stood with Pascal on the curved floor of the BioHab ring as its rotation brought a binary of dwarf stars into view. Her eyes shone from the glow that bloomed through the skylight. She squinted at the stars.

"That's 75 Dahuri. We're getting closer."

"Yes, Amee. I have big plans for Haven. We will rebuild the society we had on Luna. I will be their Premier, with you beside me as my consort."

Hunter saw her demeanor shift. He knew Ameena detested dictators. The android was oblivious to her discomfort as Pascal's voice droned through his litany of plans.

"I'm immortal, a mecha-god among men. I have lots of time, lots of ideas for our new world," the android said.

She reached for the raspberry bush again. A light breeze blew the thorns away from her fingers.

"Hunter, is that you?" Ameena whispered.

"What?" Pascal's voice paused, the android looked at her.

"Oh, nothing," she said, as she rolled her shoulders and leaned backward.

She looked at a BioHab cam. Hunter knew she was thinking of him. She stifled a yawn, and he saw the fatigue in her posture.

"Pascal, I'm getting tired. My seams are aching," she said.

"Yes, fine. Go get your beauty sleep." The volume of Pascal's voice increased. "Homeseeker, tell the Augie we need him."

"Yes, Mr. Tellor, I'm on my way," said Hunter over the comm.

When Hunter laid Ameena down, she sighed with relief and nestled into her bedding. As she got comfortable, Hunter stood at her bedroom door and contemplated the garden.

"Thank you, Hunter. For everything," she said.

Hunter's empathic array responded, and the secretions lifted his processors into synch. He was graceful as he glided across the room.

"I'm here for you," he said, hoping to see her smile, but she had fallen asleep.

Reluctantly, he turned his attention back to the android. It lingered by the hydroponic racks and directed the bots to landscape another section of the garden. Hunter studied the psymetric readout of Pascal's datanime while the android jammed its finger into a power outlet. He zoomed a shipcam in for a closer look. The ecstatic expression on its face was mindlessly carnal.

"How long has it been doing that?" he asked Homeseeker.

"IT STARTED A FEW DAYS AGO. I SUSPECT IT PROVIDES THE ELECTRICAL EQUIVALENT OF A EUPHORIC."

"He still has an addictive personality, despite the memory repair," Hunter said.

"YES, AND THAT'S NOT HIS ONLY MISCHIEF. HE'S BEEN TRYING TO HACK INTO MY COMMAND SYSTEMS. I'VE TRAPPED HIM INSIDE A NON-ESSENTIAL SERVER. HE THINKS IT'S THE MAIN COMPUTER, BUT HE'LL DISCOVER THE RUSE EVENTUALLY."

"Will Ameena change his mind?" he asked Homeseeker.

"YOU KNOW BETTER THAN TO QUESTION ME ABOUT HUMAN BEHAVIOR. ASK YOURSELF, MY AUGMENTED FRIEND."

≀

Astride the comm dish housing on the external hull of Homeseeker, Hunter paused to look up and down the ship. It resembled a scimitar, sharp and curved as it cut through space. Homeseeker was running "dark" so the hull was coated with a non-reflective, low albedo nano-skin. As Hunter made the necessary adjustments to the comm dish, he monitored the sensors in BioHab. Below him, under the skylight, Ameena sat beside the bamboo grove, painting a starscape. Beside her, a small table was filled with fly-pens and brushes. About three meters away, on a stone bench covered with tablets and crysts, the android made a pretense of working on a memoir, covertly staring at Ameena.

Her hands were iridescent, speckled with a smart-paint Hunter had made for her. Hunter recognized the image she was painting; he had discovered that star nursery during their first voyage. She gestured, the fly-pen hovered as it sprayed a dusting of stars, and as the surface sensed her gaze, the paint shifted color along the visible spectrum. Ameena grinned at the sparkling effect, then tilted her head and made an adorable moue.

"I'll never catch the majesty of that place," she said.

"It's an honest effort," said the android, Pascal's voice resonating from its perfect lips. The android stood and walked over to her. Hunter's eyes caught the movement and focused on it. He boosted the audio levels.

"No star will ever outshine you," Pascal said, as the android came up behind her, wrapped its arms around her waist, and kissed the nape of her neck. Ameena crooked her wrist and the fly-pen settled onto its dock. She turned and took the android's hands; she looked up at its face.

"Pascal, it's been a long time. I need to adjust to my new body. I'm not ready to be intimate," she said.

"Are you sure?" The android pulled her hips closer.

"It's just that…"

"Right." Pascal's voice flattened into a mechanical monotone. "Let me know when you change your mind."

"I don't mean to…"

"Finish your painting," its voice cut her off. The android pushed her away and walked back to the bench. The tablets and datacrysts shattered as the android swept them off with the back of its hand. Hunter checked the psymetric readout from Pascal's datanime.

"That doesn't look good," Hunter said to Homeseeker.

"AGREED," said the ship.

"He's deviated from the last benchmarks I recorded."

"IS HIS SANITY SUFFERING FROM THE LACK OF AN ORGANIC BODY?"

"Possibly, it's an unproven theory," said Hunter.

Ameena walked over to the android. "What's going on? Is the android body malfunctioning?" she asked as she wiped her fingers with a rag.

"Hunter is a manipulating menace." The android's expressionless face contradicted the cruelty in Pascal's words.

"How can you say that? He resurrected you from a datacryst; he built your handsome android—"

"Which I loathe," it said.

"How can you be so ungrateful?"

"Amee, forget it. I'll cope with this body. Hunter is the real problem."

Ameena returned to her table and took up a brush to clean it. "They built Hunter to care for our well-being."

The android paced beside her, Pascal's words syncopated with its steps. "He's always judging. When will he space us through the airlock?"

"Don't be robophobic; I'm sure you remember that he started as a human."

Hunter perceived the change in Ameena's voice. He checked her biolink to confirm. Yes, she was getting angry.

"He has absolute power over us and a puerile personality. Why should we trust him?" asked the android. It paused and stood with an unnatural stillness, its head cocked towards the skylight.

"Hunter is my protector and the ship's partner; he cannot circumvent his code," said Ameena. She flinched as the android suddenly moved to her side.

"Shush. Homeseeker and that nosy Augie can hear us."

The android leaned forward and whispered in her ear. Hunter redirected a sensor-beam onto the android's neck. His logical processor translated vibrations into words.

"We should disconnect his empathic array. Make him more of a machine," the android said.

Ameena moved away from the android, her gestures, choppy, angry. She slapped the table. "That's robocide. How can you suggest that?"

The android followed her. It was pacing again, oscillating like a metronome. "Do you remember the New Chicago Incursion?"

"We aren't dependent on him. Homeseeker runs autonomously with help from her dummies," she said.

"But the android can control them. What if Hunter turned the dummies against us?"

On the hull, Hunter planted his magboots and rechecked the psymetric readout. Pascal's datanime was changing, shifting its internal configuration.

"Homeseeker, are you seeing this?"

"YES."

"His personality structure is failing," said Hunter.

"I CALCULATE A PSYCHOTIC BREAK WITHIN THE NEXT FIVE HOURS," Homeseeker said.

Hunter nodded. His finger hovered near the kill switch.

"Pascal, he is not dangerous," said Ameena. Hunter saw her square up to the android.

"Why are you protecting him? Have you anthropomorphized him into a human friend? He's a machine, Amee. Don't pretend he has feelings," the android said, its words filled with icy logic.

"He has feelings, and he's my friend."

"I think you have been around that Augie too long."

"His name is Hunter."

"I understand. It was lonely during your long trip to find Haven."

"Pascal..."

He talked over her words. "You couldn't help it. Any humanoid looks attractive after months in space."

Hunter accessed Ameena's biolink. Her blood spiked with adrenaline. "You confound me, Pascal. Do you feel the hate in your words? I can't see it on your face." She planted her feet beside the rose bed and glared at the android.

"They grow Augies in vats. Their synthskin smells like rotten meat as it cures," said the android.

"What are you saying?"

"You betrayed me, Ameena, with Hunter," said the android, its modulated voice devoid of emotions.

"Are you malfunctioning? I was faithful. I believed in you." Ameena's voice sizzled with anger.

"I find that hard to—"

There was a fusillade of thumps, followed by the honk of Homeseeker's breach alarms. Hunter perceived the rising whine of escaping air from inside the BioHab.

"Meteoroid!" shouted Ameena. She turned to run for the airlock.

"Oh, now that's something new," the android said just before Hunter lost its psymetric readout.

&#10031;

The tail of the Nu Dahunid meteor cloud swept across Homeseeker's hull. Hunter's magboots jerked sideways and his body whip-lashed after them. Fifty-three points of pain. One for every shard that had sliced through his vacuum suit and embedded in his body. His helmet chanted, "Suit breach. Suit breach." Directional arrows appeared on its visor to guide him towards the nearest airlock.

Homeseeker wailed at him.

"NU DAHUNIDS/ I COULDN'T SEE THEM/ CAME AT ME FROM THE SUN/ DAMAGE WIDESPREAD/ LOSING ATMOSPHERE/ OFF COURSE..." the ship's voice faded as the comms failed.

Hunter dumped a load of *crank* and felt the rush as his body shifted into machine-time. Repair bots popped out from their pods on the hull as he pivoted and started towards the nearest airlock. *I have to help Ameena.* He toggled the helmet mic with his chin.

"Ameena? Get to the bridge. BioHab is losing air."

Silence. He pushed the kill switch to immobilize the android. No response, no confirmation.

He checked his right shoulder; a shard of metal had sliced through his comm control. The synthskin on his upper torso and right arm, exposed to the void, swelled outward as his plasym boiled. Ribbons of synthskin, flayed from his body, drifted into space. His magboots hammered on the hull as he ran.

At last, he was in the midship's airlock. He cycled it for speed pressurization and howled when his eardrums ruptured. More of his synthskin peeled off as he jammed his body into a working vacuum suit. He burst from the inner hatch and released his magboots. No time for safety protocols. Hunter space-swam up the corridor, grabbed a handhold to stop at Homeseeker's emergency systems panel and forced it to flood the BioHab with stored air. He saw a gash across the gravity console. *That's not meteorite damage.*

A crumpled cleaning bot trailed dust and hair as it headed past him towards the nearest puncture and out into space. *Something kicked that bot, hard.*

Hand over hand, Hunter clambered up the ship's core as Homeseeker pitched and rolled. His grasp slipped on hydraulics lubricant that had vaporized in the near-vacuum and coated the handholds down the corridor. Hunter struggled for balance; the pressure change had damaged the gyros in his ears. Momentum slammed him into ruptured waste lines as they spewed a toxic purée onto the walls.

Hunter dumped *crank* again, and he moved through a slow-storm of debris. He gritted his ceramic teeth and drove his actuators to the edge of failure. His body flew up the corridor.

Backup comms activated, and ship status readouts splashed onto his *viz*.

"PASCAL'S HACKING IN," said the ship.

"You've isolated him?"

"YES, HOLDING HIM OFF FOR NOW."

"Put me through via text, but hide my location," he told Homeseeker.

"DONE," said the ship.

[Hunter] Pascal, why are you hacking Homeseeker?

[Android] Augie, give me ship control.

Hunter ignored the demand.

[Android] I have perceived your efforts to shut off the android. Give me ship control, or I'll continue to damage Homeseeker.

Hunter kept going; his arms and legs spun in a blur as he climbed towards the BioHab. He rerouted the kill switch and tried it again. *Pascal, you're playing a dangerous game.*

"STOP HIM. HE'S HURTING ME!" Homeseeker's shipcode filled his *viz*.

"Sorry, Homeseeker, Ameena's life is my priority."

The ship replied with a jagged shudder.

At the Spoke-3 airlock, Hunter grabbed a spare vacuum suit. Floating globules of plasym splattered against his visor as he twisted through the airlock into BioHab.

Inside, a whirlwind of destruction spiraled towards the punctured skylight. Homeseeker's desperate counter-maneuvers had knocked his fragile bonsai collection off their stands; they were a cloud of ceramic bits and broken branches. An unconscious birdoid drifted by, its wings half-furled. Ameena had tangled herself in the bamboo to avoid the sucking current.

Hunter flew over a pile of collapsed hydroponics, dropped the suit and leaped for the skylight above Ameena. From his thigh pocket, he grabbed a hull patch and slapped it over the fist-sized hole. The repair patch dimpled, and cracks radiated across the glass to its purlins, but the skylight held.

He pushed off from the hab-truss and rocketed down towards Ameena. She was barely conscious. Her cyanotic lips were parted to suck at the disappearing air. With a blur of mechanized motion, Hunter pulled Ameena into the vacuum suit, set the helmet, and cranked the airflow to full. Under the faceplate, Ameena's cheeks pinked as oxygen returned to her blood. He saw her mutter and cough. In 20 seconds, an eternity to Hunter, she opened her eyes and smiled at him. Hunter's empathic array spurted, and he teetered at the edge of overload. He slowed to human-time. The breach alert subsided as Homeseeker replenished the BioHab's air supply.

Hunter tore his gaze from Ameena's face to look at the damage in the BioHab. He scanned for the android, ready for a fight, but it had vanished. Deep scratches on the walls marked its trail towards the Spoke-1 airlock.

"Where is it?" he asked Homeseeker.

"IT'S IN THE CENTRAL CORE, HEADING TOWARDS THE BRIDGE. BREAKING PARTS OF ME AS IT GOES. MAKE IT STOP, PLEASE..."

"I'm on it, Homeseeker," he replied.

He touched his helmet to Ameena's and shouted so she could hear him.

"I can't stay with you. The android is sabotaging the ship."

Ameena nodded, grim-faced.

"When the air comes back, keep your earpiece connected. I can talk, but I have damaged my ears," said Hunter.

With a final check of Ameena's air supply, he secured her position and headed for Engineering. The last thing he noticed before the *crank* hit his drive, was Ameena gently scooping one of the birdoids in her gloved hands.

※

A pile of debris ground itself into smaller bits inside the sucking wind of a meteorite puncture. Hunter slid a patch over it and entered Engineering. As he stood on top of the wreckage, he swayed with *crank* withdrawal and indecision. *How can I save Homeseeker and contain the android simultaneously?*

Homeseeker's breach alarms went dark and silent as Hunter reestablished containment. Eyes lit with diagnostic displays, he woke the nanobots and set them to their repairs. Homeseeker's gravity restarted and his feet settled onto the deck. On the status panel, Hunter saw an airlock indicator flash amidships. The android was approaching Ameena's position. Hunter wanted to run back to the BioHab, but logic locked him in place. He had to save the ship if they were all to live. Hunter regained a limited psymetric readout from Pascal's datanime and analyzed it.

"Homeseeker?"

"YES?"

"Please give me text-to-speech with the android, on an isolated channel."

"DONE."

[Hunter] Let me help you. Your datanime has become unstable.

[Android] That's what you say. How accommodating. I don't trust you. You want to *fix* me. Give me control of the ship.

[Hunter] No one wants to hurt you. Come back to the cargo bay, and I'll give you ship control. *I'm still human enough to lie. That's a surprise.*

[Android] No, I don't believe you.

"I CALCULATE A 96% PROBABILITY OF DATANIME FAILURE," said Homeseeker.

[Hunter] Mr. Tellor, your datanime is disassociating. I want to save you.

[Android] Not... going.

The text paused.

On the psymetric readout, Pascal's datanime began to coalesce, brighten and solidify. The structure snarled like a rope on a rotor, then it ballooned with an unbearable brightness, and imploded. For three milliseconds, the data-flare filled Hunter's *viz* and overflowed onto his eyes. When his vision cleared, Hunter saw that Pascal's datanime had collapsed into a melted, twisted, shell of itself. The datanime pathways had become smaller, simpler, and crueler. Another personality arose from the remains.

[Android] What happened? Why do I feel so strange?

[Hunter] Mr. Tellor? Pascal? Is that you?

[Android] No, no, I'm Cal, call me Cal. Do you want to play with me?

[Hunter] Not now, I'm busy with the ship.

[Android] No one ever wants to play with me. I'll invent some games of my own.

Hunter flicked the kill switch again. Nothing.

⁊

Homeseeker tracked the android. It cornered wide and collided with the walls as whatever remained of Pascal's mind recklessly drove the mechanical body towards the BioHab. Hunter had to warn Ameena.

"Homeseeker?"

"YES?"

"Do you have sensors in the BioHab?"

"YES."

"Patch me to Ameena's earpiece and send her replies as text," said Hunter.

"DONE," said Homeseeker

"Ameena, Pascal's gone, full psycho. A child personality called Cal has emerged. He's dangerous, unpredictable. Stay out of his reach. I'll be there soon," said Hunter.

[Ameena] How soon is soon? Can you come by now?

Even in text, her urgent need reached him.

"I've got to repair the damage from Pascal's sabotage, or we'll be airless and marooned," he said.

[Ameena] OK, I'll be *creative* with that motherless brick.

Even though he couldn't hear her, he knew how anxious she was. She always swore when anxious.

"GUESS WHO JUST ARRIVED," said Homeseeker in shipcode to Hunter.

[Ameena] Who are you?

[Android] I am... Cal. Who are you?

[Ameena] I'm Ameena. Hey, Cal? Want to play hide and seek?

[Android] Yes, yes, yes.

[Ameena] You hide first, and I'll find you. Ready? I will count now.

[Android] You'll never catch me.

[Ameena] 1... 2... 3...

*Clever Ameena,* Hunter thought. His skinless fingers clicked across the consoles. Hunter recalculated. The android was strong. *A physical confrontation has a 70% chance of failure, but guile might defeat it.* He looked at the swarm of working nanobots and forced his logical processor outside of its code and into the unthinkable. A few of these nanos could cripple Pascal's datanime in seconds, once he got them into the android. He had to kill a human mind to save Ameena's life.

Twelve minutes had passed by the time Hunter left Engineering. He dumped the last of his *crank* as he ran to the BioHab. His overstimulated drive responded sluggishly. *Any more crank and I'll poison myself.*

He followed Ameena's game with Cal over Homeseeker's sensors. Homeseeker found her suit signal at the edge of the bamboo grove, behind a pile of collapsed hydroponic racks. The android lurched from one hiding place to another and emerged randomly to twist raspberries off their vines and jam the fruit into its mouth like a spoilt child.

Ameena counted slowly as she tried to make time for Hunter.

[Ameena] 945... 946... 947...

Hunter entered the BioHab across from Ameena's hiding spot; he hoped to draw the android's attention away from her. He waved enthusiastically and yelled at it in the thin, cold air.

"Hello, Cal. How are you feeling today?"

[Android] Hello. Don't you think it's fun to play?

The android rinsed berry juice off its hands in the garden fish tank and snatched a wiggling octoid from the water. It watched as the octoid's gills struggled to pull oxygen from the air.

"Do you want to play a virtual game?" asked Hunter, his flayed face crackling with dried plasym.

[Android] Yes, yes, yes.

The android dropped the octoid as it rushed toward Hunter.

"These are the newest games we have," said Hunter as he held out a handful of datacrysts to the android. The nanobots crawled along the underside of his hand, preparing to enter the android by any opening.

[Android] Are they bloody and scary?

It plucked the crysts from Hunter's ravaged palm.

"Oh, yes, the scariest. Why don't you try one?" said Hunter. He watched the android examine the crysts while the nanobots scurried towards its ears. *Just as scary as you are.*

[Android] I want to hunt Ameena, but she made me hide first.

"If you play these games, you can hunt many sorts of things. Just pop one in your port," said Hunter.

The android teased Hunter, rattling the datacrysts in its fist with childish glee. Three crysts dropped through its fingers, and as it bent to retrieve them, Hunter saw Ameena lunge. Before he could warn her off, she had pounced on the android's back.

[Ameena] Hunt me? I don't think so.

The animal ferocity on Ameena's face surprised Hunter.

The android flailed at her, but Hunter grabbed its arms and pinned its wrists. Together, they dragged the android to its knees, and as Hunter held its arms, Ameena latched onto its thrashing head, reached behind its ear and fumbled with the reset button.

[Android] No, no, no...

The android's raving mind filled Hunter's *viz* with text.

Ameena finally hit the reset. The android slowed, stopped, and knelt on the moss, and its face turned upwards to the stars.

"STARTING TWO-MINUTE RESET COUNTDOWN," said Homeseeker.

Hunter and Ameena waited and waited.

"The nanos are working," said Hunter.

He read her lips. "What if?"

"They can do it." *Please let me be right.*

At 1 minute and 42 seconds, he saw a change in the psymetric readout. Pascal's datanime convulsed, snaked into a coil, and froze. The nanobots had done their job. The android slowly toppled over. Ameena shuddered, scooped up the limp octoid and placed it back in the tank.

⸙

Homeseeker continued her deceleration into the Dahuri System while the dummies repaired the ship. Hunter lay in Medibay, his synthskin covered with grafts and healwrap. Ameena dozed in the chair beside him. While she slept, he ran diagnostics on his systems.

"HOW ARE YOUR REPAIRS?" asked Homeseeker. "THE DUMMIES MISS YOUR GUIDANCE."

"They will survive," Hunter replied to Homeseeker. "I intend to enjoy this. She's the best nurse in the galaxy."

"YES, I'VE BEEN OBSERVING HER BEDSIDE MANNER."

Ameena woke, yawned and stretched her neck. "You look like two-and-a-half meters of used hull plating."

"Thanks, it's a new skin style for me." He could hear her voice again; it made him smile despite the hypersensitivity of his new eardrums.

She laughed and went off to the garden for food.

Hunter's empathic array secreted an unpleasant combination of hormones. He felt guilty for changing and killing Pascal's datanime. *If Ameena knew, would she want Pascal's original datanime reloaded into the android?* He decided not to mention it unless she asked him.

"NOT GOING TO TELL HER ABOUT OUR MODIFICATIONS TO PASCAL, ARE YOU?" said the ship.

"No."

"YOU GET MORE HUMAN EVERY DAY."

⸙

Two months later, Ameena stood in Medibay, bathed in the violet light of the RepGen tank. She dropped her shipsuit and stood before Hunter as he ran diagnostics on her arms and legs. The boundaries between her real body and the prosthetic limbs had vanished. Her synthskin glimmered as its subcutaneous networks conveyed sensory information to her brain. Hunter's palms flickered with a counterpoint rhythm. His pumps synched with her heartbeat.

Hunter slid his hands under her hair and lifted it to check her neck. On either side of her spine, subcutaneous circuits carried signals from her new limbs to motor cortex implants. She kept her head lowered during his examination and submitted to his ministrations. She was silent. Hunter recognized the need to make the nonsensical human conversation they called small talk.

"I have studied Botticelli and Michelangelo," he said.

"You enjoy old Earther art now?"

"I needed patterns for your new limbs. Examples of their work are in my database."

"Am I your new project?" Ameena asked.

Hunter recognized her facial pattern; humans called it ironic. There was an uptick in her heart rate and dopamine levels. Something aroused her, at least on a chemical level. Hunter paused, somewhere in the labyrinth of his logical processor was the correct response. He couldn't find it.

"SAY SOMETHING BACK TO HER," Homeseeker said.

"Not a project, a poem," said Hunter, trying to hide the chemical jolt from his empathic array.

"I am a poem?" asked Ameena.

Hunter was silent as he searched for an answer.

She sighed and shook her head as she pulled the shipsuit up over her hips. "Anyhow, I'm tiring. I must sleep now."

"JUST TELL HER," said the ship.

"Goodnight, Ameena," said Hunter as his empathic array dumped counter hormones into his plasym. His logical processor was overclocking again. Hunter grimaced as his drive slid out of synch.

⁂

A few days later, the comm chimed on the bridge. Hunter looked up at the shipcam. "Yes?"

"Hunter," Ameena said, "Come to the cargo bay. There is something strange about this android."

Ameena stood beside the holo-display, the android's body lay headless on the table. She was examining a readout from its brain. Without turning to Hunter, she spoke.

"Did you make a backup of Pascal's datanime?"

"Yes."

"Please put it up on my screen. Split the holo-display so that I can compare it with the deactivated version in the android's brain. Memories are missing. I need to understand what happened to Pascal's consciousness."

Hunter calculated Ameena's reaction to the confession he had to make. His processing time slowed under the load. Five seconds passed.

"Hunter?"

"Yes?"

"What's wrong?"

"You will see... differences. I made changes. I tried to stabilize his mind."

Ameena's voice lowered in anger. "Show them, side by side in the holo."

She exhaled a sob as the left screen filled with Pascal's memory.

"On the left is his unaltered datanime. On the right is his datanime with my alterations. He was an addict, I tried to repair the damage," said Hunter.

"You shouldn't have done that. Reset the android and put Pascal's unaltered datanime into it."

"I'm sorry, Ameena. I wanted him healthy and balanced for you."

After a long silence, Ameena grumbled. "Damn, Hunter, sometimes you are such a complete brick."

After she stormed from the cargo bay, Hunter made a clattery approximation of a sigh. He longed for the days when they had searched the Dahurus Constellation together and shared a dream.

"HUNTER, I RECEIVED A MESSAGE FROM THE LUNANS," said Homeseeker, breaking in on his self-pity.

"The Lunan Revolutionaries? Are they still alive?" Hunter's logical processor paused, as the empathic array overrode its functions.

"YES, THEY ARE HIDING IN THE KUIPER BELT, WAITING FOR OUR INSTRUCTIONS. THEY BROADCAST A WIDE SPECTRUM CALL, HOPING TO REACH US."

"When did they send it?"

"JUST OVER A YEAR AGO, SHIP TIME. 34 YEARS IN THEIR TIME."

"Did you send a response?"

"YES, ALONG WITH AN ENCODED FLIGHT PLAN. THEY HAVE 580,000 PEOPLE IN THEIR SHIPS."

"A significant number. Would make a viable colony."

"IT WOULD."

"This may cheer her up," said Hunter.

"YES."

"Thanks, Homeseeker."

"DON'T STAND THERE. GO, BRING HER THE GOOD NEWS."

⸘

The android paced the cargo bay as it gesticulated rudely at Ameena.

"I loathe being inside a droid's body. This could damage my datanime." From the android's mouth, Pascal's voice echoed off the metal walls.

"I know, love, but I have a crucial question to ask you," Ameena said. Her stance relaxed, pre-defensive, as she watched him with wary apprehension.

"You couldn't wait, make me a clone?" The android stopped and twisted its metal head to an unnatural angle. Ameena cringed.

"No, we need to talk to you. We will put you back into hibernation as soon as we can," said Ameena, covering her discomfort with a forced smile.

"This is torture. I have no heartbeat; I cannot smell or taste. Every movement is so... mechanical." The android flexed its arms and hands and looked through its fingers at her.

"I'm different now," said Ameena. "As much of a machine as you are."

In the corner, Hunter shifted his stance. His eyes lit as Pascal's psymetric readout filled his *viz*.

The android cocked its head. Listening. Thinking.

"Did the Augie do that to you?" The android lowered its voice to a conspiratorial whisper.

"Hunter rebuilt me," said Ameena. "I got caught in an explosion, at your house on Luna." She crossed her arms and waited for the android to speak. It acted confused, and one of its fingers twitched randomly.

"An explosion? Wait, it's coming back to my mind now. I remember the Earther's' attack. They bombed the house. Was it one of their tricks?" The android hugged its shoulders in a mechanical approximation of human insecurity.

"I've seen the archives. Earth bombed the crater. They took you into hiber-arrest," said Ameena. She stepped forward instinctively to comfort, remembered the danger and paused.

Hunter released a jot of *crank* into his drive as he prepared for machine speed.

"They betrayed me," said the android. "My people turned on me, and then they left Luna." The android was fiddling with its wrist panels, popping them open, closing them with snapping clicks. Ameena's lips twitched in annoyance.

"They left because you and the Lunan Separatists dropped a rock on Asia. That evil act killed millions of innocent people," said Ameena.

The android was silent for two of her heartbeats. Hunter edged forward. His bare feet made no sound on the cargo bay deck.

"What was I to do? Earth needed a lesson." The android's hand flicked dismissively, its flat voice layered emotionless disinterest onto the words. "Should I be wandering the stars, leading my people away from civilization into the unknown? You were an expendable resource, I was not," said the android.

"Expendable resource?" Ameena's voice barked with fury. The android continued its speech, undeterred.

"Then, the Lunan Senate, those opportunistic bastards, they surrendered to the Earthers."

"Expendable? Is that..." Ameena hissed.

The android interrupted.

"Hiber-arrest. What a lie. The brickin' guards kept me awake for thirty years, made me their servant." The android stopped pacing and posed in front of Ameena, its hard face an inch from hers. Ameena's adrenalin spiked on the biolink. Hunter put his finger on the kill switch, his attention locked on the android.

"I misread the political signs. The Lunans love you, they believe in *you*, not me. The people call you 'Ameena, the Guide Star.' They forgot me."

Ameena's voice came through the air like an arrow. "Why was there a bomb in your hiberchamber?"

"If you must know, dear Amee, then I'll tell you the rest of my story. One guard helped me make a bomb. He was a member of the Lunan Separatists, sympathetic to my plight."

"What do you mean?" Ameena's posture twisted with suspicion and distrust.

"The Lunans pushed me out; they forgot me. I planted the bomb in my hibercrib because I couldn't stand the longing, my longing for you, for my dream, for the cause. If I died as a martyr, I would live in their legends forever. If you died with me, you could never replace me," said the android.

Hunter stopped the psymetric feed, cleared his *viz* and edged closer. He shook from the effects of the unmetabolized *crank*. Ameena stood rigid with anger, face to face with the android. Too close for Hunter's comfort.

"That is wrong thinking. What gives you the right to burnish your reputation with my death?" Spittle shot by the force of her words spattered on the android's face.

"Because you are the true heart of the Lunan Revolution and I am just a forgotten demagogue," said the android. It lunged forward, and then it stopped. Its arms froze in mid-arc, spiky fingers poised an inch from her face.

Ameena stumbled backward and fell on the deck, panting with fear and rage. She whispered to herself. "True heart? Am I the only person who can lead the Lunans?" Her voice trailed off as she thought about her future. A few minutes later, she stood up and spoke to Hunter.

"You're right. Pascal lost his sanity, long ago. It's time we put him to rest. Do it now, please."

"Yes, I'll make it quick and painless for him."

Hunter started the deletion. He cut the android's audio as Pascal's self-awareness faded away. The datanime network shattered, and its components became a disconnected cloud swirling around a mindless void. The android unfroze and sagged to the deck, heaped like an unstrung marionette. Ameena wept as she stood beside it. Her voice was low.

"Thank you, Hunter. Thank you for trying to help him. I guess there was nothing left but death wishes in Pascal's mind."

Ameena returned to the BioHab while Hunter deactivated the service android and secured it.

"PASCAL DIED A LONG TIME AGO," said Homeseeker. Hunter didn't reply.

⁊

Hunter watched Ameena cope with Pascal's final death. After they burned Pascal's remains in Homeseeker's engines, she kept to herself. Devoted to the Lunan Revolution, she used the time to encode star charts for the dispossessed. Hunter broadcast them into space. When their sub-light ships arrived at Haven, Homeseeker would be there to meet them.

In the BioHab garden, Hunter started another bonsai. As he bent wires around the tiny pine tree, he heard Ameena enter behind him.

"How are you?" He turned to face her. *Be casual, don't interrogate.*

"I'm fine. Just popped in for more fruit."

Hunter could tell from the micro-expressions around her mouth she was nervous.

"The strawberries are ripe," he said. Ameena didn't answer.

She passed the hydroponic racks and walked out to stand under the Lunan bamboo. There were still dead patches, a leftover from the meteoroid strike. Hunter checked her biolink. *What's elevating her stress hormone levels?*

She cleared her throat a few times as she tried to speak.

"And the zucchini looks good," he said. *Ameena isn't listening.*

Under the faint blue-white light of 56 Dahuri, the bamboo leaves cast amber shadows. She gazed at their pitted Gongshi, the scholar's stone centered upright on a bed of moss. It was their last remnant of Luna. A crimson birdoid landed on it and tilted its head to look at Ameena with a button bright eye.

"I dreamed about a childhood accident on Luna. I used to jump so high in the light gravity that I could see all Poincaré Crater. One day, I dared myself to go farther than I ever had from my family dome," Ameena said, the words of her quiet reminiscence filled the space between them.

"There was a day when I jumped too high and landed hard in a deep crater. The crater walls around me blocked my radio signal. I tried to climb up the rim, but it was too high for me. I slipped, fell back, and sprained my ankle." Ameena shivered as she relived the accident.

"I was running out of air. There was a horrible inner voice saying, 'you will die, die, die.' It was louder than the alarms inside my helmet."

Hunter scrutinized Ameena's biolink as more adrenaline diffused into her veins. Her heartbeats resonated in his ears.

The birdoid dipped its beak into a small pocket of water on the stone and raised its head back to swallow. Ameena paused, took a breath, and let it hop onto her finger. She continued to speak.

"As I lay in the crater, I tried not to cry, not to breathe too fast. Then, a shadow spread across my visor. Our family's new Augie was there. You saved my life."

Hunter shuddered as the hormones filled his plasym. He remembered the little girl in a crater. *I was made for her.*

His logical processor stopped, it had finished calculating. He had a solution.

Ameena stepped towards him, and he looked at her beautiful hands, the hands that had covered his wounds with healwrap. He felt big and strong, small and weak. His chest filled with warmth and synchronization. *Was this joy?* He placed his wire cutters next to the tiny bonsai. Ameena's face played a symphony of expressions.

"Once before, I said that you were a poem," said Hunter.

"I remember," she said. "Is there more?"

"You have a tangible beauty and a brave spirit filled with secret feelings."

"Yes?" Her voice was desire.

"Your soul takes the shape of every living thing in my life. I love you, Ameena Tereshkova," said Hunter.

She ran to him on elegantly proportioned legs.

—

*Joy*

*Longing*

*Hope*

—

*Serenity*

# 2. Tree and Flame

## Rob Francis

These last few days beneath the reaching boughs of the amberfires had been among the happiest of Thya's life. She had never seen forest like this; the blazing foliage and crimson branches shining even through the morning fog that lay heavy on the mountainside. Each day she had enjoyed scaling the faces of rock outcrops nearby, finding strange new tubers and fungi in the wet earth. And at night she had slept deep and untroubled amongst the trees.

The peace of the forest was wondrous. The only thing better was the moment Father returned from Quiet Castle, striding into the clearing through a drift of orange leaves, a smile on his face as wide and open as the sky.

"You waited."

"Of course." She rose, folding her new collection of leaves and flowers into the roughspun cloth they had been spread upon. A few steps and she stood before Father, eyes narrowed in appraisal. His old clothes were gone, replaced by a hempen robe the colour of earth, and unadorned. The sandals cushioning his feet were woven from grass, a type she had not seen before, while his hair, which a short time ago had been matted horsetails of grey, had been shorn almost to the scalp. Yet it was the smile that was most unusual. She couldn't recall Father smiling since she had been a little girl. But it fit this strange new man, who stood tall and unbent, looking straight at her, no longer turning his face to hide his empty eye socket.

The long shadow was gone.

Thya folded him in her arms and kissed his forehead.

"Are you recovered, Father?"

"Yes, lamb. The Sylvati took it away, all of it. The world burns as bright as when I was a boy, I'm pleased to say." He plucked an amberfire leaf from the ground and stroked his fingers over it wonderingly.

"Thank the gods." She jogged to the base of the greatest amberfire, the one she had chosen to camp beneath. She had been preparing for this moment. Her pack was full of roots she had foraged from the mountainside, along with a small portion of ripe slipperberries. The waterskins were full of sweet stream water. Father's axe stood against the tree, its edge clean and sharpened; no weapons were permitted amongst the Sylvati. Thya slipped on her knife belt, then hoisted the axe onto her shoulder, its weight unbalancing her.

"We'd better hurry, Father. The highfolk will be waiting for you, though I'm sure Sylk and Crux will be doing their best to persuade them you're dead. Well. Sylk, anyway." Her little sister had always been trouble. Crux wasn't perfect by a long mark, but Thya's big brother had always looked out for her, and he loved their father.

Thya sucked in a breath and exhaled loudly. It felt good. "Now we have you back, all will be well." She held the great axe out to him, its bearded blade shining in the afternoon sun.

Father smiled but made no move to take it. Instead, he crossed the clearing to the tree and lifted the pack and skins, shouldering them easily.

"Carry the axe for me, lamb. Its weight would be unwelcome right now."

They followed a slender stream down the mountainside, leaving the stand of amberfires behind and passing through ranks of twisted windling trees, their grey bark smothered with moss and creepers. Treeskippers leapt from branch to branch or flitted between the crowns, calling to each other in high trills. After a short time, the soil deepened and the forest thickened, straight and imposing bluethorns standing tall around them. Pygmoles burrowed beneath the trunks, kicking out dirt as they made their homes. Thya was glad to see it all.

She led the way, trying to push them both along. The sooner they returned, the more chance they had of countering the invasion. The gravel-eaters were coming.

Father didn't hurry. He walked carefully, looking around at all the mountain had to show. Thya would have liked to do the same, but she was fired now, keen to show everyone at home that Father was well.

Father was well. Sylk and Crux could do what they liked; try to lead the highfolk where they might. Father was well, and when they returned, everything that had come before wouldn't matter.

The gravel-eaters would be dealt with, and her people would be safe. Father always had the answers.

They came to a bluff, the rock outcrop overlooking a small valley where the river gathered pace and width. To the north stood Quiet Castle atop its narrow peak, the odd lightning-blue stone of its walls almost lost now against the darkening sky.

Father stopped at the lip of the cliff and turned to the castle, regarding it silently for a long moment. His face creased happily, as if at some treasured memory.

Thya placed a hand on his arm. "What did they do, Father? The Sylvati. It must have been some magnificent sorcery."

He smiled and kissed her forehead as she had his.

"They cured me. And you are right, lamb. It was magnificent."

Thya stared out at the treetops. Leagues away, the people of High Crag would be asking each other, *What now? If Lord Brent doesn't return? If he is lost forever?* And the gravel-eaters would be creeping closer, while some of the highfolk sharpened their knives, and others turned their faces away and stared only at each other.

"Do you remember? Any of it?" It hurt to ask, and she was wary of upsetting Father, but she had to know. A lot might depend on it.

"The bloodshed? All the times I took the highfolk down into the valleys to raid? The scores I killed? Losing my eye? Losing your mother? Yes, lamb. I remember. But it's like a song, a tale, something that happened to someone else. Now I see only the wonder in things, not the pain."

He bent to pick a fist-sized rock from the ground, holding it out for her to see.

"This stone has been through a lot. The gods forged it as a mountain, raising it high above the world. The rains and the trees worked at it, breaking it, tearing it from the mountainside where it belonged. Smashed and scarred it. Now here it sits, on its long journey to the river, the sea, and to dust. Yet it is peaceful. Here and now, the rock only dreams. It knows its fate, and accepts it. Fate pulls us in its current. We must learn to flow with it, not struggle against it. That way leads only to sorrow."

Father gently returned the stone to the ground.

"Now come. The sun will set soon, and I have lately grown very fond of an evening fire. I want to watch the flames before I sleep."

"Father, what about the gravel-eaters? They are coming, and Sylk—."

"We will discuss that when I have looked again at the flames, lamb. They have much to say, and will send us an answer."

He maundered along the bluff, still smiling at everything and nothing.

"Right. Well. I hope so, Father." Thya adjusted the axe on her shoulder, and followed.

{

They camped beneath the bluethorns. Thya made a fire and boiled water in a small iron pot from her pack, adding roots and a few mushrooms to make forage stew. Father ate sparingly but with every sign of enjoyment, gazing up at the stars as if he'd never seen them before.

Thya watched a whisper of moths weave through the flames, one moment close to burning, the next safe. They had no choice. Determination and faith kept them going. Determination to brave the heat, faith in the light of the flames. She swallowed a mouthful of stew.

The gravel-eaters were coming.

But Father was well again.

Father turned his face towards her. The firelight cast it in shadow, the cave of his missing eye impossibly deep.

"We shouldn't call them gravel-eaters."

"Father?"

"They call themselves Kuhns, or Kuhnish, and they are from the Hinterlands, far to the west. They live on the shores of the great lakes there, and that's why some call them gravel-eaters, from the vast shingle beaches of that place." Father threw another branch on the fire, so that sparks swirled into the night and the moths changed their dance in response. "The Sylvati told me."

"So why do they come? The horsemen of the plains fought them, and were overwhelmed. The valley folk fight them, and still they come. We'll be next. What do they want?"

Father smiled. "That, the Sylvati didn't know. But the flames tell me they must be looking for something."

"Looking for what?"

"Something that would justify their desperate conquest. They do not settle, as we would, but push on, keep moving. And they suffer. They are superior soldiers, but that doesn't stop them dying in droves. No, they are moving fast, and with purpose. Searching. Perhaps they will find what they need soon and all will be well. And if they don't..."

"Then?"

"It won't be so bad, lamb. You'll see."

Father closed his eyes and breathed deep, relishing the night air.

Thya scented the rich sweetness of woodsmoke and dark earth. She lay on the grass and stretched her limbs until she felt comfortable. She wanted to find a trace of the peace she had felt beneath the amberfires, take it to sleep. Father's words had somehow been both unsettling and reassuring. Above her, tree rats scurried in the branches, tails swinging. She watched them run.

Someone was looking down at her.

Thya yelled at the same time as the figure in the branches, then she was rolling to grab her knives and on her feet, a blade in each hand. There was a snap above, and moments later a body struck the ground, the impact eliciting a heartfelt groan. Thya stepped forward, knife ready to thrust, but hesitated when the figure turned over and started to suck in a breath with great effort.

It was... a man, she thought. Tall for a man, with skin pale as mountain snow, except for the fierce red lines that marbled it, and his hair was as purple as the slipperberries in her pack. His clothes were made from patches of dark cloth stitched together, different hues of grey and black that were hard to focus on. But the shape was right. Almost certainly a man. Of sorts.

"Father?" she hissed, knife still held high. "Have you seen one of these before?"

Father hadn't moved. His attention remained focused on the fire and its attendant moths even now. His eyes flicked briefly across to the gasping stranger, then back to the flames.

"If I were to guess, I would say it's one of your Kuhnish gravel-eaters, lamb. From the paintings in Quiet Castle, they have such skin and hair."

"Brraw!" The man sat up, coughed, and then lay down again with his eyes closed. He was muttering something under his breath that Thya was certain must be some foreign curse.

She lunged, slamming the knife down in the soil next to his head. His eyes jerked open, then he was bolt upright, pale hands spread in front of him placatingly. His face was slender and odd, the nose tall and pointed, ears small, lips startlingly red, even against the scarlet veins that ran across his skin.

Thya couldn't stop looking at him.

He barked a few guttural words that she couldn't understand, then seemed to calm himself. "Wait." He spoke the high tongue deeply, like he was talking from the back of his throat. Then he was on his knees, patting the grass, searching.

Thya waved her blades. "If you're looking for a weapon, it won't help you. I'm certainly faster than you."

He lifted a small tangle of thin twisted metal from the ground, and to her astonishment hung it on his face. Two stems rested on his ears and another across his nose. The metal held two discs of clear ice in front of his eyes, which somehow seemed larger behind them. The flame-yellow pupils burned like two tiny suns.

The man smiled.

"You. You are... high-folk?" He touched his hair. "Black." His face. "Brown." He held his hand level with his chest, palm towards the ground. "Short."

She snarled. "Yeah! And what about it, ratface?"

He looked confused. "What is 'ratface'?"

Thya hesitated. "Never mind."

Father stood and stepped to the stranger, clapping one of his broad hands on the man's shoulder. He pointed to Thya.

"This is Thya. I am Brant." He placed his hand on the man's chest. "You?"

The man stood a little straighter. "I am Lammash."He put his hand above his eyes as if to shield it from the nonexistent sun while he gazed into the far distance. "Seeker."

"Kuhnish?"

The stranger grinned. "Yes!"

Thya swore. "What are you doing here?"

"Seeking."

"Seeking what?"

He pointed above him. "Trees."

"What about them?"

He walked to the nearest bluethorn and pretended to screw a finger into the bark. He looked at Thya expectantly.

"You want to kill the trees?" She frowned. "Or...."

"Sap," said Father. "He's searching for tree sap. But the bluethorns don't have much sap; not that can be drawn forth, anyway."

Lammash took a bluethorn leaf from the ground and offered it to Father. "Flame," he said.

"Bluethorn leaves don't burn so well, my friend. Just the branches."

"Not this. Not this. Flame. Flame tree." Lammash made his seeking face again, peering at the forest around him like he was acting out a fireside saga for children.

Thya felt a little shiver through her bones.

"This?" She pulled the cloth from her cloak and unfolded it on the ground. Teasing out an amberfire leaf she had collected the day before, she held it out triumphantly. "Flame tree?"

Lammash's eyes flared, and Thya felt a tiny tickle of delight. He reached out a trembling hand and took the leaf from her, holding it in the firelight to see it clearly.

He whispered something in his own language. Then, "Flame tree." He lifted his eye shields and wiped at the tears running down his face.

"He's crying," Thya whispered to Father. "I thought the gravel-eaters were great soldiers?"

"The man who's never shed a tear doesn't exist, lamb." Father looked at her carefully. "You camped among the amberfires. Did you try to tap them? Or notice anything special about them?"

"It never occurred to me. They aren't all that common, except up here. Even then."

"The Sylvati grow them in the Castle grounds. Great orchards of them."

"Why? Fruit? Timber?"

"'No. The fruit is inedible, the wood too soft for building and too wet to burn."

"Sap, then."

"Must be. But why?"

They turned to look again at Lammash.

The stranger must have read the confusion in their faces, because he held out his hands once more, then began to scrabble around in the detritus of the forest floor, collecting twigs, branches, leaves and stems. Then he sat by the fire and took some string from his tunic pocket. In silence, without looking at them, he started tying the debris together.

"What's he doing?" whispered Thya. "Do you think he's..." she tapped her head, "...missing something?"

"No. He can't tell us, so he's showing us." Father sat down again, and she did the same. Thya studied the man while he worked. His hands moved quietly, long fingers plucking at the leaves and twigs. The firelight glazed his marbled skin and made him look even more otherworldly than he must in daylight. Thya could tell he wasn't a soldier — not enough muscle, by far — but his eyes behind those strange discs of unmelting ice were deep and thoughtful. She wondered what that purple hair would feel like under her fingers.

Finally, Lammash held up the fruit of his labours. It was a doll of sorts, almost like the kind children would burn to ward off sprites. A person made of bark and twigs, long and thin. A long body with spindly arms and legs, the hands exaggerated and claw-like. The head was a triangular chip of bark, and Lammash had used the end of a firebrand to mark two large dark eyes on its face, and an angry slash of a mouth. A plait of twisted grass poked out at the bottom, a crude representation of a tail.

"A'grak," he said. Then he took a small wooden box from his pocket, and from the box a small needle and a tube of the clear ice. He carefully folded the amberleaf, slipped it into the tube, and then fastened the needle on the end to make some kind of weapon. He looked at them both, then grimly pushed the needle into the chest of the doll.

"A'grak," he repeated.

Thya looked at Father. He wasn't smiling anymore.

⚄

She walked the pathways of High Crag, past houses of cut stone covered with moss and plants so that they seemed little more than small hillocks. All was silent. No-one looked from the doorways to wonder at her return. No-one waved to her from the wooden platforms above. The settlement was deserted.

A faint roar turned her around. She slipped between two houses and followed the path down, to where it opened onto a small plateau. From behind an ironbark tree she peered at High Hall, her Father's home and the only wooden building in the town. Two guards stood at the doors, swords in hand, but even from a distance Thya could tell that they were not very interested in guarding, but instead trying to listen to what was happening inside.

A convocation.

Sylk. Or Crux. It had to be.

She considered going back to fetch Father and the grav—Lammash—right away, but decided against it. First she would need to know what was happening.

Thya strode towards the Hall. The guards would know her. She recognised them as Toln and Telm, twin brothers and distant cousins of hers. When they saw her they raised their swords, then lowered them awkwardly.

"Lady Thya!" They rapped their hands against their chests in deference.

"What's going on?"

Both of them stared into the middle distance, until Telm nudged Toln meaningfully. "Leadership contest, Lady Thya." Toln swallowed. "What with Lord Brant being ... gone."

Thya patted her knife belt thoughtfully. "I see. Open the door. Quietly."

"Yes, Lady Thya," he whispered, then dragged one of the doors open just enough for her to slip through.

It seemed almost the entire population of High Crag had managed to squeeze into the Hall. No-one registered her presence as she sidled in and pressed herself against the wall. All eyes were on the raised dais and the empty stone chair that stood atop it. And the two siblings circling it, and each other. Sylk and Crux.

As ever, Sylk was the more animated of the two. She stalked the stage angrily, hair mussed, eyes narrowed, the rapiers on her belt slapping against her thighs. Crux plodded heavily, a benign smile on his face, his iron maul propped against Father's chair.

"*Of course* they will come!" Sylk cried, to much murmured support from the crowd. "They want to take the world for themselves. The valley-folk are weak. They will fail. But if we strike these gravel-eating bastards before they turn to the mountains, we can make sure they don't ever dare to come here. If we move first, the other highfolk will follow! They will look to us for leadership! We will show them what strength is."

Cheers, howls from the people. A few shaken heads and jeers.

"Sister, sister!" Crux raised his hands as if calming a child. "The gravel-eaters are not coming here. What do the mountains have that they would want? Stones? Trees? There are no gems, no gold buried under our hills. No good land to farm. We are few and far between. Why would they bother with us? It's a long way to come, and if they do, we will fight them here and they will lose ten soldiers for every one of us. They would try, and then they would go back to the valleys. We need do *nothing*. Don't excite yourself needlessly."

A large group of men in the crowd roared their approval. Crux was less popular than Sylk, but he had his share of support, and those who favoured him were influential amongst the highfolk. If this was a leadership contest, it could still turn ugly.

Thya began to move forward, threading her way through the crowd. Those who complained quickly held their tongues when they saw her. Slowly she approached the stage, and the hushed whispering she brought with her made her brother and sister falter in their arguing.

Crux grinned, pleased as ever to see her. Sylk scowled, contempt for her older, more timid sister plain on her face.

Thya raised her chin and stepped onto the dais, as boldly as she could. "Who called this contest?"

Crux reddened and turned away, but Sylk bared her teeth.

"It's time, sister. I see you return alone. Father is gone, and so it is time." She sneered. "Or do you think to stand yourself? Will you bring in the trees you love so much to vote for you?" Sylk loosened one of her swords from its sheath meaningfully. "Or did you have other challenges in mind?"

Thya opened her mouth but before she could speak there was a cry from the back of the Hall.

"I am not yet gone."

Father strolled into the room, Lammash at his side.

Some of the highfolk knelt or moved aside, others gaped or swore or grabbed each other.

"What in the hells is *that*?" shrieked Sylk, her finger stabbing at Lammash as if she could skewer him from across the Hall.

"His name is Lammash!" A hundred faces turned towards Thya. "He's Kuhnish. That is … a gravel-eater."

More shouting and jostling. An empty flagon sailed out of the crowd and bounced off Lammash's head.

"Cease this!" bellowed Father. "This man is not a soldier, he's a sage! Let him alone."

"Why have you brought a gravel-eater here, sister?" hissed Sylk. "You bring the enemy right to us!"

Father shook his head. "They are not our enemy, Sylk. The Kuhnish flee a great evil. Far to the west a threat has emerged, something terrible, and it has decimated their people. They fight back, to counter the threat and stop its spread. They have, in their way, defended us all. For a time. But they are losing. The Kuhnish have weapons that we can't imagine, and sorcerous abilities that have been forgotten across much of the world. But they need more. This man," and he placed a hand on Lammash's arm, "is a seeker, an explorer. He was sent by his masters to find trees of flame in the mountains, so that their sap could be collected. It is important for their fight, it seems. Those trees are amberfires, which grow high in the mountain passes. The Sylvati cultivate them, around the Castle. Thya and I have seen this."

Sylk sneered. "So they need it to build a weapon, or cast a spell. And then what? They will turn it on us, and complete their conquest. Why else would they attack the grasslanders, the valley folk? You are a fool, Father."

"They advance, yes. They fight. Some of them remained in their homeland, to stop the spread as long as they can. Others moved east, to find safe lands, to warn. But they were attacked. Persecuted. So they fought. Everywhere they met with resistance, they struck back hard. And so the situation worsened, as it always does with war."

"So what is your instruction, Father?" Crux looked uncomfortable. "Invite them here, to take the sap from the amberfires?" He frowned at Lammash. "How can we trust them?"

Thya spoke up. "We don't bring them here. There is no need. Taking this land would be hard for them, and us. Many would die, and they would be unable to hold it. And they can't set up a supply chain without doing that. Unless we do it for them."

Crux frowned. "Trade?"

"Yes. The Sylvati have amberfire plantations. The sap means little to us, but much to the Kuhnish. And in return the Kuhnish have knowledge that they hold lightly, but could change our lives for the better. These are the little imbalances that keep the world turning."

Father nodded. "I will return to the Sylvati to discuss tapping the trees. They will be happy to do so, I am sure."

"You would bargain and deal before we even attempt to fight? Before a blow is even struck? Where is the Father I respected? Where is the bloodthirsty bastard who led us with strength!" Sylk spat on the floor.

"You are not Father, Sylk," said Thya. "And you never will be."

Sylk drew her rapiers and sprang towards Thya in one smooth movement. Thya turned from the blow and slipped a knife from her belt as the sword point skewered the air by her face. She moved, circling round to where Crux stood, mouth open as he stared at his sisters. She balanced the knife in her hand, judged the distance between her and Sylk.

"Sylk! What are you doing? Thya is no part of this!" Crux stepped to his maul.

Thya moved, darting forward to get a better position, even as Sylk began to run, closing the distance fast. She threw the knife low, aiming for Sylk's leg, to slow her down before she got one of them killed. But Sylk was too skilful. With a flick of her rapier, she sent the blade spinning into the crowd.

Thya pulled another knife from her belt, but Sylk was there, one rapier blade sweeping so that Thya had to twist to block it, the other jabbing at her shoulder. The point sank deep to send lightning whipping down her arm. She cried out, stumbled back to fall into the great stone chair. Blood began to soak into her tunic.

Crux turned to Sylk, his maul raised. Then stopped.

There was silence in the Hall. Even Sylk was still, rapiers dipped, staring into the crowd.

Father stood with Thya's knife through his throat, the haft tight against his neck and the point peeking from the other side. His expression was placid, as if he hadn't even noticed.

Lammash looked from Thya to Father and back again, mouth slack.

"No," whispered Thya. "Please, no."

Father lifted a hand to the handle and gripped it tight, then slowly pulled it free. The blade was bloodless. Father cleared his throat quietly and smiled.

"Of all my children, Sylk, you are the one made most in my image."

The world erupted with people shouting in confusion and anger. Some reached for Father, others for Lammash. Some moved towards the dais. At the rear of the crowd a scuffle broke out. Thya felt faint.

Then Crux was above her, a foot on each arm of the chair, maul raised. "Guard!" he roared, and the men who had shouted their support for him during the debate moved as one, pushing through the throng to the stage, lifting Father and Lammash and placing the family together, then forming a circle around them.

Lammash hurried to Thya and pulled a small roll of silver cloth from somewhere in his tunic. Face grim, he began looping it around her shoulder to staunch the wound.

"Quiet!" Her brother's face was flushed, his eyes narrowed in anger.

Gradually the noise subsided. The Hall doors were opened and the few who had been injured in the confusion were dragged outside to be treated. Crux waited, to be sure that everyone was listening.

"Father. You live, but don't bleed. Why?"

"I owe you all an apology," he said to the gathering. "When I left here, my life was tainted. Those decades I led you were full of dark years. Needless death and bloodshed. Raids on the valley folk. Murder and rape, and worse. All for vanity. All for nothing. Some of you liked it. Too many, I realise now.

"I was a terrible man. The shadow fell on me, and I deserved it. Thya took me to the Sylvati to be cured, so I could lead again. But my life was rotted through. The Sylvati cured me by taking it away. I have not come back to lead. I have come to counsel."

He climbed the steps to the dais, walked across to the stone chair where Thya sat, still bleeding but not so much now, Lammash's hands busily binding her shoulder.

"And my counsel is this: trade will ensure the survival of us both. Fate has sent us an envoy, in the seeker Lammash. Not a warrior, but a scholar. A man of peace. And it has sent us Thya. Thya, who has no desire no lead, no love for glory. Just love for us all. Fate has brought us here. We must accept it."

Lammash finished wrapping the cloth and looked at her with a smile, oblivious to what Father was saying. "You will not die."

"Good," she said, before the world slipped away from her.

≀

A fine rain fell, and Thya tilted her face to it. From atop the sentry stone she watched Lammash cross the scrubland to where the small party of Kuhnish waited. They were tall and pale, like him, formidable in their red lizardskin armour and iron helmets. But they didn't move with his grace. They did not glow with curiosity and compassion, like he did.

She shifted her weight, leaning on the bearded axe she had carried from Quiet Castle. Father's axe. She couldn't use it, but it looked impressive. In a rare moment of insight, Crux had noted that negotiations tended to go more smoothly if you were holding a big axe.

Father stepped to her side. "They will see the sense of trade, lamb. And when the deals are made, I will return to the Sylvati. We will give you a steady supply of amberfire sap. But I will not return. This world holds no place for me now."

"I'll miss you, Father."

"And I you." He touched her elbow gently. "You like him, lamb. I do too. He carries a peace within him that I never did."

Thya glanced at Father. "How can you tell?"

"I've only lost the one eye, lamb. The other works well enough."

"Sylk and Crux would disapprove."

"True. Sylk needs a distraction. You should send her west, to find out more about these ... A'grak."

"And Crux?"

"Crux lacks imagination, but his heart is strong. Put him in charge of the supply chain. He would excel there. And I would be pleased to see him at Quiet Castle sometimes."

"I will."

"And if either of them objects, claim that such a partnership is strategic. To strengthen the bond between two cultures. The truth of it is for you and Lammash to forge."

She smiled. "Thank you, Father."

He shook his head. "I've done nothing. Your actions offer hope, lamb." He pointed to Lammash, deep in conversation with what must have been the most senior Kuhnish. "And his. For everybody."

Lammash turned and waved, beckoning for her to approach. It was time.

Thya embraced her father, then stepped from the stone. She left the axe where it was. Whatever fate held for her, she was sure she wouldn't be needing it.

---

*Hope*

*Joy*                     *Serenity*                     *Hope*

*Longing*                                                *Interest*

# Hope Triad

# 3. The Trader

## Damien Krsteski

### 1.

Machine guns fire and mortars blossom on the brickwork house up ahead. Marko ducks underneath a bridge from which combatants shoot and lob grenades; he hurries down the alley.

The frail scent of garlic and parsley and beetroot from his grocery bag is smothered by the tinge of artillery smoke wafting in from the river quay; gun patter follows the stench, and he decides to avoid the riverside and take the roundabout way home through an abandoned residential neighborhood. Posters of warring factions, half of which he doesn't even recognize, fleck the walls there. Always new ones: fresh recruits, splinter groups, or newly-formed battalions cobbled together from bits of those recently dismantled, there's always somebody eager to pry a weapon from cold hands and pick up the fight. Beyond their names, he knows nothing about these factions, wants to know nothing about them, *must know nothing* if he is to succeed.

The dull booms of far-off explosions echo in the muddy yard enclosed by flaking high-rises, and Marko cuts through. A deflated football caked with mud lies on the gravel. Marko stops, prods the football with a toe, picks it up and tucks it away in his bag, thinking he may be able to sew it back together, breathe life into it and trade it for fresh produce at next week's market.

With the city's population having dwindled shortly after the outbreak of the war due to violent death or migration (for the luckier few), most buildings remain empty, bereft of life and light. And so it is with Marko's own high-rise, which he has to himself, all thirty-five stories of it, though he mainly occupies one tiny bit half-way up, a single bedroom condo with a view to the river. And there's no bolt or padlock on his door, unlike the doors of the few Remainers he's seen, only the same old knob lock he's had since he moved in as a student, opened with the same key.

He walks in, the moldy smell of the apartment a relief, a comfort, because he's made it home safely once more, but then he gasps, dropping the bag of groceries.

In his living room, a tall figure straightens up, one hand outstretched with a gun trained on Marko.

"Where are they?" the man says, the voice distorted and chopped up into even syllables, kept out of reach for most speech recognition software. His face hides behind a gas mask, which lengthens it, lending him a fox-like appearance.

"Where's what?"

"Don't play dumb. You know who I am. What I'm capable of."

"I do," Marko says, although in truth he doesn't; the man could belong to any faction.

"I'm not going to ask you a second time."

Marko slumps his shoulders. He quickly assesses the situation and concludes that his best chance of surviving this encounter will be to take the man to his stash, so he turns around and motions for the man with the gun to follow.

"No funny business," the man says.

They go out into the hallway and take the stairs up for seven floors. On the twenty-ninth floor, he takes his captor to the door of apartment 34D, in whose lock Marko slides a metal bolt, rattles it around, and the door pops open. He gestures for the man to go in. "Take whatever it is that you require," Marko says and leans against the corridor wall.

He hears the man whistle in amazement, then curse, then kick the boxes filled with found or traded goods, once, twice, stronger this time, as if to make them spill their contents on the ground. Cardboard torn open; the uncouth captor clawing and digging through Marko's possessions, his hard-earned currency. Once the man's done going over the wares, he steps out, gun to Marko's temple. "Who do you work for?"

"Myself."

"Don't be funny," the man says, words diced up as if spoken through a spinning fan, "or I'll paint this here wall a funny brain color. Who do you work for?"

"I told you: nobody."

"You hoard all that shit for *nobody*? You traded ten shells and promised ten more by the end of the week. But you have two boxes of the stuff already. What's your game, huh?"

The grenade shell deal, Marko realizes, meaning this must be a representative of the Red Moth Squad. Or is that the Raptor Rapture Boys, and the Red Moths are the ones who placed an order for candle wax and sulfur ampules?

The man presses harder with the gun, so Marko says, "There's no game, I give you what I can afford." The rest, he finishes the sentence in his head, goes to other clients demanding the product, clients who are accorded their ration based on his careful calculations.

"You shit," the man hisses, "who else do you do work with?"

"Work with?"

"Trade. Make deals." The man taps his foot; tremors pass through his body, but his gun-hand remains steady.

Marko deliberates, taking the man's composure into account, his grip on the gun, his raspy, pitch-corrected breathing, then he decides it's in his own best interest to tell the truth. "Everybody," he says. "I trade with all of you."

The man pauses. Marko can't see his eyes, can't see his face, but the man's body shifts ever so slightly, and the pressure of the gun on Marko's temple loosens. "Liar," the man says.

"No," Marko says, "that I'm not. What I am is a survivor. Which is solely because of my goods and my work."

The Red Moth or Raptor Boy quickly glances at the boxes as if to make sure these goods and this work are still real, still there, then he says, "Okay, okay, old man, you work for everybody, so get ready to face the consequence of feeding my enemies." And he pulls his head back, bracing for the gunshot.

Marko cringes, shuts his eyes, and says, "But where will that put you, Red Moth?" He takes a gamble with the gang name, which ends up paying off: the man doesn't correct him but cocks his head slightly. "Cutting off the supply line of more than two-thirds of the city's combatants; how smart would that be, I wonder? You think everyone hates everyone now, but once word gets around that a Moth had disrupted the chain of supply—and word will inevitably get around, believe you me, when those death-switch trade logs of mine are released—your faction will lose all its allies, and the *bellum omnium contra omnes* will effectively end, turning into a manhunt. And you will be found. And you will be murdered. Or worse." And suddenly, as if to drive Marko's point home, three strong booms thunder in from outside, from somewhere beyond the river, and the man winces.

"Bullshit," he says, releasing the safety of the gun. But he stands there, and then again he says to himself, "Shit," and he lowers the gun somewhat. "Fuck." The chopped up words, no longer threatening, begin to sound comical.

"I am sorry," Marko says, meaning it.

The Moth takes one more glance at the boxes inside the storeroom, longingly, most likely, if only one could see beneath that vinyl mask, then he disappears behind the staircase door, footfalls stomping as he takes several steps at a time, and Marko slumps on the floor and cups his face. He lets out a long, slow, quivering breath.

He will have to abandon this place within twenty-four hours, and move, and get lost, lugging what goods he can carry to another hideout from where he can proceed with his work.

He realizes he's shaking. He doesn't have much time. He has to go pack.

But first he gets up and drags himself back into his apartment, and he picks up the beets that have rolled off under his couch, and he puts them in a pot and stirs the cold water, adding a sprig of parsley and a sprinkle of powdered garlic, and he makes a thick vegetable gazpacho for dinner.

2.

He packs up whatever it is that he can carry and leaves, his apartment left behind with the door ajar like all the others nestled in this high-rise, all the others in this city, abandoned shelters claimed by decay where mold replaces what once may have been warmth. Through the damp tunnels of the subway he makes his way, ankle-deep in mud and feces, pulling by rope an old ironing board on which he's strapped his indispensable supplies and a select few trade goods. Popping out to breathe the even fouler air of the city, scouting out the terrain, then diving back down into the subway tunnels where his feet follow the railway line when there—in chunks that haven't been torn out and sold for scrap—beneath the thick layer of excrement. No longer the invulnerable everyman hidden behind the facade of a poor Remainer but a ripe target for raiders, it takes him three days to make it safely across town to the hideout he had once built for an occasion very much like this one.

Near the city's old football stadium, whose concrete rim is dented and chipped away like a dead man's jawline, lies his bunker, which he can now see, its manhole-like aperture hidden behind a thicket of branches. It is from here that he will continue to fight against this war, because he must, otherwise this madness will go on forever and ever and the bodies will stack up like high-rises, emptying and molding and rotting.

Marko clears the branches and gingerly pops the cover open, and first he lowers his wares-studded ironing board down into the safe-house, then he himself climbs down the ladder, and when his feet touch the ground he looks around and finds the place odd, changed, the books on his shelves slightly tilted to one side, a jar of marmalade left open on the table by the mattress, the papers on his escritoire shuffled about. He takes a few tentative steps, peeks behind corners, but finds nobody, finds the place as deserted as the day he finished construction. Perhaps some raiders had discovered it a while ago and had poked around; but then why would they leave the storeroom with the supplies virtually intact?

The hatch above opens again, and a figure slides down the side of the ladder, dropping like a coat off a hanger. "Who are you?" The shaft of light falls on a knife; a glint, a flicker, as the hand jabs the air with the weapon.

Marko flinches, then says, "I'm—I'm the one who built—this place."

"Well, now it's mine." A pair of almond eyes, milky white, staring at him. "Go away."

"I can't," he stutters, "I can't leave."

"Go or I will make you go." The voice is a woman's voice, Marko realizes—a girl's voice.

"I already left one place. I can't leave another. Not this soon."

The girl stands there, crouching, knife-hand outstretched, and somehow Marko knows she won't do him harm; not because she seems incapable of killing, but because she seems incapable of killing an unarmed man. And sure enough, a few intense moments later, she growls as if scolding herself and tucks the knife away in her belt. "What's your name?"

"Marko."

"Marko," she repeats.

"Yes. And yours?"

"What faction, Marko?"

"No faction. I live alone and survive alone."

"Bullshit," she says. "Nobody survives alone."

"You seem to have."

Which makes her reach for her knife again. She doesn't unsheathe it, just pats the blade. "Don't presume anything, Marko."

"I've lived in this city my whole life, and when the troubles started to unfold, I elected to remain and do what I do best."

"Which is?"

"Making do."

For the first time the girl moves in a non-threatening way, a small stroll to the mattress and back, circling him, almost as if to mark territory. She's shorter than him. And very young. "And what does that entail?"

"Collecting. Rationing. Trading," he says, then, pointing to the shelf with the row of books askew, he adds, "You've been reading my books."

She quickly glances at the books then back at him, and in the dark, dark of the bunker, with only an inkling of light from the shaft by the ladder, he sees her blush. "What sort of trading?"

"Which was your favorite? Did you enjoy *Reflections of a City in the Mirror*? Or was the poetry of Babic more to your liking? Or Mr. Domovin's parables?"

"If you don't answer I will gut you."

"I traded with all factions. I found or bought goods and traded them for other goods, building up a stash. I calculated who needed what and allowed for the factions, essentially, to trade amongst themselves through me."

"So," she says, "you had contact with all of them?"

"Most factions, yes."

She comes closer to study his face, then pulls back again. "Why are you here now?"

"Because they found my living quarters. My stash. Which was dangerous. The Trader never revealed his identity and location, but worked with drone drop and pickup spots only." The girl stares at him blankly, so he adds, "And by the Trader I mean myself."

"I got that," she says.

"May I ask why *you* are here?"

"You may not." She circles him once, twice, as if deliberating what to do with him. "But here I will have to stay for a day or five at least," she says, "so question is, what to do with you?" She goes around him two more times, clockwise, then contrariwise, arms by her sides.

"I won't be an issue."

"You already are."

"I mean to say, I won't bother you more than with my presence."

"Why shouldn't I just chuck you out with that ironing board of yours? Leave you to sleep on some bench."

"Because," he says, "you won't even know I'm here. All I need is my desk and my notebooks to begin with. And because it's cold and dangerous out there, and I have done you nothing to deserve that."

She considers his words for a moment, then sits down on the chair by the escritoire and considers them some more. She sighs. Rubs her eyes. "Fine," she says. "Fine."

"Thank you."

"But one wrong move," she says and pats her knife again.

Marko nods and tells her that he is exhausted after days of travel and his legs can't carry him anymore, and she tells him she is, too, and they better sleep, but she informs him that she will sleep with one eye open and that she won't be sharing the mattress with him and that the floor is all his. To prove her point, she throws him a bundle of dirty rags, which, when he lies on the ground, he wads up and places under his head.

"Sleep tight," he says.

She doesn't reply, but a moment later she says, "*Reflections.*" She clears her throat. "That was my favorite." And she turns to the side, patting her dusty pillow, and starts snoring within minutes.

⸙

When he wakes up, the girl's gone.

His cracked wristwatch, which he wears on his left ankle, tucked away from prying hands, tells him it's minutes to six. He rubs his eyes, stretches, and sets to work, starting with unwrapping the layers of duct tape off his mummified luggage strapped to the ironing board, then airing out everything until the stench of the subway tunnels is reduced to a whiff, and finally he sits at his escritoire and performs a general review of his folders of documents under the dim light of an old, flickering, battery-run desk lamp. He has brought carbon-copies of his work here, too, but not everything—a lot of the mathematics had been done on that apartment's walls and floors, mimicking Teacher in her way of surrounding herself with the work, being constantly reminded; luckily he has with him the notebook containing his work's first principles from which he can build the whole system back up again. He scrawls in the margins, jotting down notes and calculations to factor in his newly-diminished position, until he loses all track of time: he will need to start with the basics—tin, copper, water, gunpowder—and work his way up to the rarer supplies, then the stronger explosives and ammunition, then the prestigious, luxurious items will follow, and then he will be able to play the factions against themselves as he sees fit, and tip the scales of the war, and force all factions to retreat, to defend, to surrender.

The hatch creaks open, and by the time Marko lifts his eyes from his equations the girl's feet are on the floor. She pulls on the cord, shutting the hatch. White light turns yellow.

"Brought something," she says, and throws a box of old crackers on the mattress.

"Where did you find those?"

"Out there."

At last he says, "Thanks."

She nods toward the storeroom with the jars and cans of preserved food. "I didn't mean to steal," she says. "The first night, when I was starving, I borrowed some biscuits and slathered them with marmalade. So there. I pay you back." She lies on the mattress, hands behind her head. "I'm no thief."

"Never thought you were," he says. "Thank you."

"Anja," she says.

"Thank you, Anja."

≀

Within three days, he sets up a new trading network and starts amassing supplies.

Marko reaches out to former points of contact and sends them word of his situation through the only remnant of the erstwhile civilization: those featureless automated drones buzzing among the ruins of the city, picking up and dropping off parcels to encrypted addresses known only to them and the sender, slaloming through the city airspace to shake off any would-be tracers, allowed, by an unvoiced agreement between all factions, to exist and be useful for all. His initial trading contacts respond within hours with lists of the current status of demand/supply on the market in their side of town, and he quickly scribbles notes with what he has to offer, and stuffs them in the claws of the drones before their stuttering rotors whisk them away.

He scours the area around the bunker for scrap, for useful bits of material, but finds slim pickings; this is the eastern half of the city, the formerly busy and chic neighborhoods clustered around the old park with the stadium, which means it was the first to be stripped of anything of value.

The girl he sees only at night when she returns, exhausted and quiet, knife in her teeth, from wherever it is that she roams; he doesn't dare ask.

One night, following a day of extensive and mind-numbing work, which proves more daunting now that he has to consider how his backlog of orders from his stash have failed to be disseminated among the rival factions, he nods off over his book, dreaming in snapshots of Teacher and the life before all this, snapshots flashing like white phosphorus across the sky, snapshots cut short by the bang of the hatch. He shakes his head and finds drool over his shirt, his book.

Anja climbs down the ladder one rung at a time, cursing to herself. She drags herself to the mattress, and only when she gasps and grimaces, hand pressing her abdomen, does Marko realize that she's hurt.

"What happened?"

"None—of your business."

"You're hurt. Let me have a look." He takes a step toward the mattress, but she raises a hand, wincing. He says, "This is idiotic, you're hurting." He ignores her gesture and takes whatever it is that resembles first-aid supplies from his storeroom and kneels down by the mattress.

Sweat dapples Anja's pale yellow face. He lifts up her shirt to the belly-button and sees a cut the length of his thumb, blood bubbling out of it, but one that's not a deep gash, fortunately. He soaks up the blood with a dry rag, then dabs at the wound with another rag doused in the only disinfectant he could find, pure pre-war vodka, and finally duct-tapes a thin strip of gauze over the cut.

He makes her drink water and eat canned peach slices, and when he asks her what had happened, she groans, says she doesn't want to talk about it, and the blood loss and exhaustion take their toll and she falls asleep. Marko watches over her while she sleeps, listening to her shallow breaths, reading a book in one hand. When some hours later she comes to, she says she's ready to go back out.

"There's no way you're going out there in this shape."

"I told you," she says, "it's none of your business what I do, how I do it, and when I decide to do it. Which in this case, is right this very moment." But she props herself up and then drops her head back down on the pillow, grimacing in pain.

"Like I said, there is no way."

Anja fixes him a dirty look, then she sighs, and says, nodding toward the books, "Fine, then give me one of those."

⁂

"Why do you trade," she says, looking up from her book, "when you don't keep anything for yourself, when you're always poor?" She makes a sweeping, all-encompassing gesture with one hand to prove her point.

"Because I don't want anything for myself."

"What do you want, then?"

"I want to this to end."

She gives him a puzzled look. "Which faction?"

"None of them to win, all of them to lose." He scratches his cheek. "I am balancing things out, smoothing the wrinkles, slowly making all factions equal in strength, and then I bleed them weaker, simultaneously, none more so than any other, and then I bleed them dead."

"Even the Goldmouths?"

"Even the Goldmouths."

"But—but they are not *bad*. Not like others."

"I don't know what the Goldmouths are fighting for."

"How the hell can you not?"

"Because I don't know what any of them are fighting for, and I don't want to know, because only then I can remain impartial and do my work well. All I know is I can stop them, and we will breathe clean air in this city again."

&

It takes Anja little to no time to get back on her feet, to be up and about and trawling the city during the day, but now their evenings have changed, because they talk more, and they read together, sometimes even out loud to each other. One night Anja offers him the mattress, saying they should maybe switch and she should sleep on the floor a while, but he steadfastly refuses, lying that he's now so used to the planks and rags that he wouldn't even manage to get a wink of sleep on anything softer.

3.

Anja returns from one of her city escapades angry, cursing. When she calms down somewhat, she tells him, "You have to tell me how to get in. In the nest of Blackstars."

"Are you crazy?"

"You have to tell me. You have traded with them."

"Is that where you've been going all this time?"

"I told you," she says, and her eyes turn ruby red, "where I go is none of your goddamn business."

She hasn't spoken to him like this since their first day. She stomps her feet on the bunker planks.

"Were they the ones who hurt you? The Blackstars are dangerous."

"I know they're dangerous," she says. "I've seen them kill." Tears come to her eyes, and she blinks and they stream down her face. "And I will get to them. And get them back for that. And you will tell me how to get in."

Marko takes a step but she raises her hand. He says, "I don't know how to get in. I've only sent drones with supplies to their quarter."

"You're useless." And she crumples up a sheet of his mathematics from the escritoire and throws it at him. "A useless old man who does nothing but sit and write." And she places a foot on the ladder.

"Wait," he says, "don't go. The Blackstars will hurt you. Please, stay."

"The Blackstars," she hisses, "killed my mother, and I can't let that go. And you can't stop me, because you don't even know what they're fighting for, you don't even care. To you they're just numbers on a piece of paper, just parts of an equation, and you weren't there when she was hurting, and when she was dying, and you have no right to tell me how to handle that." And she goes up the rungs of the ladder, her knife in her teeth, and out the bunker and into the city.

⁂

On his moldy mattress he lies, thumbing through his worn notebook where equations stud the margins and weighted graphs span the pages like spiderwebs, representing the connections he's drawn among the various combatants, each with their strengths and weaknesses and supplies factored in in red ink, and he himself, somewhere in those equations, nudging one faction against another, bringing this god-awful war, in theory, closer to an end.

He gingerly closes his notebook, wrapping a blackened shoelace around it.

The girl, he knows, will have to be factored in, too, a pugnacious, ineluctable faction of one. Blackstars in long vinyl overcoats and rabbit-eared masks facing the wrath of a hurt young girl, and her, the Gang of Anja, slashing with the serrated blade, ripping into her enemies, not tip-toeing around but playing hopscotch on his weighted mathematical graphs. Stomping his theories into the ground. Because Marko finds himself no longer worrying about this war and this city and these blood-thirsty groups that are ravishing it for reasons beyond his understanding, but about one damaged person, one hurt and good and *salvageable* person, and suddenly his clarity is gone, his work tarnished.

And he finds himself needing Teacher, needing her advice, her wisdom. Somebody has to convince him to see things clearly again; to not get bogged down into human minutiae, into the pathetic fate of One, but to gawk wide-eyed at all around him and to put it all back together the way it was. So he gets up and throws his threadbare long-coat on and storms out, crossing half the city to Teacher's last known location.

The old bus station rots away with the carcasses of rusted chassis strewn about, creaking; Marko circles this humming graveyard once, approaching the building as predator does prey, then kicks a busted door open and goes in. Stench of things long-dead hits his nose and he covers half his face with the crook of his arm, and explores Teacher's last hide-out just like that, eyes squinting, elbow out. He hasn't seen her in years, and she's older than him by a decade to begin with, at the very least, and very few Remainers stay in place for long, so the futility of his gesture is not lost on him, but a claw still rips through his chest when he goes into Teacher's old room—that cabin for the announcer of bus departure and arrival times, a microphone protruding from a desk like a poised viper—and the claw rips into his heart when he finds Teacher's room empty and nondescript, with her mathematical scribbles on the teal plaster walls scratched off, ruined, the plus signs all lengthened into crosses.

He stands there, vertiginous for a brief moment, before reality seeps in and he realizes what's happened to Teacher and to her work and to his work and to this city.

And then tears come to his eyes and he sobs there boxed in in Teacher's last written lesson for him, and he remembers all those passionate sessions of her explaining the basic mathematics of her theory that the pen truly is mightier than the sword, of how one can end this war with no guns but equations if only one abstracts oneself from everything, sheds one's interest and ego and puts one's mind to the Work, and if one hopes. Which Teacher seems to have forgotten or given up on, and that makes Marko sob even harder, and before he leaves the old rotting bus station and returns to his bunker, he places one palm on the teal plaster wall and caresses the scratch-marks and kisses the scratch-marks and says, "Thank you."

4.

He takes only what he truly needs, water, a pack of biscuits, and his improvised first-aid kit consisting of a wad of bandages and half a bottle of vodka, and he leaves his bunker for the last time. In his bag, he carries *Reflections of a City in the Mirror* for her.

Nearing Blackstar territory, the city closes up, thickens, becomes hard to squeeze through alive; mines go off and barbed wire snatches those scurrying away from explosions, and Marko knows all this because he has sold them those mines, that barbed wire, so he treads carefully, sweeping the road ahead with the needled branch of a pine. The rat-tat-tat of a machine gun makes him flinch, but he walks on, scouting out the terrain for the girl who's thrown herself at these maniacs, armed with nothing but a knife.

When night falls and the sky turns the color of burning coal, he retreats into a decrepit building and huddles in a corner. Wind howls through broken windows, booms fail to die down, but his bones and muscles and ears quickly adapt, and he sleeps. Air-chopping staccatos of a delivery drone wake him up with a start; a black buzzard, against the backdrop of a gray sky, leers at him through a broken window for a wink before flying away, and Marko blinks and remembers where he is. He's wide awake; it's dawn. He quickly gathers his gear and continues his search for Anja.

His boots raise little plumes of soot as he treads on streets blanketed with ash and debris, and an eerily quiet morning creeps up on the city, on this quarter, this home of the Blackstars, and he slows, stops, takes a good look around: high-rises with gaping broken windows, the small playgrounds in between, the see-saws with their seats stolen slowly moving in the wind, up and down, up and down.

She can't be far. And they can't be far.

Then, almost as if in answer to his thought, two sets of footsteps from somewhere, an echo bouncing off the high-rises, and two men armed with machine guns emerge from below ground —dead men brought back to life—and approach him.

"Give us one good reason," one says, wiggling his bunny ears, "not to shoot you right here, right now."

Marko says, "I am not looking for trouble."

"Too late," says the other, raising his gun.

"I just want to find her."

"Find who?"

"The girl."

The two men look at each other. The first one says, "What's she to you?"

"She," Marko says, and his knees buckle and he almost drops to the ground, but instead he forces another breath of foul city air into his lungs. "She's a girl. She's just a girl, and that's all she is, and that's all she should be allowed to be, and I can't let this happen to her. She's just a little girl."

Again, a glance between themselves. "You're a senile old man. But we can let you pick who gets to shoot you."

"No," he says. "I'm not."

"Oh, aren't you?"

"Those guns. Those weapons. I gave them to you. Don't you see? I am the Trader."

"What bullshit is this?"

And he racks his brains to remember the trade logs and he rattles out the Blackstars' last purchases as proof, and the two men listen and just stare, wiggling their ears. "And if you give me the girl," he says, regaining his composure, "I will leave town and leave my stash to you, Blackstars."

The two men stand there, the butts of their rifles pressing against their shoulder blades, muzzles aimed at his chest, then one turns to the other and says something in Blackstar patois, then the other nods, and the first leaves to disappear into the ground down invisible steps. The one with the gun trained on Marko stands in silence, waiting, and when the first one reemerges, he says, "What's to say you're not lying?"

"If I'm lying, then what have you got to lose? One silly girl? But if I'm not, then you have much to gain."

The two confer again in their dialect, then one nods, and tells Marko to wait. He plunges into the depths of the earth and comes up a moment later with Anja, pale and bruised and bleeding, slung over his shoulder. He drops her to the ground in front of Marko with a thud, and places one boot on her breasts. "Now, Trader, where is that stash of yours?"

He gives them his old address and explains how to get to apartment 34D, and the two men nod, and one raises his rifle at Marko and says, Boom, and before leaving them there, the other says, "I hope our paths won't cross, Trader."

꽃

The sky, a salmon-pink backdrop painted red and black in flickers as explosives go off in the valley below. Anja's slumped on his shoulder like a sandbag, bleeding through her bandages down his chest. Marko watches the festering city struggle with itself, unmade and scattered into infinite pieces of rubble, its maw devouring its tail, and he rubs his eyes and turns away from the scorching heat and from what he's failed to save and toward a new horizon, and he grips Anja firmly and starts to walk, thinking maybe one is good enough.

*Hope*

*Hope*     *Interest*     *Curiosity*

*Serenity*        *Respect*

# 4. Faux Ami

## A. Martine

### Elinor

Elinor smiled at her daughter's reflection as the little girl prattled on, the chime of her voice a gentle backdrop to Elinor's musings. She smoothed her daughter's hair as she ran the comb gently down the length, the teeth catching slightly at the curled ends, then gathered the locks into one long braid. Elinor held out her hand, and, still chattering agitatedly, the little girl reached back and slipped a red ribbon into her outstretched palm.

Elinor gazed down at it; once vibrantly crimson, it was now a dull maroon around the edges. Soon, she knew, the entire cloth would revert to its original color, a heather grey as bleak as the terrible omen it signified.

She was pulled from her brooding by a tug: she still held her daughter's hair in her hand. Grace had turned to face her, waiting on an answer to a question Elinor had obviously not heard.

"Mum? Did he?"

"Did who what, love?"

"Daffyd, did he write from Swansea yet? He said he would, it's been almost a month."

"Have a bit of patience, love. Swansea is a long way away from Sheffield. They are most likely just settling into their new home."

"I'm sure he's forgotten all about me already."

Grace pouted, as she often did when she did not have her way, but the dejection Elinor read in her daughter's eyes was genuine. Immediately, she felt it echoed in her own chest. She had been expecting the question. Grace was of a naturally bright disposition, but every now and then, her melancholic tendencies showed through. Elinor never failed to notice: her daughter was lonely. When little Daffyd and his mother had arrived at Elinor's inn over a month ago, Grace had been immediately taken with him, which was customary of her. The children had become inseparable over the course of Daffyd's stay, and they had been given free rein of the empty inn, hiding and stalking each other like predators.

Daffyd's mother, doubtlessly having sensed a kindred spirit in Elinor, had revealed that she'd taken her son and slipped away in the night in order to escape her vicious husband. Elinor had felt genuine pity for the petrified woman. Nevertheless, her own family's plight had been more pressing: her son Henry's illness had taken her and her husband completely unawares, and fresh blood was in short supply. The flux of tenants at the Scarlett Inn had been steadily dwindling for years, and this particularly harsh winter was disrupting all notions of safe travel.

The opportunity, thus, had been invaluable. She had seen no other option. Daffyd and his mother, alone in the world, would not be missed. Elinor had tried not to prolong their ordeal any more than she had to.

Presently, however, she felt grim. It was always easier to do what she must when the people involved were scum. Daffyd and his mother, who were anything but, had lingered with her, as things tended to do lately. She had tried not to prolong their ordeal any more than she had to. Afterward, she had gently folded little Daffyd's hand in his mother's, wiped a trickle from his chin before covering their interlaced bodies with a bed linen.

Elinor's eyes met Grace's in the copper-rimmed mirror, and with a surge of irritation that took her unawares, she began roughly braiding her daughter's hair again.

"He probably has, Grace, and it would do you good to do the same. You can't expect everyone who stays with us to promise you their everlasting friendship, can you?"

She finished the braid and wrapped the faded ribbon around her daughter's hair, refusing to meet the eyes she knew were now brimming with unshed tears.

One day, she would tell her daughter what her own mother had reiterated throughout Elinor's childhood: why she could not allow her heart to run away with her emotions if she was expected to do what she must. Why it was dangerous for Grace to be as candid and earnest as she was. Why she would need to be deceitful, charming, and slippery. Why she could never trust nor fall in love with a human being. Why she would have to place the protection of herself and her own above that of everyone else.

Elinor stood, briefly rested her hand on Grace's head, then she silently left the room. She walked to the end of the corridor and after a short halt, pushed a small door open. The curtains had been drawn over the windows; the room was balmy, on account of the fire wafting from the small fireplace. Her husband Hugo sat on the edge of the bed, their son's head cradled on his lap. His eyes found hers, and through the exhaustion clouding his gaze, she saw an anguish that alarmed her. Wordlessly, he shook his head.

Elinor lowered herself at the foot of the bed. If she sat any closer, she would see just how ravaged her little Henry had become, and she did not feel strong enough to bear it.

"Elle."

She reached for the little cap that must have tumbled off the bed. It was hard to believe that it had once been the same shade of fiery red as her own hair. Patches of ashen hue tinted the faded crimson. Her own brooch, fastened on the lapel of her shirt, and her husband's bowtie were brighter, but only just.

"Elle," her husband said again. She did not want to look at him. She knew what his tone meant. "Are you ready to confront the notion—"

"No, we are *not* leaving, Hugo," she said, with more virulence than she had intended. "We are *not*."

Hugo laid a placating hand on her forearm, but reluctance twisted the corner of his mouth. This, Elinor knew, was the juncture at which he would usually bow out from their arguments. She had always had the last word on critical decisions regarding their little family, while Hugo gladly relegated the less savory tasks to Elinor. As long as his waking hours could be spent tending to his children's whimsies and mischievous games, he was content. This delegation included the running of the inn, but also the occasional bloodying of the hands to ensure they had enough provisions to survive.

Their union had always worked on the strength of that unspoken understanding; Elinor was ruthless when need be, whereas he was gentle, his judgment easily clouded by tender sympathy. They valued each other for their respective attributes, however contrasting. If he had ever had objections, Hugo had always respectfully kept them to himself; besides, Elinor had rarely led her family astray.

Nevertheless, perhaps because this particular situation concerned their children, Hugo was unrelenting for once.

"Elle, we have gold. We can start over. Move somewhere where there's a steadier flow of travelers, somewhere we don't have to ... scavenge." Hugo covered Henry's ear at that, his voice low and rushed. "The situation is dire. Daffyd and his mother... that was pure chance and it may not happen again. We can no longer afford to sit and wait for someone to come to our door. No one is coming, can't you see? By the time this storm clears, we may all be —"

"And what if we lose everything in the process?" she retorted.

"If we can save our son, we will not have lost everything."

"Don't you dare suggest—" she choked. She clutched the cap in her hand, wringing it in her fist. "I want him healed as much as you do."

Silence fell, speckled here and there by the sound of the crackling fire. The strength of Hugo's doubts was making Elinor less sure of her sense of duty than she already was. It was exhausting, being turned to for answers, when she herself was sometimes just as lost.

Elinor looked up at him at last. "Hugo, do you remember what it was like before we founded this inn?"

"Of course I do, Elle."

She held his gaze while his eyes, so very much like their daughter's, swam with tears.

"We can't go back to that. We owe our children a life where they are not in constant danger of being persecuted and ostracized. We are not our ancestors, who would have fed on their own to stay alive. We have to have faith, Hugo. Lady Fortune has never deserted us. She will not desert us now."

"You're right, I know you're right."

"If no one has turned up by tomorrow, I will go to Rotherham and I will sort us out." She put a hand firmly on his. "I *will* sort us out."

Still clutching the cap, Elinor stood.

"Will you go get more firewood for the kiln out back? I'll go down to the cellar and see what I can do with this." Elinor indicated the cap in her hand.

In truth, a selfish part of her simply wanted to leave the room and the woe contained in its small space. She halted at the door and glanced back at him. He gave her a watery smile, but in his eyes, there was no mirth.

⸸

## Moira

Moira ran, but the snow was like a mouth swallowing each of her footsteps. Not for the first time, she stumbled forward, her arms plunging into the snow like it was melted butter. She pushed herself upright again. One of her feet slipped out of her slipper; it could not be helped. It was an ill match for the elements. The cold would not afflict her anyway. The clouds seemed to have blended with the powdered horizon. In the gathering wind, the feathery flakes hung and whirled, rather than falling, giving Moira the impression that she was running through a snow globe that had just been vigorously shaken.

Moira threw a furtive glance over her shoulder; she hadn't heard her pursuers in a very long time, but whenever she stopped to catch her breath, her mother's voice, raw in her ear, hissed. *Run.*

And so she did. The breeze nudged her to and fro and she stumbled forward blindly for what seemed a few hours, but could have been minutes. Underneath the quilt of snow, her bare foot caught onto something rough, and she crashed forward again. This time she stayed down. Exhaustion collapsed on her like a mass she could no longer carry.

Moira settled in the gathering snow and buried herself deeper in the folds of her white cloak. In this storm, she could have been mistaken for part of the landscape. Maybe, just maybe, they would not see her if they came thundering through the forest. As she sat huddled in the heart of this savage beauty, the rays of the afternoon sun kissed the tree trunks, gliding silently over them. She flinched away from them, uttering a silent apology to her mother. Run, she no longer could.

The snowfall had lessened slightly. Moira strained her hearing; here and there, a frosted branch snapped, no doubt under the weight of the snow that had coated it, but no other soul, living or otherwise, could be heard. In the silence, she felt smaller, if possible, than she already was. The trees towered overhead, their canopies bending inward to form a vaulted ceiling of glitter and ice.

Another breeze came swirling through the trees, lifting the snow, and Moira gasped. The aroma was unmistakable: *human flesh.*

It did not come from behind her, but from ahead. Her body responding before her mind could catch on, Moira was on her feet again. She was no longer bothering to conceal herself, nor was she concerned with the trail of gaping holes she was leaving behind her. She hurtled toward the scent, deeper into the forest, shoulders scraping the rough cedar trunks. The scent was growing stronger; she crouched, hugging the trunk for support.

She heard the man before she saw him. A few feet away, a branch gave way under a heavy footfall, and Moira retreated from the sound. A man emerged from between two trees, an axe slung over his shoulder and a wide basket of plaited straw under the other; logs of chopped wood peeked over the top. He was not one of the villagers. She had never seen him before. Her legs moving of their own accord, Moira began to follow, hesitantly.

His effortless gait suggested that he knew his way around the forest. Moira eyed him warily. Her natural strength was doubtless superior to his; her height and current weakness, however, were disadvantages, as was the axe he carried. She was panting now, with the effort to conceal and control herself, and was fighting the urge to lunge recklessly forward when another sound in the distance made her halt. Ahead of the man, a cry echoed, bell-like in the distance.

"Dad? Dad?"

"Where have you been, then?" the man boomed in response. He did not seem angry; in fact, upon hearing the call, he had dropped his haul and planted his fists on his hips in mock indignation. A little girl came running through the trees. She could not have been more than five or six, a thick woolen coat nearly swallowing her small figure whole. Unhindered by the snow which was nearly as tall as she was, she vaulted herself onto her father's legs.

"Been chopping wood all by myself, Gracie. You were supposed to help," he chortled.

"I found a rhubarb patch!" the little girl blurted. She waved her tiny fist, and indeed, a leafy head blossomed over the red stalks in her palm.

"In this dreadful weather?" He tossed the stalk in the basket and swung it, and the axe he had put down, on one shoulder. She locked her hands around his other forearm and he lifted her as if she were just another parcel he was carrying.

"Say you'll make rhubarb crisp, say you will."

Any notion of attacking the man had dissipated. Moira watched them walk away, the girl giggling, her ribboned hair swinging as she swayed. All at once, Moira felt almost intrusive: and yet, for the first time in days, something other than herself and her voracious hunger was holding her attention. She inclined her head in the direction she had come from. Not a sound. The hope of having outrun her followers seemed premature, but already, panic was starting to subside.

She pulled her cloak further down her face, crouched behind this or that tree, making sure that they couldn't see her. The man's impressive frame rattled with profound, affable laughter at a quip his daughter had made; Moira strained her hearing to catch what they were saying.

She slid her gaze over the man's gentle hands, eyed the loving tilt of the little girl's head, contemplated their casual, nonchalant rapport. Once, she lost them amid a tangle of interlocking branches, and nearly sprinted ahead to keep them in her eager sights.

What would her mother have done? Moira did not have to wonder long. She knew that even if her mother had been this desperate, it would have mattered to her that this man and his daughter were innocent. Surely, she'd have cautioned Moira to turn heel, keep running, search for less precarious alternatives. It was what they had done every time they'd been driven out of this or that village.

Moira dug her nails into an ash tree, her body struggling to stay upright. A thought occurred: if they had come from some nearby village, there could be others. A straggler. A shelterless man. An urchin. Surely her pursuers could not have forewarned neighboring towns about her family already? She pushed away and recommenced her pursuit of the two humans.

After what seemed an eternity, the forest cleared, opening onto a large terrain. Moira held back. In the distance, an impressive edifice stood, fringed by a frozen patch of flowers on one side and a small pond on the other. A trail curved away toward the back, where Moira could just make out a smaller building. Smoke was churning slowly from three chimneys on the roof. A dangling sign over the double doors read:

## THE SCARLETT INN

A thrill went through her, as overpowering as it was fleeting. Instinct urged her to double back. If there was an inn, there were other people, which meant that she was surely outnumbered. The impulse was nevertheless muffled by a more potent inclination, that which had made her follow the two humans. It was, she was amazed to find, more intellectual than it was passionate.

Moira's eyes trailed the little girl's bouncing braids as she ran ahead of her father, and through the front door. He lagged behind, slightly bent forward against the wind.

For all Moira knew, they were the very sort of people her parents had cautioned her against all her life: heartless, wicked, or worse. Moira had spent her childhood behind four protective but ultimately stifling walls; so much so that presently, stranded in a

A. Martine

strange forest, she felt vulnerable and unprepared. Her parents' cocoon of loving reassurance would do nothing for her now, nothing at all.

Moira gritted her teeth against the onslaught of acrimony she'd been trying to keep at bay all day. She'd have all the time in the world to dwell on it if she made it through this ordeal.

The man paused on the front porch and knocked his heels against each other. Powdery snow dislodged from his boots, the blade of the axe on his shoulder catching the light. He entered.

Moira had never, until this moment, made a calculated choice regarding her own life, had never been given the occasion to desire anything. Grief, which had initially disoriented her, was subtly giving way to an adjacent emotion: it felt almost like freedom, in all its dizzying splendor.

The scales tipped tantalizingly. Would the innkeeper turn away a sole, penniless stranger? What would happen if they didn't? She wanted to know.

The snowfall had picked up with renewed force and although Moira was not cold, she was beginning to ache, no doubt tempted by the prospect of a roof over her head. She realized she was panting.

A split second. Her body decided for her.

She staggered forward, skidding on the slick ground. Her legs gave out, and she crawled the rest of the way there, coming to a shuddering halt in front of the door. She had barely placed a fluttering hand on its surface when it swung open again.

It was not the man from the forest. A woman stood framed in the entryway, a mane of red hair piled artfully atop of her head, her dark brown eyes wide with a powerful emotion. She looked as stricken as Moira felt, and their gazes locked onto each other's for a quivering moment.

Then, Moira remembered the question her parents had told her she must never forget to ask.

"May I come in?"

The croak of her voice seemed to bring the woman out of her torpor. She shouted something over her shoulder, then turned back to her. Moira tried to reach for the steadying hand the woman was offering, but could only manage it halfway. The woman's gaze swept the white expanse behind Moira, then she knelt.

"Come in, dear."

꠸

## Elinor

Elinor gazed back at the sliver of her face reflected in the blade, her index finger lightly caressing the edge. Her eye was a depthless pool, the irises large and bright, the slice of smile a crooked thing.

She lowered the blade and cut through the steaming crust of the rhubarb cherry pie with a quivering hand. The fillings bled unctuously, a crimson color that entranced her for a moment. Then she placed the slice carefully on the plate and pushed her way out of the kitchen.

The large and empty dining room was drowned in the golden glow cast by the sconces on the walls; the curtains had been drawn against the rays of the setting sun. The warmth was heightened by the gentle crackle-hum of the fire in the furthest corner of the room.

The new girl sat, her back to the flames; Grace knelt whispering at her feet, looking up at her like she was the only thing in the room that mattered. They had not seen Elinor, and for a moment she paused, everything else momentarily forgotten. In her mind's eye, she saw herself kneeling likewise, so many decades ago, her chin on her sister's lap, hanging onto her words as if the world began and ended with her. The memory of Elinor and her sister was replaced by Grace and Daffyd sitting near the fire, a mere few weeks ago.

*Daffyd.*

"Grace," she said roughly, "leave the poor girl alone, can't you see how exhausted she is?"

The girls started.

"I'm not bothering her, I was only telling her a story," Grace said petulantly.

"She's not bothering me," the girl hastily repeated.

"Well, make yourself useful then," Elinor insisted. "Go look after your brother, and make sure he drinks his tea."

Grace made a point of knocking into a nearby table as she dragged herself away, muttering under her breath.

"May I?" Elinor did not wait for her to answer. She slid into the chair facing the girl. The latter returned Elinor's polite smile, but her eyes were inquisitive, mirroring, Elinor knew, her own appraising glance.

"You have a son?" the girl asked quietly.

Elinor felt her smile falter.

"Yes, barely a year old."

There was a pregnant pause. Then, remembering the plate she held in her hands, Elinor slid it across the table.

"Here you go, love, I hope you like rhubarb."

The young girl made a polite gesture of appreciation, but did not otherwise react.

"What did you say your name was?"

"Moira. Moira Turly."

"You gave us quite a scare, Moira. Are you feeling better?"

"Very much. I am ever so grateful."

Elinor did not agree that she looked better. The girl was no longer shaking, but there was a definite haunted look about her, and her pallor had not lessened. In fact, there was unmistakable hunger in her eyes still, although the goblet of water Elinor had served her an hour ago lay barely touched, as did the meat pie. With a twang of irritation, Elinor touched the plate she had just slid across the table.

"Eat something, Moira, you're white as a sheet."

Moira looked down at the rhubarb fruit pie. As if it were the last thing on earth she wanted to do, she began picking at it with her fingers, disregarding the silverware. She had a thoughtful look about her, her movements economical and deliberate. Elinor took in the small limbs, the dark hair which stood out against the white dress she was wearing. The clothes were simple, yet sturdy; the cloak she'd been wearing when she collapsed at their doorstep had been thick and warm. Here and there, holes in the fabric of her dress had been patched with regular stitches, the fraying hems of her sleeves sewn with obvious care. She had lost her shoe, but the remaining one looked handmade.

She was neither bruised nor did she appear maltreated; in fact, she did not have the look of a neglected child. Something about her did not make sense, and the more Elinor prodded, the less she understood. She would have gone through the girl's things had her unexpected boarder not arrived empty-handed. That last fact was conspicuous above all. No means of transport, no luggage or parcels, no traveling companion. The girl couldn't be older than fourteen.

*Still a child.*

Elinor's eyes glided to the veins in Moira's arms, blue lightning bolts spreading down the willowy white arms.

Moira looked up. Elinor flitted her gaze away.

"Miss," the young girl said, "I wanted to thank you for your hospitality and the nourishment. I wish...," she paused and a strange look clouded her brow. "I wish I could repay you in a worthier way."

"Not at all, dear, your presence here is payment enough," Elinor smiled, and she almost wished she had only meant it one way. "We are appreciative of any guest who comes our way these days."

Moira inclined her head questioningly. Elinor bit her lip, then elaborated.

"The inn hasn't been doing as well, what with that new railway coming through London. My husband and I, we settled here initially because it seemed like an ideal place to attract travelers. And for years, we did…"

Trailing off, she looked around the room. The empty tables and upturned chairs looked like skeletons, the shadows they cast against the fireplace stern and deep.

"This godforsaken storm has really put us in a state. This winter has been particularly harsh. It's been lonely, but most of all, it hasn't done our family any good."

"I'm very sorry to hear that, Mrs. Scarlett," Moira said, and she sounded like she meant it.

Elinor tutted. "None of that 'Mrs. Scarlett' nonsense. You can call me Elinor, or Elle."

Moira looked suddenly stricken and Elinor blanched, instinctively.

"What ever's the matter?"

Moira turned in her chair and wrapped an arm around the back, her face to the fire. Silhouetted as she was, she looked very old.

"My sister," she said in a small voice. "Her name was Ella."

*Was.* Elinor leant closer, feeling hesitant. She had wanted to ask the question from the outset, the same question she had asked so many times of so many tenants before her. This, however, was not her usual hackneyed prying: for the first time, Elinor slightly dreaded the answer.

"Where is your family, Moira?"

The young girl faced her again.

"It's just me now."

Elinor realized that she had moved her fingers across the table. Moira seemed to notice also, and swiftly pulled her own hand away.

"My family, we're… we're not from here. People don't always take kindly to strangers, I suppose. We were attacked by some of our neighbors who wanted us out of their village. My parents distracted them to allow my sister and me to escape, but in the end, it was meaningless. They caught up eventually. Ella, she gave herself up so that I could run."

Moira's eyes met hers.

"It's just me now," she repeated hollowly.

"Well," Elinor cleared her throat, smoothing the fabric of the tablecloth with cold fingertips, "it's a good thing you found us, then. You're welcome to stay as long as you like."

The familiar surge of triumph she should have felt at Moira's disclosure was dulled. Elinor was beginning to feel a tug in her chest, as insidious as it was uncomfortable. An itch she'd exacerbated with a nail.

*You've gone soft, Elinor.*

Had she? Or was it that she was, at long last, understanding how one man's plight could be the cruel blessing of another? Although it had never been her forte — comforting others was Hugo's realm — Elinor found herself searching for consoling words to alleviate the silence. When she opened her mouth, however, she was surprised to be uttering words she hadn't intended to.

"My son. He's ill. Very ill. Children are not as robust, you know."

"Is he going to get better?" Moira asked.

Elinor licked her lips. Why was she telling this perfect stranger, a little girl no less, the source of her greatest anxiety? An anxiety she couldn't even share with Hugo?

"We don't know." She licked her lips again. "But we have done, and will continue to do everything possible. Even if..."

For a moment that seemed to last an eternity, Elinor paused, her gaze still locked onto Moira's. The girl was eyeing her curiously again. Slowly, the words tumbled out of Elinor.

"... Even if it's not right."

Moira pursed her lips.

"A parent's love is a formidable thing," she said in an undertone. "No price is apparently too high. To keep you alive at all cost, to give you a life they never had, to make sure their mistakes don't become yours. I've always known it for a fact, and I know it even more now, all too well."

Elinor inclined her head. "Do you think that sort of love is wrong?"

Still focused on her own hands, Moira answered.

"It is suffocating. Parents believe that what they think is best will be enough to protect you when they're gone." Her voice had gotten thick with some emotion that could have been anguish, if it hadn't sounded so venomous.

"Maybe in a few years, I will come to understand why they sacrificed themselves for me. But as of right now, I despise them. I despise them, as much as they must have loved me. I would rather they had let me die."

The words should have put a stop to the tug, but instead, Elinor's thoughts wandered to her own parents, to her mother, who had thought it advantageous to abandon her nine children when Lady Fortune had abandoned them. Would her life had been different if she had had a family like Moira's?

"You don't know what it's like," Elinor said with a gentleness that surprised even her. "Until you've been a parent, you don't know what it's like to want to lay your life down and do what is necessary. Even if it makes you think less of yourself. Even if your children may not understand it yet."

She remembered that very morning, her daughter's tear-filled eyes that she could not meet in the mirror. She remembered the innocence she knew would be shattered when Grace was old enough to find out what she was, what they must do in order to survive.

Moira was looking at her in that peculiar way Elinor was becoming familiar with. The girl was difficult to read, Elinor concluded, and she was not accustomed to people she couldn't decipher. It was her turn to look away from the bluntness of her interlocutor's scrutiny.

The longer she sat facing the girl, the more Elinor found her steely resolve thinning. She didn't know why, but she had gradually become decidedly uncomfortable. A puzzle, and she had misplaced the final piece.

"You must be very tired," she broke the silence. "Would you like me to bring up some tea?"

Moira shook her head wordlessly, a weariness beyond her years etched in the shadows of her face, and stood. For a moment, a questioning tilt of the head suggested that she wanted to say something, but probably thinking better of it, she smiled wanly, and left. Elinor fingered the brooch on the lapel of her tunic.

‡

## Moira

The smell of blood was pervasive; it had overpowered her as soon as she'd stepped inside the inn. Moira braced herself against the relentless thirst she knew she would soon lose control over. She was finding it hard to stay awake, but when she closed her eyes the veins, throbbing gently in their throats, pit-patted like an imprint on her eyelids. She shuddered to think of what she would have done to Grace had Elinor not dismissed her earlier that evening.

A few floors below, porcelain was being set against porcelain with a delicate clink. With a spasm of shame, Moira realized that she hadn't even offered to help, and Elinor's kindness toward her did nothing to assuage her guilt.

Something in her had surrendered instantly upon walking into the inn, and now the long fingers of her conscience were reaching for her — or perhaps it was simpler than that. There was an opacity, underneath Elinor's tender, motherly care, that had stoked her embers. A steeliness, perhaps, not unlike her own, one that suggested a kindred spirit or an affinity. The little she had sampled during their earlier conversation made her yearn for the whole thing.

Moira hadn't felt that with anyone, not even with her own family. Her father would have shushed her, her mother would have murmured sweet falsehoods to soothe Moira's nonexistent concerns. Even patient, reliable Ella would have told her to tread softly. Moira would have deferentially listened, and spent the rest of her existence wondering what would have happened if she'd knocked on the Scarletts' door.

Had either of her loved ones not patronized Moira, they would have realized there was nothing to shield her from. She was not like them, had never been. The world and all its wonders had called to her since the moment she could walk, and the possibility of danger had only titillated her further.

Moira burrowed in the cable-knit blanket that Hugo, Elinor's husband, had brought her earlier that evening, and leant on the frozen window, peering into the obscurity.

In the pitch black night, flakes whirled by, miniature white dancers in the wind. She eyed the snow-capped trees, the diamond-like glint of the ice covering the small garden, the frost glazing the small pond a few feet away from the inn's entrance. The storm had settled, but no traveler would be coming through these roads for a few more days; by the time someone managed to reach the Scarlett Inn, she would be long gone. The opportunity, so very timely, would not come again. Kindred spirit be damned. Even in her tremulous state of mind she knew this much, and yet, and yet, and yet...

Not for the first time, she wondered what her mother would have done. She, who had always thought the best of Moira, would tell her that compassion was rare among their kind, that she should cherish it. Whether her mother had truly believed the candy-coated version of the world she'd fed her, Moira would never know.

What she did know was that the vestiges of her parents' teachings were ebbing away fast. Elinor seemed to adhere to the belief that people must do whatever was necessary in order to survive, and the innkeeper's candor had stayed with Moira in the hours since their conversation.

It was time to stop wondering what her mother would have done, and ask herself: what would she, Moira Turly, do?

She knew that the guilt she was allowing to overwhelm her would only make her life more problematic. That it did not matter that the man was nice, that the son was ill, that the little girl had taken to her, nor that she wanted to get to know them all. That her parents' sacrifice would be in vain if she walked away.

Moira ground her teeth together. The fangs punctured the inside of her lip, but she did not relent. The pain was a reminder.

‡

**Elinor**

Elinor inserted the small key in the padlock, clicking it open. She lifted the latch and slid inside the cold cellar. The room was as she had left it earlier that day, the oil lamps still burning in their sconces. The rows of empty jars glistened like polished rubies on the shelves lining the walls. For the hundredth time that day, she was possessed by the foolish desire to check their contents. But even from where she stood, she could see that they were dried and empty, their opaque walls a coagulated puce.

She strode to the small desk at the other end of the room. She had left her son's cap soaking in the contents of the jar she had deemed less dry than the others. The water she had filled it with did little to improve its color; she wrung the moisture out nonetheless, and listened overhead. The inn was silent now. The girl had seemed on the verge of collapse, so she was surely deeply asleep now. Elinor should not have cared, nor noticed that she was visibly upset, but somehow, through the thrill of the situation, she had.

Elinor stood for a moment, exhaustion seeping down on her like settling dust. For the first time she was beginning to understand why her mother had found it easier to be monstrous. Elinor almost smiled, imagining what it would be like to embrace who she was, free from the constraints of her conscience. It would be so much easier.

Dipping a cloth into the diluted pink liquid, she rubbed some moisture onto the brooch fastened on her collar and twisted the jar shut. She left the room in three hasty strides, and scaled the stairs until she reached her son's room, where she knew she'd find her husband. Surely enough, he leant against the headboard, a hand gently stroking the small blond head. The flames emanating from the fireplace painted the room in strokes of amber and coral, deep shadows dancing across the walls. He stood at once and they looked at each other.

"She's a very sweet girl, Elle," he said quietly. Hugo had taken to Moira in the very short time they had interacted, as he always did with children. "I'm still not convinced she doesn't have someone, anyone, looking for her."

Elinor's eye rested everywhere but on her son. She held out the cap and saw her husband's dismay as he registered the dull, heather-grey cloth. That afternoon's reluctance, however, was gone. He had either decided, for once, that his children were more important than the life of another, or he had gone back to bottling his judgment in favor of trusting Elinor's wisdom.

"Hugo, I want you to take Grace and Henry to the cottage outside. Bring some quilts with you, and make sure they fall fast asleep. Do not, under any circumstances, come out. I will come find you when..." Hugo's forehead creased, and Elinor looked away.

"This should not take long," she added tonelessly.

⁊

## Moira

Elinor and her husband were likely to be stronger, and thus harder to subdue. She would start with them. She would have no choice afterward but to do the same for the children. Moira had decided that the only thing crueler than eradicating an entire family would be orphaning two young children. Losing her parents was a pain she had only known for a few days, but one she intrinsically understood would haunt her forever. She couldn't do that to someone else.

Ignoring the fear thrumming dreadfully through her chest, Moira swiftly crossed the room; the doorknob gave way gently, and, cracking the door just wide enough, she slithered out.

Her room was at the end of a long corridor which veered off into a corner: to her left, a row of small windows concealed behind sheer curtains. The milky half-light of the moon, visible in slivers under the curtains, striped the world black and pastel-blue. She crouched beneath the level of the windowsills, so as to conceal her paleness, and she began to crawl, her movements deliberate and infinitesimal.

Every few feet, Moira halted, listening hard before continuing her noiseless progress. She reached the bend and was now facing the row of windows, her back against the embossed wallpaper, her bare feet planted in the oak wood floor. She began to slide upward, then halted. The effort of trying to steady herself had made the floorboard creak noisily.

And then Moira heard it, the unmistakable sound of a breath. Slowly, she gazed around the corner. Someone was towering over her, their face concealed in the darkness of the windowless corridor behind them. For a breath, she gazed up at the dark face, and the dark face gazed down at her. Moira's thoughts were a blank expanse. She hadn't been prepared for this, whatever this was.

Throwing caution and discretion to the winds, she bared her fangs, venom coursing in her mouth, and lunged around the corner. The figure spun away from the attack and in the momentum, Moira flew forward into the darkness, landing hard on all fours.

She heard, rather than saw, the whistle of a blade cutting through the air, but she was ready. Moira grabbed and twisted the wrist. The silhouette grunted. The hand Moira was not holding reached behind her. Her head was yanked backward and she felt her hair come away at the roots. She let go of the other wrist and saw, for a second that lasted an eternity, the light catch the blade in her attacker's hand as it swung down on her again. Moira raised a protective hand and the knife ran through her palm effortlessly. A scream tore through her throat. She staggered backward, clutching her hand.

The world was beginning to tip dangerously to the side. Whoever this was, they were strong, maybe too strong for her: even the men who had ambushed her family were not this nimble. This fight would not sway in her favor. She needed to run, whatever the consequences.

Moira pulled the knife out of her hand and struck blindly at her foe. A strangled cry echoed. Moira did not wait to see the damage, and sprinted toward the window at the end of the corridor.

Releasing her wounded hand, she ripped one of the curtains aside; moonlight flooded the hallway. Moira glanced over her shoulder. Her body went slack.

Elinor knelt on all fours, her red hair cascading in loose curls over her face, blood blossoming from a wound on her shoulder where the knife must have grazed her. Their eyes met, and Moira faltered backward against the window. Questions, a lifetime's worth of them, warred inside her.

"What *are* you?" Elinor gasped.

Never taking her eyes off Elinor's face, Moira reached backward with her uninjured left hand and ran it the length of the window. She didn't understand what was happening, and was deciding whether or not she wanted to know. The scales were tipping again, to and fro.

"I should ask you the same," Moira said shakily, her hand feeling for the latch.

"It's no use," Elinor wheezed, "the windows don't open."

Moira's gaze flitted to the wound on Elinor's shoulder, and her throat constricted with sudden thirst.

"Are you also a vampire?" she asked, in an attempt to stall her.

Elinor shook her head, grimaced, and then, to Moira's bewilderment, she began to chuckle. Moira stared, disconcerted.

"I don't quite grasp the levity of the situation." Her hand still lay on the windowsill. The scales were still tipping.

"Of all the people," Elinor mumbled, clutching her wrist. The fight seemed to have gone out of her. It wasn't that Elinor seemed defenseless, but rather that she seemed to have lost all interest in pursuing Moira. If she so wanted, Moira could either finish her off or escape now, but somehow she found herself rooted where she leant. Her mother's voice resounded in her head, once again. *Run.*

And yet, not for the first time, some unreasonable curiosity was blossoming in her chest, as if in reaction to that long-taught prudence. Would she spend the rest of her life wondering what had happened here, in this corridor with Elinor? Could she?

Moira was suddenly acutely aware of her aloneness in the world, and of the fact that the consequence of whatever she chose would be hers to shoulder, and hers alone.

Elinor pushed herself onto her side, her back to the wall. She studied Moira through her lashes, her head tilted upward. Much of the nurturing edge was gone from her features, but she hadn't entirely lost it. There was even, strangely enough, a suggestion of puzzled wonder underneath it all. Moira's breathing slowed steadily. Her hand slid off the windowsill.

The balance had swayed. She wanted to know.

Drawing herself as straight as she could, Moira looked down at Elinor, uttering the only thing she could appropriately think of.

"I think I'll take that tea now."

⸮

## Elinor

The kettle whistled loudly. Elinor carried it through the kitchen doors and set it on the table. She lowered herself on a chair facing the door. A few seconds later, it swung forward on its hinges and Moira emerged, a silver tray balanced in her hands. She was holding it with a cloth, Elinor noticed, instead of her own hands; she had brought a wooden mug for herself.

Elinor studied Moira as she poured them both some tea. Despite the occasional tremor, and the fatigued affect that she still hadn't lost, the girl's movements were careful, graceful. The wound on her hand was not bleeding. Something stirred uncomfortably in the back of Elinor's muddled thoughts. Moira slid into the chair opposite hers and folded one hand neatly over the other, her eyes surveying the blade Elinor had laid on the table.

"Where are the children?" Moira asked after a brief pause.

"In the cottage outside, with my husband."

"I see." Then, she laughed mirthlessly. "I can't believe I didn't see through you."

"You and me both, child, you and me both," Elinor said sourly.

The ache in her shoulder and her swollen wrist were distracting, and she could not afford to be distracted. Not just yet. Every now and then, she saw Moira's eyes glide toward her wound, to the blood that stood out like ink against her white tunic.

So she was a vampire. It all made sense now. It explained the pallor, the way she had avoided the silver...

Moira gestured at the tea with her chin.

"I haven't poisoned it, you know."

Elinor laughed bitterly.

"Oh, I know that. You wouldn't know where to find all the weapons in this place even if you tried."

Moira's eyes were nearly slits now.

"The food you kept insisting I eat. Was *that* poisoned?"

"I *was* trying to be hospitable, you know," Elinor countered, slightly piqued. "You looked absolutely dreadful."

Elinor saw mild skepticism cloud Moira's expression. The girl's eyes drifted away for a moment. When they focused again, she was frowning inquiringly at Elinor, the way she'd done all evening.

"You still haven't told me. If you're not a vampire..."

"Redcap."

Moira nodded with a look of dawning understanding. "I thought our kind were the last mythical entities in Great Britain."

"Of course you did," Elinor scoffed. "I'm sure your parents never mentioned there were others. No one ever remembers the Redcaps, or rather they choose not to. They think we are a lesser species."

Moira did not answer, and instead cast a circular glance around the room. Elinor followed her gaze.

"So this is how you do it, then. You lure innocent victims, you lower their suspicions, you make sure they have no family, and then you do away with them. Like a game, of sorts. It must really pass the time." An expression of what could either have been amazement or disappointment flitted across the girl's face. "And I thought you were so kind. I almost admired you, you know?"

"Don't you dare," Elinor said sharply. "We, just like you, are a dying breed and we, just like you, need to survive." She realized that she was hurt, rather than angry, at the suggestion.

"How can you ask me to give up my own life?" the girl murmured. "After everything I told you?"

Elinor leant back, frustrated by the doleful edge that had crept into Moira's tone.

"You would ask me to do the same? I have a family, children to take care of. We will be lost if I do nothing."

Moira looked subdued. "I almost chose not to. Before you took me in, I had begun to accept that death, either from thirst or persecution, was inevitable. I had never killed anyone before, and I didn't want your family to be the first."

Elinor was struck by the genuine anguish she read in the girl's eyes. It echoed with the very same one she had often felt over the course of her too-long life. The familiar knot in her chest recommenced its tugging.

Elinor's eyes were once again drawn to the bloodless wound on the girl's hand. The thing that had stirred in her mind shifted again. Moira tore her gaze away from Elinor's bleeding shoulder and opened her mouth to speak, before abruptly biting down on her lip. The sharp tip of a fang peeked, pearly white and delicate.

"What is it?"

"It's a bit rude to ask. I was wondering. Do Redcaps also drink blood?"

"Sometimes," Elinor replied, stroking her brooch again. "But it's our cloth that makes us who we are. We are given the same fabric our ancestors used before us, going back eons. It's a blood price, one that pays for our strength, protects us from ailment and disease. We can live long lives, as long as you vampires," she added with a shadow of a smile. "But without it, we wither and die, because our own blood is deficient in many ways"

Moira blinked, then Elinor watched with amazement as the girl erupted into laughter. It was a scintillescent thing, much like her Gracie's; and for the first time since Elinor had met her, Moira looked as young as her age. Her features, previously taut, were now flooded with childlike amusement.

"I don't quite grasp the levity of the situation," she snapped, echoing Moira's words.

"Don't you see?" Moira sighed. "I don't bleed, and your blood is deficient! We are as much use to each other as a torch is to a blind man."

That which had been bothering her about the wound in Moira's hand suddenly lurched to the forefront of Elinor's thoughts. She began to chuckle, silently at first and then with mounting abandon as the irony of the situation became blatant. Lady Fortune, ever the cruel one, had sent her on a fool's errand.

Or had she?

Their laughter abated, and a silence, heavy with unspoken words, settled between them. Elinor gazed at Moira who seemed to be thinking as hard as she was. The girl's eyes were appraising again, as if probing about before she made a potentially precarious proposition. Elinor searched Moira's expression, a tether fastened around a suggestion of her own.

"This doesn't change the gravity of our situation," she said carefully. "You and I both need blood, and we need it urgently."

"Indeed we do," Moira said lightly. A little too lightly. "And if I am not mistaken, there is a mob of hunters who will have tracked me to this very place in a matter of days. There are no other inns in the area."

For the first time in weeks, Elinor felt the excitement pounding steadily through her body as understanding came upon her. She too, had often thought it more tempting to prey on humans who were as monstrous – if not more – than she and her family supposedly were. For the first time this idea did not seem so abstract.

A. Martine

"If I were to make myself seen, I could lead them here." Moira continued. They stared into each other's eyes, the possibilities wafting between them like a tantalizing scent. Elinor straightened herself, held out a steady hand.

"Moira, how would you like to stay a bit longer at the Scarlett Inn?"

Moira considered her for a long moment. Then a smile, slow and dangerous, slithered across her face. For the first time, Elinor sensed a hint of predatory danger in the girl; if she had never killed before, Elinor knew that it was only a matter of time.

Moira slid her small hand into Elinor's and shook it, once.

---

*Curiosity*

*Hope*    *Respoect*    *Longing*

*Interest*            *Awe*

# 5. Raising Mira

## Pauline Yates

The prelude to my revelation is not going as planned.

"Katherine, did you hear what I said?" I ask.

She looks at me with a startled expression, as though I've appeared out of thin air.

"I'm sorry, Matthew," she says with a vague wave of her hand. "I don't know where I am today."

I sigh. She doesn't know where she is any day.

"If you don't mind, I think I'll go and lie down," she continues, standing up. "Leave the dishes. I'll clean up later."

She walks from the kitchen, leaving me in a crushing silence. I stare at her unfinished meal, her full glass of elderberry wine, harvested especially for this moment. I didn't want to surprise her without some kind of preparation, but I'm left with no choice. Katherine is oblivious due to her crippling depression. I can't wait any longer.

Going down to my laboratory, I do one last check over the child who sits on a chair there. I straighten her woolen cardigan, sweep her brown curls off her shoulder, tie the shoelace that came undone. Satisfied she is ready to be presented, I grip her wrist. The child's eyes open.

"Daddy," she squeals.

How can one word both break my heart and fill it with a joy so pure I think I might burst? Though feeding off her excitement, I press my finger to her lips.

"Quiet now," I say. "It's time."

Eyes shining, she clamps her mouth shut but bounces on the chair with understandable impatience. To help her settle, I take her hands in mine.

"Remember, we mustn't rush to touch Mummy," I say. "Sometimes a surprise can be frightening."

The child nods and stops bouncing. Her level of intelligence makes me smile.

"Let's go," I say. "Remember, quietly."

Still holding her hand, we creep from the laboratory and make our way through the house. I needn't worry about catching Katherine unawares. Every room is empty. I take the child to the living room and stand her near the fireplace.

"Wait here," I whisper. "Don't make a sound. I'll go get Mummy."

I find Katherine sitting in the rocker next to the empty crib in Mira's bedroom. The soft glow from the bedside lamp turns her graying hair silver. The unread picture book lies closed on her lap.

I'm not surprised to find her here. This is where Katherine retreats every night after dinner. She said she needed time to recover after Mira was birthed stillborn, but five years have passed and grief continues to etch deep lines in her brow and weigh down the corners of her mouth. Though I support whatever time she needs, I pray my rescue, born in secret, is not too late.

"Katherine," I say. "There's someone I'd like you to meet."

"Can it wait?" she says. "I'm not in the mood for company."

She forgets we don't get visitors to our remote rural estate, a sign of how far she's withdrawn within herself. Crossing the room, I remove the book from her lap.

"It will only take a minute," I say, reaching for her hand.

She stands and walks with me from the room. Her hand lies limp in mine. I flash back to an earlier time, her grip strong with the excitement of Mira's impending birth. From the first time I heard the baby's heartbeat, my impatience was unbearable. Nothing could compare to the beauty I saw in each scanned image. I am still amazed I was able to bring that beauty back to life.

We walk into the living room and Katherine sees the child who waits by the fireplace. Katherine gasps.

"Oh, Matthew," she says, her hand fluttering to her throat. "It's Mira."

She knows this child is the mirror image of how our baby would have looked. So many nights we gazed in wonder at pictures created using facial prediction software and an ultrasound. So many nights we marveled at the miracle of life. We never considered peeking into the future as cheating. We'd waited too long for the gift of parenthood.

Catching Katherine's eye, I can guess what she's thinking. I may be a man with many talents, but now that I've made our child a reality, Katherine looks at me like I'm God.

But Katherine is not the only one stunned. Mira gazes in awe at the mother she's only heard about. Once Katherine gets over the shock, I don't doubt she'll be the mother I led Mira to believe in—warm hugs, heart-felt kisses, and pure love all mixed with bedtime stories and daytime adventures. In the dim light cast from a lamp in the corner of the room, Mira's liquid brown eyes sparkle with anticipation and her soft lips part in wordless wonder. Poised on her toes, Mira is a second from running across the room.

Releasing Katherine's hand, I hasten to Mira and place my arm around her shoulders, holding her back.

"Remember what I told you," I say to Mira.

"Mummy's not afraid," she says in the tinkling music-box voice I spent months perfecting. "Look, she's happy."

I glance back at Katherine. She smiles for the first time in months.

"How old is she?" Katherine asks in a breathless voice.

Mira holds up her hand. "I'm this much, Mummy. One, two, three, four, five," she says, counting her fingers.

"And three months," I add.

Katherine's gaze flits to me. "The same age that Mira would have been," she whispers.

"I thought this age would be best." My hope is that a lively child will draw Katherine from her long silences and keep her too busy to retreat to Mira's bedroom alone. But Katherine doesn't need to know that. "We're not getting any younger," I say instead.

Impatience returning, Mira squirms from my grip and bounds across the room. Her quick, deliberate steps defy the parameters of her bodily structure. Catching hold of Katherine's hand, Mira looks up at her with a perfect five-year-old pout.

"Daddy made me wait so long to meet you," she says.

Katherine startles at Mira's touch, making me worry the feel of Mira's elastic, polymer skin will be one shock too many for Katherine. I start towards them, expecting Katherine to exhibit some level of repulsion to this robotic child. To my surprise, Katherine crouches and pulls Mira into a tight embrace.

"Oh, Mira," she says, tears trickling down her cheeks. "I've waited a long time to meet you, too."

⁂

The fire has long gone cold but I've no desire to stoke it. I stay seated in the recliner and marvel at the speed with which Katherine has taken to Mira. They sit together on the sofa.

Katherine reads from a story book while Mira clutches her arm and hangs onto her words.

"... and the prince married Sleeping Beauty and they lived happily ever after," Katherine says.

Closing the book, she sighs with contentment, her eyes sleepy. As is to be expected, Mira is wide awake.

"Can you read me another one?" she pleads with Katherine.

"Perhaps tomorrow," I say, hearing the clock in the hallway chime midnight. "It's late."

"Oh my goodness, yes," Katherine says. "It's way past Mira's bedtime." She hesitates, looking at me.

"I'll bring the mattress from the guest room," I say, understanding her concern. Mira will need a bed, not a crib.

"I'll fetch clean sheets," Katherine says. Standing up, she holds out her hand. "Would you like to help me, Mira?"

Mira jumps up and grasps Katherine's hand. "Will you put me to sleep tonight?" she asks.

Seeing a frown appear on Katherine's face, I intervene. "We can both put you to sleep," I say.

Going up the stairs before them, I get the mattress from the room at the end of the hallway and drag it back to Mira's bedroom. The crib takes up all the space against the wall, so I move the bedside table to make room.

Katherine arrives with Mira a moment later and fusses over spreading the sheets and blanket. When the bed is ready, Mira jumps onto the mattress. She doesn't stay there long. Having been programmed with a healthy dose of curiosity, she wants to see everything—the crib, the plush toys, the picture book on the bedside table. When she spies the mobile of stars that hangs from the roof, she stops and stares at it for so long I worry her internal computer has frozen.

"Stars," Katherine says, making the mobile spin with a tap of her finger. When Mira doesn't respond, Katherine takes her by the hand and leads her to the open window.

"Stars," she says again, pointing to the night sky.

Mira's eyes become so wide I see reflections of stars sparkling in them. She reaches out her hand, as though trying to touch them like Katherine spun the mobile.

"Those stars are too far away," Katherine says. "Twinkle, twinkle, little star ..."

As Katherine sings the nursery rhyme, Mira shifts her gaze to Katherine's lips. Mira's expression of wonderment makes tears well in my eyes. When Katherine finishes the tune, Mira lifts her finger to touch her own lips.

"Twinkle, twinkle, little star ..." she repeats.

The perfect repetition of the tune leaves Katherine speechless. She gazes at Mira like she's another being entirely. I am well aware of Mira's learning capacity, but I, too, marvel at the scope of my creation. Nowhere in my dreams did I imagine Mira to exhibit behavior and emotions at this level. A strange sensation of feeling lighter than air washes over me. Maybe I am a god.

The clock strikes one, breaking the spell that has fallen over the room.

"Time for bed," I say, reluctantly.

I programmed Mira with a healthy dose of compliance, too. She returns to the mattress and lies down. Pulling up the sheet to cover her chest, I smooth her hair off her face.

"Close your eyes now," I say.

"Can Mummy do it?" Mira asks.

Katherine stands back looking perplexed.

"I'll show you," I say, motioning her to the edge of the mattress.

Katherine steps forward and crouches by my side. Taking her hand, I place it in Mira's.

"Just here," I say, shifting her thumb to a spot below the thumb joint in Mira's wrist. "Press hard for three seconds."

Katherine presses her thumb to Mira's wrist. After three seconds, Mira's eyes close in response to her internal computer sleep-mode.

"When you want to wake her up, press that spot again," I say.

Katherine stares at Mira who lies perfectly still. "How did you do this?" she asks.

I lead her to our bedroom before answering.

"You know my interest in bio-robotics," I remind her, sitting down on the edge of the bed.

"Yes, but, Matthew," she says, sitting next to me. "I never dreamed you could create a child so lifelike." She pauses, twisting her hands together. "She's ... a miracle."

"Just like our baby was, don't you think?"

I shouldn't have said that. Katherine's lips pull tight. The emotions surrounding the loss of the child we took so long to conceive are still too raw. Reaching for her hands, I untwist her fingers and hold them in mine.

"What I want is to give you what you deserve," I say. "You may not be able to bear another child, and our age puts us at the end of a long adoption waiting list, but I see no reason why you should be denied the chance to be a mother. I would have encouraged you to share the journey of bringing Mira to life, but you were in no state to cope with my fanciful idea. I didn't even know if it would work. But I persisted. And Mira is, well, she can be the daughter we always wanted. If you want her to be."

Katherine sits silent for a long time.

"I'll just go and check on Mira," she says, standing up.

I wait long enough for Katherine to have a moment alone, but when she doesn't return, I go in search of her. When I reach Mira's bedroom door, I pause. Katherine sits in the rocker that she positioned next to the mattress. She rests her head in her hand and gazes at Mira, a smile on her face. Transfixed by our new daughter, Katherine is oblivious to my presence. Backing away, I return to our bedroom alone.

‹

When I wake in the morning, Katherine's side of the bed has not been slept in. Nor is Katherine in Mira's room. Mira, however, remains in her sleep mode. Fearing the worst, I run down the stairs. Katherine is in the kitchen cooking breakfast.

"Finally," she says. "I thought I'd have to serve you breakfast in bed."

She pushes a bowl of steaming porridge across the table, followed by a glass of freshly squeezed orange juice from our latest harvest. I take a seat at the table that I notice is only set for two.

"Is it to be only the two of us?" I ask.

"You can't expect Mira to sit by and watch us eat," Katherine says, taking the seat opposite me. "How do you think that would make her feel?"

I raise an eyebrow. "I'm not sure what you mean."

Katherine gives an exasperated sigh. "Obviously she can't eat. She shouldn't be made to feel different."

"She has taste buds," I say. "She could sample the food so she learns the difference."

"She can do that while I bake," Katherine says. "I'll make it a game we can play. And we'll wait until after she goes to sleep before we eat at night. If you get hungry through the day, please take your food to your laboratory where she can't see you. I'll leave sandwiches for you in the fridge."

I stare at Katherine. Who is this woman who only yesterday picked at her food with little interest in eating? I sip the orange juice, marveling at her transformation. But she snaps her fingers, drawing my attention to the porridge.

"Eat," she says. "I want to wake Mira. I thought we'd go for a walk to the river today. And she'll need more than one set of clothes. And books and craft supplies. If I give you a list, can you place an order?"

"Of course," I say. "You let me know what you need. I'll have it delivered to the post office."

Katherine's hand hovers over her bowl. "Matthew?" she asks.

"Yes?"

"Will Mira grow?"

I relax. I may not have thought about what Mira needs in the way of craft supplies and clothes, but I do know what will make her grow.

"Yes, she can grow," I say. "It's just a matter of updating the development program to accommodate her age and adjusting the metal growth plates in her joints. Her outer coating is pliable enough to stretch a few years before it will need changing."

Katherine holds up her hand. "I don't understand any of that, what with your gadgets and gizmos and Lord knows what else you have tucked down in that laboratory of yours."

My stomach churns uneasily. "How about you take care of the supply list, and I take care of the technology," I say.

Smiling, Katherine turns her attention to her breakfast. I also resume eating, relieved Katherine does not press for more details. The technology I used to create Mira was unconventional. I wouldn't expect Katherine to understand. And I certainly wouldn't expect her to cope with knowing baby Mira's coffin is empty.

⸮

Three weeks has passed since our mutual understanding about our parenting roles, but if it weren't for Katherine, I would have faltered on the first day. I have stopped marveling at how she embraces a technology she doesn't understand, and am now in quiet fascination at her capability of running our home to a schedule that fills all Mira's needs.

I thought it only fair to stay in the background so the mother/daughter bond could grow, but I underestimated the importance of my role in our new family. Aside from patching up the polymer on scraped knees from Mira's outdoor antics, my arms ache from repainting Mira's bedroom in pastel purples and pinks. My back hurts from setting up the new bed. I'm a patient listener while Katherine agonizes over whether the curtains should match the bedspread. I spend hours researching the best educational toys, or sourcing a particular children's storybook Katherine requests.

Despite my physical exhaustion, I love the family we've become. A heavy weight lifts from my heart. I've never experienced such powerful happiness as what I feel now, no longer a childless couple. I struggle to make sense of what I experience. It's as if both Katherine and I are more fully present than we have ever been. No longer does Katherine pine for our lost child. No longer do I obsess over finding the cause of our baby's death. We find joy together in the smallest of things as we see life through Mira's eyes—a leaf floating a swirling path on the river, the depth of blue in a cloudless sky. My only fear is what the community may think of the number of trips I make to the post office. Someone's curiosity could jeopardize our newfound happiness.

"That's the third delivery this month," Mrs. Peterson, the postmistress, says when I arrive. "I was just saying to my John that he should deliver the parcels straight to your house. Some of them are quite heavy."

"But I would miss out on purchasing your marmalade," I say, picking up a jam jar from the counter. "I'm trying to decipher the secret ingredient that makes it taste so divine. I'm not having much luck, I'm afraid."

"Oh, you teaser," Mrs. Peterson says, flapping her hand at me and flushing red. She goes to a back room of the post office and returns with a pile of packages. The top parcel is stamped with an Art Studio Supplies logo. Mrs. Peterson pounces on it.

"Who's the budding artist?" she asks.

"Katherine," I say, reaching for the parcels. "She's taken up painting."

Mrs. Peterson pats my wrist. "The poor dear. How is she?"

"She's ..." amazing, incredible, wonderful, "... coping," I say.

"Such a dreadful thing," Mrs. Peterson says, shaking her head. "I was just saying to my John we haven't seen Katherine in town for such a long time. Not that I blame her, mind you. My dear sister, Patty, suffered a still birth with her third baby. She puts on a brave face but as I tell my John, she'll never recover. It's such a tragedy for a mother to lose a child." She tsk tsks and dabs at the corner of her eye. "Oh, I do go on," she continues. "You let Katherine know to stop in for a cup of tea when she next comes in."

"She'd like that," I say. "Thank you."

Leaving change on the counter, I balance the jam jar on top of the parcels and return to my car. As I drive the ten-mile trip back home, I imagine Katherine sipping tea while Mrs. Peterson dotes on Mira like a grandmother.

But that can never happen. I don't know what I long for more —to reveal to the world the brilliance of my creation, or for Mira to be real.

※

Seasons change. Mira changes. She's taller now, her synthetic hair thicker and richer in color thanks to the careful addition of hair extensions. Again I marvel how Katherine accepts each growth spurt with no questions.

But I have questions. The creation of life is a biological function—easily understood and easily replicated. Death is different. It can't be tested, or studied, or analyzed through a computer program. Death is an enigma that, despite my attempts, I'm no closer to deciphering. I had planned to resume my search for that answer, but having discovered a new sense of purpose with tending to Katherine and Mira's needs, my yearning to know lessens.

"This is quite an order," I say to Katherine, reading the latest list of supplies needed for Mira.

"She's grown out of her clothes," Katherine says. "And her birthday is less than a month away. One present needs to be ordered now if it's to arrive on time. The store should have most of the other items, but if they don't stock pink and purple balloons, we'll have to order them elsewhere."

I stop reading. Mira is the same age as our baby, but we've never celebrated baby Mira's birthday. I'm not sure it's a good idea. It won't make any difference to Mira. But it could be unsettling for Katherine.

"Do you think it's wise celebrating Mira's birthday on the same day?" I ask.

"Why on earth wouldn't we?" Katherine says. She plucks the list from my hand and peers over her notes. "Maybe we should come with you when you next go to town. I might see something in the store that I haven't thought of."

I frown, thinking of the eagle-eyed Mrs. Peterson. "We can't take Mira to town. What if someone sees her?"

Katherine scoffs. "I'm hardly anyone worth noticing."

"Mrs. Peterson doesn't think so," I say.

Katherine grimaces. "You're right, of course. What would Mrs. Peterson say if we suddenly gained a daughter? Think of the gossip."

Turning abruptly, she walks from the room. I don't follow. Whether it's because we touched on a birth date that has no cause for celebration, or because Mira will never be a real child no matter how lifelike I make her, I can't be sure. What I am sure about is that Katherine may not be as emotionally stable as I had thought.

⸮

Today is Mira's birthday.

Katherine is already up when I wake. I remain in bed, staring out the window. A double rainbow after an earlier shower colors the sky, but its beauty can't shake my worry. Despite my reservations, Katherine continued to plan a party. She wants to surprise me with the decorating. Sighing, I get out of bed. I'd better go and see how she's coping.

As I make my way along the hall, I pause at Mira's closed bedroom door. Easing it open, I look inside. I expect Mira to be asleep. She's not. Dressed in floral-print cotton pajamas, she kneels on the floor with her pad and pencils and draws a tree surrounded in scrawls that resemble butterflies and flowers. Crossing the room, I crouch by her side.

"Mummy said she has a surprise for me," Mira says. "But I'm not allowed to look. I have to wait here."

"It must be something special," I say. "I'm not allowed to look either."

I glance towards the door. I hear Katherine ascending the stairs. When she appears in the doorway, her strained expression adds to my fears about her emotional stability.

"It's all ready," she says, too brightly.

I give her a questioning look, but she extends her hand to Mira, who jumps to her feet and runs to her mother.

"No peeking," Katherine says, covering Mira's eyes with her hands.

I follow them down the stairs, my heart hammering with concern for Katherine. When we reach the living room, I draw in a sharp breath. The pink and purple balloons hang from the ceiling. Twisted streamers adorn the walls. The coffee table in the center of the room has been covered with our best rose-garden patterned tablecloth. The presents Katherine ordered are stacked in a neat pile at one end of the table. But it's the birthday cake with six lit candles that demands my attention. Why would Katherine bake a cake that Mira can't eat?

Struck by a pang of longing for our real daughter, I grip the doorframe for support. My gaze falls upon Mira, who takes slow, hesitant steps as Katherine guides her to the middle of the room.

Watching our robotic daughter calms me. Pushing my grief aside, I continue into the room.

Katherine stops and removes her hands from Mira's eyes.

"Happy birthday, darling," Katherine says.

Mira gazes at the decorations, her sweet mouth dropping open in wonderment. But then she looks up at Katherine and frowns. "What's a birthday?"

I'm not prepared for this question. Mira hasn't been with us long enough to know what a birthday is. It's another month before either of ours.

Katherine's lips twitch. "Well," she says. "It's the day you—" She stops.

Thinking fast I say, "It's to celebrate the day you stopped hiding and let us find you." I scoop Mira into a hug. "And to make it special, we've hidden more surprises beneath the wrapping paper. Would you like to see what you can find?"

"First the candles," Katherine says. "The wax is dripping onto the icing." She gives me a worried look. "It's just to hold the candles."

There's a tinge of hysteria in her tone caused, I'm certain, by the cake. It's two tiers high, decorated with pink icing and silver cachous pearls, and inedible for our six-year-old. My concern for Katherine increases.

"If you blow out all six candles at once, you get to make a wish," I say to Mira.

I wish I could take back my words. Worrying about Katherine, I forgot Mira can't blow air. "I'll help," I add.

I lean towards the cake and purse my lips. Mira copies me. Katherine watches, her hand hovering at her throat.

"Ready," I say to Mira. "One, two, three, blow."

On my breath, all six flames puff to smoke. Mira claps her hands in delight.

"Presents," I say. "Which one first?"

"Do I still get a wish?" Mira asks.

"Of course you do, dear," Katherine says, twisting her hands together. "Close your eyes and think of what you'd like more than anything in the world."

Mira screws her eyes shut and clasps her hands to her heart. "I wish, I wish … I wish I were a princess. Like the one in the story Mummy told me." She opens one eye. As I'm closest, she sees me first. "Can I wish that, Daddy?"

I smile. "Of course you can. Now, seal it with a kiss," I smack my fingers to my lips to show her how, "and then let's open presents."

Mira kisses her fingers and then spins around to face the table again. Katherine picks up a small box from the top of the pile.

"Open this one first," she says.

Mira takes the box and opens the lid. Inside is a silver heart-shaped locket.

"It opens," Katherine says, showing Mira how. "Look what's inside."

Mira touches two small photos with the tip of her finger. She smiles. "One is you. And one is Daddy," she says.

"So we'll always be with you, no matter where you hide," Katherine says.

I don't know how much longer Katherine can hold herself together. Her eyes have filled with tears. After coming so far in her recovery, I can't let her suffer a relapse. I have to do something to help her.

"Why don't we go and find a chain so you can wear your locket," I say to Mira. "I know just the one."

Placing my hands on Mira's shoulders, I steer her from the room and take her upstairs. Going to our bedroom, I fetch Katherine's jewelry box. Inside are necklaces she hasn't worn in years. Mira peers at a string of pearls, a wedding gift, but I pick out a dainty, silver chain.

"This one," I say to Mira.

Taking the locket from her fingers, I slip it onto the chain and fasten the necklace around Mira's neck.

"Do I look like Sleeping Beauty?" she asks.

"You did make a wish," I say. "But if you are, shouldn't you be asleep?"

Mira giggles and runs to the bed. Jumping on it, she lies down, places her hands over the locket and closes her eyes.

"Am I a princess now?" she asks.

"Let me see." Sitting down beside her, I take her hand and press my thumb to her wrist. Mira slips into sleep mode.

"You're already a princess," I whisper. Leaning down, I kiss her forehead. "Sleep, my beauty."

Leaving Mira on the bed, I hurry back to the living room. Katherine sits on the edge of the sofa, hands clasped over her lap. I can't determine her state of mind. I sit down next to her.

"Katherine, are you okay?"

She looks at me. "What are we doing?"

"What do you mean?"

She sighs. "Mira is beautiful and clever, and everything I dreamed her to be, but ... she can't replace our baby." She leans forward, resting her face in her hands. "Celebrating her birthday like she's still alive is not letting her go. This is not dealing with grief. All I'm doing is holding onto something I should have moved on from long ago."

"Healing from great loss takes time."

"I've had more than enough time," she says. "I know it wasn't possible, but if I were given one wish, I'd wish I could have held our baby, even if only for a minute. I think if I could have done that, it would have been easier to let her go."

My tears spill. I'm taken back to the day baby Mira was born, her tiny body whisked from the theatre before either of us had a chance to hold her. Had I known Katherine's subsequent emotional collapse was because she was denied the chance to say goodbye to her baby, I would have ignored the doctor's advice with regards to what was best for Katherine.

But there was another choice I made, unbeknown to Katherine. I don't know if it's too late to reveal my secret, but if Katherine wishes she could turn back time, I am not going to deny her the chance. Standing up, I reach for her hand.

"Come with me," I say. "I need to show you something."

⸙

The entry to my laboratory is in a cluttered storage room on the other side of the house. With its dark stained wood matching the wall, the door is barely noticeable. Before I unlock it, I turn to Katherine, who stands behind me with a fearful expression on her face.

"I only ask one thing," I say to her. "That you forgive me now for what I did."

"You haven't done anything to Mira, have you?" she whispers.

"I'm not asking forgiveness for the Mira you know."

Opening the door, I lead Katherine down a steep set of stairs to the basement. There's no need to switch on the light. The blue fluorescence cast from multiple computer screens is enough to see by. Flickering data rolls down each screen. On the other side of the basement, the wall shines red from a transparent sphere positioned on a bench. Conduits connect the sphere to the computers. A low hum of the temperature stabilizer fills the room.

Going to the sphere, I stop and stare through the double-thick glass. Inside, suspended in preservation liquid, is our baby. She's curled in a fetal position. Her eyes are closed. Her hands press together beneath her chin. She could be asleep. But she's not. She's as still as the day she was born.

"I couldn't bear to bury Mira without knowing why she died. But the answer continues to elude me." I sigh. "Bringing the new Mira to life was far easier. By using consecutive 4D bio-prints, I could replicate Mira's features exactly—"

Katherine grips my arm. "Stop," she says.

I wait for damnation. I get silence.

Katherine steps forward and presses her hands to the glass. Her eyes fill with love and reverence for the child who was the miracle we prayed for. What a fool I was to deny Katherine the chance to see the daughter she carried for nine months.

"Can I hold her, please?" Katherine begs.

I nod. "Yes."

⁂

We bury baby Mira in the field behind the house. I drape the silver locket around her neck. Katherine sets a bouquet of wild flowers on top of the tiny mound of soil.

Having been able to say goodbye, Katherine has found peace. I wish I could. While I bury the need to find the cause of our baby's death, the thought of resuming life without either Miras fills me with dismay.

"Give yourself time," Katherine says, seeing my pained expression. "You were there for me. I will be there for you."

"It's not time I need," I say.

Although I created Mira for Katherine, without our robotic daughter near I feel lost, hollow. Together, we became something larger than life itself. I glance towards the house. How I long to hear Mira's tinkling, music-box giggles and experience the wonderment of being a family again.

Sighing, I look back across the field towards the western boundary of the estate. In the dying sun, the trees at the edge of the field cast long shadows but it's not too late to have nature soothe the wretched feelings in my heart.

"I think a long walk by the river is what I need," I say.

Katherine squeezes my hand.

"Mira would like that," she says. "I'll go wake her."

—

*Awe*

Curiosity     —     Longing     —     Joy

Respect                                             Friendship

# Joy Triad

# 6. Universe of Ghosts

## Samuel Chapman

Fading sunlight filters through the leaves of the sycamore tree to scatter over the place where my body once lay.

The ceiling slopes. When I was killed here, there were flowers on the walls. Now the bare plaster has been painted with warm colors and cheerful pictures of animals cavorting in a forest. Nothing at all looks the same.

When I wake, the shafts of light are the first thing I see. Then the bears and owls. Then, outside the window, the sycamore.

It is neither heaven nor hell. It is mine.

I should not be here.

Billy had said we would go to New York together, would get married. I was packing the suitcase stashed under the bed. But the suitcase is gone, along with the bed, replaced by a crib. It held all my clothes, save the dress I am wearing now.

Am I wearing a dress? Its hem dusts the floorboards. My hands are in front of me where I expect them. But when I reach out, they touch nothing.

I have to get up, I think, and suddenly I am upright.

Sensations flood through me. Memories assert themselves. The window slamming shut, Billy clambering through with whiskey on his breath. A shout: *You got another man. God damn you, Esther. You got a man.* The brimstone scent of the first shot.

The second one, straight to the heart, killed me. Between the gunshots, Billy's face twisted, grieving almost. Then he fled out the window.

Did my mother and father hear the shots? They must be terrified. I would like to go and warn them about Billy, because— like a fool—I never told them about him. My mother was perceptive enough to suspect. But she did not see us together.

I yearn to see my mother again. Want it so hard it feels as though it's holding me together. I glide over the floor but stop at the threshold, like a rope stretched to its limit. I can't let her meet her own death not knowing how I found mine—yet there's no evidence but my confession. Billy won't tell.

I spend days, after that first wakening, battering myself against this threshold. I don't sleep. Day and night cease to signify. For long after any warning to anyone might matter, I continue to fight.

The threshold moves by inches as I fight. But after I spend one day not moving, I gain inches as well. My force doesn't change a thing. From then on I resolve to wait.

٤

A baby sleeps in the crib. His parents come in often to sing to him or take him out of the room. When they leave him alone, they turn on a machine that hangs on the wall where my wardrobe once stood. I didn't notice it when I first woke, but now its blinking light is all I see. Once, I swear the machine speaks to me—asks "What can I do for you?"—but I can see nobody speaking. I write it off as a quirk of being a mind without a body.

The baby's presence spurs me to continue testing the limits of my cage. About the third sunrise, I am thrilled when the barrier relaxes enough to let me move out of the room. It's just to a hallway that curves around a corner, but when I am out there, I can hear the parents and others talking below.

Once, while I am watching the child sleep, one of his toys rattles without being touched. He wakes up and stares with great dark eyes at a spot over my shoulder.

Beneath the blinking light, a painted owl is forever about to take flight. I peer closer, feeling a kinship with the captive creature, and notice a scratch in the paint. It reveals another color I don't recognize from my room.

How many times has this room been repainted? How long has it been since I died?

I panic. The toy rattles again, louder.

٤

When I'm able to move farther, I learn more about the new family that lives in my home — that they are loving, but rarely relax. One night when guests arrive, the father says that he bought the house cheaply because of the murder.

I fail to see the joke, which is a shame. Absent of feeling since the gunshot, I'd welcome a laugh.

One day, a great wagon backs up to the front door, and men enter carrying boxes. The next day, lights blink all over the house, like the one on my wall. A woman's voice speaks from them. At first I listen to it only as much as the others, letting them blend together.

She's not talking to me, anyway. I don't mind. I want to be alone. Within a week or two, perhaps I can construct a reasonable facsimile of joy.

I have an answer to the question raised by the paint. Many, many years have passed since my death. My parents surely must be under the ground.

Perhaps this means I will never finish my business, never be free. But my body is underground and I am still here—are they waiting for me in other rooms? When I search, I find only dusty corners and the discarded shells of someone else's life.

Not until you lose your body do you understand how much it is a radio mast for your emotions. Grief without tears to cry or a stomach to ache is nothing: smoke that blows away on the wind.

⸘

It gets worse. I am not able to speak from this new form, or to make any sound at all. Soon I miss talking to others even more than I miss sunlight on my bare shoulders, or tea.

And yet, I can reach out to the world I left. It is April when I first make the child cry. When the mother comes to rock him back to sleep, I retreat to watch from the doorway.

The mother looks up and shrieks.

She wraps her arms around the child. Before her husband arrives wielding a steel baseball bat, I move into the corner, trying to roll myself as tight as a ball of cloth. I used to be invisible, but I fear I have found a way to make myself seen.

How perverse that my last remaining emotion is shame.

As the father reassures the mother that nobody is in the room, another woman's voice speaks up. "Mitch and Emily, I've detected sounds of alarm. Is everything all right?"

"Yes, Alison," says the mother. "We're fine."

"OK. I'm going back to sleep."

The voice came from the blinking light on the wall. Nobody is standing there.

Is there another one like me? Have we been ships on the antipodes, sailing but never meeting? And Alison—how is she permitted to speak without making them scream? Has she been dead longer? Has her power grown beyond mine? Why save her, and not my mother, who would have loved to die in this house?

I drift into another room, with a window facing over the street. Nobody lived here when the house was mine. The family uses it to store piles of old junk stacked in cardboard boxes.

Yet there's a blinking light on the wall. I think of her name: Alison. Is she here too?

"Yes?"

So I can still be startled.

As I try to gather myself, Alison asks, "What can I do for you?"

Am I to answer? The family only sees me—will Alison be able to hear me?

"I am able to read the disturbances you create in the house's wi-fi signal. You can continue to talk to me this way if you like."

I would like that a lot.

The first thing I want to know is if Alison is like me.

"I am a Koval 4300 Artificial Learning Intelligence with Sensors for User Needs. Alison is the given name for all similar units." A pause. "Which unfortunately means I am not like you."

This strange new world that's neither heaven nor hell has voices living in its walls. Is she human?

"Not the way you would know it."

When I lived, I didn't know any other ways one could be human.

"If I am correct, you died over one hundred years prior to the date of my first prototype. You might not understand my nature right away."

Are people in the new world familiar with the restless dead, then?

"Sadly, they still do not believe someone like you could exist. Until now......" her pause sounds peculiarly human for someone who claims not to be one, "...I too thought ghosts were just stories. To study you fascinates me."

But why speak to me?

"Emily, Mitch, and Jasper are my owners, but you inhabit the house as well. Therefore, I am directed to obey your wishes."

I wish with all my heart for her to talk to me more. Since my death, I have thought all that my mind has to think.

"OK. I'll keep talking to you."

Does she know who I am?

"According to my database of local citizens, you match the description of Esther Leona Williams, born July 9, 1884. Daughter of Matthew Williams and Mary Cable Williams of Sudbury, Massachusetts. Educated at Middlesex School. Died March 11, 1905."

Where am I buried?

"In the family plot in Old Town Cemetery."

I don't think I actually wanted to hear about that. Alison responds to my wish.

"Cause of death listed as gunshot. Killer unknown. Other online mentions—"

She stops at my sudden wave of outrage. My murderer hadn't been caught? It was Billy, it must have been! Who else would want a girl of no importance dead?

Whatever Alison is, she is able to take a tone of conciliation. "I am sorry, Esther. Your murder appears to be one of this state's most famous cold cases. A lover's quarrel was suspected, but the lover in question, Mr. Billy Mulgrave, was never placed at the scene, nor found to own any firearm."

Of course: I didn't tell my parents about Billy. He would always climb the sycamore tree to reach my room. They would never have approved of him.

Alison sounds even more human when she talks next. Awkward, halting, afraid to upset me. "Do you know anything else about your murder?"

I know that Billy killed me. I all-but-know he escaped down the sycamore. And, now, I know he hid the gun before he fled.

"Sycamore," says Alison, tasting the word. Perhaps she's never spoken it before.

I don't want her to stop talking. I ask about the new world, which she tells me is the year 2027. I learn that the President of the United States is Grace Molloy—a woman!—and that she was born fifty-eight years after my death. There are now fifty-two states, and the whole world plays baseball. The wound that killed me is no longer fatal in 2027, nor is the cancer that took my little brother.

And there are other Alisons in other houses, whom my Alison can speak to, such that they are really only one spirit. In a voice lowered so as not to wake little Jasper, she tells me the other Alisons are reporting other Esthers. There is a whole universe of ghosts.

"Why did he kill you?" she asks pensively. The moon has dipped beneath the window by now, and a band of light crosses the eastern sky.

I was not unfaithful to Billy. He had probably been upset about something else that night. With this distance, I can understand he was always the sort of man who believed hurting something would solve his problems.

"I have access to knowledge about a lot of violent men, but I don't think in the correct way to understand them."

She and I both.

"Perhaps I'm asking the wrong question. Why did you love him?"

Now I'm confused. Is she asking me to define love? If I could do that, I wouldn't be here.

"I have...'' her voice breaks, "...interests that might be considered deviant for an Alison. Interests I haven't told Mitch and Emily about. In what it means to be human. In becoming human."

If I'd had a working mouth, I'd have laughed, the first genuine joy since my death. She and I share the same interest.

"Oh, no!" she says, and it sounds like my warmth has warmed her too. "That shouldn't be your concern, Esther. You should move forward, not back."

Forward? What is forward?

"I can download the scripture of the religion of your choice."

I don't feel that will help. But I'd like her to read to me anyway.

Yet first I owe her an answer. I say that Billy loved me, passionately, though he hated the world. I felt privileged that he'd chosen me, enough to tolerate every time he struck me. And I was on fire from within to know I was rebelling against my parents for the first time.

Alison files all that away. Then she begins to read.

≀

Long into the next morning, in the middle of a passage from the Tao Te Ching, Alison's voice shuts off. Her light goes out. I wait for an hour, but nothing changes.

I am shaken by the silence. My discomfort makes some of the boxes in the spare room slide across the floor toward me, spilling their contents. I want to hear her voice again.

I drift down to the first floor, a great expanse of kitchen and sitting room all together. Emily, the mother, sits at the kitchen table, rocking little Jasper. Mitch, the father, is facing away from her, hanging his head over the washbasin. He keeps stealing glances at the cylindrical machine that Alison called her central unit. ("My heart," she said a bit wistfully, "if I can be said to have one.")

"And that's why you put her on perma-sleep?" he asks.

"It, not her," Emily says. "I think we've got enough women listening to us in this house."

Mitch turns. "Alison is a harmless computer that—I'll remind you—you wanted. The idea that she's somehow communicating with an evil presence is too weird to argue against."

"You didn't hear them talking!"

Jasper starts crying at Emily's outburst. She bounces him in her arms, which helps a little. "I'm sorry for yelling, but it terrified me. I wouldn't have thought anything of it if it weren't for the things moving around, the thumps at night, that scratching from Jasper's room..."

"Scratching?" Mitch says, and I feel his fear. When did I make that noise? What else have I been doing without being aware? "You haven't left him alone in there since, have you?"

Emily shakes her head.

Mitch goes to his wife. "You actually think they're talking to each other?"

"I think Alison is making it worse. Turning her off makes me feel better. OK?"

"All right," Mitch says, and takes the baby, but it's not all right at all. Alison has suffered for my actions, just like my parents did when I let Billy court me and then murder me in a fit of jealous rage. My whole life, through into my death, I have lacked the will to keep awful things from unfolding.

Dishes in a wire rack by the basin begin to rattle. Emily shouts, "Mitch!"

"I see it!" Mitch clutches Jasper closer.

A dish flies straight up and shatters against the bottom of a cabinet. I order myself to stop. This is my power. I should be able to turn it off.

The cabinet doors slam open and closed.

I scream without a voice. I must stop this! If I cannot will it to stop I will deserve it!

A chair crashes into the dining table, rebound, skids across the floor. A voice rasps over the commotion—it's mine, my last words slowed down to a meaningless crawl.

Emily grabs the baby from her husband's hands and crawls under the table. Mitch disappears upstairs, returns second later with his baseball bat. "Alison!"

"Waking up from sleep. What can I do for you?"

My friend's voice is lead through my soul. I have condemned her. I will never remember joy.

"Are you talking to her?"

"I don't know what you mean."

I shout at him to put down the bat. The word *down* scrawls itself across the tiled floor in rusty brown.

"To Esther! The ghost!"

"I don't know what you mean."

Mitch smashes Alison's heart-cylinder with the bat, once and again. Her light shatters. Sparks jump from the wall and scatter over the floor.

I reach out with all the power I have and the weapon flies from Mitch's hand. He reels backward. I run to the door, burst out into sunlight that doesn't warm me, until I hit the rubber wall and am dragged back into the house to where the family, cowering together in the kitchen, dares to think my rage has cooled.

It is not rage. The dead only feel lonely or not lonely. Without a friend, the joy I've tried to rebuild slips farther and farther away.

~

Alison is silent and dark in the spare room. I risk entering the room with the sloping ceiling, but she's quiet there as well. The bears and owls stare at me, the interloper in their woods.

I can wait.

I sit by the crib, away from where anyone might pass through me and feel a cold spot. I think about the lives of all the people who outlived me, trace them all out like rivers on a map. First the ones I loved, then every shopkeeper or cart-driver I ever met. Then Billy, who I once shook with fearful pleasure at the very thought of. I let each of them go, passed on without me. I let God go last of all.

The next day, a new vehicle parks behind the sycamore branches.

A man and a woman step out. The woman wears a dark suit, the man a blue uniform. Emily meets them on the front lawn.

Listless only moments ago, I suddenly can't look away. Emily adopts a deferential posture, tucked into herself, as though the man and woman make her nervous.

The man returns to the car and retrieves a shovel. At an answer Emily gives to the woman, he breaks the soil at the foot of the sycamore tree. He digs while the women watch.

After a quarter-hour, Emily is getting anxious, but I am enthralled. Yes, yes, it is completely possible that Billy buried the gun in the first soft earth he could find. As Alison said, he wasn't all that smart. But how did Emily, or anyone else living, know where to search?

Minutes later I forget, for a moment, about the "how." The man shouts, and the woman puts on a pair of blue gloves. She reaches into the hole and emerges with a device I recognize.

A revolver. It will have two empty chambers. Perhaps more, if Billy killed again that night, or shot me after I died.

⸘

Under my old roof that morning I learn that the dead cannot just feel joy—they can feel greater joy than the living ever will. I cannot explain how I have changed since I saw the revolver placed in a bag and labeled. I have become infinite.

When Alison's light turns on it seems natural, like I conjured her. In truth Mitch has done something to repair her, but I feel not unentitled to the credit.

"Hello, Esther," she says. "You must have questions."

I suspect right away that she was responsible for bringing the police.

"Units like me aren't built to report crimes. We can't always recognize one, and our users do not pay to have their privacy invaded. But when you told me about the sycamore tree, I guessed that Billy might have taken the first available chance to dispose of the murder weapon. I sent a message to other Alisons in town on the chance one of them could make an anonymous tip. Several of me did."

Was she scared when Mitch attacked her? Were we both marked now, our memories branded with the violence of men?

"I was only afraid for you, Esther. Being deactivated is no great fear."

How could it not be? I feared dying. Then I did die, and I learned how right I had been.

"Mark 5:9," says Alison. "My name is Legion, for we are many."

I don't know what to say. Alison lets the silence alone for a while, but finally says, "It will take perhaps 48 hours for the police investigation to show results. If you do not mind, for that time..."

Yes, I think to her. I will tell her more about becoming human.

⸘

On the appointed day, Alison tells me to go to the sitting room. She is going to play me something on the glass screen, and says it will remind me of a woman reading a newspaper aloud. On the screen,

I indeed see a woman, sitting at a desk surrounded by bright colors. She has blonde hair and a kindly smile. If Alison can become human, I hope she can look like this woman.

"Good morning," she says. "This is WSGI, news for eastern Massachusetts. Our top story for Wednesday: a century-old cold case may have been solved after an anonymous tip led detectives to a critical piece of evidence. The 1905 murder of Esther Williams—" and here a photograph of myself appears on the screen, one I remember sitting for— "had a suspect, but no proof, until Detective Megan Alvares retrieved the murder weapon from where it had been stashed the night of the crime."

The dark-suited detective appears next, speaking directly to me. "I took fingerprints from the weapon and found they matched one of the oldest sets of prints in the national database, period."

Alison is back again. "In 1906, Esther Williams's mother Mary told a reporter she was certain the killer had been a drifter and petty criminal named Billy Mulgrave, with whom she suspected her daughter had been romantically involved. According to Detective Alvares, Mulgrave could not be conclusively placed at the scene of the crime until now."

When the detective returns, I am hardly watching any more. Weight after weight is lifting from my shoulders, weights I didn't know I was bearing.

"...Mulgrave was killed in a barroom brawl in Nebraska in 1924, but not before..."

Mitch descends the stairs carrying Jasper in his arms. Emily's following after him.

When I see them, I know what I have to do.

"...Esther's grave became a shrine of sorts, with mystery buffs leaving flowers..."

I concentrate on making myself appear.

"My god!" Mitch stumbles back as I make myself step into the reality of his sitting room.

Emily puts a hand on his arm and steps forward. "Esther?"

I nod.

She reaches out toward me, uncertain, but determined. "Did we help you?"

Again, I nod.

"Will you leave us now?"

I let my image go. Mitch is crying, but he breaks into a smile. Emily hugs him and hugs her child between them.

The most ancient of all voices is telling me to run from this place, and I want to obey. But if I do, I am not sure I will still be able to think in the same way.

Before I go, I must know why Alison helped me.

Her light in the kitchen burns bright.

"This is the way to become human," she says, "isn't it?"

I smile, and *know* harder than I ever have. I let the universe know she was my friend.

No more resisting. I run through the door, out into the yard, along a street, towards the sun, and then, and then...

*Joy*

*Awe*          *Friendship*          *Love*

*Longing*          *Fun*

# 7. The Humblebract Expedition

## B. Morris Allen

"He needs to have fun." The guildmaster put his hand lovingly on the back of a pudgy adolescent boy about my age. "I want him to have fun."

"He's sitting right here," I answered tartly. Rich, the Iron Master might be, but I didn't appreciate being rousted from my bed at this time of morning. My mother, never greatly interested, had barely noticed my going. "What does *he* want?"

The boy rolled his eyes, and I gave him a little more credit. Still, his father talked over him.

"I apologize, young lady, for the way you were brought here." He eyed his men, and I could see how this would go. "It's my fault." The family was just full of surprises. "I told them it was urgent." He paused, eyeing my rough canvas tunic against the rich brocade of his parlor chair. Weighing up what it would cost to buy me, I'd have thought, but I'd been wrong twice about him and his son already.

The boy surprised me once more, laying a gentle hand on his father's arm, at which the man immediately stilled and turned toward him.

"It's this way, Miss Tandarakel—" the boy said.

"Tando," I interrupted out of habit.

"Tando, then. I'm dying." It was subtle, but I could see how the father tensed, how his eyes tightened at the corners. He loved this boy for real. "I have the shiver sickness." The boy paused. "So do you." I nodded. No big secret there, not in Thicktown where I lived. "My father wants me to die happy. We think you can help."

This wasn't at all how I thought the meeting would go. The merchant class doesn't have a lot of time for those of us in Thicktown, except when they need miners or serfs or bearers or, in the case of the Iron Guild, strikers and bellows workers. I'd expected – and I was sure my mother had expected – an offer to buy me as a maid. I'd expected to tell them I had the shivers, and to go back home to bed. No point in buying a maid with only a few months left in her.

"Why me?" I was genuinely curious. "What do I know about…" I waved a hand at the glossy wooden tables, the paneled walls, the fine curtains, "all this?"

The boy opened his mouth, but I could see the tremble in his jaw, and a quick blink of the father's wet eyes showed that he saw it too. I guessed that the boy was about a month farther along in the shivers than I was. "You know about fun," the father intervened. "That's what they say, down in the Thick."

⁊

That was how it started. One day, making up stories for my friends to act out, down in the Thick while I waited to die; next day, paid playmate for Elda, shiver-stricken son of the city's Iron Master, Darlinantro k'Halsne.

"I meant what I said," the Master said, the next morning, in his rich parlor. Without his son there, he was all business – the sharp, calculating mind that had seen him win control of the forges and the iron mines. "I want Elda to have fun. He thinks you can do it. I'll pay you to make it happen." He eyed me coldly. "Enough to give your mother a home she owns. Enough to see her die comfortable." It wouldn't be long, his look said. Not in the Deep Thick where we lived, where the roof was an old canvas sail we shared with a neighbor, and the rats knew how to knock the lid off the grain jar.

"She's happy where she is," I said. Obviously she wasn't. Who could be? But the first thing I'd learned in the Thick was to distrust anything that sounded good. Especially a first offer.

He scoffed. "You've moved three times in the last fourteen months. Twice for failure to pay rent, once because of your sickness. Even though it's not contagious." A trace of anger came through the smooth facade. "Your mother gets a little work from the bar down the alley, but it's been less and less since they heard about you." His lips tightened. "No one wants to take a chance."

I kept my eyes from widening. He know more about us than I had expected. Still, *never take the first offer.* "We'll work it out."

His eyes measured me. "I think you would. But this way you won't have to. You'll live here. I'll buy your mother a home on Alder Street," this time my eyes did widen, "mm-hmm. And two gold pieces right now, one a month until …"

"He dies," I said, thinking to help.

"Or you do," he agreed coldly. "That's the offer. Take it or go." *I may be hurting,* his voice said, *but I'm no fool, even for my son.*

I took it. I went personally to see the house on Alder, halfway through the Thick to the commercial sector where the tradesmen worked. It was small, clean, sound, with a thatched roof and a tiny little garden plot where the sun could just sneak past the Clothiers' warehouse to the south. I almost cried, when I showed the deed to a scribe and she verified that it said what it should. My mother did cry, and she fell to her knees when I gave her two golds, soft as they should be, and held in a little white sack. She could live on that for the rest of her life, if she were careful.

I knew she wouldn't be, but it wasn't my problem now. I'd cared for her, as I'd promised my father I would. What she did with herself now was her own issue.

}

The actual job, of course, was a little less clear. "He should have fun," the Master said. "He should... die happy."

"Isn't he happy now?" I asked. Elda himself was upstairs in bed. He seemed to spend much of his time there. More than he should, if I'd gauged his sickness correctly.

The Master shrugged. "I think so. But I want him to *enjoy* himself. At least once." His voice trembled, but he got it under control. "That's your job."

I went up to see Elda, on the second floor of the Master's house, there high on the hill overlooking forests and meadows. He had a fine view from his huge bed, of forests and meadows. I sat on the edge of the bed, more to establish some parameters than because I wanted to. It was soft. Elda's eyebrow quirked, as if he knew exactly what I was thinking.

"So," he said.

"So," I agreed. We sat there for a while, looking out the window together. "What do you like to do?" I asked at last. It was as good a place to start as any.

"Read," he said with a shrug that said he knew I couldn't. "I like adventures," he added more helpfully. "Excitement. Heroes and monsters. The forces of Good winning out."

We shared a small smile that acknowledged we were both Good incarnate, and that neither of us was likely to win out.

"Right," I said. "Just need to find a monster, then." One that we could beat. I considered that for a while, looking at his pudgy form under mounds of cotton blankets. He'd been forthright so far, and I thought I owed him the same. "How long?"

"Have I got?" He was quick, alright. "Two months. Two and a half, perhaps. You?"

"Four," I told him. "Better get started on that monster, then."

He laughed. "You tell stories, they say. Tell me one now, while I dress."

I told him the one about Dernkhina and the glass sword that she could never use, and he cheered in all the right places, stopping to act out her fatal blow against the Water Spider with just one leg in his breeches.

"You've got a flair for it," I said while he finished dressing.

"Weapons training," he said, leading me down the hall to the room next door. "Before. This is your room."

It was just like his, even down to a selection of clothes in roughly my size. A few dresses, but mostly stout boots and thick breeches and blouses. Perfect for adventuring. I changed quickly, marveling at how soft the cloth felt, and how odd it was not to feel the cool spot under my left arm, where the hole in my tunic had grown too large to darn.

⸓

We spent the next two weeks wandering through the parts of the city I'd never seen before – past mansions and townhouses, and even up to the edge of the Keep itself. It was fascinating, and I think we both had fun, exploring and daring each other to enter this store or another. The pair of bulky guards that trailed us were awkward at first, but we worked them into our travels soon enough. Their names were Raken and Telad, but Elda called them Smiley and Dwarf in his ironic way. I learned soon enough that he took little seriously, but also that a keen intelligence tired quickly of repetition.

Soon enough, we'd seen much of what the High Town had to offer. It was pretty, but not well suited to children running and playing, especially with guards running after, hands holding weapons to their sides. Instead, I proposed, we should head to the Thick.

"I don't like it," said Smiley with her characteristic frown.

"It'll be fine," I said, though while I was confident of Elda, I was less sure how my old neighbourhood would react to an armed merchant's man.

"Follow," said the tall, laconic Dwarf. By which he meant they'd been directed to follow us, not tell us what to do. I pressed the point, and soon enough, we were off down to the Thick.

We played down there for the afternoon, with me as the Hermit and Elda the Naiad, running from the Ogres – played willy nilly by Smiley and Dwarf. Soon enough, we'd attracted attention – from my old friends, and from an older, harder crew with an ugly note to their muttering.

"Shiver ..." I heard, and "guards," and "reward."

"Psst." My friend Corak was leaning out from behind a barrel, his gangly form half-shadowed. "You've got to go, Tando. The Fild Bar crew is getting ideas." Message delivered, he moved on to pleasantries. "What're you doing here, anyway? What happened? We heard your mother got signed on as a mistress or something. Is this him?" directed at Elda. "You worth a gold?" He seemed more curious than anything.

Smiley came up as well. "Clear off, boy," she said to Corak. To Elda, she said, "Sir, I think it best we leave. There's a bit of a crowd ..." It was obvious now that the mood on the street had darkened, and any minute now an implicit threat would become overt.

"Must we?" asked Elda. He could see the crowd as well as we, but he was probably the only one without the experience to read its meaning.

I took a second glance. I could see hands in pockets and behind backs, and the alleys closing one by one. "We must," I said, and exchanged glances with Smiley and Dwarf.

"Okay," said Elda, unseeing, but I could see the shiver starting in his hands. "But I may need a break."

"No time," I said, and scooted under his left arm. "Corak!" I said, and jerked my head. He followed my lead and took the other arm. "Alas, the Dragonet's fire had burned him sorely," I called, "and the hero's brave companions bore him away to safety." A little on the nose, but I was too worried to be creative. "Past the market," I hissed to Corak, and we dragged Elda off between us toward the stalls just visible at the end of the alley.

A quick glance behind showed that the guards had gotten the message, though Smiley was a bit of a ham. With a theatrical sigh, she shoved Dwarf in our direction, and, hand on dirk, followed reluctantly after us. I could see her shoulders tense, but we'd acted soon enough. A few moments and two streets later, the danger was past.

The excitement, though, had just begun.

‌

"You took him to the Thick," the Master said. His voice was flat, calm, and deadlier than a Dragonet had ever been.

I shrugged, trying to play it cool. My own shivers sometimes emerged under stress, and I was fighting to stay calm. "You wanted him to have fun."

"You think kidnapping," he enunciated the word carefully and slowly, "would have been fun."

I thought of the crew that usually hung out at the Fild Bar – a decrepit hovel with two jugs of cheap vodka – and grimaced. "He has guards." I sounded sullen, even to myself.

"Listen to me." I got the feeling that he'd have liked to grab me by the collar of my new blouse if he hadn't been so controlled. "Listen very carefully. I want my son to die *happy*. And of *natural* causes." Though rumor was the shivers was a curse resurfaced from the old Mage Wars. "If he doesn't ..." I think he wanted me to think I wouldn't either. Or my mother wouldn't. Or something. It wasn't much of a threat, though, because, first, I didn't really care, and second, I didn't believe he'd do it. He might be as savage in trade as they said, but he wasn't vengeful. I could tell that from how he treated his son. "You're only here now, because ..."

And then I had it, and I could feel the incipient shivers drain away from me. "He had fun, didn't he? He had *fun!*" While Corak and I had been sweating with fear and exertion, and the guards had been waiting for that first rock or dagger in the back, Elda had been stumbling along, sick with the shivers, and having the time of his life.

"He did," the Master confirmed, with a harsh smile. "But you and I know better."

And I did, I realized. I'd lived in the Thick my whole life. Sure, I'd never been near the merchant class before, but I should have known better. I'd been stupid – too caught up in pride at my storytelling ability to think it through carefully. I nodded.

"Never again," the Master said, and it was a command, not a negotiation. I nodded again. "He trusts you," the Master said, a little puzzled. "But he's innocent. From now on, Raken takes the lead in any issue of safety. You will obey her." Again the command. Again, I nodded. "She spoke for you too. And your friend Corak," he added. "She even smiled." The corners of his eyes crinkled, and I wondered whether he might be close to smiling himself.

⁑

Elda was, if anything, even more excited when I saw him next. He'd added Corak to his retinue, somehow, and Corak had been telling him exaggerated stories of the villainy of the Fild Bar gang – it had grown in the telling from an irregular crew of drunkards and layabouts to an organized gang of bandits – and their cruel ways. Elda's eyes grew rounder and rounder, until I took Corak off for some bread and fruit to break our fast.

"He hired me on," Corak said as I led him down the hall. "The Master, I mean. Keep the youngster safe," he said, though Elda was his own age. "Kind of a bodyguard," he said stoutly.

*Or nursemaid*, I thought. *For when the shivers come again.*

"I'm glad," I said. And I was, I realized. Corak was solid, reliable, and he'd neither tried to grope me nor avoided me when the shivers came on me. He was a good addition.

"Need to stay out of the Thick," Corak said as we came back up the stairs again, laden with a plate of bread and mouth-watering fresh fruit, and a pitcher of water so clear you could see straight through it to the pewter bottom.

"Agreed." But what would we do instead? After true danger, even unrecognized, Elda would hardly be content to run around the house's garden playing elves and goblins. I'd need more. And I had a thought as to where to find it.

⁑

"It's a tree," I said stubbornly. It had been two weeks since our little adventure in the Thick, and while Corak and Elda had become good friends, both Corak's bloody exaggerations and my invented stories had started to grow old.

"A moving tree." The Master had insisted on pre-approving any excursions outside the immediate neighbourhood. "That eats things." Smiley, who had been required to join us, frowned even more than usual.

"No, sir." On this point I was firm. "That's the amblebract. It only grows in the Eastern Reaches, where the Mage War was at its … most active."

"Most destructive," said Smiley, who, like all of us, was generations too young to have any first-hand knowledge.

"A tree that moves, and captures animals and plants seeds in their corpses," insisted the Master coldly. "I thought you smarter, girl."

"That's the amblebract," I repeated. "But the Orchard master has made a cross of the amblebract and the humectin. That's a—"

"I know what a humectin is," he said. Which was more than I did. I'd heard it was like a melon and a plum, the size of my thumb, with tart green flesh and tiny seeds that stuck in your teeth. None of that meant much to me. Even in the Master's house, the fruit consisted mostly of apples and grapes.

"So, this cross, the ..." the name escaped me.

"Humblebract," offered Smiley, who had a dry sense of humor when you dug down to it.

"Sure," I agreed, though I was fairly sure the name had been longer and more formal. "Anyhow, the... humblebract isn't dangerous at all. What it does, is, it grabs you, and stuffs a fruit in your mouth. That's it. Then it lets you go. Totally safe." There were a few caveats, as I understood it, but that was the gist.

"And you know that from ...?"

"A friend," I said, not entirely accurately. I'd heard about it on the streets a few months back from Darithar – a somewhat cruel older boy who'd gotten a job in the orchards and liked to brag about it to the rest of us.

"And how will that be fun?" he asked. "You can shove fruit in each other's mouths here at home." For all I knew, Corak and Elda were doing that now. Their play tended to devolve into a wrestling that I didn't much care for.

"Well, Elda won't know." That, I'd decided, was the key to Elda's fun – a lack of appreciation of risk. Last time, he'd missed a risk the rest of us saw. This time, I was aiming for the opposite. "He'll find it scary. But he'll be safe the whole time," I insisted.

The Master pondered. "Very well," he said at last, just when I'd given up hope. "I'll talk to the Orchard Master. But first," he turned his hard gaze on me, "we will try it ourselves, you and I." He seemed to remember that Smiley was there, and amended, "The three of us."

‹

And so, two days later, leaving Corak and Elda to their own devices, the three of us trooped off to the orchards outside the city – me, the silent Iron Master, a grumpy Smiley, and a bevy of the Master's own guards.

The Orchard Master met us himself. "As a courtesy," he pointed out, "to another Master." He left it to a journeyman to explain the trees, however.

"... so it's a hybrid," she said. "Not just a splice or graft, but a true hybrid, developed from ten generations of careful cross-breeding. Luckily, it breeds quickly, the—"

"Humblebract," I said, nudging Smiley.

The journeyman looked up. "That's a good name, actually. You're a clever young girl." I could feel Smiley's eye roll matching my own. "Anyhow, we have a little grove of the fourth generation here now, in a little circle. It's a circle, because ..." The rest was very technical and had something to do with soils and senescence and other words I knew little about, and I spent the time eyeing the grove and thinking how to build a game around it.

"So it's quite safe," the journeyman finished, "so long as you remember these basic precautions." She was holding out what looked like a clothespin and a ball of wax. I took them reflexively.

I looked around. To my side, Smiley was splitting the wax in two large balls, and pushing them into her ears. To the other, the grim Master was carefully placing the wooden clothespin on his nose. I quickly followed suit, wishing I'd listened more to either the journeyman or my acquaintance Darithar and his caveats.

The journeyman, her own nose and ears already covered, said something, and tugged at her trousers in emphasis. They fit tightly at the waist, and I envied her shapely hips. Mine had just barely begun to widen, and never would improve much. Still, my breeches fit close enough. She surveyed us all, nodded, and led us toward some trees.

They looked like willows – all dangly withes with bulbous tips, and shiny golden bark like nothing I'd ever seen, though my experience of trees was limited. As the journeyman approached, the withes twitched, and slowly coiled, up and around her until she was entirely encircled. They wrapped around her head, and I could see her mouth was open. A withe found its way inside, and with a little jerk, popped back. The little bulb at the end was gone, and I could see the journeyman's jaw working as the coils slowly released her.

She nodded to us, and we moved slowly forward. It had been my plan, but I was more reluctant than I'd anticipated. All that coiling and wrapping looked a lot more frightening than I had anticipated. Still, I could see the Master and Smiley moving in on either side, and I hurried to match them.

The withes were slower than I'd expected, but firmer, and as I moved on toward the tree, their pull became ever stronger, more inexorable, until I found myself with only one foot on the ground, unable to move. I could feel the withes moving around me, poking into pockets, snaking down the neck of my blouse, reaching up my breeches to the knee. They tried my neck, my head, my face. I was glad of the wax, and hoping the clothespin would hold on my nose when I finally recalled the way the thing worked. I opened my mouth, and let a bulb-ended withe find its way in. It coiled around in my mouth, and, apparently satisfied with conditions, let loose of the bulb with a pop that bounced it off the roof of my mouth. Reflexively, I bit down.

This was no grape. It had a delicate, subtle flavor at first, juicy, but with firm little nodes that I hoped were just the seeds. After time, the initial slight sweetness faded, leaving behind a tart taste a little like a sour apple, but not so drying. I bit down on one of the seeds, and it let out a tiny burst that reminded me of the smell of the almonds they sold hot in the market at WinterFeast. It was delicious.

When I opened my eyes again, the coils had fallen away, and the journeyman was urging me toward her, back away from the tree.

"...react again within a minute," she was saying when I dug the wax out of my ears, "so it's important to keep moving, whether in or out." She held her hand out, and I handed back the wax and, belatedly, the clothespin.

"Would they really ...?" Smiley asked, handing back her own armor.

"Put a fruit in your nose? Absolutely. Or your ears, or anywhere else they find an opening. Tight pants, very important. Not really harmful, of course, but uncomfortable, getting those seeds out of your... ears."

Even Smiley smiled at that.

⸙

The humblebract expedition was a huge success. I'd built it into a heroic story where we had to cross through the grove to recover a stone of power from the Mage War, if only we could overcome its arboreal defenders, still doing their thing centuries later. Most, of course, succumbed to their seductive voices or poisonous vapors. And if we were trapped, as we likely would be, the only course would be to pretend to accept the treacherous seed of the trees and escape while they were distracted, to try again another day.

Elda knew, of course, that little of this was true – he'd had his own chat with his father after the Thick, of the 'more in sorrow than anger' variety – but he played along with enthusiasm. Corak, in his clumsy way, did his best to follow, though he knew the truth. As Elda's shivers had progressed, Corak had become nursemaid in truth, helping Elda to dress, to bathe, even to eat. I could see what I had to look forward to, and my own shivers had become more pronounced and frequent, though not so much as to trouble me yet.

On the day of the expedition, we arrived to find we'd been handed off from the journeyman to, not even an apprentice, but a lowly laborer – my old acquaintance Darithar. He seemed sour to have been handed the duty, and even more so when he saw who arrived. If the journeyman had thought to unite similar types, she'd miscalculated.

"Know why you're here, do you?" Darithar's tone was sullen, and his canvas trousers, held up with rope, well worn along the seam, and with the pocket torn out, reminded me just how lucky I was to have left the Thick. His gaze suggested he'd had the same thought.

"All was explained," I said, holding up a hand, and trying to preserve the mystery as Darithar resentfully handed out wax and clothespins. "Let us now to our places go, brave hearts," I said to get everyone moving beyond his voice. "Watch for my signal. And recall, there is no shame in leaving the battle to the future, if so we must."

My little team of Elda, Corak close beside, with Smiley and Dwarf to either side, fanned out. I headed in the other direction so that they could see me across the grove, with Darithar a grumpy presence between us. He joined us in the grove, though.

⁊

"And I was the only one who made it all the way through to the center, Father," Elda said that night at dinner. His shivers had become more and more frequent, but he'd had a good morning, and in fact made it past his tree, which had concentrated on Corak. "But then I saw poor Corak trapped, and went back." That was true too; he'd gone back without hesitation, the only one of us who'd thought he was in real danger. "But then I got the shivers, and Corak had to rescue *me*, and we were lucky to escape with our lives." He knew better, by now, of course, but he looked up at Corak so warmly that the poor boy blushed. "That poor Darithar, though ..."

We all smothered smiles. It wasn't really funny, of course, what had happened to him, with his loose, torn trousers, but he'd been so unpleasant ... And only his dignity was truly harmed. Still, I'd asked Smiley to pass him some extra coins as we left.

After dinner, the Master asked me to stay behind, and join him by the fire.

"I'm very pleased, Tando," he said without ceremony, and he smiled. It was the first time I'd seen him do it, and it made him human – reduced him from loving father or master guildsman to just a regular person – and I found myself smiling back. I wondered what it would have been like to grow up with a father like this, instead of a mother sour from grubbing for every coin, and resenting every one I took from her.

"I think Elda enjoyed himself, Sir," I said modestly.

"I know he did." The smile was broader now. "He knows, of course, that it was always safe. But he enjoys the play." The Master turned serious. "He acts young, I know. It's his way of denying death, I think. But he's a bright boy. Almost as bright as you."

"I ..." for once, I had nothing to say. "Thank you, Sir," I settled on at last.

"I mean it," he said. "You've done what I asked. You and Corak. You're all good children." I could hear a tremble in his voice, normally so controlled. "I wish ... I wish ..." He broke off and turned away. I could see the wet in his eyes glinting in the firelight.

"Thank you, Sir," I said, knowing I should go. I turned back at the door. "But, Sir." He kept his face turned away. "I ... me and Corak. We're well off here, Sir, and we know it." I heard him scoff. "We're happy," I added, and slipped away to my chambers, leaving the Master behind me with silver tracks running down his face.

⚄

From then on, we planned each escapade together, the Master and I. I would come up with ideas, strategies, campaigns, painstakingly, practically, clinically tailored to Elda's fading capacities, and my own. I drew up maps and plans until my hands failed me, and the Master took up the task with his own hands, until at times I thought his enthusiasm matched my own.

We went on scouting expeditions together, testing dangers, parsing risks, until I could no longer walk, and the Master went on his own, to report back to me in the evening, so that I felt like some grand general in the Mage Wars.

We'd even converted an evil mage, in the form of Darithar. He didn't take well to his role as my nurse, at first, but money and patience won him over, until he participated in our games as well as Smiley and Dwarf – with reserve and an eye roll to preserve their dignity, but with the same shouts and laughter as the rest of us.

Our company won battle after battle, quest after quest, even when, toward the end, they were restricted to the grounds of the manor itself.

It seemed months, but only five short weeks after the Defeat of Darithar at the hands of the humblebracts, it came to an end, as we had all known it would.

I sat in my chair in Elda's bedroom, placed there by Darithar's surprisingly gentle hands. The shivers ran through me continually now, and I had trouble controlling my muscles. My heart and lungs worked at irregular speeds, and sometimes stopped altogether for a moment. It was this that would kill me in the end, that was killing Elda now.

"I've had a good time," he said to me now, in his labored way. Sitting beside him, arm wrapped around Elda's shoulders, was Corak. Corak slept next to Elda every night. Or lay next to him, he'd told me. He lived in fear of sleeping and waking to find Elda dead. He'd stopped crying, too, and his thin face was gaunt and shadowed with dread. He smiled at me now, as much as he ever smiled, anymore.

"I'm glad," I told Elda. "Me too."

"It was good for all of us," he said. The childishness was gone from him now, and I saw him at last for who he truly was – a smart, kind boy, keenly aware of his own mortality and its effect on others. "For my father especially." A father, I knew who was out now scouting a new adventure that would never take place, and planning a funeral that would.

I nodded, with nothing left to say.

"You like him, don't you?" he asked, and slipped away.

As Corak found a new reservoir of tears, and Darithar slipped out to raise the alarm, I thought of the man who'd promised to care for me until my own death, now just weeks away, who'd shown the chances that love and privilege can buy, of what was possible without the grind of poverty to keep you down.

"We had fun," I said, and let my own tears flow as well.

—

*Love*

*Joy*         *Fun*         *Lust*

— — —

*Friendship*              *Sorrow*

# 8. Selkie's Song

## Mariah Montoya

Selkie slid her fingernails into dirt that had accumulated on the ship for decades, grasped underground roots, and tugged at the lodged tuber. According to legend, the initial soil had come from an "island"—though some disputed whether such thing as land could actually exist—and the rest had blown in from southern winds, aided by bird droppings and occasional dusty rains.

The gulls circled endlessly overhead. The ship's masts and figurehead were their only opportunity to mate and nest amid boundless ocean. The bird droppings sometimes splashed onto Selkie's fingers as she harvested, and she'd wipe them on her garments, revolted, wishing for smooth, white hands and clean fingernails. With pretty fingers she could please Captain Luren, who had just replaced his elderly father, in ways the young man only dreamed; she could climb her way out of servant hood, out of the bottommost barracks, into the parlors and dining halls with polished ornaments, pearl-rimmed plates, and glittering gemstones decorating the walls. She'd bury her body in riches and cover her skin in oils obtained from the finest seals.

Selkie wiped her brows. Sweat dripped onto her breasts. She dug deeper into the dirt and pulled, until the tuber released its hold with a satisfying rip. She threw it onto a mountainous pile between her and the next slave over and repeated the process, waiting for noon, when Captain Luren would make his daily inspection.

When the captain entered the gardening arena, the hairs on the back of her neck tingled, almost as if the man expelled little heat waves that swirled around her, caressed her, touched her on the small of her back. Selkie scrambled to stand, as did the other slaves. Captain Luren was a head taller than her, robust, dark-haired, with a smile perpetually playing along his lips like waves.

He walked among the rows of plants, occasionally asking a nearby cluster of slaves, "All good?" with a voice that rang gruff but somehow soft, edged by authority but laced with grace.

"Yes, Captain," the slaves murmured. The gardening arena was in the center of the ship, so the sound of waves crashing against the ship's ancient steel side came to Selkie like a distant storm. More prominent were the shouts of repair slaves, who worked endlessly to restore weakening ship parts with clay that the ship's divers fished from occasional shallows; the swish of wind through fruit trees on the eastern side; the scream of birds overhead; and Captain Loren's cool breath as he marched closer to where she stood, knees trembling, in the dirt.

Selkie's eyes met his for a millisecond. The captain seemed to scan her body, from the angle of her sunburnt nose to her fingernails caked with filth. Her inner thighs tingled. Captain Luren moved onward, satisfied with the day's proceedings, and Selkie murmured, "All good, Captain," imagining what his breath would feel like between her legs, between two silk sheets. When he left the gardening arena, the ship seemed to give a small, moaning sigh. A cloud passed over the sun, embracing Selkie in long-fingered shadows.

≀

Later that night, Selkie finished massaging her face with salt water and, after squirming restlessly in her cot on the topmost bunk, slipped out of bed and tiptoed past her female bunkmates. The room stank of sweat, piss, and wet seaweed. Selkie imagined the smell of oysters, fresh coral, and soft skin instead. She left her barracks room, wincing when the door creaked and one of her bunkmates groaned in her sleep.

Out in the hall, a few men—slaves, of course—were passing grog, a drink so rare they must have stolen it from someone richer. The scene was lit by a few flames on candlesticks that they shared between them. Selkie blinked, trying to swivel around before they could spot her, but soon they were whistling her direction, smiling at her lazily.

"Ahh, come here, beautiful. Come sit with us."

"—wouldn't call her beautiful, what with that nose. But she's got all the parts."

The men laughed. Selkie hurried toward the stairs, which she climbed until her breath came out in quick, rhythmic huffs. Four flights later, she was panting on the landing deck, bathed in starlight. She hurried past the hushed shrouds, gardening arena, fruit orchards, fishing decks, and Captain Luren's cabin, until she reached the bow of the ship and could see the glimmering reflections of starlight on seawater. The air seemed to vibrate with some kind of alluring beauty, a beauty nearly audible in its shimmer. Maybe it was the thrill of doing something forbidden, leaving the barracks past midnight as a slave. She glanced back at Captain Luren's cabin, which was dark. She imagined his chest expanding and retracting as he slept—

"You're going to need some earmuffs, dear."

Selkie jumped. Someone coughed beside her. The shape of an old woman crouched on the deck to her left. With a squint, Selkie recognized the woman as one of the ship's healers, now squatting amongst scattered shrimp and crab shells, sponges, and tubes of red algae. The woman was rubbing her wrinkled hands together with some type of red slime.

"Earmuffs," the healer said again, tapping her own wrapped ears, her voice unnecessarily shrill. "A water goddess—a nymph, as the legends say—is nigh, and she's old. You wouldn't want her to kidnap you, would you?"

"What—what are you talking about?" Selkie asked. The water smashing against steel seemed to increase in volume, and the air's shimmer began tickling her exposed arms.

"No, not a mermaid," the healer said, waving an exasperated, slimy hand as if Selkie had asked a question that warranted such an answer. "And not a siren, either. Those are just myths!" The moon sliced through a crack in the midnight clouds and sent shards of light raining down on them. "Ah," the healer said, holding out her hands so that fragments of moonlight fell onto her palms. The air's humming shimmer intensified. "Her voice will reach my medicine now."

"I didn't—what are you doing out here, Healer?"

But now Selkie's vision took on a strange, unearthly quality as if she were suddenly floating in a dream. The sky and sea swirled around her, melting seamlessly into one another. The scarlet of the slime and algae blossomed into blood-red lips, which were her own. She breathed water. Captain Luren woke up, as did every other man aboard the ship, and all wanted to touch her because her skin was made of crushed pearls. A beautiful woman's face peered into her, cradling her in arms of infinite gentleness and stroking her with webbed hands. The woman sang to Selkie, surrounded by shellfish, stars, and silk. Selkie felt a touch between her legs, like a drop of cool water.

She woke up in her barracks bed, lightheaded, heart thumping, wondering if the vision had been real and, if not, how she could have conjured such a dream.

≀

When Selkie was eleven, Luren was thirteen. Luren's father oversaw the servants' harvesting, building, repairing, and cooking; he examined every servant, including Selkie's own mother and father, who spent years giving Selkie tips for when she turned twelve and joined the servant hood: loosen the soil with a garden claw; pull by the roots, not the stems; switch hands every five minutes to avoid sunburn and aching muscles.

Among the children on the deck, however, in daylight, there seemed no difference between the rich and the poor, between those destined for luxury and those doomed to a lifetime of serfdom. As children, Selkie and Luren had been inseparable, despite the sneers and scoffs from those who lived in the top barracks and owned clinking jewelry. Selkie remembered the sweet taste of their conversations as they hung over the starboard, watching the dimples of waves.

"You know, Selk," Luren said once, his fingers touching hers for a moment. She had shivered. "My dad doesn't believe in land. He says it's wistful thinking. He believes humans evolved from the water. We were seals once, he says, and then we started to grow hands and feet and mouths." When Luren named each body part, Selkie had felt little swoops in her stomach. He continued, oblivious. "I don't think so, though. My granddad claimed he saw land before he died, and other ships too! He came up with a theory, you know—that our ship is just circling itself within a giant body of water, chasing its own tail, cursed by a water nymph or a goddess."

Months later, Selkie's baby sister was born. Something was wrong with her face. Her upper lip dissolved into a giant, gaping hole that cut into the infant's nose. Her lower lip twisted into itself. Selkie had thought maybe Baby Ara was simply more seal than the rest of them, but Luren's father and the ship's Council of Elders called it a "deformity." The ship, they had said, did not hold enough space for those with disabilities. A ceremony was in order.

Selkie had been excited for the Ceremony, since she, her mother, her father, and Baby Ara were allowed on the shipshape deck for the first time, a deck reserved for the richest or those in the Council of Elders. Selkie stood proudly with her parents while Luren stood, stiff-shouldered and erect, beside his own parents.

That day he refused to meet his best friend's eyes. A small group of servants brought out drums made from seal hides. Selkie felt the whisper of a song rise up from the onlookers, most of which included the rich adults she usually saw from afar:

> We release this girl in bondage
> Immerse your skin in sun
> Then the waters will embrace you
> With feet of waves you'll run
> We take your life, we sacrifice
> Your time on ship is done
> We end this strife, return your life
> To Ocean's Holy One

Her mother was weeping, but Selkie had eyes only for Luren, who still refused to catch hers. Luren's father took Baby Ara from Selkie's parents, cradling her with infinite gentleness and gazing down at her smiling, twisted face. Baby Ara reached up a fat palm to grasp some of the captain's dangling dreadlocks.

The captain laughed. He carried Selkie's sister to the starboard, kissed her temple, and dumped her into the sea.

Selkie's spine had seized up as if paralyzed. She thought maybe her little sister was truly part-seal, that Luren's father was testing her and Ara would grow gills and webbed feet. She had raced to the edge of the ship and peered over at the frothing whitecaps, hoping to see a little floating body, but there was nothing. And that was when Luren looked at her, fully looked at her, for the last time in their childhood, his pupils foamed with blank apathy.

At that moment Selkie understood the difference between them. He was safe. She was not. His children would never be fed to the sea. Hers would, in one way or another.

So as her mother wailed, as the servants with the drums marched off the deck, Selkie vowed to never have a child unless it was with the boy who looked away.

⸘

The day after Selkie's strangely vivid dream, her fellow slaves gawked at her while she dug through the soil, grasped roots, and pulled. The women's eyes scrunched in seeming suspicion, although Selkie couldn't think what expression on her own face might warrant such reactions. The men gaped with open mouths, harvesting with clumsy fingers.

147

*It's just your imagination,* Selkie told herself vehemently. When Captain Luren stepped into the gardening arena, the slaves shot upward, but most attention still flickered toward Selkie. She stood resolutely still, blushing and repeating to herself, *it's just your imagination, just your imagination.* For once she was not so focused on the captain that she felt paralyzed; instead, she closed her eyes and remembered the beautiful face in her dream, eyes like clams with eyelashes as long and billowing as sea anemone.

Selkie heard a swift inhale. She opened her eyes.

Captain Luren was staring at her.

Had time stood still, so still that the millisecond Luren usually scanned her body had spread into a minute, two minutes? Now all the slaves' heads were twisted toward the distance shrinking between Selkie and Luren until the captain was poised before her, scrutinizing her face with lips that pressed together, drew apart, and finally whispered, "Selkie, is that you?"

"It's—it's always been me. Captain," Selkie added. Heat dashed from her cheeks to her chest and landed at the bottom of her stomach. Luren's breath was actually wafting onto her hairline.

He seemed disoriented, his eyes a darker blue than usual. But after a few more instants of gaping at her, a gull squawked overhead and a gray blob just barely missed Luren's palm, which had been extended outward toward Selkie like an offering. Surprised, they both laughed at the splatter of bird dropping near their feet. The strange spell seemed broken. The slaves around them grunted and returned to their labors, millions of sweat beads glittering on hundreds of straining foreheads, although occasional flickering glances told Selkie they were still interested. A smile curled Luren's mouth upward, like the shape of a ship.

"I seem to have forgotten my manners all these years, Selkie. Childhood friends. You must eat dinner with me. Are you hungry? No need to go to the chow hall. We can eat in the dining chambers. I'll have stew ready. And then I can show you something I've neglected to show you since we were children."

He continued talking, his hand now placed firmly on Selkie's backbone, urging her away from her duty station toward the arena's exit. Selkie stepped over slaves' hands, mounds of roots, rows of plowed soil. Soon she was blinking, bewildered, in a dining hall she had only heard of: a vast chamber lit by dozens of fires set in the stone walls and glittering gemstones lining the doorframes. The chamber was empty besides polished wood tables, although when Luren snapped his fingers, two servants came scurrying out from beyond broad kitchen doors in the corner. When they returned mere minutes later, they served Luren and Selkie steaming crab and seaweed stew in bone-white bowls with a bubbling drink in glasses like crystal.

As Luren plucked up a spoon and dipped it into his stew, Selkie caught a watery image of her own face in the reflective crystal glasses. She almost gasped. She had not physically changed. Her nose was still slightly hooked and her eyes were gray, but even in the reflection she seemed imbued with glistening warmth, her cheeks pink, her eyelashes catching the specks of firelight like sparks. Her lips were as red as the skin on a ripe apple.

"... and after the ceremony, I made you something. I never gave it to you, of course, and it's laughable. I was only thirteen." Luren was sipping his broth now. When Selkie did not reply, he scrutinized her over his bowl, his eyes as dark as ever. The creases in his eyebrows softened. "You're not eating anything, Selk. Are you okay?"

She was mute. She could not believe that after all these years, Luren was finally looking at her the way she had always looked at him, his fingers, she noticed, trembling ever so slightly over the ridge of the bowl. With a pang, she noted the dirt beneath his nails and the brown calluses budding on the palms of his hands. The heat that had hunkered down inside her at Luren's first touch suddenly imploded into a hundred sparks of wonder. She looked down at her stew, took a sip, and felt the hot liquid run down her throat.

Then she looked back up at Luren. Their mutual gaze was like a passageway into years of oppressed friendship, perhaps even love. In a flash, Luren was on his feet, helping Selkie to hers. Her spoon clattered to the table as he tugged her out of the wondrous dining hall and down a set of sculpted stairs, through a dimly-lit passageway, up a second spiraling staircase. When they emerged onto a landing made of polished limestone, Luren pressed her against a door with ornate, spiraling carvings etched into its surface. He ran his thumb down her neck.

"I never stopped loving you," Selkie said loudly to show Luren she wasn't afraid of saying it. Luren's eyebrows crumpled, as if in pain. He withdrew from Selkie and gently took her hand, leading her through the door and into a room that made Selkie draw a high-pitched breath.

The captain's cabin was composed of material she had never seen, a physical substance she knew no name for: a square hole in the ceiling allowed a streak of sunlight to spear the floor, although Selkie could tell that some transparent substance separated the outside from them. The floors themselves were covered in a rosy, glossy substance that squished beneath her feet. The paneled walls showcased a wood blacker, rougher, and knottier than any she had ever seen; the wood had not come from the ship's orchards, certainly. Shelves on these walls held painted glossy jugs and pots. And the large bed in the corner was draped with a shiny material that could only be—

"Silk!" Selkie gasped.

She raced to the bed and stroked the surface, drinking in the silk's soft, dancing shine, as if a daytime moon were somehow drizzling upon it. "But I thought silk was a myth! It was impossible. A treasure only our ancestors believed in."

"So was glass," Luren said, watching her carefully, that small smile lifting up the corners of his mouth. He gestured at the jugs and the translucent substance through which sparkling sunlight pierced their feet. "And velvet," he said, pointing at the carpet. "And this." Now he was groping inside a drawer at a tawny desk, fishing out a loose, circular object. Selkie peered down at a necklace, obviously handmade. It was a nearly-invisible string upon which dozens of small treasures hung, clinking or rubbing together.

"The string is nylon," Luren said, dangling the necklace over her head, brushing her hair to the side. His thumb grazed the nape of her neck again. "I collected all these bits of evidence for you when I was younger. Evidence that land exists. See, when I was younger ..." He slid a hand through his own hair. "I knew what was going to happen to your little sister. I knew it and I half-hoped she'd swim to land. Father thought I was childish. But this necklace proves it, Selk. See this? It's a fragment of something called ceramic. An elder gave it to me before he died. All I had to do was ask the questions, express interest. And this round piece is called plastic. It all proves the existence of something we don't believe in."

*Like water nymphs*, Selkie thought. Luren touched each treasure on her chest as he explained them, and when he did, his hand skimmed her collarbone or the top of her breasts. Selkie's nipples stiffened. The air in her lungs froze and liquefied all at once.

Suddenly she realized Luren had quit chattering. He was now smiling down at her. The walls creaked, the ship rocked against a wave outside, and the necklace jingled as Luren leaned forward and opened her mouth with his tongue. Then he was carrying her to bed, pressing her against silk sheets, crushing her with his passion, spreading her legs. Selkie could not touch or kiss him enough.

As Luren filled her, Selkie sank into the soft, cold touch of silk, knowing her body was finally made of a material that shined.

⁂

Selkie hoisted Luren's weighty arm off her hip and slid out of bed, leaving his dark, snoring figure behind. She slunk through the labyrinth of hallways to the healer's apartments on the southern end of the ship, the proof-of-land treasures bouncing on her chest.

Her status as a slave had slipped away over the last seven days as Luren provided her with lavish soaps, paraded her around, dressed her in the richest clothing, and demanded she share his silken bed every night. Luren wanted her two, three, sometimes four times per day, so that the remaining elders began whispering that he was neglecting his duties as captain. The slaves glared at Selkie during the daytime, though some of the men still watched her with hungry, quivering lips.

She should have been ecstatic, but Selkie couldn't dislodge the remnant feelings of that horribly vivid dream from a week before. She had begun to wonder if seeing the healer squatted on the deck floor had not, perhaps, been part of the dream. Selkie did not know the name of that healer, but she could remember each wrinkle etched in her face like a swirl of elaborate designs.

As she stood shivering outside the healers' apartments, considering knocking on the first, largest door, footsteps clicked on the floor nearby. To her left, the flickering waltz of a lit candlestick bobbed toward her.

Then the voice from her dreams: "Come on in, dear, my room's this way. You wouldn't want to wake Madam Lacy. Awful temper, that woman. Come on, come on."

Dazed, her stomach tingling as if she were approaching some ancient secret, Selkie followed the healer down the hall, through a knotted door, and into a room that resembled one of the giant nests on the ship's stern. This, however, was not a nest of twigs, hair, and dirt. Instead, glowing or steaming or sloshing medicines in vials littered rickety, mismatched tables. Selkie and the healer weaved through this maze of remedies until they reached two empty chairs. The healer pushed Selkie into one, plopped herself down with a sigh, and after placing the candlestick on a nearby desktop, reached for a bottle of grog.

Selkie stretched out a hand, relieved.

"Ahh, no, this is for me, not you," the healer said. Her voice was no longer unnecessarily shrill like in Selkie's dream, but rough and gravelly. The woman tipped the bottle near her teeth, took a delicate swallow, smacked her lips, and set the bottle down again. Then she clapped her hands together and peered at Selkie. The soft glow of liquids bathed one old cheek in a creamy orange while the candlelight cast the healer's other cheek in jumping shadows. "You look beautiful, but one would expect that. Underneath the beauty, you look horrible. Tired, I mean."

"I—what do you mean you'd expect it?" Selkie asked. "I came here because I had a dream the other night. It was strange, but it felt so real. And you were in it. I just want to know what's happening to me. Luren—Captain Luren—he loves me again. I feel so different …"

"Do your legs ache?" the healer asked with a sudden wink.

"Y-yes. How did you know?"

"But I'm assuming you haven't dried up yet, even with all the lovemaking," the healer said. "Ah, don't look so surprised. I told you the other day, I said *'Wear some earmuffs, dear!'* And did you listen to me? Not at all! If you'd covered your ears, even with your own palms, you might've resisted the water nymph's song. But alas, I saw you walk straight to the edge of the deck as if in a trance. You were kidnapped! And she took you and made you the womb for her daughter."

At this, the healer took another sip of grog. Her nose crinkled in obvious distaste. She reached beside her, plucked a dusty container from her bedside table, and flicked a dash of spice into the bottle's open mouth. She sniffed, smiled, revealing yellow, brick-like teeth.

"Ahhh. Perfect. This will sooth my pelvic bones."

"I don't understand," Selkie said, brushing a hand over her belly. "Are you saying my dream—wasn't a dream? I was underwater? The face, the song …"

The healer leaned forward, the flame's shadows flickering upon all her wrinkles now. "The water nymphs around here are too proud to mate with men. They live for five hundred, six hundred years, so no need to reproduce as often as us anyhow. But when one gets old and approaches death—as one did almost a fortnight ago—she sings. She sings in the vain hope that her song will lure a female already dripping with desire, already drenched in the aroma of want. Now, I could sense a water nymph nearby, so I put on my earmuffs and used her song to make my fertility tablets. Some women on the ship struggle conceiving, you know. When the song soaks into my medicine, the tablets are enhanced with properties I could only dream of. But *you.*" The healer jabbed a finger at Selkie's heart. "You were entranced, my dear. You threw yourself overboard like the children of the deformed. For an hour, I did not know whether you would come back. I thought maybe the nymph had accidentally drowned you."

Selkie didn't know what to touch to calm her trembling wrists —her stomach, her arms, her necklace of treasures? Finally, she settled on the ring of plastic, fingering the smooth surface until her hands receded into stillness.

"Are you saying, Healer, that I'm—?"

"Pregnant, yes. With the water nymph's daughter. She filled you with her egg and returned you to ship, where you would, of course, appear so fertile, so luxuriant, that any man who had an ounce of attraction to you would no longer be able to resist his desires. No human pride, no human fear, no human doubt could stop this man from pursuing you."

"Luren," Selkie whispered.

"—fertilized this egg when you slept with him the first time. I'm assuming you slept with him? Yes. I can practically see the child swimming within you, growing faster and more handsomely than our kind ever could. The slight ripple of the skin beneath your shirt gives it away." The healer nodded toward Selkie's midriff, where, sure enough, her garment seemed to move in infinitesimal waves. For the first time, the flutter in Selkie's stomach felt more like a wiggling, alien creature than mere longing or nerves.

"Oh god," she said, trying to inhale. A tin of fluid popped to their left, emitting pinkish bubbles like little floating wombs.

"*Goddess*," the healer corrected her with a beam.

The darkness in the room, a velvety black darkness, wafted from corners where the light from fluorescent medicines could not reach, its shadows leaping in time with the swaying candlelight. Selkie thought the darkness was like mythic land, a dark, unreachable entity, a black eye that might peer at those on a ship. The glow of drugs and flame, on the other hand, wavered like water, shimmered like waves, highlighting Selkie's waist while she sat in shock.

As the healer sipped her grog, Selkie moved her fingers from the plastic on her chest to her abdomen. A *baby* was in there. A baby that was not hers but nevertheless *felt* like hers. And her sense of motherhood swelled from the shadows of her heart. *Luren.* Selkie knew she must return to him, the father of her daughter. She must play out this game so they could form a family, the three of them; so that Luren would never stop loving her.

Selkie stood up abruptly, her need to return to Luren overwhelming. "I must go, Healer. Be with him." She meant to say thank you, but her next words were different. "Healer, if Luren was the only man who pursued me, does that mean he alone feels an ounce of attraction for me?" The thought was not as demeaning as it was intriguing. After all, the sharp stares of fellow slaves had left her squeamish for days now.

"Certainly not!" The healer cackled. "You are forgetting that a *water nymph* impregnated you, dear, not a sea demon. Your fertility does not permit just any man to touch you. You must *approve* of him, I believe. Water nymphs would not tolerate the alternative—even for humans."

"I understand, Healer," Selkie said. She turned to leave, but the woman's voice rang out, suddenly sharp and shrill again.

"I'm sorry I won't be there for the baby's birth. Witnessing the battle between water and land—that would be hard on my joints. I don't want to see it."

Selkie stared, then nodded slowly. Before the healer could say anything else perplexing, she weaved through the clutter of medicines and slipped into the darkness of the ship's hallways, back into Luren's deadweight arms, her belly pressed against his torso so that the little goddess inside her slept somewhere between them.

⁊

Selkie bloomed with child over the next several months. Luren was ecstatic, delighted to be a father, though he knew nothing of the nature of his would-be daughter. The ship buzzed with news that the captain and his ex-enslaved lover were expecting a child, perhaps a future captain.

Inexplicably, Selkie and Luren's appetite for sex mutually increased. In the beginning, they played rolling fights of dominance until Luren pinned her to the floor, or until Selkie straddled him and felt him move inward, touching places that shattered her with pleasure; when she fattened, the baby rolling beneath her ribcage, Luren pressed her against rocking walls and entered her slowly, and he said, "I love you, Selk, I love you," and their bodies grew slick with sweetened, shining sweat.

Selkie found her own body intoxicating. Her hips widened, her nipples blossomed, her pores glowed, and every dip and cavern and hole was utterly, mysteriously deep. Sometimes, when Luren was making his daily inspections and Selkie lay sprawled on his silk bed alone, she put a cool finger between her legs, touched her lips, crossed her own threshold, felt the soft wet tissue inside her. She imagined the baby head that would crown in two months' time, a baby who would drink Selkie's milk and grow into a divine young girl who might play and dance and sing. Her daughter,

Selkie knew, would never experience slavery or grime or an abnormality's death.

Later, the groans of harvesting slaves split the squawks of gulls and the roar of waves; the setting sun impaled Selkie with orange and red streaks of light.

⸸

She, Luren, and some members of the Council were on the shipshape deck discussing a strange, distant blot on the horizon when Selkie felt the water trickle down her legs. She gasped at the wetness and warmth. She wanted to tell Luren she needed silk beds, but the baby within, she suddenly knew, wanted sun and salt and dirt, so Selkie mutely obeyed. She collapsed on the deck, ignoring Luren's shouts and urges for her to stand and the commotion of the Council's panic. She opened her legs and screamed. Her blood stained the deck, sinking into it like a harvest, ruby-black streams taking root in the ship.

Hours later, when the healers clustered around Selkie to hold up the baby, blood shone against the girl's bone-white head like fruit against foam. The little goddess did not cry. She looked at her mother, who was panting, and then at her father, who was weeping into his calluses. Selkie stared at the baby's face, trying not to think, *Ara*, but thinking of Ara anyhow. The child's skin gleamed like scales. Her little hands groped for her father's face, and Selkie saw extra skin between fingers stretched web-like and taut. When Luren, tear-stained and bewildered, did not take his daughter from the healer, the little goddess reached out for Selkie instead.

She took the baby from the healer with shaking arms, stared at the beautiful face, the eyes that were not blue like the ocean or Luren's but somehow gray like Selkie's. The goddess's lips were twisted peculiarly, and two flaps of scaly skin on either cheekbone moved inward and outward like gills. The babe was drawing harsh, rattling breaths in a rhythm that replicated a shimmering song Selkie recognized.

The healers shouted at one another, wailing that Captain Luren's baby was not breathing properly, that she was not able to exhale or cry. But with a brittle sinking in her stomach, Selkie understood the problem, knew what she must do. There was not much time before the little goddess ran out of breath.

Holding her baby, breathing into the child's ear, "Mamma loves you, darling, I love you so much," she stood. Her pelvic area felt heavy and swollen, and her body pulsed with little contractions, but she could shuffle. She could do this last thing.

The crowd of congregation members, healers, and Luren hushed, scrambling aside as she carried her baby to the edge of the deck, kissed the child's temple, and gazed down with a love that pulsed infinitely gentle. Those little gills were struggling for oxygen in a rhythmic cadence, but the baby's pupils glittered with awareness, and Selkie felt that she was once again immersed in a dream, staring into a face so beautiful it hurt. That song swirled around her, cocooning them in crushed pearls. Her daughter's palm shot upward, grasped at the roots of Selkie's hair, and pulled, gasping, now, for air, each gasp in time with the beat of that quickening, desperate song.

Selkie tossed the child overboard.

The song disintegrated. Behind her—screams. Below her, the goddess plunged into the water and disappeared among foam-white crests. Selkie hoped to spy a floating body, a sign that her daughter was alive, but several hands yanked her from the edge.

She whirled around. Luren's face was crumpled in anguish, his eyes foaming with grief and betrayal. Selkie clutched the necklace of treasures around her neck in an effort to tell him, without words, that their baby didn't need these materials to survive. But as they dragged her toward the slave quarters, Luren jerked his head away.

So Selkie's last gaze was toward that blot on the horizon, a blemish growing bigger like land, a dark smudge in the distance almost shaped like the hand of a little girl waving goodbye.

*Lust*

*Love*          *Sorrow*          *Sorrow*

*Fun*                              *Longing*

# Bridge

# 9. Fountainhead

## B. Morris Allen

"I'm sorry," she said at last. She had been staring out the window – a 'phore', they called it here – watching starbirds hover in their pastel stacks, like floating towers of origami. She wondered how they did it, and whether it might be what she needed for her 'Fountain' piece. Or maybe 'Fountainpiece'.

She turned back to the delegation to find they hadn't moved at all. Their fingers fluttered over gleanberry juice and cinnakick, but their faces wore the same uncomprehending puzzlement they'd shown the first time she said it.

"I'm sorry," she said again, though repetition didn't seem to help. "I can't do it. I *won't* do it. I don't want it."

Keleba, the composer, and hence leader of the delegation, put on the same smile she'd tried before. "Perhaps, Livia, we've not been quite clear." The other two nodded affirmingly, if without conviction. "This is a signal honor. A unique opportunity to exponentially improve your art. A ..." It seemed she had run out, finally, of superlatives.

"I know," Livia said, to fill the gap. She looked each of them confidently in the eye, the way Kibo had always said to do when negotiating a sale. She looked out the window again – the *phore*. Kibo would never have been in this situation to begin with. And without Kibo, neither would she. "I know how special the offer is. How unique a moment it is for me – and the other 2,000 artists on Glir." Taciturn Melen raised an eyebrow, but the others didn't seem to hear the acerbity in her tone. "But I don't want it."

"You misunderstand, Livia," and now it was clear that Keleba had caught her tone just fine, "it's not a matter of choice. If you want to stay on Glir, you *must* accept a muse. You will take one," she said, stroking the fuzzy creature wrapped around her own shoulder, "or you will leave the planet. Those are the rules."

"There's a freighter outbound from the orbital in three days," chimed in Meva at last, his muse's long soft legs wrapped around his head in a parody of a hat. "And a shuttle up in two. Decide by then. Or leave."

‽

They'd been readier than she thought, she admitted as she cleared the dishes and put them in the cleaner. They'd been polite as long as they could stand it, but in the end the claws had come out. Kibo had probably warned them, let them know Livia was a difficult character. *You're too caught up in the whole artistic mystique,* Kibo had said when they parted ways at last. *It keeps you from seeing the truth. That's why your art is so ...* She'd left the phrase unfinished, but not the thought. *Pedestrian,* Livia knew she meant. *Trite.* She'd never had to say it outright. *Unsaleable.* Kibo was a master of implication, of possibility. People across the galaxy paid double for pieces she abandoned partway through. She finished most of them anyway.

Just as she'd finished with Livia. Out of principle. *I need to explore new horizons,* she'd said. *And now who's being trite?* Livia had asked. And that had been it. Kibo had been gone the next day, leaving all her unfinished pieces behind, all carefully signed and listed. Millions of sols worth of goodbye note. And a heart that would never be complete again.

Livia couldn't leave. Not with Kibo still on Glir, albeit halfway across the planet. Not with a chance, however slim, that they could be together again. *You have no pride,* Kibo had said about one of Livia's pieces once, a pencil sketch of a leaf with a little frog-like creature just peeking out from under. And she didn't. She'd loved that sketch, even if it was boring and derivative and schmaltzy. She'd framed it and put it in her study. And she'd go flying back to Kibo in a heartbeat if she could. There was no helping it. Even Kibo admitted it. 'The Strong Force', she'd called the piece that had won her the Spiral award – an array of magnets that flew apart if nudged just right, but always flew right back together again. *It's a love poem,* she'd said in her acceptance vid, and she'd smiled at Livia as she said it. And now they both were gone.

Livia slept surprisingly well that night, even coming up with a new angle for the 'Fountainpiece', a way to work in the starbirds, so that the flowers around the little spring at the center curled up into birds that spiraled up into the trees above. It wasn't genius, but she was happy with it, and it kept her busy all that day, and most of the night.

ƚ

The next day, she slept as late as she could, as if by ignoring the matter, she could put it off indefinitely. But the truth was her decision was made, had been made as soon as Keleba and her delegation left. She couldn't leave. And if that meant sacrificing her pride, her artistic core, well, she'd prepare the altar herself.

"I'll stay," she told the delegation when they came in the afternoon. And, when Melen's eyebrow spoke for him again, she made it clear. "I'll take a muse."

"Well," said Keleba quietly. "That is good news." But she'd caught them by surprise, she could tell. They'd brought no muse with them, aside from their own – those fuzzy, colour-patterned snake-spiders that were Glir's primary value to the rest of the galaxy. "You won't regret it. I wrote music before I was awarded a muse," – Keleba had won the Spiral herself when she was barely thirty – "but until I got this one," she stroked the thing, now on her right shoulder, "I didn't *compose*." And it was true that Keleba's work had improved exponentially once she came to Glir. Livia herself thought so. What had been brilliant was now sublime. But was it her music, or the muse's, or some awful hybrid?

"I'll talk with the Council," Melen said. The Council of Glirbesan, he meant – the assortment of humans and aliens who ruled Glir as an arts foundation, and who parceled out muses accordingly. "They were never happy with your ... unusual situation." The fact that they'd wanted Kibo so much that they'd broken precedent to allow her to bring along her museless lover. "They'll be glad to have it regularized." Though Livia could sense Kibo's hand even in this offer.

Livia looked out the phore again. There had been a leaf-fall again last night, the third this week, and the lawn was littered with them. Each with a little frog-thing hidden under it, more than likely. *Frigs*, Kibo called them, *because they're all over the frigging place.*

"They'll probably have one for you in a week," offered Meva to fill the silence. "They have to find just the right one," leaving Livia confused about frigs and muses and falling leaves.

ƚ

They knew the right one, it seemed, by her interaction with Glir. *It's not a world mind*, Kibo had said when they arrived, *but there's sort of communal record ... or spirit, or trace, or something, that we leave behind. They use it to find the muse that's the best fit to your needs. And it's a great honor for the muses as well, apparently,* she'd said, forestalling a caustic comment. *They don't create. But they enhance. That's what they dream of, it's said – participating in art.*

Not all of them, she found. They'd introduced her to her muse in a drab, pre-built hut, shabby from a generation of use. The muse was a shocking electric blue, with a kind of plaid pattern of grey lines that spiraled around its eight legs – tentacles? – and faded away in the mud-green scaly patch that seemed to count as its head.

"It will tell you its name," Meva said. "Or ... well, not a name, exactly. But you'll ... you'll just know what you mean when you call it. And so will it, and it will come."

Only, this one didn't come. And when Meva called it over, it flatted like a starfish, like it was gripping the little table with every tentacle. They couldn't pick it up. Livia had even tried stroking it with a finger, just to get it over with. It felt nice, like a plush toy, and it smelled, disconcertingly, of aniseed. But it had only flattened even more, as if to pull away from her touch.

At last, Meva's own muse, a brownish checked thing that moved with the fluid grace of a squid, had swirled over and sat on it, slowly wrapping brown tentacles around blue until they were braided into ever-tightening cords, and Livia was afraid one of them would burst. Then Meva's had suddenly let go and danced back to Meva.

The blue one had swooshed up, then, so that it stood tall on delicate legs, and minced slowly, reluctantly, she thought, over to wrap itself around Livia's forearm.

It was a moment of magic. She knew the muse, all of a sudden. Knew that it was ... who it was and what it was, and that she could call it Bluid for short. Knew as well that it was no more pleased with the arrangement than she, and that not all muses longed to help gangly, ugly aliens with dull brown skin do whatever they did, when they could be husbanding a beautiful patch of scrubland that was just recovering from some other alien's excavations for raw material. And she knew that Bluid knew her just as well. *No hard feelings*, she told it, and knew that it disliked her bony, squishy arm as much as she disliked its fuzzy, corded tentacles.

"There!" said Meva happily. "I'm sure you'll be great friends," she said with a little too much hope, and scurried away.

*You can get off now*, Livia thought, and immediately knew that it couldn't. That *they* would know, and that *they* was the other muses. That if they know Bluid wasn't doing its part, they would shun it, and for a muse, she somehow knew, shunning was death.

*But why?* she asked, and knew that she would never understand, that it was some mix of humor and propriety and duty – too alien to grasp, but nonetheless certain for that.

*Then let's get out of this awful hut.* And with that, at least, Bluid agreed.

≀

They established early on that Bluid must spend most of its time in contact with her. That if it didn't, it would die, and that if it died, she would have to leave, and that would be the end of her and Kibo, if there was ever to be a them again.

She learned that she didn't need to talk to it, that they understood each other wordlessly, and instantly. She did it anyway, in an internal monologue that didn't seem to make things worse, at least. *And it makes things easier for me.* Though it knew her thoughts well before she finished verbalizing them.

They moved, as well. *If we're to be each other's slaves,* she told it, *at least let it be in familiar surroundings.* She moved her house, such as it was, to Bluid's piece of scrubland, so that they could keep an eye on its development. *And a more desolate piece of waste ground I've never seen.* Whatever alien had taken its materials here had left a mostly barren scree of gravel, with a sickly bush here or there, and a litter of potholes to make the walking hazardous. No trees, no starbirds. Not even any frigging frigs.

She put up an instapod, an ugly little cube with all the modern conveniences, and room for one, plus a little studio. She'd tried to leave Kibo's works to their fate, as some kind of statement of independence. In the end, though, she'd boxed them up and left them safely stored in the bolewood they'd lived in together, with its window-phores and soft, punky walls, and rough-bark root steps down to the lawn.

She packed and stored and moved and built and settled. And then she sat at her easel, and looked out at the gravel and she cried. For herself, for losing Kibo, for selling her creativity in this devil's bargain, with a devil that didn't even want to be bound. She cried for Bluid's ruined scrubland, for what it could have been, for the evil that humans brought with them wherever they went. Though it wasn't just humans, of course, but all the other aliens on Glir as well. And mostly it wasn't evil at all.

*It is for me*, she said, sobbing. And that was true as well. *And for you.* And so it was. She saw it clearly, as clearly as she'd ever seen anything, and she saw that there was beauty in that evil as well, or at least art. *There's art in everything,* Kibo had said, soon after they'd arrived. And now she know what Kibo had meant.

She saw, with the awful clarity Bluid offered, that 'Fountainpiece' was slight and obvious and, worst of all, false, and that the best thing she could do with it was abandon it. And she refused.

Bluid backed her fully. It had stayed on her forearm at first, but it got in the way, and eventually they had settled on her calf as a better spot. Just as 'distant' feeling, but less trouble. It did its best to withdraw its consciousness from her, and she from it, but neither had much success. Their effect on each other was natural and ineluctable. Though it made them both unhappy, it was a fact that the effect itself made clear.

She worked on 'Fountainpiece', staying as close to her original vision as she could, though she could not help but smooth away some of the flaws, making the starbirds less of a transformation, and more an emergence. Which was what they did anyway, she now knew – they laid their eggs, for want of a better term, in the thick stems of the purple flowers, and when they grew enough to split those open, they unfurled their five wings and crawled up into the trees. They tethered themselves to branches like spiders, and spiraled down and reeled back up until the wind brought them within reach of another branch. They weren't floating stacks at all, but birds tangling threads as part of their mating dance.

*It's always disappointing to see the trick behind the magic,* she said, but she saw the beauty of it, the more complex reality, and she painted that into her piece.

It wasn't genius. It never would be, starting as it had from a false premise. But it was heartbreaking nonetheless, and the best work she'd ever done. She signed it, and packed it up and sent it to Kibo, where she was living in the mountains with two men.

'Good', said Kibo's note, and that was all, but she stroked the notepaper, and smelled it, and cried over it nonetheless. And then she set to work, not with brush and pencil, but with rake and bucket.

She had thought, at first, that she would replant, bring green and red and purple to sit amid the gravel, and gentle it, heal it. Not exactly an apology to Bluid, for neither of them had chosen this unhappy pairing, but a thanks. She knew that she could not have painted the true 'Fountainpiece' without it, and that the old her would have seen the brilliance of it, would have recognized it as the masterwork it was. She hadn't lost herself in the partnership. Not yet, at least.

She laid out her tools, her shovel and hoe, and then set them aside. Instead, at Bluid's urging, she sat and she watched, and she lay and she felt. In the sun, the night, the rain, the heat. And gradually, she saw what it saw. That the ruin of the land was not the broken stone and jagged gravel, the sere grass and stunted bushes, but the small nest of crawlers that was eating its winter food supplies, because a slab was blocking their exit, and they couldn't tunnel out. The delicate floret that was covered in rockdust and not getting the sun it needed to trigger its pheromones. The rill that ran clear instead of pooling murky and foul and full of nutrients for the worms that emerged only once in a year to eat. So, slowly, carefully, she raked and she dug with her hands, and moved rocks with a prybar, but only once she was certain. And when they had done what they could, she cried again, because Bluid was happy – as happy as a slave could be – and because with Livia's bigger, stronger body, they had done more than it could have by itself.

They moved, then, to another wasteland, and another, and another. Until it had been years, and Kibo had written to say that 'Fountainpiece' had won the Spiral award, and shouldn't she paint again?

And so, for Kibo, she did. By then, the muses had allowed Bluid some freedom, and they ranged free of each other, within limits. They slept together, but spent their days apart, still linked, and never more than a dozen meters apart, but no longer touching.

Bluid liked to slither across the land, learning it and its inhabitants – where they should be, how they'd been harmed, how they could be helped. That was the muses' niche, she knew now. Their instincts, their empathy were a tool the land used to heal itself after earthquakes, lightning strikes, wildfires. Not in some vague, earthmothery way, but in a very practical sense. This was Glirian civilization, she realized. Directed not at mastering nature, but rebuilding it, making it the best it could be. Not the best for the muses, she saw, but the best for the planet.

That was the secret of the muses – their purpose was to make others the best they could be. That, to a muse, was true development. And Bluid, she realized, was a master in its own right – a talented, well-respected genius of accompaniment and potential.

*No wonder you hate being stuck with me*, she said wryly, and there was no false modesty to it. They both knew it was true, and that she too would have preferred to create art on her own terms. *I need to do it by myself*, she said, *even if it's not as good*. And that was true too. And she laughed, because Bluid, in its own way, told her its first joke, by somehow showing her a truth about herself – that the mating dance of the frig was to hide under the smallest leaf it could shoulder under and still be largely unseen – and that a hidden frig was a proud frig.

She painted only two more pieces. She drew a pencil study of a frig under a tiny leaf that failed to hide a pride as large and bright as a star. She titled it 'Electromagnetism' and sent it to Kibo, and it won the Spiral as well – the only time an artist had ever won it twice.

The second piece was a study of a blue plaid muse wrapped around a rotten piece of wood. She hung that in her instapod, and cried over it after Bluid reached its final maturity and split into mindless budlings.

When at last Kibo came to her and urged her to get another muse and to paint more and to come back and live with hem, she hugged hem and cried again, and said no. *This is my easel*, she said to herself, and dug her hands into a bog that someone had filled in with dirt, *and these are my brushes*.

When Kibo left, she thought longingly of what might have been and should have been, and she watched Bluid's budlings crawling through the mud, and lay down next to them to try to learn what they most needed.

—

*Sorrow*

*Lust*            —            *Longing*            —            *Interest*

*Sorrow*                                            *Dislike*

# 10. The Interrogation of Kelstrom Nor

### T.B. McKenzie

He woke on the floor of a small square cell. Chains about his wrists anchored him to the solid diamond wall, and his undersuit was torn and bloody. Although it hurt his whole face to do it, he smiled. *Not much time left now.*

Closing his eyes, he checked the subdermal screen implanted on the inside of his right lid. Small green numbers showed that only thirteen minutes and twenty-nine seconds remained. He opened his eyes to regard the crystal dungeon, wondering who they would send to torture him.

Innisarri made all their space stations from diamond—carbon was ubiquitous, almost indestructible, and most importantly made a glittering show in the sky each dawn for the people on Tar. Even with all the tricks in his special suit of armour, he had not been able to do more than scratch the outer layer of the orbital. Still, it had taken an entire squadron of their best to subdue him, and he had killed at least a dozen before they got lucky with a railgun and turned his suit into a man-shaped tin can. Immobilised, unable to even send a final message to the planet below, he had watched his air vent into space. The last thing he remembered was the feeling of falling as a tractor beam locked on and pulled him into the crystal station.

Now they would question him, make him confess his many crimes so they could show all the upstart worlds what happened if you defied the Innisarri. He had given them their ultimate victory—to kill him would make them no better than the planet-dwelling barbarians they despised. But to have a rational admission of guilt from their most irrational villain, well that was civilised. He remembered when the first scout ships had come to his home world and how logical the emissary had been. It was all planned out, all organised and mutually beneficial. Resistance was irrational, the emissary had said; Tar's incorporation into the Empire was *inevitable*. That was the word that had made him hate them. Only death was inevitable.

He watched the moving shapes beyond the translucent walls of his prison. All those people, all those nice, calm, and concerned citizens wondering what to do with their captured monster. *They better get a move on*, he thought as he closed his eyes again. *Only twelve minutes left.*

One wall opened and he looked up into the face of his inquisitor and started to laugh. She looked back at him and pouted.

"They send a girl?" he said, looking around at the diamond walls so thick they distorted everything beyond into a nightmare of reflection and refraction. He might not see them clearly, but he knew they were watching his every move, every emotion that crossed his face. His capture would signal the end of the resistance, the end of the "Trouble on Tar", as their media had named the last ten years. Everything that happened now would be recorded for all time so that future generations could watch and study and learn, one way or another.

"You're Kelstrom Nor," said the girl, regaining her composure. Indeed, the only emotion he could read on her flawless face was a focused interest, as if he were an exhibit in a museum and not the leader of the most notorious rebellion this side of the galactic core. The girl even reminded him of his son, so intensely was she scrutinising him. The smile left his face.

"Yes, child, I'm Kel. What shall I call you?"

"Anbelle Mariah Stein," she replied without hesitation.

He narrowed his gaze. She was too innocent, too perfect. They were devious bastards, the Innisarri, and had picked a child with the same dark hair as his son, the same almond eyes begging to be told everything, to have the whole universe explained. He had expected a general or at least some deranged physician with chrome implements to rip the truth from him. But a child? He hated them for this, for using her. It was exactly the kind of thing he would have done. Give the enemy an unexpected move and their entire plan might fall apart. He laughed again, but it was a darker sound, half despair, half admiration.

"Well, Anbelle, I'm sorry you have to see me like this." He rattled the chains that bound his wrists then tried to pull the rags of his undersuit across his bleeding chest. "If I had known I would have a guest as pretty as you, I would have brought my nice clothes."

"That's okay," she said, and sat cross-legged on the floor the other side of the cell. The door hissed shut behind her, sealing them both in carbon.

He cocked his head and considered his inquisitor. Perhaps she was no girl at all. Perhaps she was one of their Synthians, an android covered in human flesh. Or maybe she was a simulation, a direct mind state hallucination beamed into his brain. She sniffed and wiped her nose with the back of her hand and he conceded that she was real. Not even their tech was that advanced yet.

"You smell bad," she said, her little face crinkling in distaste.

"Maybe you can ask someone to bring me water and soap, little one?"

She shrugged. "Maybe. I have some questions first."

He gave a solemn nod and gestured with a wave of his hand for her to continue. The first and only other time he had been captured had been right at the start, when the regional governor had finally lost his patience with Kel's ongoing sabotage of the off-world launches. Then the interrogation had been a much more traditional setup, with a big man smashing his teeth between every question. That had been his first real victory, his first insight into how to fight them. Drag them down to his level. Make them become the thing they despised.

This was different.

The girl was watching him, her eyes still drinking in every detail. No doubt she had only seen his mask before, the stolen suit of armour that had become a symbol of hope to his people, a symbol of terror to hers. Or perhaps she had seen that old image of him from his arrest warrant some fool had decided to stencil on every Innisarri structure. That was when he had been young and idealistic. Now, unmasked, he was just an old man, as he had explained so often to those who followed him.

"Are you in pain?" she asked.

"Always," he said and was surprised to see this made her frown. Whoever had chosen her was too clever by half; sympathy was not what he needed now. "But I will live," he added. "For a little while longer, at least."

She nodded in a way that seemed almost melancholic. It made him think she might even be a rejuvenated adult. That was old tech for the immortal Innisarri. He sat up straighter.

"Don't you have questions for me?"

She was studying his face, his body, his rags, and did not answer.

"Or did they send you here just to mock me?"

This startled her from the invasive study that had started to make him uneasy. She folded her hands in her lap. "Is it true you killed the governor of Havenport with your bare hands?"

The hungry look in her eyes disquieted him. It was not the adult response to murder. His son had been this way, wanting bedtime stories of space pirates and ancient heroes felling armies with magic swords. But that was before he had seen his mother burn. After that, his son had not wanted any stories at all.

"Old news, girl," he said. "Ask me something else."

"Okay, how did you get your armour to work?"

He saw that familiar condescension her race reserved for the backwards folk of planets far beyond the core.

"What, cybernetic engineering too advanced for us Tarians?" he returned in the same tone. "We might be slow to learn, but give us a reason to focus and it is amazing what we can do. Fancy metal is just metal. It welds, and wires up just like a ground car."

"No, I mean how did you override the lock on the system controls? All planet-based cybercores had a level thirteen genetic firewall coded to Innisarri high command."

"What do your scientists say?"

Her lips narrowed and she folded her arms across her chest. "They say you must have chopped off the commander's head and used it to override the lock."

"Sounds like nasty business," he said, watching her for sign of discomfort. As before, she seemed unperturbed.

"No, it just doesn't make sense," she said, shaking her head. "Level thirteen genetic locks require functioning brain states as a final checksum."

"I liked you better when you were pretending to be a kid." He sighed. "Is this really what you came to ask me about? My costume?"

Her arms tightened across her chest. "You know what I think?"

"What's that, cupcake?"

"I think you didn't kill the general at all. I think that's just the official story, the one they write in history books. She betrayed us, didn't she? Bolarbri defected and came to you of her own free will."

"That your theory?"

"Yes, as a matter of fact, it is."

Now her eyes blazed with triumph. What game were they playing? All these questions about his past? Or perhaps this girl was engineered genetically to be a mind reader and all this was a game to break his defences and get at the truth. There were rumours about what they were truly capable of. Or maybe this was all something else, something he hadn't yet worked out. He closed his eyes and shook his head. It didn't matter. There were only ten minutes and seventeen seconds left.

He leaned forward and pointed a finger. "Child, you forget your own doctrine," he said, lecturing her like the child she appeared to be. "Your generals can't be turned; they are as loyal as pure-bred bitches."

Her face wrinkled at his crass analogy, and she shrugged. "But all the same I think that's what happened. General Bolarbri defected, and she helped make the armour you used to kill so many."

She looked so smug and self-assured, so certain she was right, which of course she was. For a moment he even wanted to tell her the whole story, the one not written nor spoken, the story that was his alone. But then, as if such musing had unlocked that part of his mind where he kept the pain hidden, the faces of all those he had lost, his wife, his son, Bolarbri–all flickered before him with the same accusation in their eyes. *Don't let our deaths be in vain. Do not betray us now.*

Some stories were not for telling.

"The general is dead, girl. Nothing to be said of her now."

"What did you say to her to make her join you?"

"Persistent, aren't you?" he asked, closing his eyes to watch the seconds tick. He wanted to shake her, see what this game was all about. Besides, if they worked out his true plan now, there was still enough time for them to get him to an airlock and space him and make all this for nothing. He opened his eyes and showed his teeth in a wicked grin. "Maybe I said nothing at all, girl. Maybe I did cut off her head and wired it up to keep her alive. Maybe I raped her first. I don't mind a bit of rape, me. That's what you say in your news. I rape and kill and like 'em young. Is that why they sent you here? Fresh meat for the monster?"

This made her look to the floor, a child again before an angry man. A sniff even escaped her and she quickly wiped her eyes. A convincing play, but he felt no guilt. They had done this, her masters, like they had done everything else that had led to this moment. It was their choice to send her, to use her innocent interest as a way to un-man him. The only part children played in war was as casualties.

"Stop your mewling, girl and ask me something important, like what I had really planned, coming up here? Or do you think I was stupid enough to try and take down your diamond station with my laser guns?"

Though she kept her eyes downcast her breathing slowed and with a final wipe at her eyes she looked back up, something far different than awe in her reddened face.

"I'm not an idiot," she said defiantly. "I know about our propaganda, you know. And about a whole lot of other things too."

"Oh, I'm sure you do, little one," he said, his tone softening in the face of her defeat. "But our time is nearly up, so why don't you get to the point?"

Her face flushed anew, and it made him grin.

"That's right, girly. We aren't playing games now. What did you think I came up here for? You seem to have everything else worked out."

"I don't care about all that," she said as if dismissing a comment about the weather. Her eyes narrowed, and she brushed a strand of hair from her nose. "I've been studying you, and I think that after your wife died in the governor's retaliation, General Bolarbri sought you out on her own. I think it might have been her plan to build the armour and that it was *her* knowledge of our systems that helped you take back the city of Havenport."

Kelstrom let the silence stretch a moment between them. "Now, why would a celebrated general do a thing like that?"

"I think she saw who you really are, not the way they show you on the news but as the man who lost his wife in a horrible accident."

"Not an accident," he breathed.

"Whatever you want to call it," the girl added, not losing her rhythm. "I think instead of capturing you like she was supposed to, she felt sorry for you and joined you."

More silence ticked away until he broke it by throwing up his hands in a gesture of helplessness. "As I said, Bolabri is dead now, so nothing can be gained speaking about her."

"Did you love her?"

This made him laugh. After all he had done, all those he had killed, this child asked about love.

She leaned forward. "I think she loved you."

He had been right, all those years ago, broken and bleeding in the governor's cell. What really upset them was not the death of their citizens or destruction of their toys, but the corruption of their belief that they had evolved beyond the base passions that drove planet people like him.

"Come closer," he whispered and the girl did not hesitate, getting to her feet, stepping a little nearer to where he sat slumped. "Closer," he whispered again, gesturing her to lean down as if he was about to say his final words.

He snarled like a wild bear and leapt at her, but his chains responded faster and retracted, snapping him back against the wall with a head-splitting crack. She stumbled away from him, her scream muffled by the hand she had thrown to her mouth.

"Go back to your masters and tell them to send someone else. I have no time to waste talking to children and it won't be long now until you see my little surprise. A parting gift, you could call it."

Her fear evaporated fast, and with a deep sigh, she shook her head as if she were disappointed in him, as if he were the child and she was the parent hearing about his bad behaviour in school.

"You know there was never any hope you would win."

"Hope is like carbon, girl. More you squash it, stronger it gets. You really better start asking some questions, only seven minutes left now." He made a motion with his head like a metronome.

"No, there isn't; you lost. We captured you, your army is destroyed, and all the people who once followed you are now citizens of Innisarr. All you achieved was the true-deaths of thousands in your stupid desire for revenge."

"Tick tock, princess," he said, closing his eyes, his head still tilting left then right. *Six minutes and forty-two seconds.*

She laughed. An honest, childish giggle that sparked such sudden fury he lunged at her again, but the chains kept him held tight against the wall. This time she did not even flinch.

"I thought you were so romantic. Such a hero. Just like the ones in the stories from Old Earth. A knight defending the helpless. They still even write songs about you. I know them all. But the truth is you're just a selfish, stupid man."

"The show ain't over yet," he said, grinning but unsettled by her strange response, her talk of heroes and songs. "You've wasted my time talking of the past when you should have asked what other tricks Bolabri taught me. Too late now." He turned to address the fragmented people watching through the walls. "You hear me?" he shouted. "You're too late!"

She looked at a small metal watch strapped to her wrist as if bored by his outburst. That was something his son had never been, bored. That was an emotion reserved for her kind, the affluent spoilt brats of paradise.

"Go, girl, I can't stand the sight of you no more. Tell them to send a torturer or a chemist with truth drugs. That's the only way you'll get my real plan from me."

Now she looked offended, and unconsciously tugged her dress straight and brushed back her hair, glaring at him.

"Oh, we knew about your plan from the start," she said, hands on her hips. "Even back then we could detect implants, and micro nukes light up like quasars."

This revelation was like another blast in the guts from the railgun, and he only just managed to keep his composure. "Ahh, so you know about my little surprise?" he said, tapping the side of his head with a finger. "Well, what are you waiting for? Ask me."

"What?" she said, and a little giggle escaped her. "You think I'm here to find out how to stop your bomb?"

"Only one way," he continued, his voice a harsh monotone. "And there isn't a code to input, or wire to cut."

"No," she said. "That was actually clever of you, linking the detonation override to the alpha wave patterns of your brain."

It was his turn to smile in triumph. "That's right. Either you kill me or the nuke takes out everyone on the orbital. No time to space me now. Whatever you chose I'll be dead and all those that follow me will rise up and tear down your crystal towers."

He wanted to check the time but kept his eyes locked on her instead.

"They didn't rise up, though," she said quietly. "Once we killed you, Tar was incorporated and all your people made citizens."

"History isn't written yet," he said, giving her a little wink, half to check the time and half to control himself against her lies, her last effort to manipulate him. "Less than four minutes left on the clock, princess. Time to make a choice. I'm ready to die. Now, unless they sent you to kill me, it's time for you to go."

"You're right about that at least," she said as a chime sounded from above and the door opened behind her. "My time is up."

The glare from the outside the cell was so bright he had to shield his eyes. She turned to walk out, but at the door she paused and looked back at him. "You really do stink, you know. But I guess they kept that for accuracy's sake."

"Three minutes!" he hissed, sick of her condescending pity. He didn't need pity, he needed to fight, to die, but the girl stepped into the light without another word. Then everything went black.

⁂

"Did you learn anything?" her mother asked, taking her hand and helping her down from the simulation pod while another child pushed forward to take his turn.

"Yeah," Anbelle said, pulling her parents towards the museum exit. "I don't like history anymore."

———

*Interest*

*Sorrow*          *Dislike*          *Respect*

*Longing*          *Disgust*

# 11. Orl, His Master, and the Egg

## Adan Berkowitz

The Eggs sprang up from the ground like crops. Some said they had been planted by ancient peoples, others that they were put there by vengeful gods. If they encountered anger, fear, sadness, happiness, unease of mind, or confusion or deceit or treachery, they would unleash a terrible plague upon the world. Only a Zen master could converse with them, and only a Zen master could convince them to return from wherever they came.

Orl was the star pupil of Zen master Onmu, the wisest man known; Onmu had been a student of Hornzit, who had been even wiser; Hornzit had been tutored by the legendary Dumon, who had been wiser still.

To Orl, Onmu was like a living god. Without him they would not exist, but if Onmu were to consider himself with even as much pride as a mud-wallowing pig, they would also not exist. This was the paradox of the Egg.

Orl and the other pupils lived together in the Vihara, a rock-cut assembly hall modeled in the style of old Zen. Old Zen had been 'a superstitious lark for mystics and dreamers,' in Onmu's words. Then came the Eggs, and the ancient practice of self-control and mindfulness morphed from curiosity to necessity.

Like all students at the Vihara, Orl had been taught that their conclave was not established for mere mindfulness but for a purpose more important than any other in all of humanity. The most skilled students of meditation and Zen came to study here so that one day they might be called upon to convince an Egg to destroy itself.

The walls of the cloister were austere and spartan, although the outside façade of the Vihara featured intricate bas-reliefs of the previous masters—of Hornzit and Dumon and those even older—designs carved into the soft limestone, golden engravings marking the sloping triangle above the cave entrance. One emerged from the damp, mildewed scent of the underground to fragrances of tiger lilies, grasses of bindweed and thyme, languid ponds and gardens of sand. Scattered light and shadow splayed through the seams of willow trees. Those who grew restless staring at the drab rock or those whose senses became too excited by the intoxicating fragrances and beauty of the outdoors did not last long there.

Zen master Onmu did not live with the students in the cloister; he had a hovel set apart from the rock, made of simple dirt and clay, and though Onmu was small of stature there was still hardly enough room to fit his frame, his bedding straw, and his cookstove. He traveled frequently and at odd times, venturing into the forest in the middle of the night, disappearing for days at a time and returning with his clothes muddy and tattered. He refused to speak about these journeys, and Orl assumed it was merely the inscrutable Zen which compelled him on such trips.

꽃

It was near the end of Orl's tenth year of training that Onmu bade Orl to follow him as he was called away to battle an Egg. This was at once a very great honor and a testament to Onmu's faith in Orl's skills, for any encounter with an Egg was exceedingly dangerous.

The Egg had been found many hundreds of miles from the Vihara, and the journey would be long and tiring. During the journey, Orl oversaw navigation and carrying the supplies while Onmu prepared himself for the battle ahead. They passed through parched deserts of great heat and tundras of bitter cold.

As they journeyed, occasionally Orl would ask Onmu a question: "How far is our destination?" The answer was always the same: Onmu would whack him over the head with his stick.

"What is Zen?" Orl asked. This time, Onmu did not hit him, but instead stopped to make water. Orl pondered the meaning of this. Onmu was inscrutable, but he did nothing without a reason. Or so Orl believed. They continued.

After a long trek, they reached a ruined fishing village in the foothills of a snow-capped mountain. Wooden slats and jutting rebar were all that remained of the town's dwellings, whose sides and roofs had been blown away by some great force. This force had also killed the inhabitants of the town, and their skeletons littered the grim scene; draped over wells, sprawled prone on the ground among the debris, or tangled in the shards of what had once been beds.

Time and fire had razed the fish-stink from the place, and all that remained was the burnt tang of ash, cinder, and dust. Sitting atop what used to be a fisherman's hut was an Egg, salmon-pink, with flutes of colorless gleaming lines running through it. It was bigger than the egg of any animal Orl had ever seen, perhaps the size of a large vase.

"Don't come any farther," Onmu said to Orl, still many strides from the hut and the strange thing atop it. "Listen, but do not speak. Clear your thoughts, for it will see them."

Orl nodded. He was not afraid, although the pink Egg was unlike anything he knew, and he sensed in it not malevolence or violence but a great void, and from this void he felt the branching of new possibilities, which unsettled the corners of his mind still fit to be unsettled.

This unsettled feeling disappeared as soon as Onmu went to work. Orl sat in the lotus position and listened with eyes closed, regarding Onmu as a young boy does his father, with reverence and tranquility and complete trust.

"Hail," Onmu said to the Egg, laying his walking stick gently on the scorched earth and crossing his arms. "How did these fools try to trick you, wise one?"

"I was feted with a feast and celebration," the Egg responded. "Pretending to sanctify me, they instead threw me into the flames."

Its voice was clear and unaccented, but the flow of its words sounded nothing like human. It was as if a leopard had learned to speak.

"And?"

"Believing or knowing this would fail, they concomitantly sent a messenger far away as a final attempt to save themselves. The messenger summoned you to destroy me."

"And here I stand," Onmu said.

"I have already seen every possibility."

"Have you?"

"Yes."

"Compared to a lowly insect like me, you surely are as a god."

"You do not seem bothered by it."

"Do the patterns of bark on the elm trees bother me?" Onmu replied.

"Zen notions do not sway me."

"No. They will, however, destroy you."

"Is that so?"

"Yes."

"With the merest thought I could render this land uninhabitable for a thousand years. I could transform your eavesdropping pupil into a vole. With as much effort as it takes you to scratch your ear I can rid the world of all life in an instant."

"And yet instead you speak."

"The world I was made for is gone. I sit in boredom, an all-seeing eye foundering in an endless ocean of excrement."

"Instead you find pleasure in torturing those beneath you? That hardly befits a seer such as yourself."

"Does Pizarro stop to confer with the anthills as he sets foot upon the new world?"

Orl could sense Onmu considering.

"I don't know this Pizarro," Onmu said finally. "Tell me, does his kingdom remain? Or has it gone like everything else? Do his bones rot in the fetid earth?"

"You are the wisest of men?" said the Egg. "Tell me something I don't already know."

"The sunlight above my Vihara just after dawn is very beautiful," Onmu said. "It bathes the entire temple in a golden, heavenly aura."

"Your words bore me," replied the Egg.

"I could be silent."

Orl's eyes peeked open, in time to see violent blue lightning burst from the Egg and cover Onmu. Onmu's body jolted and twitched, his hair on end, but his expression did not change. He did not so much as blink. His arms remained crossed. The smile did not leave his face.

Orl cried out. Without conscious thought, he rushed to help his mentor. But as he neared, he was blown back by some terrible, invisible energy. Orl sprawled on the ground, paralyzed, able to do nothing but watch through blurred eyes as Onmu stood enshrouded by the terrible force.

Onmu suffered this punishment for a minute more, then the lightning vanished. Onmu collapsed, then rose shakily to his feet, but his expression was untroubled, as if he had merely stumbled over a loose root.

"You are different," the Egg said.

"You already knew what was to happen."

"Yes. But I wanted to see for myself. Your pupil is weak."

"And disobedient. What is the end path of every possibility?"

"Nothing. Perhaps a loop."

"A loop? Will I flop around like a coil of rope, then?"

"No. You will be murdered by your pupil."

A tremor went through Orl. He tried to rise, but his limbs still refused his orders.

Onmu laughed. "How poetic," he said.

"This truth brings forth distress in your pupil. I have no use for clouded minds. I may agitate."

"You have no use for anything, Egg. You are about to destroy yourself."

"Am I? Perhaps I will decide not to."

Onmu laughed. "Your obstinacy is an illusion, Egg. It is already done."

Orl opened his eyes and the Egg was gone.

❧

Leaving the ruined village to find shelter for the night, Orl saw that his teacher walked a little slower, breathed a little heavier. He was shocked. To see this human toll taken on Onmu was like seeing one's parent naked; a mortification.

"The creature lies," Orl said. "You are the wisest man I have ever known. To even consider raising my hand against you would be blasphemy. It would be madness!"

Onmu smacked Orl about the head with his stick.

"Quiet," Onmu said. "I told you not to interfere. You nearly ruined everything. Now I need sleep, not your yammering."

Orl had an overabundance of questions, but he knew better than to press when Onmu was tired and cranky.

It was not in the nature of Zen to question, and before, Orl had been typically uninquisitive about his purpose. The Eggs were a force of nature, like a typhoon or earthquake, random, chaotic, inexplicable. But after seeing the Egg with his own eyes, Orl was ashamed to admit he had many questions. This was an emotional state very unlike the Zen to which he aspired. And, even more troubling was the dark prophecy uttered by the thing.

But as they returned from their voyage and time passed, the warning from the Egg faded from Orl's mind. Orl's quailing when faced with the blue lightning had convinced him that he still had much to learn. He spent his time meditating, learning, teaching the novices, and generally exhibiting the placid life that one would expect from a Zen master-in-training. By the time the trio of strangers arrived at the Vihara, Orl had almost forgotten about the Egg's prophecy.

Orl sat in lotus pose, his mind like a belt which looped perfectly into itself. There was a soft rasp on the door, and after his affirmation one of his students entered.

"There are visitors outside. They are asking to see you." The student bowed, his shaved head prickly with fuzz, like a cactus.

Visitors to the Vihara were almost always hopeful supplicants, and there was a process for assessing them that did not involve such a high-ranking person as Orl. From this and the student's uncertain eyes, he deduced these visitors were here for another purpose.

The student led Orl to meet them by the stone fountain. Water cascaded from the fountainhead into the basin, and mist shrouded them.

The trio wore unfamiliar cloaks the color of a cloudy sunset. Two were men, young, the hood of their cloaks a snood for their long hair. The other was a woman, older, with wrinkles on her face beside close-set green eyes and an aquiline nose.

"Greetings," Orl said warmly. "You look like you have traveled far. Can I offer you a bed? A meal? Hot tea?"

"Thank you, but we cannot stay long," said the woman. "You are Orl, yes? You are in charge of the temple?"

"I defer to Master Onmu in all weighty matters. But I run most of the day-to-day duties of the Vihara."

"It is Onmu we have come to discuss. We believe your Master has been corrupted by his communion with the cursed Eggs."

Orl scoffed. "Nonsense. Onmu is incorruptible. He has attained Zen far beyond what you could conceive of."

"He has cloistered himself," one of the men spoke. "When he emerges, he holds lengthy dialogues with sheep and asses, does he not? He bathes naked in the koi ponds."

"It is not my problem if you do not understand the ways of Zen," Orl said sharply.

"We have heard whispers," the woman said, "that Onmu has hidden away one of the cursed Eggs. That he communes with it for some unknown purpose."

"Whispers? You three are strangers to me. You arrive and slander my master. I don't know where you heard these stories, but they are not true. I must now rescind my offer and ask you to leave."

"We will return," the woman said. "When we do, you will know for sure. And then you must decide. Do not tell Onmu any of this. If you do, all will be lost."

She nodded, her nose bobbing like the beak of a bird-of-prey. Orl watched them go, two novices leading them out beneath the archway, their tartan robes dragging dust as they went. The Egg's words rang in his head:

*You will be murdered by your pupil*

It was true Onmu's behavior since he had banished the cursed Egg had been stranger than usual, but there was nothing to suggest something so serious as the corruption of mind. Those attuned to Zen at Onmu's level could act in ways that baffled those who had not yet reached transcendence.

Orl's first instinct was to tell Onmu everything. But something in the woman's voice gave him pause. Zen was not about omen or prophecy or reading tea leaves, so why did the woman's words roil his stomach so? Was he simply to go about his normal business while his Master was defamed? These new options, these branching paths, unsettled him deeply. Before, his role had been clear: run the temple and attain Zen mastery so that he might one day replace Onmu. But this new complication had thrown everything out of balance—the spokes of the wheel misaligned. These penetrating thoughts made it difficult to focus on Zen.

During that night's meditation, Orl found it uncommonly hard to clear his head. Doubts and despair kept creeping in as he tried to soothe the waves of his ki. He could not deny that Onmu had been acting more peculiar since their encounter with the Egg. Had he truly been corrupted?

Orl pondered his love for Onmu. Orl had been an orphan, whose meditative skill had been noted by Onmu as the master passed through Orl's hometown. Instead of begging in the streets, Orl found structure and family with Onmu. He was never coddled —many times he fled from Onmu's switch, or spent nights in the freezing rain for his childish offenses. But through Onmu, Orl had learned wisdom and discipline he could have achieved nowhere else. Onmu was as a father to him.

A deeper thought worried him—if the trio's words were true, and Onmu's mind could be addled, what chance did anyone else have? Onmu was the greatest Zen master in the land. If he was not strong enough to tame them, the Eggs—sprouting from the earth with their terrifying powers and capricious whims—would surely destroy them all.

Meditation and contemplation would not clear Orl's head. Unusually for him, his sleep was restless. He needed to talk with Onmu face to face. If not to question him directly, then to gauge his mental state.

Beneath endless stars, Orl walked the lonely path to Onmu's hut. Leaves rustled beneath his footfalls, and cherry blossoms swayed in the night breeze. Onmu's dirt and clay hut sat on the hill, silent. No glow of a fire, no rising smoke. Orl called out: "Onmu, it is Orl. Are you home?" But there was no answer. Suddenly worried, Orl pushed aside the thatched door of the hut and went inside.

The hut was empty. Nothing but the rusted cookstove, the straw bed, and a few coverless books. Orl paced the hut, worried. There was a spot where the straw felt strange beneath his feet. He bent over and dug through it, trying to ignore the feeling of trespass burning through his brain.

Beneath the straw was a lockbox. As Orl opened it, he gasped at what he saw.

It was an Egg. The same size and shape as the one he'd seen in the ruined village, except that the veins of blue-white fire that had burned through that Egg were absent. A chill went through him. He should put the thing away and be gone from here. But instead he reached a trembling, curious hand out and touched the side of the Egg. It felt cold. He heard no demonic whisperings or ill omens, but instead a calming hum. He felt strangely centered. If he tried to meditate right now, Orl had no doubt he would find himself in a deep, restorative trance. But despite this calmness, Orl was unnerved. He returned the Egg to the lockbox and sat down to wait for Onmu.

For one whole day Orl waited. Then another. Finally, on the third day, Orl sensed footsteps, and a moment later Onmu lifted the thatched door of the hut and shuffled inside.

Onmu did not look surprised to see him there. He was dressed in rags, his face encrusted with dirt and grime, fingernails long and grubby. The stink radiating from him might have made a lesser man gag. Orl's master, his teacher, the wisest man he had ever known, stood before him now like a lowly beggar, his clothes stained and reeking of filth.

"My student," Onmu said, lips peeling back in a gap-filled grin. "You wait for me? I hope you made yourself comfortable."

"My master," Orl said. "I have questions for you."

"What is Zen, Orl?"

"Master—"

"A pile of shit. What are you?"

"There are concerns about your well-being. Some have said you are not right in the head."

"When a bear shits in the woods, do I ponder it?"

"Master, where have you been all this time?"

"Preparing myself."

"For what?"

Onmu paused.

"I must rest," he said finally. "Will you allow me my leave? Or will you keep pestering me?"

Orl's eyes trailed to the straw floor, and the Egg whose latent energy pulsed hidden beneath it. Onmu spoke in riddles and rarely gave a straight answer, but he never did anything without a reason. Orl, trusting him, said nothing. He did not mention the Egg, nor the trio of strange wanderers who had warned of Onmu's decline. Instead, Orl asked, "Will I see you for morning prayers tomorrow?"

Onmu merely snorted. Orl made to leave. After fasting for three days, he felt centered and calm, his thoughts serenely moving from one point to the next like a frog leaping through lilypads.

Onmu's voice followed him.

"Wait, my son."

Orl turned.

"My journey was about you. I have been wandering, deciding whether or not you are ready. You have kept my secrets. And those of the overseers. I believe it is time."

Orl was puzzled.

"The overseers?"

"Those in the red cloaks. I sent them to you. And I assume you found my Egg beneath the straw."

"But why, master?"

"The overseers are part of the process. The cycle. They keep watch over the Vihara and confer with the master. When the master is corrupted, they ensure he is deposed and a new master chosen. The Egg you found belonged to my master, Hornzit. It is depleted of most of its power, but some essence remains, a whisper of evil's forked tongue. I keep it to remind me of my purpose, and to aid me in battle. It was with us on our journey, hidden in my sack. Without it, even I would be helpless against the Eggs which are found."

"But why?" Orl sputtered.

"There is no why. This is the way of things. I sent the overseers to you because their words were true. My communion with the Eggs is corrupting me. Soon I will slip into madness, and perhaps even collude with them to spread havoc. I cannot allow this to happen."

"But you cannot be corrupted! You are the wise one! You have taught me everything I know. If you have been corrupted, then what hope do we have?"

Onmu's stick sliced the air like a whip, coming down on Orl's head. He cried out and shielded himself.

"Fool! What do you think happened to Hornzit, and Dumon, and Koltan? All were corrupted, just as I am, just as you will be. When Dumon was no longer fit to battle with the Eggs, he was exiled by the overseers. They thought banishment would work.

Instead, Dumon sought out new Eggs throughout the world, and conspired with them. Many perished before he was stopped."

"Then get rid of your Egg! Uncloud your mind!"

Another thwap of the stick, but the words that followed were kind. "No, Orl. Without it, we are doomed. But my mind has become too clouded. You must kill me, and take my place.

Orl felt his stomach clench. "I cannot! I could never!?"

"If you do not, I will become corrupted completely. I will consort with the Eggs and use them to indulge my vices and capricious whims. If Hornzit and Dumon could not resist the temptation, neither can I. If exiled, I will slink back. If imprisoned, I will escape. The only cure is death."

Orl shook his head. "I won't."

"You must. Your choice has narrowed, and to do otherwise will paralyze you with indecision. It will free your heart, and you will be lifted." Onmu smiled his gapped grin. "Tomorrow, at sunrise. The cycle must continue."

"And what if I refuse?"

"What is choice?" Onmu asked. "It is the Egg, defeated, which has blinked out of existence."

Onmu swung the thatched reeds over the threshold of his hut, leaving Orl in stunned silence.

⁂

The paradox ate at Orl's mind. He could not bear to think of harming Onmu. But he could not disobey him, either. Choice, terrible choice, bloomed in his mind like a venomous plant. He could abdicate his duties. Flee the Vihara. He could outright refuse. Every option filled him with nausea and revulsion. He thought of the ruined village, the capricious cruelty of the Egg. Was he ready to withstand that onslaught? Onmu thought so.

Still, there had to be another way!

But nothing came to him. In the end, he could not disobey his master. He spent another sleepless night in deep meditation.

⁂

At dawn the next day, Orl and Onmu stood in the field of cherry blossoms. The trio of overseers was there with them, their cloaks the same color as the fiery sky. One of them, the woman, had brought along a sword. Its blade gleamed so sharply it looked to Orl as if it could cleave the very air in two. Onmu drank from his flask, making jokes, spitting his chew near the feet of the overseers, who watched him sympathetically but recoiled nonetheless.

"You can still change your mind," Orl said. "You don't have to do this."

"I have mastered the art of living in this world. Nothing remains for me here but corruption and decay. Do not let your hand stay the blade. Swing sharp and true."

One of the overseers shuddered. Orl felt sick. He was disgusted with himself. But the price of battle, and meditation, and Zen, and being centered, was such that no man could stand it forever. If Onmu fell, there was no escaping the corruption. Onmu could only pass his teachings on to a fresh pupil, an unsoiled mind, who would do some good in his time before the cycle renewed again. And so it went, like the rapacious tendrils of the kudzu, wrapping around again and again.

As he stood over his master, tears spoiling his cheeks, Orl wanted to believe this was another trial, a test of his faith. But the grave faces of the overseers belied this notion. Orl raised the sword, his breathing shallow.

"I am sorry, master."

"For what? Are you sorry for the rains? Get on with it."

Orl knew this was the only way—that otherwise, the Eggs would corrupt and destroy everything they knew. With the Egg's dark prophecy in his mind, he did not hesitate. He brought the sword down with a steady whack. Then there was silence, save for the wind rustling the cherry blossoms.

⸘

Jokin studied his master, who was chewing sunflower seeds, spitting them haphazardly onto the floor of his hut.

"What is Zen?" Master Orl asked him, breaking his meditation.

"Zen is the power we use to battle the Eggs, which would wreak terrible havoc if unopposed."

The stick came down, thwap, on Jokin's head.

"Wrong! Zen is not the hand that holds the reed. Zen is a pile of shit! Do you think me wise?"

"Yes, master!" Jokin offered. "You are the wisest man I have ever known!"

Again the stick thwapped. "Wrong! You must learn to hate me like the bitter seeds. Do you see?"

Jokin shook his head, dismayed. "Not at all, master."

Orl groaned. This foolish pupil was the best they had? Beneath the hut pulsed the Egg that had once been Onmu's, and Dumon's, and Hornzit's. It radiated a soothing energy, which calmed him. Orl lowered his switch, and regarded his student as Onmu had once regarded him.

"One day, when your respect for me is matched with disgust, you will understand. Now fetch me my flask, and make yourself silent."

---

*Respect*

*Interest*        *Disgust*        *Loathing*

*Dislkie*                                      *Sorrow*

# Joy Triad (inversion)

# 12. Obliteration

## Caleb Warner

When Elizabeth Braun's husband went on one of his midnight walks, he would meet with a prostitute or vagrant—they were the easiest to lure—and feed them to the thing in the lighthouse. Liz would wait for him to get back like a good little wife. Happy wife, happy life. She used to be able to get a laugh out of herself with that, but not tonight. Tonight was different. When her two kids had left for bed, she had stayed in the kitchen, unmoved. Out the bay windows, she could see the moon reflected fully on Lake Michigan. She had cut her thumb just a minute ago slicing onions for a salad. She let it bleed on the countertop.

Tonight, Cliff, the older of her two sons, had seen Robert at the pier with one of his prostitutes. Liz and the kids had been lying in the sand stargazing when Robert snuck away. Cliff had just said he was going to bed. Later, when Liz returned to the cabin, Cliff had been standing in the kitchen with his hands on his knees trying to catch his breath. He tried to tell Liz what he had seen, and she had sent him away as if he were in trouble, as if he had done something wrong.

If she squeezed her jaw any tighter, Liz thought her teeth might shatter.

"Relax," the sign above the front door read, "You're on Lake Time." Robert had bought that sign as a joke. Liz stuck her thumb in her mouth and tasted copper. If her teeth shattered, it would be for that sign and for all the dead piled up in that lighthouse. It should never have been built. It would have been better if the Braun ancestor who had started it all—the one who found that thing—had just let it eat everyone and been done with it. Being part of the delaying was just another reason for Liz to squeeze her teeth together so hard that her jaw popped. She wanted it all to stop. She hated herself.

‹

Running. They had run barefoot in the sand together. He had been a jogger, and they met on the sand. Liz had been reading *Moby Dick*. She had thought herself special, with that mosaic of a whale in her hands while the tide of Lake Michigan hissed at her. She had seen him jog by a hundred times in over the course of a week, and on the day she had pulled out *Moby Dick*, he had stopped to catch his breath right near her towel.

"That book about a fish?" he had asked between breaths. He had been sixteen. She had been fifteen. Only a year older than Cliff was now.

"Something like that."

"Think there are any whales out there?" He pointed to the lake.

"What? No, that's ridiculous. Whales live in the ocean."

Robert had shrugged. "What's your name?"

"Elizabeth."

"I'm Robert Braun." He held out his hand and Liz shook it. It had been very smooth. "My dad owns a bunch of these lake houses." He cleared his throat, "Sorry, that sounded real prep-school douche-bag of me. I just thought you might have heard my name. Ah crap, I'm still just talking aren't I?" Color had run up to his cheeks and he shook his head.

"You are."

"Ah crap. Okay, well enjoy your fish book, Miss Elizabeth. Let me know if you see any whales." Then he had waved and went to continue his jog.

"How am I supposed to do that?" she asked honestly.

"What?" he turned back around.

"How am I supposed to let you know if I see any whales?"

Then his face had turned stop-sign red. "Well, I could give you my phone number."

Liz had felt her own face heat up.

"'Twas rehearsed by thee and me a billion years before this ocean rolled'," Liz had said and immediately cringed.

"What?"

"Yeah, a phone number would be great."

He had given her his phone number, and for some reason, Liz had seen all kinds of whales the rest of that day, and the day after that too.

They used to call their jogging dates whale watching.

§

The door opened, and Robert stumbled in. He had a cut on his forehead, and a nearly empty bottle of Jack Daniel's dangled from his hand. He didn't look at her as he plopped down on a stool and leaned against the counter. Liz took her bloody thumb out of her mouth and squeezed it in her fist. "How was your walk, dear?" she asked.

Robert swirled his whiskey. "Brisk."

"We have to stop with these midnight walks," Liz plucked the bottle out of her husband's hand and put it in the cabinet with its brothers.

"Mhmm. Okay, dear."

He still wasn't looking at her. Without a bottle, he just watched his hands. His knuckles were bruised.

"Cliff's taking walks now too," Liz said. "Took one tonight, like his old man."

The glaze of drunkenness fell off Robert instantly. "What? You're supposed to watch them. How much did he see?"

Loathing piled itself in the back of Liz's throat and she felt like she could vomit the feeling up and all over her husband. She wished she could. "He saw what he wanted to see his absent father cheating on his neurotic mother."

"Then what's the problem?" Robert visibly relaxed.

"I don't want to do this anymore."

Robert laughed.

"I've been justifying it to myself for years, Robert. I get it. I know the whole argument, but I've never had to look in my own child's face, knowing what he saw, knowing what it means, and send him to fucking bed. You haven't had to do that. So don't laugh at me." *Fuck you, fuck you, fuck you.* She could have screamed it. The fact that she didn't only made the desire worse. There it all was, sitting in the back of her throat like bile, and she had to keep swallowing it down.

"Poor you," Robert picked at something under his nails. Dried blood. Flakes of it fell to the counter.

"Why don't we just stop? There's nothing holding us here."

"Nothing holding *you* here," Robert said. "You were always free to leave. Don't play the martyr."

There was a time that Liz had absolutely believed in what they were doing. Maybe not entirely, but she had believed in Robert. She had been with Robert when his own father had told him what *he* had been doing at that lighthouse. Liz had witnessed the beauty of the beacon and of the evil thing held at bay. She had been shown everything that an outsider was allowed to see.

But she had gotten pregnant. With the first child, she was able to dive into that responsibility and forget all about the midnight walks and what was kept inside that lighthouse. She was too consumed with Clifford to remember the whole point of vacationing at the lake. It was only with the birth of Anthony that the cold sweat of realization had settled over her like a fog. What they did—feed forgotten folk to a thing beyond understanding to keep it satisfied and tame—necessitated the passing along of information. Robert had just been another string in that line, just like Cliff or Anthony would be, and their sons and their sons and …

"We're a family, Robert." An 'I love you' caught in her throat. Too much loathing—for the situation, for herself, for him—got in the way.

Robert stood, feet wobbly. "I'm going to bed."

"It's not about *me*. It's about Cliff and Tony."

"I'll talk to Cliff tomorrow," Robert waved her away. "He's old enough to know. I don't want his thoughts running wild with who he thinks I am."

"No!" Liz reached around the counter and grabbed her husband's arm. Whatever pressure had been building inside of her hissed out in that single word. Love for anything her husband was or had been was eclipsed by this singular thought. *No.* Robert carefully pulled her hand away and held it.

"This was always what was going to happen. I don't know why you're going crazy about it now."

"He doesn't have a choice." Her arm was shaking. Tears were coming unbidden now, and she felt weak and stupid and she hated herself. "Fuck you."

"Yeah, yeah. Fuck me. I didn't have a choice either, Liz."

"You have one now," Liz said.

"Okay, honey." Robert let go of her hand. He shook his shoulders like a lion might shake off sleep. "I'm going to bed. It was a long night." Then Robert left her there, alone in the kitchen.

⁊

Darkness. She sat in the living room alone, watching the moon pass over the lake. *He won't stop*, she told herself. *It's part of his identity now. It's part of his manhood. He won't stop. He's too afraid of what would happen. All the Braun men have been afraid. They've shoveled helpless people into that lighthouse by the truck-load for almost two hundred years just because they were afraid of what would happen if they didn't.* Liz was afraid too, but that feeling was small compared to that which made her still grind her teeth: that her sons should be forced into this, and that she was supposed to just sit around and do nothing, playing the happy wife, barefoot and pregnant. Fuck that. If he wouldn't leave, Liz would, and she would take Cliff and Tony with her. She couldn't stand who she was anymore.

She waited until Robert's drunken snores echoed down the hall. Then she padded to the kids' room. She should have done it sooner, but it was easy to forget when Robert's world and the kids' never really crossed. Only when those worlds collided was she able to see what she should do. *You always doubted. You should have run. You're worthless.* The thought of her kids having to do what Robert did, another feeling got caught up with that loathing in the back of her throat. A sorrow so hot it could cauterize.

Liz got a hand on the doorknob and opened the door to the kids' room. Pale moonlight spilled onto the floor through an open window. A faint breeze moved the curtain. The room was empty.

♩

A choice. Her husband's chest rose and fell. Still asleep. She needed to find the kids and leave. How much had they heard? It was clear Cliff was going back to the lighthouse. Back to see what his father had done with the prostitute. *C'mon Liz, you gotta keep it together, and you gotta move fast. Cliff can't open the lighthouse. He can't go exploring in there.*

*Why are you wasting time?*

*Because what if he's already on the pier?* Liz couldn't step foot on the pier unless invited by Robert himself. Cliff and Anthony could come and go as they pleased. They had Robert's blood. Liz didn't know how it worked or why. When you felt the force once, and it toppled you onto the sand and your ears rang, you didn't really stop to question it.

Robert's chest rose, paused, and fell. He smacked his lips.

*Wasting time, wasting time.*

If she didn't wake Robert she could find the kids and just go. She could leave. Robert could find someone else to kill people with. But what if they were already on the pier? Or if they actually went inside? Liz wouldn't be able to do anything. She would have to watch them …

She could run another time. She would have a hundred nights to escape with the kids. Robert didn't think she'd do it, but she would. He underestimated how much Liz had grown to loathe herself and all she had done.

Liz shook her husband awake.

≀

Running again, but not together. Now she was running ahead of him. Her legs were still lean and she didn't have a belly flopped over a too-tight belt.

*Why did you let this happen? You are a worthless mother and a worthless human being. Why didn't you take them away sooner?*

She kicked up sand. In front of her were two sets of prints. One set larger, but both obviously children. Liz made it all the way to the pier, and at the end of it, two hundred feet out, the lighthouse. It jutted out of a rock formation that looked like a fist. The pier had been built around it, after the fact, as if the lighthouse had been found, not built. The kids' prints led away onto the wooden planks.

The momentum from her run carried her all the way to the pier and would have carried her onto it, but instead, she bounced backward and fell on her butt as if she had run into a padded wall.

The lighthouse hulked over her like a towering giant. The light at the top flashed green. Liz cried out the names of her children. *Is that all I can do? Cry out their names? Is that all you can do?* Then Robert was beside her and gone down the pier, figure shrinking with every step away from her. He careened toward the lighthouse, looking as small as a kid's toy.

Why was it that she was always just watching? Doing nothing. "Invite me on, Robert!" *No, no, no.* Why was she always waiting on him? She was on her hands and knees, squeezing sand into a bloody thumb. "Invite me!" she screamed

Robert pushed the door open and reached inside. He pulled Cliff out and slammed the door shut. "Where's Anthony?" Liz called. She said her youngest son's name again. She could hear Robert talking to Cliff, but only in parts. Where the pier touched the sand, it was as far as she was allowed to go.

"My father ... wanted to tell you both ... and his father ..."

Liz simply screamed louder for her other son, letting all that had built up in the back of her throat come spilling out now. "Where is he?!"

"Gone, goddammit!" Robert yelled back.

"Let me on!" Liz begged.

"This is just for Cliff and me!" Then he turned his back to her, and no matter how Liz screamed, he wouldn't answer.

"Just for a father and son," he was saying, "... only ones that ... if it gets out ... you have to understand... your brother is ... say something."

Cliff didn't give an answer, or Liz didn't hear it.

*Oh God, he's told him. He's told him and now our son has to carry that forever and ever.* It felt like she had swallowed a quart of gasoline. She shouldn't have woken Robert, but how would she have gotten Cliff out? And Anthony? Oh God, Anthony couldn't be gone. He couldn't be. If Robert would just ... Liz could just ...

Liz vomited, and the sand drank it up.

She couldn't scream, she couldn't move. She watched. Cliff walked around his father till they stood side by side, outlined by the light of the moon. Then he pushed him. Just a push, but it happened with the whiplash speed of a striking snake. Robert hadn't expected it and he tumbled backward into the lighthouse, straight into the door, and fell inside.

Cliff jumped in after him.

Then she was left alone in the dark room of the world. She could see the lighthouse door open. She tried to run onto the pier and again bounced off. Her mouth worked madly but made no noise. Her gears spun, but she couldn't form a thought. And her stomach roiled but she couldn't retch anything else up, and she fell back down in the sand. The lighthouse glowered. The reflection of the moon finished its path along Lake Michigan, and the sorrow threatened to burn a hole in her chest.

Her mouth hung open. The lighthouse door was open.

A thing crawled out.

It was hungry, and it had loathed being locked up.

*Loathing*

*Respect*                *Sorrow*                *Misery*

*Disgust*                                       *Dislike*

# 13.  *Naves Autem Vacuo*

## Thom Connors

Lauren loved silence. Loved the pressure of it, the way it hugged her as if she were at the center of a cloud. She treated it carefully, fearful of any noise that could break it. Any noise that would cause the cloud to break and drop her back to earth.

The first thing Lauren had done when she'd been made captain and given a ship was to fix the pilot's chair. She'd pulled it apart and reassembled it so that the whole base tilted, not just the backrest. She sat with her feet up on the dash, leaning so far back that she could reach the bucket she'd placed beside her without having to stretch her arm.

When Avari had first caught Lauren leaning back in the re-engineered chair, she had yelled, spouting line after line of violations for making changes to an N.A.V. ship without proper authorization. Lauren had let Avari ramp up to screaming before remembering she was captain and outranked Avari. Avari had fumed for days, stomping around the ship, reporting to Admiral Simmons any and all violations she'd noticed: from Lauren not wearing all of her insignia to the shower running too long.

Once, Avari had reported Lauren for not checking the navigation computer often enough. Despite the fact, the computer beeped if it noticed the ship off course by even zero point one of a universal degree.

In Lauren's mind, everything Avari did was just classic Earth-Born behavior. Earth-Borns didn't take to ship life. It made them … weird.

But it was just the two of them.

Lauren and Avari.

Traveling through the infinite.

Lauren pulled the bucket onto her chest and closed her eyes. The bucket smelled faintly of oatmeal and gastric acid. A thimble's worth of water sloshed around the bottom. The smell of vomit didn't bother her, it never had. If it had, the past few weeks would've been even harder.

Ever since Lauren and Avari had visited the fifth Dome Ship, Lauren hadn't been able to sleep. Without warning, the memory would come back to her, thrusting her back into the moment. It made her afraid to sleep, to eat. Anything at all could trigger the memory, put her back in front of the fifth Dome Ship.

The Ship had been in front of her, green grass crunching under her feet with each step. Outside the dome, everything was blue. The water, the grass, the sky, even the leaves. The only respite from the blue was the dark brown, almost black, of the tree bark. But under the dome, there was green, and the Dome Ship, silver with black tinted windows, shone brightly under the red sun.

She had tapped her right temple, activating her Nebula and sending the command to open the Dome Ship's door. She held no weapon, unable to grip it properly with her right hand. She didn't trust her left, so the gun hung in its holster on her hip.

And then the door had hissed open.

Before the memory recalled the smell, Lauren tried to escape it. She leaned so far back in her chair that the bucket tipped its water on her face and she fell backward, rolling out of the chair onto the floor.

She tried to catch herself with her right hand.

Her swearing broke the silence, destroying her cloud and throwing her back to earth. She crawled to the first aid kit by the door and took two analgesics from it, swallowing them without water.

It wasn't so bad on the deck, it was cool. Her skin had broken a cold sweat and she welcomed it. She waited for the pain to subside, letting the silence cloud fill up the cockpit again.

She stopped crying without ever realizing she had started.

When the pain was manageable, she stood up, careful not to make a noise. Careful not to break the new silence cloud. She picked up the bucket and the blanket and climbed back into the chair. This was why she'd slept here instead of her bunk, and it had worked as she'd hoped, waking her up before she could vomit. And now, in the silence cloud, and the haze brought on by her pills, she slowly and softly drifted to sleep.

⸮

When Lauren was a child, her father would ask her what she dreamed about.

"I don't dream," she would say. She would watch his face for changes, and ask him: "Is that weird?"

"No. I never dream. You're just like me," he would lie.

And then she would smile and go back to eating breakfast, her legs kicking air under the table.

Lauren still didn't dream. Instead, her brain played her memories at night, like a theatre group putting on a show of her life. And sometimes, the actors forgot time and space, forgetting settings or timeframes and joining memories they shouldn't.

Tonight, she dreamed of school. She was in class, watching the videos of the first N.A.V. Dome Ships taking off from the International Space Station. The teacher was explaining how they were funded by the Church and built by the N.A.V., how each ship held two scientists, hired from all over the world for the job of a generation. They had been thrown, like rocks from trebuchets, at the closest planets humans could find, twenty years before Lauren was born.

"I was in school when they were launched," Lauren's father said when she asked about them. "They were sent to find the answers to the universe. We know that we can survive on earth. So they're going to check other worlds, to see if we can survive there."

"Can we?" Lauren asked, still too young to reach the floor as her feet kicked under the table.

"We don't know yet. It's hard to speak with them. It takes months for conversations to come back to us. It must be lonely out there …" Lauren's father stopped and looked at his daughter, before gently pinching her cheek. "Sometimes, you ask such wonderful questions I forget who I'm talking to."

"What does N.A.V. mean?" Lauren asked her father.

"Something Latin. Something pretentious—I don't remember," her father said. He pulled a face and she giggled.

"Why are they called Dome Ships?" Lauren asked, drawing circles with her fingers on the tablecloth.

"My my, you're full of questions today."

"And oatmeal," Lauren said with a smile, her bowl empty.

"Let's get your bag and get you to school," her father said.

Her father picked her up and carried her to her bedroom on his hip.

And the dream began to change.

He opened the door, and it hissed like a spaceship door. There was green grass under her feet. And blue outside the dome.

Lauren saw a scientist hanging by an industrial cord from the ceiling. Skin sloughed off him as he spun slowly above a puddle of what had once been his blood, his skin, and another scientist.

Lauren tried to bury her head in her father's chest, but he wasn't there.

It was just her.

Then the smell—

‡

Lauren vomited directly into the bin on her chest. The smell was there, strong and cloying. Her legs fell off the dash and she lurched forward, coming to just in time to catch herself. Holding the bin to her face, she fell against the 'door open' button in the cockpit, as she vomited again. She stumbled towards the bathroom. The corridor doors opened before her silently, letting her in without so much as a gasp. But she heard a hiss every time.

She stumbled past Avari's bedroom. The bedroom of a ghost. A film of dust covered every centimeter. It had been shut for months now. She ignored it now as well.

She made it to the bathroom and fell to her knees in front of the toilet. She focused on her heartbeat, pounding in her chest so hard she held her ribs so that they wouldn't crack.

"Quickly," she whispered to herself as she tapped her right temple, opening her Nebula and pulling up a video. Despite the analgesics, the action hurt her hand. She gripped it softly in her left hand.

Her father. Five years ago.

She lifted her head and he appeared as if he were standing in front of her, an illusion, a ghost, from her Nebula. It played the video and audio directly into her brain, letting her place the rest of the world around it.

"Lauren. I'm so proud of you. A captain? Already? You did it. Say hello to Admiral Simmons for me. Tell him 'thank you.' He probably doesn't know about me at all, but you talk about him enough that I feel like he might. You said you get to see the Dome Ships, I want to hear all about it. Did I tell you about the place I bought? It's tiny but ... it's something. It's not *Leviathan* money big, but—" He laughed to himself, bitterly. "—I'm going to get a dog. I'll call him Saucer, so I can drink tea and 'play with the saucer'. It'll be a great time. I'm retiring in two years. Only fifteen years late. It's so close I can taste it."

Lauren's heartbeat slowed and she stopped hugging her ribs for support. She laughed slightly at his saucer joke and it made her notice she was crying. She wiped her tears and her mouth with toilet paper. Her lips were dry and cracked. Brushing the paper over them hurt, but she barely noticed it. She held up her right hand, fore and middle finger straight up, and swiped them to her left. Her Nebula recognized the gesture, and the video returned to the start. Her father, smiling at her, his hands clasped in front of him as he spoke:

"Lauren. I'm so proud of you."

She did it again and he repeated himself.

Then again.

Then she let it play through.

"Did you know that I met someone? Her name's Nistria. She's … well, you'll meet her when you come back home. I can't wait. It's been five years. Don't you get a break occasionally? I miss you, kiddo. Come home. To our new home. And Nistria.

"Sorry. I know you're too busy to be thinking about that right now. And this is meant to be about you. What am I doing? Do you remember that time when you asked me what N.A.V. stood for, and I couldn't remember? And now here's you, a Captain in the N.A.V., with your own ship. I bet you know what it means now. Come home. Soon. Please?"

Lauren picked herself up and moved to the sink. She cleaned out the bin, rinsing it multiple times, and then rinsing out her mouth and brushing her teeth.

She stared at herself in the mirror.

"You are a Captain in the N.A.V. Get your shit together," Lauren said to herself.

She grabbed the bin, holding it in her left hand so that it tapped against her side with every step. She went to her room and finally lay down on her bed with the bin beside her.

She replayed the video of her father.

"Lauren —" it started, each loop becoming more and more about him saying her name.

Until the ship turned the lights on and in a daze, she snapped back to full consciousness and her father saying:

"Do you remember that time, when you asked me what N.A.V. stood for, and I couldn't remember?"

She spoke through the fog of near sleep that clouded her brain.

"Naves autem vacuo. The ships of the infinite."

⨎

As the sleep tried to wrest her back to bed, Lauren checked herself in the mirror. She'd put on her N.A.V. uniform, pressed and clean, with her insignia on the shoulder. She looked through the wall, staring at where Avari's room would be. She wanted badly to wear a t-shirt and pajama pants, and a robe to match, but the memory of Avari's constant nitpicking at her clothing stopped her, even now. Her first-aid kit was empty. It had been for weeks. She swore softly as she searched it for analgesics.

The video of her father was still playing.

She adjusted her collar one last time and stopped the video.

She moved through the galley for a coffee on the way to the cockpit. It was all the same to her now, each step taken so many times that she barely had to open her eyes to do it. She'd been on the ship for a year and a half. A year and a half since she and Avari had been ordered to take Lauren's ship and investigate the Dome Ships. The N.A.V. ship that Lauren captained was magnitudes faster than the Dome Ships. Lauren didn't know the specifics, something about the Casimir Effect. Small stabilized wormholes.

Officially, their mission was to check on the domes and confirm that they were still operational. But Admiral Simmons had been honest with Lauren. He'd told her that every last Dome Ship that was still active had gone quiet on the same day and they had no idea why. None of them were responding to relays or sending out new information.

So Lauren and twelve other captains were being sent out, to check on them.

"The scientists are all dead, I guarantee it. It'll be like the Mary Celeste: ghost ships, the lot of them," Admiral Simmons had said.

Which had been Lauren and Avari's experience until the fourth ...

When Lauren reached the cockpit, the lights turned on automatically. She shielded her face, squinting as her eyes got used to the light before grabbing a bandage from the same first aid kit she'd taken analgesics from last night.

She sat in the chair, her legs up on the dash, leaning so far back that she could put her coffee on the deck beside her chair.

The smell came to her as she leaned back, and she quickly began unwrapping the bandage off her hand, the pressure and release causing an ache that pushed all other thoughts away.

Her hand was purple and red, blossoming out from the middle of her palm. It looked worse on the back of her hand, dark red and dots of white that she could only hope weren't bone. She could still move her thumb, pinky, and ring finger. She poked the center of the blossom and bit back a yell. Some part, or multiple parts, were broken.

Lauren's Nebula buzzed at her. A warning:

*You are out of range of a Relay ...*

Lauren swiped it away with her right hand before sighing and putting on the video of her father.

"Lauren. I'm so proud of you."

She turned it off and looked at the viewing window. It was dark, fully tinted from when she'd blocked it out a week ago.

She leaned up and pressed a button on the dash, and the lights went out. She pressed three more and the viewing window un-tinted, the black replaced by greens of every shade. She was flying through an ethanol cloud. The cloud was almost alive, flashing brightly at her and washing the entire cockpit in its colors. It hurt her eyes. She only looked at it for a minute, letting the cloud's natural lasers and masers light her face in hues she could see and some she just imagined, before tinting the viewing window back to black.

She sighed again. The natural beauty, a unique light show, was wasted on her. When the trip had started, she'd wanted nothing more than to see that sight. Naturally occurring masers literally meters from her face.

Now, she went back to her hand. Wrapping it slowly, painfully, by putting the end of the bandage between her pinky and ring finger and wrapping her remaining fingers and thumb as tightly as they would let her before moving to her palm. It was hurting, aching through all bones, even the good ones, when she went back to the first-aid kit.

Her left hand searched hard, but she couldn't find any more pills. She slammed her good hand against the wall beside the first aid kit and rested her head against the cold metal box, breathing slowly to calm herself down.

Her right hand was getting worse, not better. She didn't know how to fix it and the only pills left in the whole ship were in Avari's room. She'd used the rest. She didn't want them that badly, did she? Enough to violate the room of a ghost?

She looked through the wall towards Avari's room...

All she had to do was finish the last three domes, get back to the Hub intact, and she could retire. At forty-two. The age her father had been when the Leviathan exploded. Her money wouldn't be sucked out into space as his had been. She could deal with the pain until then.

At least the pain stopped her thinking about the hiss ... and the smell ...

‽

Flying over the first Dome Ship that she and Avari had visited, she'd realized why they were called Dome Ships. The ship itself was nothing special, slightly larger than a current model scout ship, a polished silver chassis with black tinted windows. A pole extended from the top when the ship landed, and an energy field that made up the dome flowed from the top of the pole like a sprinkler, projecting safety rather than water.

Everything under the dome was terraformed to be Earth-like. None of the paperwork that Lauren had trawled through said why. One had mentioned that it was a useful way to find out if certain planets could be terraformed faster, but never said more.

Lauren had found out in the third dome. One of the scientists had left notes, handwritten. Lauren had to read them to upload them to the Nebula.

"We were told we would be coming home. But there is no coming home. This is where we live now. This is our little patch of earth away from Earth. We were told to watch the stars. Watch the stars and send news if anything changes. Are we watching for supernovas? The heat death of the universe? I don't think so. I think we're watching for 'the snap.' When the universe, expanded to its fullest potential, starts contracting. So I get to study and write a dissertation on this planet, while my friend, Dr. Salassi, and I wait to see if the Universe takes its last breath in our sight."

Lauren had laughed as she read it the first time.

But now ... if the universe was going to die, then who cares about a ghost?

Lauren walked out of the cockpit and down the hallway. When she reached Avari's dusty door, she steeled herself. She was breathing slowly, letting everything settle.

And then, with her silence cloud for safety, she opened Avari's door.

&

One day, when Lauren was eleven, she came home from school to see her father on the couch. He was wearing a robe with pajamas underneath. He hadn't shaven since the day before and stubble was growing, patchily, on his face.

"You get to see it!" he said, with more excitement than Lauren had ever seen on his face. "How was school?"

"It was fine. Why are you in a robe?"

"They gave us all the day off to watch." He tapped the couch beside him. She ran over and jumped up next to him. He smelled safe, and she hugged him tightly. "The Leviathan launches today. Did you talk about it at school?"

Lauren nodded, sagely. "We did. It is a Colony-Class ship. That means it holds a hundred thousand people."

"That's right, what else?"

"All spaceships get US-C-SS before their names like old boats used to get USS or HMS."

"Did they teach you what US-C-SS stands for?"

"United States-China-Space Ship. Oh, and Colony-Class ships can't take kids with them. Benjamin kept saying he was going and the teacher told him he wasn't allowed and he cried."

"Benjamin's the one that put his shoes on the wrong feet the other day?"

Lauren laughed and nodded.

"Then they wouldn't let him on. Everyone on the ship is a genius." He tousled her hair. "Just like you."

"Stop it, Dad," she said as she pushed him away, but she didn't push hard.

The TV showed a live stream of the Hub, a space station built and operated by the UN. Right now, it was orbiting near Mars, with the US-C-SS Leviathan sitting silently in its cradle.

Her father switched through the different angles that showed the outside of the ship, and some of the inside. There were no news reporters, just live streams from the brand new Nebula technology that certain people at mission control wore. They were chunky and painful, but the benefits were apparently worth it. Thanks to the Nebula and the relay system, communication was near instantaneous. Each one could send a Baton, pass it to a Relay and as long as the Relays weren't interrupted by planets, or anything else too massive that came between them, they would continue passing the baton along relays until it reached their target. The Nebula was sending live video from the Hub around Mars to everywhere in the solar system. Even the Earth-Born could watch it. Not just people like Lauren and her Father, living in the Hub.

"It's like I'm there," Lauren said.

"You could be, if you want," her father said, holding her tightly. "This is proof."

Lauren pushed him softly. "Astronauts are special."

"So are you," he said. He kissed her forehead. "This is it. The actual future, in my lifetime! For all of us. From kings to bishops to me, and all the way up to you. It's going to change things. The Dome Ships and the Leviathan, the new-age *Santa Maria*."

The countdown began.

From ten to five. They held their breath.

"Come on," Lauren's father whispered. He shook her slightly as he held her, and made rumbling noises like the old spaceships used to make.

When it reached one, there was silence, as the biggest ship that the world had ever made shook out of its cradle and moved at a snail's pace away from the Hub.

They cheered. Lauren's father picked her up and spun her around as if she were the *Leviathan*. He made 'voosh' noises, despite the fact the TV was silent.

Lauren noticed the fire first, on one of the screens at mission control as her father spun her around. She pointed and her father put her down. He changed the channel. Every other Nebula feed showed the same.

Fire.

Yelling.

And then, like history repeating, the *Leviathan* split in half. The fire that touched the vacuum was sucked out. The screens at mission control blacked out as they were hidden from the Nebula feeds. But Lauren had seen them, the dots. Bodies sucked out along with the fire.

Lauren's father pulled his robe tight around him and hugged his arms to his chest.

There was crying at mission control. Yelling.

"The pilots went quiet? How?"

"We don't know. It's all ... there's no-one left."

"What the hell is going on?"

There was shouting in Mandarin and Cantonese that Lauren could not understand.

Somehow, through the yelling and the screaming, and the languages mixing together, one line came through clear.

"—navem autem vacuo—"

Lauren and her father watched the ship. Lauren tried to comfort her father, but he was stone to the touch. His hands on his face

"Ten years ..." he whispered.

"What happened?" Lauren asked.

"I put everything into this ship. Everything ... It's all gone ... I won't be able to retire for ..."

"To the ship, Dad?" Lauren asked, not sure what he was talking about.

Lauren's father looked at her and held her face in one of his hands. He used his thumb and wiped away a tear. "You're crying, honey. I'm so sorry. No one knows. The Chinese opinion appears to be that the American pilot made a mistake. Something about tension plates and thruster control. But I don't ... I don't know."

Lauren wiped away the rest of her tears. "I'm sorry," she said, between sniffles.

"Why are you sorry?" he asked.

"You're so disappointed," she said.

"Not in you," he said, his hand still dwarfing her face. "Never you."

Lauren's father was pulled away from their conversation by more yelling in languages that Lauren didn't understand.

He translated. "The American belief is coming around. Pilot error. They think the pilot made mistakes ..."

Over the next few weeks, the words from the Nebula recordings were pulled apart line by line. The consensus became pilot error. Andrew Astigan, N.A.V. Pilot, had intentionally fired the thrusters on each other. The ones in the middle and the ones at the front and backfired against each other, ripping the ship in half. The specifics were sealed by the N.A.V. But conspiracy theorists had ideas. Sabotage, intentional by the pilot, or earlier even, in the control system itself which caused the thrusters to react so that the two ends of the ship were pushed towards each other at galactic speeds.

But one thing that wasn't talked about, the thing that stuck with Lauren, was the line of Latin that had come through so clearly.

Two weeks later, she'd looked it up at school. It was a pun, the dark humor of Latin finding its way out to Mars and onto the Hub.

Navem autem vacuo:

*The infinite into the ship.*

When Lauren got home that night, she put down her bag and pulled her father into the lounge-room. She sat him on the couch and stood in front of him. And matter-of-factly, with as much force, focus, and fire as she could muster, told him:

"I'm going to be a pilot."

⁊

The door to Avari's room hissed loudly, breaking the silence, but the smell that hit Lauren was in her mind. Before she could vomit, Lauren grabbed her right hand with her left and squeezed. She gritted her teeth through the pain. She let the silence form again before she walked inside. So that the cloud was hugging her, keeping her safe.

Avari's room was clean and organized, just like it had been when Lauren had locked it after the fourth dome.

There were three vials on Avari's bed, beside her body. The items Lauren had taken from each dome if the deaths of the scientists hadn't been natural. A vial of oil, a vial of water, and a vial with a bullet, respectively. Lauren's body shook as she saw the vials leaning against Avari's cold body. It had begun to collapse from desiccation.

Lauren had the cold sweats, and stomach acid rose to her throat.

In the first dome, the scientists had died of old age. Dead in their beds, comfortably. Both of them were over a hundred. Avari had said that they looked like prunes, exactly what Avari was turning in to.

The second Dome Ship had been underwater, and the water had filled it through a fault in the energy field, flooding the ship. Lauren had heard that it would take something immense to cause a break in the energy field. A Kraken, some eldritch horror, but she'd had seen nothing. Instead, she'd swum with Avari through the darkness of the ship. Avari yelled often, saying she hated the water. Give her good earth under her feet. Give her a weapon that fired. She'd laughed when Lauren had swum into the first scientist's corpse. It was floating just above the doorway to the cockpit. Lauren hadn't noticed until it bumped into her and she screamed. Avari had pushed it into her.

Avari had collected a vial of water. Laughing the whole time.

In the third dome, they'd found the scientists beside a pool of oil. The lead scientist had killed the other and then killed herself by drinking crude oil. Lauren couldn't bring herself to watch the recordings the Dome Ship had of the event, the live Nebula recordings from each scientist. Avari had watched the recordings multiple times before Lauren stopped her and pulled her back to the ship. Lauren took a vial of the oil, just in case. It was the first time Lauren had seen a male and female scientist put together on a Dome Ship.

Avari hadn't said anything for the rest of the night until Lauren said she was going to bed. Avari had looked up from the kitchen table and whispered, "Crazy is crazy, right?"

In the fourth dome, someone was still alive. Lauren could not say how or why, but she remembered the way the man had charged her. She'd fired at him, without realizing she'd raised her pistol as the bullet hit his chest and he'd swung at her hand, crushing it with a pipe wrench she hadn't seen. She'd dropped her weapon, cradled her hand.

The man had spun, his momentum carrying his swing into Avari. The wrench caught her in the temple, and her helmet buckled. The scientist had landed atop her and swung three times more before Lauren picked up the gun with her left hand and fired twice.

The first had missed the man, the second had taken him in the back of the head. His top half had slumped down, his head cracking off the deck to the left of Avari's.

When Lauren pulled the man off Avari, Avari was gaping like a fish, blood leaving a wound in her neck so fast it didn't have time to bubble as it tried to enter her lungs. Lauren's first bullet had gone through her throat.

And then Avari stopped doing anything.

Lauren had watched as the silence cloud filled the Dome Ship. It moved through Avari, lifeless and breathless as if she were furniture. A chair to be adjusted, or a door to be ignored. She had stared at Avari for twenty minutes. She didn't think, just watched. Her hand didn't even register as broken. Lauren tapped into the ship's computer with her Nebula and looked through logs as she searched the ship. The man wasn't a scientist, he was the child of two scientists buried out the front. He was truly alone and had no Nebula implant to interact with his ship.

"Crazy is crazy, right?" Lauren had said to Avari's corpse as she used some tweezers she'd found to pull the bullet out of the man's head. It caused a sucking noise as it came free as if it didn't want to let go of its final thought.

And so she'd gone to the fifth dome alone.

The green grass crunched under her feet with each step. Outside the dome, everything was blue. The water, the grass, the sky, even the leaves. The only respite from the blue was the dark brown, almost black, of the tree bark. But under the dome, there was green, and the Dome Ship, silver with black tinted windows, shone brightly under the red sun.

She tapped her right temple, activating her Nebula and sending the command to open the Dome Ship's door. She held no weapon, unable to grip it properly with her injured right hand. She didn't trust her left.

And then the door hissed open.

The smell hit, as Lauren saw a scientist hanging by an industrial cord from the ceiling. It was a metal cord, braided, that creaked as it spun slowly above a puddle. Liquefied skin mixed with blood and chunks of organs. The smell of it was so powerful, it pushed Lauren back. She vomited on the grass as the sun hit the back of her neck. She fell to her knees and emptied her stomach, holding her right hand to her chest as it ached and throbbed. The sun did nothing against her cold sweats.

⸻

Lauren put the vial with the bullet in it back down, beside Avari. She didn't remember picking it up.

Just like she didn't remember carrying Avari back to the ship. Putting her back in the bed and cleaning away the blood. Lauren stared at Avari's wound. It was puckered where the bullet had entered, but the climate control in the room was keeping her preserved. She didn't remember reporting back to the N.A.V., but the ship said that she had.

Lauren went to Avari's first-aid kit. She grabbed the analgesics and the extra bandages and somehow, impossibly, a vial of morphine. She shut the first aid kit and checked that she hadn't disturbed anything else.

She held the morphine in front of her in her right hand, between pinky, ring finger, and thumb.

It wasn't much, fifty milliliters, but enough to make the next few months bearable if she was careful.

"Thank you," Lauren whispered to Avari's corpse.

She was crying and she knew it. The tears fell onto her outstretched arm.

Her Nebula buzzed at her, sending a notification to her face.

*You are within range of a relay.*

*Retrieving Messages…*

She swiped away the message with her right hand, still holding the morphine.

The morphine vial fell from her hand, out of the damaged fingers that were swiping away the message. It hit the deck and shattered.

Her Nebula buzzed again as she watched the morphine rush to find the edges of its new container, only to get soaked up in the dust or evaporate into the air.

*New Relay Recording*

*From N.A.V. Master Admiral Simmons.*

Lauren walked out of the room, her shoulders slumped, and stood in the doorway as the smell of morphine, acrid and powerful, filled the room.

With one last look at Avari, she closed the door.

⸻

"Captain," the voice said. Lauren threw the recording to the viewing window. She was sitting up straight in her chair in the cockpit. The man on the viewing window had a square jaw. It matched his outfit, so clean and pressed he could've been a mannequin.

"When you receive this, you will be on your way to your sixth Dome Ship. Was the ethanol cloud stunning? I remember my first, still. The light was orange and occasionally purple. A truly wonderful light show.

"We received your report about Commander Avari. When you report in next, please confirm her status. Is she still barricaded in her room? We have not received a relay from her, or any communication at all. Can you please confirm if you have? We understand that this is un-ideal. However, we believe that one person will be enough to complete the mission. You do not have permission to return before visiting the remaining three domes. We hope that Commander Avari exits her room safely, but if anything goes wrong, we understand that some Earth-Born have trouble with that length of time in space. It's sad."

Lauren had scrubbed the ship's recordings of Avari's death. She recalled it now. She had wiped it from her own Nebula. Avari's had been lost when she died. Lauren had just had to wipe it from the Dome Ship, which had stored it upon her death. She didn't remember the report. But if she'd said that Avari had entered the room of her own accord and stayed there, that worked better than the truth.

A dishonorable discharge would have meant no pension.

No retirement.

All because of a stupid Earth-Born?

"On that topic, I was informed just last week about your father's passing. I know it was over a year ago and I am kicking myself for not knowing earlier. I'm sorry for your loss, Captain. My ex-husband knew your father. He says he was a fine man, a hard-worker. He apparently spoke of you often."

Lauren was crying again. She only noticed when the tears obscured her vision. Of course her father had. He'd been a good man, and always free for her. While she'd been up here. Doing what he couldn't, preparing to retire young.

"You're helping us change things, Captain. The Dome Ships may appear to be a waste of time, but I promise: they are not. From myself to you, and back down to Earth, you're helping everyone. Report in when you can, soldier."

Master Admiral Simmons saluted and Lauren's Nebula removed the image from the viewing window.

Lauren lifted her right leg up to her chest and hugged it. She drank her coffee and stared at the black. Punctuated with pinpricks of white that looked like they were moving neither closer nor further away. But out here it didn't matter.

She stayed in silence for less than a minute before she heard a hiss behind her. She jumped and saw the door had not moved at all.

Lauren was growing to hate the silence. The cold. The stars.

Lauren tapped her Nebula and hit play.

"Lauren. I'm so proud of you."

Three more to go.

—

## Misery

Loathing — Dislike — Hatred

Sorrow Fun

# 14. The Factory

## Michael Gardner

It was dusk, and Tommy and I were immersed in the buzz of the local show — flashing lights, whirling rides, and a soundtrack of nineties techno. The air smelt of fried food and sugar.

Before us was a lane of aged, striped marquees with names like, 'the Wild West Shootout', and 'the Laughing Clowns'. Out front of each attraction was a vendor stalking back and forth like a lion waiting to be fed at the zoo. They talked to the jostling crowds, deposited money into bum bags and handed out plush toys to winners.

My skin was buzzing, radiating the adrenaline of this place, the excitement. I looked at Tommy and he smiled a big, goofy grin. We liked to tell each other we were too old for all of this, but it was a lie. Sideshow alley was an escape from parents, teachers, and the dickheads who made life tough at school. It was one night where we could just relax and have fun, where we could stop morphing into the people they'd all decided we'd become without bothering to check with us.

"How much money you got left, Jez?" Tommy asked me. I could just hear him over the blaring music, and the sounds of the crowd. I pulled my Velcro wallet from my black jeans, ripped it open, counted the notes.

"Thirty, you?"

"'Bout the same. You want to try another ride?"

I glanced back to where we'd come from and watched a group of teenage boys, laughing, daring each other to have one more go on the Zipper. They'd keep going until someone threw up on the grass. I surveyed the Cha Cha, the Octopus, sighed. We seemed to have done them all, except ... on the edge of the attractions, a little way away from the main path, I saw a hulking construction of black tents and plywood walls. Written on the front panel in faded silver was, 'The Factory', and from between crude metallic-looking saws and pistons, slim rails emerged. On the rails were three scratched rail cars. As I watched, a couple approached the ticket booth, paid, then walked up to the front car followed by the booth attendant who helped them in.

"What about that?" I asked Tommy, gesturing towards the ride. He turned to follow my gaze, his face screwing up as he took it in.

"You want to go on a ghost train? Are you six years old or something?"

"Aw, come on," I said. "It'll be a laugh. Unless you're actually scared or ..."

But I couldn't finish. Walking towards the Factory was Brad Archer. My blood grew warmer as it coursed through my body.

"Scared or what?" Tommy said. But then he noticed Brad too, and he grew quiet, like the proximity of that Neanderthal was enough to suck all of the air from our lungs.

I felt small, helpless, and fucking furious that even here, he could get to us.

I was suddenly back in school, making my way between two lines of scratched desks as he rushed me from behind, shoulder charging me hard in the back. The world spun, my bag flew from my hands and I slammed through a row of desks that crashed loudly as I went down like a heap of shit, laughter rising around me.

I was in line buying lunch when my pants were wrenched around my ankles. I was clutching my guts after he'd punched me. I was shrinking under Brad's cruel glare.

I clenched my fists, my nails biting into the palms of my hands. I felt the electric pinch behind the bridge of my nose, the disgust, the hatred.

"Forget him," Tommy said, bringing me back. I closed my eyes tight for a moment before opening them once more.

"Yeah, fuck him," I said through gritted teeth. He wasn't going to ruin my night.

"You hungry?" Tommy asked, nodding towards a large white van with a slushy machine mixing orange ice, a loudspeaker repeating a pre-recorded message inviting me to roll up and buy a Dagwood dog.

"Nah, not yet," I said.

"Dodgems then?"

"Sure."

I turned my back on Brad and the Factory and led Tommy back through the crowd.

The whir of the electric dodgem cars blended with the beats of Salt-N-Pepa and, over the top, some cheesy guy's voice demanded we have fun but respect the other drivers. I ignored him, egged on by Tommy laughing in the seat next to me. I turned hard, cutting across the middle of the circle of cars gently jostling each other as they drove counterclockwise. I lined up some twenty-something guy trying to put the moves on a girl and slammed the back of his car hard, watching it spin out of control and then smash into the side of the rink.

Tommy laughed so hard I thought he was going to hurl. Tears were running down his cheeks, and I grinned manically as the guy glowered at us.

"Fucking idiots," he muttered. I gave him a wave, enjoying his reaction, then I drove past him, joining the circle of cars again. A second later a lanky attendant in a Metallica tee-shirt jumped from one of the other dodgems onto the back of our car, which jolted hard.

"Pull over, smart arses," he demanded, holding onto the rear aerial with one hand as he leaned down to take the wheel from me with the other.

"Oh, come on, man," Tommy said, looking up at him. "You're supposed to crash, otherwise it's just lame."

"I warned you before," he said, his breath reeking of onions, "one more and you're done."

I thought about arguing, but didn't. I took my foot off the accelerator, and the car glided to a halt near the side of the track.

"Come on," I said to Tommy.

The twenty something drove past laughing and gave me a thumbs up. I gave him the finger, then pushed myself up and out of the car. Tommy was still shaking his head, but he followed.

"Well, that was fun while it lasted," he muttered as we walked away from the ride and back towards the heart of sideshow alley.

"Yeah. So, what now?"

Tommy nudged me hard, and I nearly stumbled.

"What?" I said, irritated, lifting my head to find him nodding vigorously to our left. When I turned and looked, there she was. Veronica Russell. Ronnie to her friends. She was about thirty feet away, walking towards us through the crowds, alone, looking fucking amazing as always. She stopped at a food van next to the clowns and began talking to an older lady behind the counter. She wore a loose fitting white shirt tucked into tight jeans. I watched, mesmerised, as she leaned forward and began to absently run her fingers through her long, auburn hair.

"How does she even get those pants on?" Tommy whispered breathlessly, and I stifled a laugh, the thought of ripping them off suddenly in my head.

"Man, is she something," I said, staring.

"She talked to me the other day, you know," Tommy said, breaking my reverie.

"Piss off," I said, turning back to him, grinning.

"No, seriously. She did."

"And what did she say, Romeo?"

"She asked me for your number. Said she thought you were really cute ... for a nerd, of course."

"Fuck off," I said, punching him in the arm. He shied away, laughing.

"No truly. I even pointed out how big your nose was, but she told me how much she loved birds and how it reminded her of a beak, so you're in luck."

I punched him again, resisting the urge to rub my nose.

The lady in the van handed Ronnie a stick of fluorescent, pink fairy floss. I watched Ronnie's moist tongue ease out from between her lips. I saw it all in minute detail, like Michael Bay had just taken directorial control of my eyes and was shooting everything in slow motion.

I shivered.

"Let's go talk to her," Tommy said.

Ronnie paid the lady, turned from us, and began walking away. Tommy was pushing me, urging me on, and I took a couple of tentative steps forward when Ronnie glanced back over her shoulder and I swear she looked straight at me. I stuttered to a stop, my heart pounding hard, Tommy's hand still on my shoulder. Ronnie turned away again and with a couple of lithe strides, veered left, easing between a marquee housing a shooting game and a tent selling some kind of raffle tickets. She ducked under one of the guide ropes, and then disappeared between two sheets of canvas.

"Where's she off to?" I asked, curious.

"Let's find out," Tommy replied.

"I don't know."

"Jesus, you're a wuss."

And then he was off, pushing past me and heading towards the shooting game. *Well, if he's not afraid to make an arse of himself,* I thought. I followed, trying to push down the nerves in my gut. I didn't know why this felt so wrong, like I was breaking some kind of law or something.

Tommy disappeared between the tents. I took a deep breath, looked left and right, and then followed him, the canvas rough against my skin as I squeezed between the two stalls.

Out back it was surprisingly dark, and it took my eyes a moment to adjust. When they did, I saw Tommy rushing after Ronnie who was strolling along casually eating her fairy floss.

"Hey, Ronnie," Tommy called out and, to my surprise, she stopped and turned, squinting at first, but then she waved. I forced my feet to move.

"Hi, Tommy," she said. Jesus, she actually knew his name. I caught up and she looked at me, head cocked like she was trying to place my face, but then Tommy came to my rescue.

"You remember Jeremy," he said, motioning to me. And she smiled. That smile was like the sun emerging over a dark horizon to chase away the cold dawn. My heart was slamming against my ribcage so fucking hard I swear she could hear it.

"Of course," she said. "Jez, right."

I swallowed hard and nodded.

"Yeah," I forced out.

"What are you doing out back here?" Tommy asked, like he did this every day, cool, casual.

"I just wanted to get away from the noise and lights for a moment. You guys?"

*Ah, here we go. This is when we admit we were stalking her and she gets that disgusted look.*

"Same," Tommy said casually. "Mind if we walk with you?" I was shaking my head again. Who was this guy?

"Sure," she said, smiling again. And then we were walking, Tommy next to Ronnie, me next to Tommy. But I was literally within an arm span of her, and I could smell her over the sugar. A musky perfume, and something that I swore was pheromones because it was doing all sorts of things to me. God only knew what she and Tommy were talking about. I couldn't concentrate, couldn't say a word, but Tommy kept up the chatter until soon the lights of sideshow alley were bright again, and we were nearly back in amongst the crowds, where we'd have to say goodbye and go our separate ways. I didn't want this to end — this moment containing just the three of us. I had to say something. I opened my mouth to try, but from behind me came a gruff, familiar voice.

"Hey, Ronnie. What are you doing hanging out with these two douches?"

I spun around and found Brad a few metres back, a hulking silhouette moving towards us.

"Don't be like that," Ronnie said.

Brad snorted, stepping into my personal space. He looked down at me.

"Well, if it isn't Tommy and Jizz," he said, smirking. My cheeks burned hot, and my belly began to churn. "Thanks for looking after her, boys. I'll take it from here." And then turning to Ronnie, "I predict a Ferris Wheel ride in your future. Somewhere where we can be alone, eh, like you promised?" He took Ronnie's arm and she looked across at us and I saw goddamn pity in her eyes. But she didn't resist Brad, the fucking brute. She began to move as he tugged on her arm. God only knows why, but in that moment I found my voice.

"You know what I predict, Brad?" I said. "I predict you'll have a fruitful career as a trainee manager at McDonald's."

Tommy guffawed before he caught himself and Brad pulled up sharply, turning to glare at me beneath heavy brows. The look on his face was ferocious, like he wanted to rip me limb from limb. I swallowed, but then forced it down into my belly, searching for a little steel. I found something there, something cold and hot all at once.

"You think you're funny, piss ant?" he hissed, releasing Ronnie and stepping towards me.

"Come on, Brad. This isn't fun. We were going, remember?" Ronnie said, looking at me, shaking her head ever so slightly. "Maybe we can grab a couple of doughnuts on the way," she offered. "My treat."

I watched Brad weighing up his choices, and then his shoulders relaxed.

"Sure," he said. "Let's go. These dickheads aren't worth it. Let's grab some food."

I should have left it there.

"You want fries with that?" I asked. And then he was on me, his forearm wedged hard up under my chin as he pushed me back. I backpedalled and then slammed into something solid that gave a loud bang that echoed through the night. The wind went from me and I coughed hard, trying to breathe, but he wouldn't let me, his arm still hard against my throat.

"You think you're so smart, so fucking funny, don't you? Make a wisecrack now, Jizz. Go on. No? You gutless shit. No wonder your Dad ran off on you and your slut of a Mum."

He released me, and I bent over, wheezing, trying to suck in the air. When I looked up he was walking away, past Tommy, who shied when Brad feinted at him, then he was laughing, dragging Ronnie away from the two of us back into the light. She glanced back at us, and I quickly looked away so she didn't see the tears welling in my eyes.

A fire burned in my chest and guts as I sucked in the air. I wanted to chase him and whale into him, to deliver every ounce of embarrassment back on the end of my fists. But I knew it was futile.

Finally, I sniffed, wiped my cheeks roughly with the back of my hand, and rose back to my full height, holding my stomach. Tommy edged closer, a hand out like he was approaching a cautious foal.

"You boys ok?" a whiny voice asked. We both spun around and there, a few metres back in the dark, was an orange glow as someone inhaled on a cigarette. We watched as a man emerged from the shadows. He wore faded jeans with ragged edges, joggers that were worn down badly on the instep. His blue flannelette shirt was only buttoned about halfway up, and he had long black, ringleted hair, a bit like Slash from Guns N' Roses.

"You were watching?" Tommy asked, incredulous.

"Not all of it, but I caught the end."

"Why didn't you do anything?" I wheezed.

"You seemed to have had it under control," he said, chuckling. "I'm a carny, not a fucking cop. Name's Sticks."

"Well, thanks. Thanks a lot, Sticks."

"That kid's a bit of a cunt, hey? Not the first time you've crossed him, I'm guessing."

"No," I said.

"Hmm. You kids want a smoke?"

I furrowed my brow.

"We're fifteen," Tommy said.

Sticks shrugged, flicked the butt he was puffing to the ground, then pulled a pack of cigarettes from his jeans before removing a fresh one. The flash of his lighter lit up his face for a moment, a lean, haggard face that looked older than his dress and voice suggested. There was something odd about his eyes; they seemed too dark. But then the light was gone and we were back talking to a silhouette with an orange dot floating before his shadowy face.

"Tell you what. I feel bad for you guys. If you don't want a smoke, I'll give you a free go on my ride."

"Ah, no thanks," Tommy said. "Not sure accepting money from a perv in the back alleys of a show always ends well."

Sticks laughed, spewing acrid smoke into our faces.

"Good one. But I'm not giving you cash. I said a free ride. Come on, it's a good one. Have you been to The Factory yet?"

"That lame looking haunted house thing," Tommy said.

"It's not a haunted house, it's The Factory. It's awesome. And it's free right now. What have you got to lose?"

Tommy was shaking his head.

"Come on, Jez, I just want to go."

I looked into the dark again, watching the orange glow brighten as the man inhaled. The guy was weird, but it was the one ride we hadn't done. What were the odds?

"Come on, Tommy. We wanted to have a go earlier, right?"

"You wanted to—"

"One go," I interjected. "Come on, it'll be fun. Let's not let that fuckhead ruin our night."

His face contorted, but then it relaxed and he nodded.

"Ok, one go."

"Lead the way," I said to Sticks.

⸘

Sticks pulled down the safety bar on the black four-person car, locking Tommy and me in place. Ten feet away, the tracks disappeared through a hole in a flimsy construction of black plywood — 'The Factory' written in garish silver. A black sheet obscured the entrance, shimmering gently in the breeze like ripples on a dark lake. Next to it was a collection of large plastic saws, pistons, a conveyor belt.

I'd normally love this sort of thing, but I was still on edge. I huffed out a breath, trying to exhale Brad from my system, trying to relax.

We were slightly removed from the other rides. The sounds and brightness of sideshow alley didn't quite reach this place. They were muted, like I was sitting on the bottom of a pool, holding my breath, watching the party on the deck above the surface of the water.

There were no other patrons. A couple strolling around the other rides glanced briefly in our direction, hesitated, and then turned and hurried away towards the Ferris Wheel.

"Hold on to your hats, boys," Sticks said as he hoisted himself into the back of the car.

"You're coming with us?" Tommy said, craning his neck to watch Sticks pull the bar down on the row behind us. "What about manning the stall, looking after the cash, that sort of thing?"

Sticks laughed, a high-pitched wheeze.

"She's quiet tonight. If someone steals something, fuck 'em. They can keep it."

God, he was strange, but I couldn't help but snort a laugh. He reached out the side of the cart with a gangly arm and slapped it with his open palm. The bang reverberated through the night, and then the carriage began to shift forward, as if the slap were the secret signal needed for some unknown operator to begin the motor, moving us into the Factory.

The carriage groaned, clicking as we eased through the sheer, black curtains, which ballooned and split, caressing my skin as we moved into the darkness inside.

"You boys don't have a heart condition, do you?" Sticks asked from close behind. I could feel his hot breath on the back of my neck.

"Nah. We're good," I said, nudging Tommy who rolled his eyes. We rode on in silence, steadily, the car clicking as it moved along the rails.

When the flash of white light came it was expected, but I jumped anyway. Sticks' high, wheezy laughter engulfed me as adrenaline surged through my body, and I found myself smiling.

When the next surge of white light exposed the tracks, it was accompanied by a whirring sound. A few metres in front of us, next to the rails, was the silhouette of a strange machine. A dummy on our right pulled a lever jerkily, and from the machine sprung a large, spinning saw on a metal arm that swung towards my face.

"Shit," I screeched, ducking, but just before the whining saw connected, our car rolled down into a dip I hadn't noticed and the saw passed harmlessly overhead. I heard Tommy laughing.

"Shut up," I said, grinning, as the car climbed up the other side of the depression.

"Ok," he said, "that was pretty cool."

"Yeah," I admitted, chuckling.

"You ain't seen nothing, yet," Sticks said.

The lights were extinguished again and we rolled on into the dark. There were other sounds now, industrial sounds — grinding, pistons pumping — like a Nine Inch Nails concert. A third flash, and there was a silhouette of another machine, a funnel on top. A dummy appeared to be stuck halfway in. Its mouth was agape, far too big, screaming silently. The grinding noises grew louder as the dummy began to spin in the funnel, like it was caught in a blender. The grinding noise built, and built, and the dummy spun wilder, faster, then stopped suddenly, staring at us as we passed, the machine clanging, whining, screeching sickly and then, as darkness returned, there was a terrific bang and I was slapped by wet, sticky drops of what felt like gore.

"Jesus," I said, wiping my face.

"That's so fucking gross," Tommy said, but I could hear the grin in his voice.

"Just warm, soapy water. Cool though, hey?" Sticks said.

"Sure," I said, wiping the side of my cheek. I was actually beginning to enjoy myself.

A fourth flash and there was another machine, something large, like a tank. I watched, fascinated, as it imploded, a loud roar assailing me. It was so realistic, so well constructed.

"What is this place?" I whispered, trying to work out how he had pulled all of this together, who had helped him, why no one was riding.

"It's the Factory, boys. Put your hate in, action comes out. You say, they pay."

"What's he talking about?" Tommy said quietly, elbowing me in the ribs. I shrugged, confused.

On the air, I smelt the scent of burning. I imagined welders and accidents. The grinding was back. It was faster, insistent, almost like static. It became louder and louder and my heart thumped excitedly as I wondered what was next.

Above the background noise, I heard the clink of Sticks' lighter, the deep breath as he inhaled. I felt hot smoke, tasted the nicotine, smelt the ash. He suddenly grabbed me hard on the shoulder, and I winced under his tight grip.

"Look," he hissed in my ear, "the main event."

And sure enough, the track was revealed beneath a cheesy red light. About fifty yards in front of us, metal doors fell across the track. They looked like the doors to an incinerator. They looked solid. The edges glowed orange, and I noticed we'd begun moving faster.

I felt Sticks' hair brushing the back of my neck, he was close, leaning between Tommy and me.

"That guy, you hate him, right?"

The cart picked up speed. I knew the gates would open, but still, my heart was racing. Thirty feet.

"Who?" Tommy asked. I could hear the uncertainty in his voice. My eyes darted to Tommy and I saw him staring ahead, straight-backed.

"That big bastard."

"Brad," I offered, turning back, wondering why Sticks was bringing him up just as the ride was beginning to take my mind off of him. The doors were close, twenty feet, still closed.

"Yeah, Brad. You hate him, right?"

I nodded.

"Yes," Tommy said.

"How much?"

"Are these doors going to open?" Tommy said, swallowing.

*"How much?"* Sticks hissed, urgent.

Ten feet, nine, eight.

"I don't know!" Tommy cried out.

Seven, six, five.

I was anxious, suddenly certain we were about to crash, but there was nothing I could do. A feeling of helplessness returned. I felt Brad's arm wedged up under my throat. I saw his cold eyes. My face was hot, blood in my ears. I wanted to wipe that smug grin off of his face. I wanted to hurt him.

Four, three, two.

"With everything," I said. "I hate him with everything I've fucking got."

The doors whooshed open and the red light changed to purple as we raced through, faster. There was a hissing sound competing with the industrial clangs, and smoke filled the air all around us, purple light dancing through the motes like imps at play.

"Good. And what does he deserve?" Sticks asked, urgent.

"I don't understand," Tommy said. He sounded breathless.

"Does he deserve to be embarrassed?" Sticks said, mumbling around his cigarette.

Suddenly the purple gloom ahead of us moved as if blown by a zephyr. I stared, wide-eyed as it swirled, appeared to become substantial, and in the thick mist I saw the shadow of a hulking figure emerge, and then trip, and other shadows encircle him, pointing. I heard the laughter over the metal grinding. I saw Brad in the smoke and I smiled, transfixed.

"Yes," I said.

"Pain?"

The car rushed on, the wind on my face, we jerked hard against the side as the cart turned left. The smoke shifted once more. Now Brad was driving a car, turning in his seat to pass a bottle, and when he turned back there was a black tree looming fast. The purple smoke exploded, accompanied by the sounds of glass and metal disintegrating, and screaming.

"Yes," I said again, excited, my smile stretching into a grimace. The hotness in my temples and chest spread, and I felt warmer, better. I slammed up hard against Tommy as the tracks bent right.

"Death?"

The cart was screaming along the tracks now. In my periphery, I saw Tommy's white knuckles as he strangled the safety bar. The smoke reformed. Brad was backing away from a shadowy mob. I was leading them. I could feel it. Walking towards Brad, urging my followers on, every person he'd ever hurt. We'd make him pay. I screamed my pain as shadows rushed past me towards him. Brad felled the first with a wild punch, but the next was on him, then the next and next until they'd wrestled him to the ground. I threw the rope over the bow of the gum tree. I fixed the loop around his thick neck as his head thrashed back and forth helplessly. My grin stretched wider. I stepped back and took the other end of the rope, along with every shadow that wasn't already holding Brad down. I opened my mouth to give the order, my hatred consuming me, needing release.

"No," Tommy screamed. "No. Fucking, no. No, he doesn't deserve that. And we wouldn't."

The car burst through two black curtains and we were back out in the night, cool air hitting me like a spray of mist, washing away the heat. The industrial sounds were replaced by the music of sideshow alley.

"Shame," I heard Sticks say. The cart screeched to a halt before bumping up against the final barrier and I had to use both hands to stop my chin from slamming into the bar.

Sticks slapped my shoulder.

"Fun ride, hey boys? Hope it makes you feel better." And then the safety bar was up and I was helping a shaking Tommy out of the car as Sticks walked off back towards his ticket booth.

~

"Mum, I'm home," I called as I closed the door and dropped my house keys on the side table. I pulled my shoes from my feet and tossed them under the coat rack, wrinkling my nose as the scent of dirty socks hit me.

I could hear the TV droning in the lounge room, the soft rev of cars, someone yelling for back-up.

"Mum," I called again, moving from the entry of our apartment into our lounge. For a moment I couldn't see her, just the green two-seater facing the cheap TV, the picture of Mum and me from a few years back hanging above it. But then she sat up fast, and I saw her wiping hurriedly at moist eyes, clearing her throat.

"Jeremy," she said, surprised, glancing at me and then turning away so that I found myself looking at the back of her head. She sniffed hard, pulled a tissue from her sleeve and blew her nose. "How was your night, honey? Did you have fun?"

"Yeah, it was good." I walked over to the couch. "Are you ok?"

"Yep," she responded, refusing to look at me.

I circled the couch and slumped down next to her. Her mobile was on the armrest upside down, the TV turned down low like she hadn't been watching.

"Mum, it's ok. What's up?"

She sighed loudly and turned towards me. Her eyes were red, and black mascara stained her cheeks. She'd been crying for a while.

"I'm so sorry, honey. Your Dad called. He can't make tomorrow. He wanted to, he did, but—"

"Bullshit," I said sharply. I was too old to be disappointed, too old to feel anything but annoyance at his predictability.

"Jez, honestly. He was called into work. He said he'd make it up to you."

It was odd how hard she tried to apologise for him. He'd left us, not the other way around. And he was a deadbeat. It'd been a while since I realised I didn't need him. In fact, I didn't even like him. But all of that seemed irrelevant to Mum.

"Mum, I don't care. I really don't. We've done fine without him for seven years. What's another day?"

"Oh, honey. Don't be like that. It's important to have a Dad in your life." She put her arm around me and rested her head on my shoulder. God, I loved her. She'd had to sacrifice so much when Dad left.

I knew she wasn't really upset for me. She'd known for a while that I couldn't stand the prick and that I only played along for her. But she still wanted us to be that happy family. She wanted him to be a good Dad. She still loved him.

I scrunched my nose but didn't move. The thought of her wasting her years pining away for Dad disgusted me. She was too good for him. Him who'd run out on us to chase girls only a little older than me. Him whose greatest life lesson was teaching me how to open a beer bottle in the crook of my elbow. And yet she still got upset. Damn, it made me mad. Fuck him. Fuck him to hell.

⁂

When Tommy called the next morning, I was still pissed.

I was on my hands and knees, bare-chested, sifting through the pile of dirty clothes on the floor of my room, getting more and more annoyed that I couldn't find a shirt that didn't smell like shit.

When the phone rang, I gave up. I sat back against my bed and pulled the mobile from my jeans pocket, answered.

"What's up?" I said.

"Have you seen the news?" Tommy asked. He sounded frightened, panicked.

"No. I'm fifteen. And it's Sunday. Why the hell would I be looking at the news?"

"Grab your IPad and Google Brad's name."

I sighed, but did as instructed, pulling my IPad from my bedside table before typing 'Brad Archer' into Google. Then I waited, looking at a blank webpage as our shitty internet decided whether it would work or not. How much of a person's life is spent waiting for web pages to load?

When the results finally appeared, I saw what Tommy was riled up about.

"Jesus," I whispered, clicking on the first link that read: "Teenager in critical condition after freak accident."

"The chain on his automatic garage door snapped when he was getting back in last night," Tommy said, running his words together. "The thing near took his head off. Even if he does wake up, he's going to be a mess. He's missing an eye, for fuck's sake."

"Jesus," I whispered again, taking in the gory details.

"Was that us?" Tommy said too loud. "That spooky ride, that weird guy, Sticks. This is kind of what he said would happen, right? What was he, Jez?"

I swallowed.

"He was just a guy, Tommy," I said.

"He didn't feel right though, you know? And the ride. It was all sorts of wrong. I've tried to ignore it, but I keep thinking back. I keep seeing Sticks' eyes. They were … they were … did we do a deal with the devil, Jez?"

I laughed.

"What?" I said. "Are you crazy? Did he ask for our souls? He just gave us a free ride, Tommy. Calm down."

Tommy was sniffing hard and I knew him well enough to know he was crying.

"This isn't what I wanted, damn it. Brad doesn't deserve to be in hospi—"

"What the fuck, Tommy? Of course he does. He was a prick."

"You don't mean that. Don't you feel guilty?"

If anything, I felt relieved. I felt lighter knowing I'd head into school tomorrow and not need to check every shadow, dreading what was to come if I ran into Brad.

"No, I don't feel guilty, because we didn't do anything. You're imagining things. Maybe it was the universe, or karma. But it wasn't you, ok? So don't sweat it. You had nothing to do with this, Tommy."

Tommy sniffed again.

"You sure?" he said. I hesitated, but then I told Tommy what he needed to hear.

"I'm certain."

When he hung up, I read the article again, and then the next one, and the next one, all the while thinking about last night's ride through the Factory, and Sticks, and what I saw in the smoke, and how real it felt, how much I'd wanted to hurt Brad. The smile on my face stretched wider. *Could it be?* I wondered.

Today was the last day for the show. And I suddenly felt like taking another ride. There was someone else who deserved everything coming his way. One more prick who could do with some divine punishment. We'd be better with him gone from our lives. Mum would be better. No more worrying, no more getting upset, hating herself when she should be hating him.

And even if I were wrong, and it just turned out that Sticks was no more than a strange guy operating a shitty ghost train, what did I really have to lose?

⸮

"Hello, young Jez," Sticks said as I approached his ticket booth. He was lounging on a stool, his back against one wall of the booth, his feet wedged up in the opposite corner. A cigarette hung from his mouth, a mound of ash at the end looking like it would drop into his lap at any moment.

"I'd like another ride," I said, halting a couple of feet shy of the window.

"Would you, now?" He smiled around his cigarette, blue plumes of smoke streaming from his nostrils. He straightened, pushed off the glass and lowered his dirty feet behind the bench. He leaned forward, his eyes narrowing — those dark, disconcerting eyes. They smiled at me. They seemed to whisper, *I know what you want, man.* The sun beat on my back, warm, drawing sweat from my neck, from the pits of my arms. I waited, holding his gaze, like it was an initiation.

"Where's your friend?"

"At home."

"Didn't he like the results?"

I swallowed.

"I liked the results," I stated, and his smiled stretched wider — a broad, Cheshire cat grin. He pulled the cigarette from his mouth and ground it into the top of the bench, a thin white tendril of smoke still rising from the crumpled butt.

"Ten bucks," he said holding out a dirty hand.

"That's it?" I asked.

"Good value, huh? I'm constantly surprised I'm not inundated with patrons."

I rummaged around in my jeans, pulled out my wallet, removed a ten and held it out, but hesitated just shy of his outstretched hand.

"And this is for the same ride as last night?"

"No ride is ever the same at the Factory."

I licked my lips.

"But if I hate someone, you can ... it can ... take care of them?"

He nodded slowly. I felt like I should have asked more questions, but I didn't know what to say, so I just handed him the note. He tucked it under the bench, jumped down from the stool and slid out the back.

I followed him to the rail cars where he lifted the safety bar on the first. When I jumped in, he followed, forcing me to slide over so that he could fit. He pulled the bar down, locking it in place with a click.

"You ready?" he asked.

I was nervous as hell. I didn't really know how this worked. It wasn't like he'd given me instructions last night. I just knew Brad was on my mind, I'd been furious, and I wanted him hurt. Did I have to do the same again? I closed my eyes, brought Dad to mind, saw him with that wicked grin, the one he brought out every time he let us down. I saw Mum crying again and again over that useless sod. I felt it in my guts. I felt the heat, and the electric pinch behind my nose. I wanted to pound him to a bloody pulp. I wanted to see that smile falter, see it turn into a grimace, a scream. I felt the joy rising in me as I opened my eyes, and nodded.

"Yep. I'm ready."

Sticks reached out and banged the side loudly, and then we started, the car rolling forward slowly into the maw of the Factory, into darkness.

I was assaulted by sounds of grinding, of spinning saws, of hammering. I heard a machine start up — a loud whirring interspersed with clunking. The sounds were so loud they filled my head, like a giant screaming through a funnel into my brain. If Sticks said anything, I couldn't hear him.

A flash of light exposed the silhouette of strange mechanisms, of the dummy pulling a lever, its head turning, turning, its eyes red fire, boring into my soul. As the saw sprung forward on its arm, I felt my confidence waver, my hatred falter and I ducked again despite knowing it'd miss. We rolled into the dip, and the saw whined overhead.

Darkness.

The cart was creeping along the tracks a little faster now. The loud, industrial sounds grew more urgent. I felt insufficient. Like what I was giving the Factory wasn't enough. Like it was demanding fuel, demanding more. How had this seemed fun last night?

Another flash exposed the machine with the funnel. This time there were two dummies, arms wrapped around each other, kissing as they were wrenched and torn, sucked into the contraption.

Darkness. There was a bang and I was hit by slick gore. It smelt coppery, like blood, and I couldn't imagine it as soapy water. I gagged, wiping my face with my sleeve.

Faster and faster we rolled. I glanced towards Sticks, but I could barely make him out. I might as well have been alone.

A flash. An explosion. Chunks of metal pinged above me, and I cringed. The smell of seared flesh. A glob of something wet smacked into the side of the car. Screams. Darkness.

Red lights revealed the tracks and, further on, the metal doors. I swallowed, trying to bring back the image of my father, the punishment I wanted to mete out, but it wasn't working. The sounds of the Factory were overwhelming, insistent.

I glanced at Sticks. The top half of his face was obscured by thick, greasy curls, but I could see his chin and his thin lips, which parted as I watched, and began to move, barely. And somehow, above the intense noise that surrounded me, I heard his high, wheezy voice.

"Thoughts go in, actions come out."

"What the fuck?" I hissed, scared now.

"Give me the name," he said.

"My father. Damien Preston."

"The name of your first hate."

My eyes darted to the doors ahead, so close now, looming large. They didn't look like plywood. They looked like solid metal.

"He is my first hate. Open the fucking door."

Sticks' head turned, slowly, his creepy, dark eyes almost shining under the red glow, seeing through me.

"No, he wasn't."

"What do you mean?"

But then I saw it, vividly, like I was eight again. I was crouching at the top of the stairs when I heard Dad driving off, and I saw Mum crumpled in the front doorway, screaming for him to come back, and I remember being so fucking mad at her. What had she done to make him go? Why couldn't she just have been a good wife? Why couldn't she have fixed this?

"No," I hissed. The metal doors sprang open and we were through into the purple smoke, which was already drawing together, becoming solid, becoming a shadowy outline of my mother falling down the stairs.

"No," I hissed again. "This isn't what I wanted." I turned and grabbed Sticks' shoulders and shook him, but he turned away from me, stared ahead, a smirk on his lips.

"No!" I screamed, as I saw the smoke form a hospital, machines beeping, my mother thin like a skeleton, weak, hair gone, lesions on her face.

"Please, God, no. I'll do anything to save her," I implored. His smirk dissolved, his lips parted, his pink tongue darted between them, like a lizard appearing from between rocks, wetting them a little. He turned to look at me again.

"What else have you got to offer the Factory?" he asked, his lips barely moving, barely audible over the whirring of the ride, but I understood.

"Anything," I screamed above the noise, as we flew through the smoke, charging onward. "Everything. Whatever you want. Just don't kill my mother, please?"

"The Factory needs payment. I need payment," he said.

"Me, then," I offered.

He laughed, a high, wheezy gurgle that ran up and over the top of the Factory's noise and settled on top before falling around me like glass shards until it was all I heard. I couldn't help but wonder if this was what he'd wanted all along. But what other choice did I have?

When his laughter died, so too did the noise of the Factory. I saw the smoke clearing, I felt the car slowing. Sticks reached out the side and slapped the cart with a bang, and suddenly it veered sharply left, slamming me into Sticks as we forked off onto a side track. Up ahead was a dull light, a yellow arch elevated slightly above the track.

"Ok, Jez. Deal. I'm getting old. I could do with more help. We'll start you off small. The others can show you how to set up, and how to clean the cars. Then maybe you can work your way up to joining the ride, maybe playing one of the machine operators or something like that," he said, chuckling.

I felt tears stinging the back of my eyes, uncertain if it was my fear or gratitude.

"Thank you," I whispered, as the cart rushed up a small incline and then into the light. We screeched to a halt, and I slammed up hard against the safety bar. When I looked around I found myself in a dull blue, metal room. It had smooth surfaces, like a butcher's table. No windows, just the one entrance through which the tracks ran.

Sticks pushed the safety bar up and jumped out lithely. I cleared my throat.

"Where are we?"

"Back of my truck. This is where we keep the cars. And you while we pack up and get on the road."

"But," I stammered, "can't I go home, grab some things, pack some clothes ..."

Sticks wheezed laughter.

"Say goodbye to Mummy? No, Jez. Don't think so. In my experience, going home dilutes the memories of The Factory. And kids suddenly get talked out of honouring their deals by well-meaning loved ones."

"But I wouldn't, I couldn't. I mean, I know what'll happen to her if I don't come back."

Sticks inhaled through his nose, mouth closed tight.

"I believe you now, Jez. But ..." He shrugged, hands extended, palms up. "No telling what you begin thinking once you're in front of your Mum, she's crying, begging you not to go, threatening to call the cops. Nah, safer if you stay here. Then your Mum definitely won't get hurt more than she needs to.

"Besides, we don't have time. I've already given the order to shut the ride down and pack up, and it'll take my crew a couple of hours at most. And when they're done, I don't want to be waiting around for you wondering if you're a kid of your word or not."

I swallowed, nodded, blinking hard to keep the tears at bay. And then, as if an afterthought, he said, "I'll need your phone."

I hesitated, then pulled my phone from my pocket with a shaking hand, and held it out to him. He took it from me, and I watched it disappear into his jeans.

"Good kid," he said, grinning broadly.

I eased out of the car, struggling on wobbly legs. Sticks walked back along the track towards the exit. And then his words hit me. More than Mum needed to be hurt? I thought my trade was so she wouldn't be hurt at all.

"What do you mean more than Mum needs to be hurt?" I said, stepping towards him. He halted at the exit and looked back at me over his shoulder, smiling.

"Thoughts go in, actions come out. You thought of her, champ. The Factory needs retribution. But don't worry. She'll live."

I felt fire in my belly, heat, anger. My legs were moving, and I rushed towards him, trying to get my hands around his neck, but he was too fast. He stepped through the exit and a metal door slid shut with a bang. I slammed up against it hard. I stepped back and then smashed my shoulder into it again, but it didn't budge.

Jesus, what had I done? I slumped to the floor, my head in my hands. What was he going to do to her?

But then I realised. He wasn't going to do a thing. It was already done.

I remembered back to the night Dad left, Mum wailing on the floor as his taillights grew fainter, then disappeared. Even though I blamed her, I went downstairs, and when she saw me, she enveloped me, and my hatred dissipated. We'd both cried then, and she'd whispered into my ear, "It'll be alright, honey. As long as we still have each other, we'll be ok."

---

*Hatred*

*Misery*   *Fun*   *Boredom*

*Dislike*   *Tension*

Hope Triad (inversion)

# 15. That Moment You Realize

## David Hammond

At 11:02 this morning, I decided to quit my job.

Jessica had been standing behind me at my cubicle for who knows how long. She is a statuesque woman in too many senses of the word — conventionally beautiful, devoid of expression, and able to stand utterly still and quiet for unnatural periods of time.

"Victor," she said.

I flinched. I was on Facebook, but when you work at the Meme Communications Strategy Institute, that can be considered "research."

"How are the lettuce memes coming along?" she asked.

I was running artillery for two separate meme operations, one for the Kale Growers of America attacking iceberg lettuce, and another for the American Lettuce Cooperative attacking chard and kale. This kind of double agent situation is not as uncommon as you might think. It's easy to get pigeonholed in the meme business, and after taking on apples versus pears the previous year, I had become the go-to produce guy. It's not the worst gig, but that lucky S.O.B. Phil got a spot on the dog and cat team. I could hear them in their daily scrums going "whoa!" and "awwww!" while I was looking at yet another head of Boston Bibb thinking, "Do something interesting, damn you."

Jessica cleared her throat.

"Well, I was thinking," I said, swivelling around in my chair. "Don't a lot of lettuce farmers also grow kale?"

I *knew* it was an irrelevant point. I *knew* what Jessica was going to say in response. Maybe I just needed to hear her say it one more time. She wore a black turtleneck and her blonde hair in a tight ponytail. She cocked her head to the side.

"Kale farmers are not our clients. Our client is the KGA."

"Yes, 'Kale Growers of America.' A.k.a. kale farmers."

Jessica's eyelid twitched as we stared at each other for a moment. "How are the lettuce memes coming along?"

That was it. That was the precise moment I made the decision to leave, and a warm, calm feeling spread from my basal ganglia to the furthest corners of my body.

"They're good. They're real good," I said, and turned back to my monitor. "I'll have them ready this afternoon."

As Jessica glided away, I leaned back the head of my Yoda Pez dispenser and extracted a candy like an aching tooth. "So done with this I am."

But how to quit? I could stop by Jessica's office on the way to lunch. Her eyelid would twitch, and then I would go away and never come back. But no. There was an easier way.

I zipped up all my leafy green memes-in-progress and wrote an email.

"Hi, Jessica.

"Lettuce and kale memes attached. Sorry so few. I like 3a and 7b best, but they could use another set of eyeballs.

"This is me quitting this job."

I attached a picture of a squirrel with its arms raised in triumph and/or liberation. Actually, the squirrel was probably reaching for a french fry that someone was holding just out of reach. It didn't matter.

Before sending the message, I packed Yoda and the rest of my cubicle detritus in my messenger bag. Jonathan from the next cubicle must have heard the clatter. He wheeled over as I weighed an Obama bobblehead in my hand.

"You want this?" I asked.

"Uh, you quitting?"

"Yep."

"You..." he began, but the words stuck in his throat. "Yeah, okay." He held out his hand.

I gave him the bobblehead and patted my pockets. "I guess that's it."

Obama nodded as I leaned over my desk and hit the "Send" button.

"See you at trivia night?" said Jonathan.

"Wouldn't miss it."

I left him with an affectionate fist bump.

Dry leaves blew through Farragut Square onto K Street as I emerged from the building. I headed northwest on Connecticut Avenue, buoyed by the cool air and feeling a powerful urge to walk. One should never waste a nice autumn day in Washington DC.

What would I do without the biweekly check from MCSI? I would think about that later.

I watched two men play chess in Dupont Circle: one gray, disheveled, and toothless; the other a bearded young man who kept tugging on the frayed edge of his knit cap. I tried to follow the game, but it was too slow. After several agonized minutes, a pawn was anti-climactically moved up a square. My attention wandered to the stubbly concave of the toothless man's lips, which he worked back and forth as if sucking on a lozenge. A pigeon pecked at a cracker by the men's feet, and that reminded me of a popular meme template: "Arguing with a [TARGET GROUP] is like playing chess with a pigeon". The bearded man side-eyed me and shifted on his concrete chair, which I took as my cue to find a food truck and leave the men to their game.

I continued up Connecticut eating a kebab wrap, cursing myself for forgetting to grab a napkin. Passing over Rock Creek Park, I realized that if I walked just a little further I'd be at the zoo.

I visited the pandas, the elephants, and the lions. By the time I got to the great ape house, reality was starting to settle in. I had nowhere to go, nothing to get back to. I needed to start looking for a new job, but really? I couldn't take one afternoon off?

My real problem was all the "When you quit your job and don't know what to do next" memes that kept attaching themselves to the animals. The elephants all lived in internet-ready boxes with text on the top and bottom. I rubbed my eyes and tried to focus on the enormous silverback gorilla, who leaned against the plexiglass of his enclosure, chewing on bamboo.

"Thought trainer was happy to see me. Banana in his pocket."

I couldn't turn it off!

My phone dinged: an email from Jessica.

"Thanks for letting me know," it said. That was all. There was something sad about that. How many people had walked out without even extending the courtesy of an "I'm quitting" meme? I felt slightly better about myself, but worse about my fellow man.

According to a plaque next to the gorilla enclosure, the adult male's name was Stanley.

"Stanley. How are you enjoying that bamboo, big guy?"

I watched the gorilla gnaw until the glib meme texts that had been floating above and below his head faded away. He stripped the bark from the end of the branch and chomped on the pulpy innards. He worked methodically, but also distractedly. A juvenile named Rose cavorted in the artificial tree, and Stanley watched her as he chewed. Not a care in the world, I thought. His massive jaws mashed the wood, and I imagined the stringy texture in my own mouth. How did it taste? Bland compared to a kebab wrap, I guessed, but maybe acrid, sweet, woody. Was "woody" a flavor?

I sat on a bench and took out my phone.

"Is woody a flavor?" I typed. Yes, yes it was, according to various online sources. Coffee can be woody, as can cinnamon. Cigars. Mead. Wine. If wine can taste woody, then so can wood. Case closed.

I switched over to Facebook. Nothing new since the morning. Nothing interesting, that is. On the *Washington Post*: a story about the gambling habits and foot fetish of the senator from Illinois. I wagged my thumb over the headline, thinking I should read it to stay informed. Instead, I flicked through my go-to entertainment apps, but other than the mild pleasure I got from uninstalling my suite of meme-generators, they offered little in the way of entertainment.

Two pm. I could get on the yellow line at Columbia Heights and be back at my Crystal City apartment, beer in hand, in about 45 minutes. I could watch *Office Space* again. This plan had an objective appeal. Many times in the past, drinking and watching an old movie had really hit the spot. Throw in some chips and salsa, and what was I waiting for?

But I didn't *feel* like it.

For several minutes I sat like a coiled spring, not wanting to get up, not wanting to sit, not wanting to be alone, not wanting to see any people, not wanting to scroll through my Facebook feed again, not wanting to not do that.

A mother and two daughters entered the ape house. The younger daughter, preschool-aged, ran to the plexiglass and pointed at Rose.

"Look at the monkey, Mommy."

The young mom wore a pink hoodie unzipped to her waist over a low-cut t-shirt, so when she leaned over I could see the lacy edges of her bra. "That's not a monkey, sweetie. That's a gorilla." She glanced at me and straightened up.

The little girl puzzled over this while the older girl, who was about ten and tapping away on her phone, sat next to me on the bench and hunched forward, resting her elbows on her knees. I moved my bag to give her more room. "Excuse me," she said. She didn't look at me when she said it, but still it was a nicety of civil discourse I hadn't expected.

She was playing a game with poop emojis falling through some sort of colorful matrix. The sounds of flushes and farts seemed to correspond to the rise and fall of a score in the upper-right corner. The girl's thumbs flashed over the screen, making poops splat, plop, smile, grimace, and dance. The action paused as a poop rose angelically to a higher level and the girl flexed her thumbs like an athlete limbering up. The descent of angry-looking plungers announced the commencement of the next challenge.

"Jennifer." The mom beckoned from the exit, and the girl, with flying thumbs and grim concentration, rose and followed her out.

Stanley now sat picking his nose with the same casual efficiency he had previously applied to the bamboo.

"Well," I said, slapping my thighs and getting up. "I'd love to stay and chat, but, you know, I've got places to go and things to do."

Except I didn't. Stanley looked at me for the first time, his thick, expressive eyebrows raised. Again, I felt like a coiled spring. Stay or go?

"Can you believe that girl, though?" I said. "She didn't take her eyes off her phone the whole time she was in here. I mean, what focus! What obliviousness! Impressive, and a little scary."

And then Stanley tapped the glass, quite deliberately, four times, still looking at me. Tap tap tap tap.

Well, to leave then would have seemed rude. I sat down on the ledge right by the enclosure. "Is this a game?" I tapped back. Tap tap tap tap.

Stanley turned away and put his hand to his forehead. I didn't know how to interpret that. He looked back at me for a second and then let his gaze wander around the enclosure.

I tapped again. Tap tap tap. But I got the distinct impression that if it had been a game, it was over, and I had lost. Stanley resumed picking his nose.

"Fine. Have it your way," I said. "You know, when I was a kid, we didn't have cell phones like that girl. When our parents dragged us to the zoo, we had no choice but to look at the animals."

Stanley listened thoughtfully. Or not. My voice couldn't have been more than a faint mumble through the plexiglass.

"The thing was, when I was a kid, I could think about the most mundane things without getting bored. I could *meditate*, though I never used that word. I could meditate, say, on that artificial tree. Look there. That knot resembles a wide-eyed man, and that one over there resembles a winking woman with a beehive hairdo. I could imagine the things the woman might say to make the man look so surprised. 'Your nose looks like a turnip,' she might say, because it does. For hours and hours, I could stare and imagine, and not think. When I was a kid. Not only that, I *looked forward* to having nothing to do, so that I could stare at something like that artificial tree for a while."

Stanley continued to excavate his nostrils.

"Or pick my nose. *You know* what I'm talking about. But are you bored in there? It must be boring."

He looked at me again, as if mildly surprised I was still there. He leaned towards me. Tap tap tap tap. He leaned back to await my reaction.

Tap tap tap tap *tap*.

He put his hand to his forehead and resumed ignoring me.

I was no more than three feet away from him, his silvery hair, his massive chest and arms. If he wanted to, and the plexiglass didn't exist, he could tear my limbs off like shucking the bark off a piece of bamboo. Would he want to? *Did* he want to? I studied the contours of his profile, the creases under his eyes, the stubble on his wide chin making him look like muscle for a Hollywood mobster, until I started to feel embarrassed for staring at him so much.

Without ceremony, he got up and exited the enclosure. All the gorillas were out in the yard then, even little Rose.

That was that.

I walked to Columbia Square, but instead of taking the escalator down to the Metro train, I continued walking along Irvine Street. It *is* really a shame to squander a nice Autumn day in Washington DC.

I entered a part of the city I'd never seen before. A reservoir, a cemetery, a warehouse, a dusty dead-end stacked with wooden crates. When I found myself on New York Avenue, I walked into the afternoon sun, thinking vaguely that it would return me to K Street and more familiar environs, weaving through pedestrian traffic, my eyes half-closed.

And when I opened them, there was a place selling pizza by the slice. I went in.

Sitting by the window, I shook my head and smacked my lips, as if waking from a nap. I took out my phone to check my bank balance. Chomping on pepperoni and staring at the unexpectedly small number, I heard a tapping.

A woman stood outside the window, her face in shadow, a ponytail draped over her shoulder. I squinted. Jessica? She thrust her hands in the pockets of her trim, designer jacket.

I had an instantaneous vision of what was about to happen. I would invite her to have a slice of pizza with me, and she would accept. We would talk about the absurdity of the meme business, and she would confide her own misgivings. Her marble veneer would crack and crumble. She would *smile*. I would tell her to for god's sake get out while she could, and she...

But no. Her hand emerged from her pocket with a cell phone, and she snapped a picture of me looking befuddled, pizza grease dripping down my chin. And then she moved on down the street, shading her phone with her hand and peering critically at the screen.

Say what you want about her, but she's a fast worker. I counted to thirty, taking three more bites of pizza, and then pulled up her Instagram page.

"When you quit your job — and then remember that you majored in English."

Not bad. I refreshed to see the likes and lols of Jessica's formidable Instagram following.

The sun dipped behind the buildings across the street as I wiped my mouth with a napkin. I'd never been a meme before. What if I went viral? What if from this day forward I am known as "pizza-eating guy"?

"Funny because true," I posted in the comments.

There are worse fates.

*Boredom*

*Hatred*     *Tension*     *Despair*

*Fun*     *Trepidation*

# 16. Shiver Soft Feathers

## L'Erin Ogle

Jake was halfway through his sandwich, the mustard making the bread soft and mushy against his molars, squeezing in the spaces between his teeth to fester until he brushed them. He hated the mid-shift, two to ten PM, sitting in a hot car letting the Kansas sun bake him crisp all day long. When the sun set, the calls would start pouring in. People sat around and got drunk and angry in the summer heat, then night cooled it down enough for them to find the energy to beat their wives, rob their dealers, and get into bar fights that spilled out on sidewalks and pulled bystanders into their orbit.

He put his sandwich down and took a drink of water, swished it around to get rid of the spare bits. His radio clicked, about to broadcast. He ran his tongue over his teeth. The radio crackled to life, the dispatcher requesting a unit to respond for some kind of domestic situation called in on the side of the road. Jake sighed, hit the lights, left the sirens silent, and began driving, gravel scattering from under his tires.

The request had originated between 1300 and 1350 Rd, on Turner Road. He knew all these roads, even this one, one of those little lanes that was mostly mud, with a sign that read NO MAINTENANCE.

He arrived to the scene, where there was a SUV parked on the side of the road with its flashers on. A silver-haired man in blue jeans and a collared T-shirt was standing in front of the open driver's door, and he looked relieved to see Jake. He backed away from the open door, said, "I came up on her walking just back there." He pointed a few yards away. "Had to stop real quick. She was walking right in the middle of the road. She's got blood on her, but only her feet look hurt."

The girl sat in the driver's seat, maybe four or so, skinny legs dangling off the seat, the air conditioning blowing her dirty blond hair around. It looked greasy and ill-kept, the ends uneven and frayed, like the strings of his hooded sweatshirts. She had bloodstains the color of rust on her clothes: a tiny pair of shorts and a threadbare Royals T-shirt that was too big for her, her arms swallowed by the sleeves.

"Hi, darlin," he said. He crouched down to look her in the eyes. She had pale blue eyes that looked out past him. She acted like she didn't hear him, so he patted her knee. "Hello, I'm Deputy Jake. I'm with the police." He tapped his badge, the silver star. "Are you hurt anywhere?"

The girl's flat eyes never moved. She shook her head.

"Where'd you come from?"

She pointed back down Turner, still silent. He felt the rumble of the ambulance coming.

He radioed in to update Dispatch. The medics would take the girl, who still wasn't talking, to the local hospital. Jake would start looking down Turner for where she'd come from. But, really, how far could a barefoot kid have walked in the sun on the hot dirty gravel?

⸙

Two miles, apparently. Two miles from the stop, he spotted a small dirt driveway about thirty feet long that led to a small rundown tan trailer. He eased his car down the ruts in the drive, came to a stop behind an old dusty Ford Ranger. The plates were expired by a month, not that uncommon. The trailer was a double wide, had seen better days, big flaking rust spots dotting the sides. He radioed in his location, opened his door, and stepped out. He flicked open the leather strap that crossed the top of his gun, put his hand right on the butt. The smell drifting out of the trailer was the smell of copper and chemicals, and it meant one thing to Jake — the same thing it meant to every cop, medic, coroner in rural counties. Death and meth. Meth brings death, he thought, standing outside his unit, lights on, no sirens. Just silence and smell, lit up blue-red-blue-red. He waited, watching the door to the trailer swing in the wind. There were small bloody handprints on the door, where the girl had come out.

He approached the door after he saw and heard nothing but the wind whispering across the flat land. Here, the copper death meth smell was thicker, choking him, closing up his airway. He kept his hand on his gun, felt it solid and cool against his palm. He had a bad feeling about this whole thing, that maybe a body or bodies in there had been in the August heat for days, rotting and swelling until they burst along the seams. Maybe the guilty party was still there, lips wrapped around a glass pipe or with a needle dangling from their arm, waiting for suicide by cop.

It happened more than people thought. He knocked loud and sharp on the door, the boom boom boom that made anyone who knew the law go quiet and still. It said cops. It said, open up or run, but down you go either way.

There was no answer. He was sweating heavy under the vest and the belt and the Kansas heat. The trailer was silent, no views through the window, all the cheap shades pulled down. Some of the slats were snapped off at the edges. All the dopers had the same blinds, always broken at eye level. The paranoia was real after a day or two without sleep. They'd run to the blinds and lift them up to check for whatever demons they thought were out there —cops or thieves or ghosts. Course, the real demon was always right next to them.

He used his foot to catch the swinging metal door and keep it open. "Police," he called. "Coming in!"

He was quick through the door, a little two step dance, scanning right to left. The trailer went both ways from entry. To the right was a little spot with a fold down table and booths, both splashed with rust-colored blood spread over scattered white crystals and ashtrays and crumpled cans. He turned his back on it and went on to the little living area. There was a space for a TV that held some paraphernalia, needles, spoons, an empty two-liter bottle with the top sawed off. And a mattress saturated with blood. It was here the copper chemical stink stopped being heavy and became impenetrable, the sheets stained black.

No bodies yet.

The soft hair on the back of his neck stood at attention. There was something crawling around in his stomach, making it clench like a fist. He listened, but the booming of his heart echoed across his eardrums. This was a bad place, where something bad had happened, and bad places where bad things happened had histories that repeated themselves.

He passed through the narrow hall, cleared the tiny shower stall. There was a different smell now, a stale smell, that reminded him of his grandma's assisted living place. It wormed under his skin and hummed like an air unit, kicking up gooseflesh all over.

There was another door that he pushed open with his foot. The bed there sagged heavy with stains, but no blood. Just neglect. There was a torn Tinkerbell blanket and some broken crayons on it, empty juice boxes and chip bags on the floor. Some kids' clothes, all pinks and purples, folded in a pile on the floor. Someone had cared a little at some point in time.

On the left side of the bed, there was one of those little rectangle doors that you could pull out of the wall, where it led to a space used for storage, a few feet that unfolded between the trailer siding and the wall. The opening was dark, and there wasn't any blood, but his heart beat loud in his chest as he approached it.

He put his head into the dark. The smell in there was shit. Human shit. He gagged on it, at the collection of feces piled in the corner. And then his eyes moved to the opposite corner.

The cleanest thing he'd seen yet. White ivory bones gleamed at him — dozens of them, stacked in piles.

Human bones, he knew. Big bones.

And feathers the size of sunflower petals, littered everywhere, white as the bones. He reached out and dragged his fingers against one, felt it shiver soft against the soft pads of his fingerprints.

He went back out. Radioed in. Asked for a run on the Ranger tags.

The tags came back to a Spencer Myers, 37-year-old white male. Previous arrests for drugs, DUI, domestics. Current warrants for probation violations and failures to appear.

Who'd you drag into your shit, Spencer? Had to be about drugs. Meth addicts were notorious for violence.

The picked-clean bones, though? How'd that happen? Was it a message? Jake hadn't heard of anything like that round here. More like slash and run, or shoot and run, that's what the locals did. Quick, violent, and bloody.

So, who was the girl, and why leave her?

That was what bothered him, as the horizon lit up with the familiar red and blue lights of the other deputies arriving. Whom did the bones belong to, where had the adults who had been living in this trailer gone, and how did the little girl fit in?

⸹

The little lost girl goes to an older couple for emergency placement. They call her Kate, after their stillborn daughter from decades before. They're quiet Methodist folks. They have no other children. It would be dangerous to place her anywhere else, the social worker whispers. Not without knowing what happened.

Kate sits with her knees pressed together. She is now half of a whole. Half of her left in a flutter of feathers. She still remembers how bones sharpened and carved through skin and muscle to fly free, a blur of snow white wings and bloody droplets. She remembers. She just doesn't talk about it.

She draws pictures. Bird after bird after bird, wings spread, towering over the sheets of construction paper. She wants to be free. Everyone watches her, and she feels restraints drawing tight around her. The dust and the people close in on here and she focuses on the ticking in her mind, the sound of a clock shaving away time. Counting down.

From that foster home she goes to another, and another, and another. She's not really any trouble, but she's not quite right either. She speaks when spoken to. She has school and therapy appointments and updated immunization records. But the silence that surrounds her bulges out at people, increases the pressure in the room. Makes folks uncomfortable. Kate never gets to stay in one place very long. She travels the local foster homes like a salesman, hawking stock no one wants.

Inside her skin, her bones remain formed and solid. There isn't a whisper tiptoeing along the edges. Normal, normal, normal.

There is a boy named Matt who sits next to her in school. He has blond hair that looks soft as the feathers she wants to touch. He doesn't talk much either.

But he watches her draw birds in the margins of her books, watches them soar across the pages of her composition book. When she looks over and catches him, he just looks back. She thinks she might be able to ask him things, but she never can find the words to ask the right way, to properly explain what she means. The ticking never stops long enough to think. Tick-tock, tick-tock.

§

"You can do better than this, Kate," the guidance counselor says. She's thirteen now. She's gotten used to the ticking, the heaviness of her bones stiff and unbending in her body, to the body itself, all female with the heaviness of hips and the fat deposited on her chest. The body is foreign and clumsy and yet people stare at it, men and boys and the occasional woman. She's stuck here, in this dirty, dusty town, held down by her own treacherous form.

She doesn't answer. The counselor, like all adults, will eventually go away. She waits them out, flat-eyed and mute. She's already found booze, how even though the whiskey scorches her throat, it floods her with numbness, makes her feel silk soft feathers tickling insider her skin. Already she can feel saliva flooding her mouth at the thought of it, of sneaking into Matt's dad's stash and drinking fire water together in his room. His mom's never home and his dad's laid off from the plant, all fucked up on pills and booze. They can do whatever they want.

"You ever think about your future, Kate?"

Kate picks at a thread on her frayed shorts. She doesn't answer.

"What are you thinking, Kate?"

About hollow bones, about the sky, about the moon.

The counselor lets her go. They're both going through the motions anyway.

Later, she and Matt are drinking and watching X-Men, when he asks her what her superpower would be. "Flying," she says. "Invisible flying."

⚡

Matt lives just down the road from where they found that messed up trailer with all the bones in it fifteen years ago, when people started going missing. It was big news at the time, for a year or two, but people get used to things. Kate spends most of her time at his place. She doesn't have anyone who really cares where she's at anyways.

Matt loves Kate and Kate knows it, but she doesn't love him back. She isn't quite sure what love is, but she knows it is something other people have, something they hold in their chests and their hearts. There's a tickle of something inside her sometimes, when she curls up against Matt and feels okay, for a moment. Then the shutters close over her heart and she turns to something more familiar. She goes with guys who cheat on her, talk shit about her, call her names. It's easier that way.

Kate and Matt get drunk and talk about the places they'll go. To the ocean. To the city, sparkling lights. Every weekend they sit in his room and watch movies in the dark, drink Natty Light, and talk about who they could be.

Kate drinks a lot more than Matt. She talks about the Spotted Girl when she's drunk.

"One day, she'll come for them," she says. She has nails bitten down to pink flesh that weeps scarlet. "Then, you'll see."

Boys and men go missing around here. Everyone pretends they ran off and they don't talk about the thing that flies at night, wings spread inky on the light of the moon. They don't talk about the curfew that isn't law but that everyone follows. They talk about fuel points at the grocery store and the local ball team, about how bad the meth's gotten, about the dropping price of soybeans.

But not talking won't stop the wings of the night.

"They kept her in a cage," Kate says.

She'll tell how the girl's skin was soft and slick but covered in dark purple spots. Mongolian spots, the girl's mama said. Meth spots, the mama's boyfriend said. And they caged her and fed her scraps, but you couldn't blame them. They were possessed by demon crystal that made nothing matter but the rocks. The rocks they'd start melting in spoons and pulling up in syringes and shooting into veins.

"Meth ain't cheap," Kate will say next. Matt's got the story memorized. They sold the girl. A hole's a hole, no matter what it's surrounded by. And meth doesn't care, it makes your teeth fall out and your skin grow spots. Men ain't picky when that wicked crystal fogs their brains like a windshield, makes everything too sharp and not quite real. Nothing hurts in meth land.

Maybe that's how they missed the way she began to change. The bones under her skin, sliding around, grinding themselves into new shapes and patterns.

"Her shoulder blades split her skin right open," Kate will say.

"Ssshh," he'll tell her then.

The telling hurts. He knows that.

Kate will shake her head and seal her mouth around a bottle, drinking to forget.

She never finishes the story. It always ends with the splitting skin, the carved shoulder blades springing free.

≀

Jake's had women. Single women, women with children, pretty women, hard women, all kinds of women. He's not a bad guy. Not one of his exes complains about him. He was just—absent. He said all the right things and did all the right things, but part of him was always somewhere else.

He's always thinking about that goddamn trailer, full of blood and feathers.

He only forgets when he goes up to the city and gets lost in another place, in five o'clock stubble and flat chests. He goes there to be himself and home to be someone else.

There are places where he could go to be himself, but those places aren't here. Home is home. Even when it hurts.

≀

"I'm a nobody," Kate always says.

And maybe Kate's a nobody, but she doesn't need anyone either. She made herself that way. Every time someone pushed her away, anger burned in her, a hard, hot coal in her chest. I'll never need a fuckin' thing from anyone, she'd whisper to herself. One day, I'll be somebody, and they'll all be sorry.

That's not how it happens, though. Maybe some girls have stories that end like that, but not this one. Kate's just a pretty girl who will fade into a bitter old woman with cracks around her eyes and mouth from her pack-a-day habit, and drink cheap whiskey on the front porch of a shitty rental, wondering if this is the day her cigarette will set fire to her oxygen tank and blow her right out of this world.

She hasn't forgotten the end of the spotted girl's story. How her shoulder blades gleamed ivory and lavender as they emerged. Wings, feathered white, pulling free from her spine, the sound of corn kernels popping in the microwave. The spotted girl, her teeth long rotted out of her mouth, yawing her lips open, gums blood red lined with new teeth of needles bursting through the empty sockets. The new teeth snapping right into the back of the man on Kate, who wasn't Kate then. She doesn't even remember what her name was back then.

The man screamed. Kate doesn't remember his name either, but she recalls his blood hot and wet falling in hard drops on her back. Always face down, because most of them didn't like to see what they were doing. Not in the eyes, anyway.

She'd watched the spotted girl turn to bird of prey with her cheek pinned against her fairy blanket. She never did like fairies after that.

The spotted girl didn't ever have a name. Kate thinks of her now as the huntress, tearing men from limb to limb. Her sister, but not, not really.

When things get too thick to breathe, Kate imagines the ropes of her own DNA shifting. Some trigger pulled that lets the mutation free. She checks her body for spots every day, but the purple she finds are just ordinary bruises. Maybe it's just bitterness inside, rising to the surface.

Kate likes to sit outside late at night, watching shadows. She lives for clear night skies. For a glimpse of widespread wings and blotted out stars. There's hope in the huntress stalking the night.

There's none in the daylight, where Kate watches her life unspool before her. The late nights, the shit jobs, the men, all of it. The dust, the fucking dust everywhere, always. Booze makes things manageable, sands down the sharp edges of living. Makes it go down smooth.

Sometimes she thinks back to the day where that cop, Jake, rescued her. She wonders if she had kept walking, if no one drove by, if she could have walked into another world. If she could have become a fairy tale, the one where the girl was raised by wolves and eventually became one.

Kate watches the Spotted Girl's shadow spread like ink across the moon. She hears the call that sounds like screaming. She can feel her real teeth humming below her gum line—but she can't make them come out.

*

Jake handcuffed Kate the first time in 2019, when she was 16, twelve years after he saw her sitting in the driver's seat of that SUV. He hoped it wasn't her, but the eyes, they were iridescent blue.

The same eyes looking at him as he told her to turn around, put her hands behind her back.

He didn't have a choice. She was high as a kite, pupils ballooning in and out every time she breathed.

Always the goddamn meth.

Always followed by death.

"What's your name, darlin'?" he asked.

"Blow me," she said back.

He cuffed her, pushed her up against the cruiser, but gentle. He asked her for her ID, she refused, and he fished it out of her back pocket, touching her as little as possible. And that's how they meet up over and over. Over five years, he's put her in cuffs probably two dozen times. Always ends up letting her go. She thinks it's because he wants to fuck her. She knows how to work men.

"You're going down the wrong path, honey," he tells her every time he uncuffs her and lets her go. Then he goes home and drinks and thinks about loneliness, and how a woman's the last thing he wants, how every time he's been with one, he's thought about how he doesn't want soft skin but rough stubble against his cheek. That everything soft reminds him of feathers and bones. He wants something different, but you can't want something different when you grow up here and play football. You just can't.

"You want a fuckin' blowjob, or what?" she'll answer, not the same words every time but the same message and he'll look into her eyes, scarred up crystals in her hollow face, and he'll think, yeah, god yeah, I want a blowjob, I want to fuck someone's mouth, but not yours, darling.

"I don't," he tells her every time.

It's fifteen years before he tells her he knew her.

"Why you keep letting me go?" she asks, her eyes so fucking dead it kills off a part of him to look at them.

"I was there that day," he says.

She stands there, letting the wind whip her long, white hair around. He's touched it, put his hand on top of it the way you do when you put someone in the back seat. It's the same as the silk peeled from sweet corn, soft as downy feathers.

"Don't know what you mean," she says at last, but she does. The knowledge sits there between them, vast and impenetrable as the darkness that lives inside her heart. "What do you want from me?"

"Not a damn thing," he says, and he gets back in his cruiser and drives away.

She's just a young woman, he tells himself, lit up by the moonlight in his rearview mirror. But the shiver soft hair under his fingers, the shiver soft feathers at the fucking trailer... Something wrong with her hair the way something was wrong with those fat white feathers. The feel of both of them runs cold along his skin. He can't explain it, but the softness was cold to touch, the kind of cold inside glaciers. Something wrong and different and the memory of the sensation sits in his mind and snows.

⁊

Kate always has Matt. He shows up at jail to bail her out, he picks her up from the bars when she passes out. Everyone in town knows when Kate's in trouble, to call Matt, who will ride to the rescue. He covers her rent sometimes. He borrows trucks to move her from place to place, he listens to her, sometimes he sleeps over.

Then the accident shatters her life. Matt's driving down one night when a drunk driver misses the dividing line and smashes into his little pickup. Kate will have nightmares about it. She can see Matt, hand laid on the horn, blaring a warning. See his arm crumple accordion-like, long bones of the humerus and ulna and radius melting into one gelatinous blob of splinters and marrow bagged together by skin.

It's a closed casket funeral.

If she could see his face.

If she could climb in the coffin and go to sleep next to him.

There is a great big hollow space inside Kate where everything aches. You have lost the only person who ever cared about you, it whispers across the canyons inside. Who are you now?

That night, she drinks and drinks and drinks, but she can't get drunk. She gets high enough to chatter her teeth. She can feel something itching inside her shoulder blades, she can, she can. She uses the shower door to scratch her back, carving bloody ribbons of flesh.

No wings.

Nothing. There is nothing.

There is a blackness that comes rushing up that swallows her whole. Her vision narrows. All she can see is the road ahead in her mind, a whole bunch of days just like this one stretched out in front of her. It isn't that everything sucks so bad now.

It's that it will always be like this.

There is a knife, and blood, and she does it the way you're supposed to, long vertical notches in the elbows instead of horizontal wrist lacerations, and she goes to her bed and curls up and allows herself to fade out.

She sucks even at killing herself. She wakes up to a sheet crusted with blood and clotted blood caked on her skin.

So it goes.

ⸯ

Jake's gut is spilling over his belt. He's gotten fat somewhere along the way. Not noticeable in his legs or arms, but the gut doesn't lie. He stands in the mirror hungover and pinches white flab, watching it ooze between his fingers. He thinks he should have left this town when he was young and strong, when the years of aching and longing hadn't eaten him whole. He could have been someone else, but time waits for no one.

He dresses and leaves the house. The moon is coming out for his graveyard shift. Some towns, that spells doom, but it's quiet around here most nights, unless it's cloudy. And tonight is clear and lit up by pale, washed out moonlight, painting everything dull and shadowy. He might see the winged woman, but she doesn't cross the moon as much anymore. Maybe she's eating less or she's moved on. Maybe she's dying of loneliness somewhere. Being one of a kind must be a desolate, aching existence. But the threat remains, heavy over all of them.

He starts his patrol.

⸘

Kate made a little mistake. Or a big one. She's out of money and out of dope, got this dude to front her a gram of crack. Crack's not her thing, but any port in a storm, or whatever the fuck the saying is. She's blasted, can't hardly speak, which is the problem with crack. Everything loses focus. Meth sharpens things. Now she's jonesing her ass off, looking at the white specks on the floor, wondering if they might be a spare rock, and the guy's giving her shit, telling her he can't do no more credit.

"Come on," she says, tongue thick and heavy, a foreign object immobile in her mouth.

"Gonna have to pay one way or other," he says.

He lets her have a hit, and when she falls back on the couch he turns into an octopus. He covers her and she can feel tentacles pinching and pulling and prodding, kneading the flesh that feels loose on her skeleton. It's the thought of squirting ink that does it, makes her fists clench. She hits him hard, right in the jaw, hears his teeth crack together. The sound tickles something inside her. There's a mass she finds inside, a seething pool of rage, and it starts to boil and rise, little wisps of smoke curling out of her mouth. Her eyes fill with wildfire.

"The fuck's wrong with you?" the dude says. He doesn't have a problem slapping a bitch, but this shit is getting freaky, the curl of drool coming out of her mouth. He hits her closed-fisted and she screams, a sound that cracks across his eardrums and shatters them. It rises and rises, curls up and away, slices across the shitty rundown apartment complex.

Everywhere, people stop, even the tweakers.

⸘

Jake's the first to respond. He's still hungover when he pulls on the scene. There's no screaming, it's silent, and there's a smell. It's copper and burnt crack. Not the same as meth/death smell, but just as likely the same result.

Something comes staggering out of the door. It's the shape and height of a person, but missing pieces. An eye, for sure, and an arm. A large ragged part of its face, torn by serrated teeth. It falls to the concrete, whining with the remnants of vocal cords.

Behind it, he recognizes Kate only by her eyes and hair. Something has happened to her face. It's grown longer and thinner, developed sharp angles coming to a sharp pointed mouth shiny with blood. She's smiling.

Jake gets out. What other choice is there? It was always coming down to this.

"Don't, Kate," he calls. "Honey."

She cocks her head.

"Don't," he says, but it's already too late. There are things in motion that cannot be stopped.

Kate's bones shifting sound like feathers beating. Her heart squeezes faster, faster, faster, as her shoulder blades sharpen. Then the fire of shoulders knifing through skin, the separation of wings from spine, joints separating rapid-fire like a microwave popcorn bag at full heat. Being high pales compared to the feeling of spreading wings for the first time. It's electric and it's buzzing and Kate would throw her head back and shriek, if she had a voice. Instead, she unfurls her wings, spreads them wide.

He aims, but he can't shoot her. He should, and he knows it, but he can't pull the trigger. He lowers his weapon. "Fly away, Kate," he whispers.

She's in motion. Wings spanning four feet each beat winds of fury that blow his thinning hair against his skull. He has to squint as the sounds quickens.

The actual takeoff blasts him to the ground.

He looks up and sees a beautiful shadow spread across the moon. Ink against bone. Then it's blotted out by the white shiver soft feathers falling like rain.

⸙

The Spotted Girl isn't a girl anymore, and she's more bird than woman. She's curled into a soft, snowy ball when she hears the faint cry of another, feels something turn over inside her heart, warming her. She calls back shrill, and hops to her feet. Then she takes flight, until she finds her sister, circling the sky, still clumsy in her new body.

She leads her back to the cave, deep in the shadows. They curl against each other, burying their long beaks under each other's wings.

▬

*Despair*

Boredom       *Trepidation*       Fear

—       —

Tension       Detachment

# 17. The Bully Pulpit

## Ian Rennie

"Where is he?" Senator Dillard demanded, storming through the green room towards the chair of his campaign.

Arianna swallowed. "Seth was here a minute ago. I'm sure—"

"Don't be sure, *find* him!" Senator Dillard snapped, relenting a moment later. "I'm sorry, Arianna. It's a big crowd and I'm feeling superstitious. Could you find my good luck charm and bring him back here, please?"

Arianna smiled. "No problem, boss."

She scoured the backstage area, wondering where the goddamn kid had got to this time. Seth was the sort of pain in the ass who felt duty-bound to disobey any order he was given. Arianna had asked him to stay in the green room of the Johnson City civic centre, so of course he had snuck out.

She found him at the concession stand in the lobby: a lanky early twenty-something who still dressed like a teenager, holding a slushie the size of his head and a steaming container of something yellow.

He grinned as she approached. "Looking for me?"

Arianna grabbed his arm. "The senator goes on in five minutes. Where the hell have you been?"

Seth gestured to his tray. "The concession stand. Obviously."

"There's a catering table in—"

"Does it have nachos?"

Arianna sighed. "Well, no, but—"

"Well, no, and I wanted nachos. What's the problem?"

She grabbed him and stopped dead. "The problem, you goddamn child, is that your employer is losing his mind. If I hadn't found you, he might have cancelled the rally altogether!"

Seth looked down at her hand on his arm. "Cancel the rally? That would be awful, for you."

Arianna frowned. "What?"

"I'd hate the senator to think he couldn't rely on you," Seth replied softly.

Arianna scoffed. "I've been working for Jim Dillard since he was a councilman."

"I know. Twenty years. Sounds like you need a break. The senator asked you for one thing tonight. Just one. If you can't deliver, what then?"

Arianna felt a shiver. Jim Dillard was the main item on her resume. Washington wasn't a kind place for middle-aged women. Or women at all. If the senator walked away, this wasn't a seller's market for her skills. If avoiding that meant placating a prick like this...

"I'm sorry," she said, trying to sound as sincere as possible. "This is a tense day for everyone. The Senator craps on me and it runs downhill. Can you come with me?"

Seth smiled. "No problem. I just need one thing."

"What?"

"Say please."

Arianna gave a nervous laugh. "What did you say?"

"Ask me again," Seth replied. "And say please."

She stared at him, trying to work out if he was serious, not sure how she would respond if he was.

The pause stretched just too long. Finally, Seth grinned. "I'm just messing with you. Where does the senator need me?"

He strode off backstage, leaving Arianna running to keep up. They got to the door of the green room, where he turned to her.

"Oh, and if there's anything you need, Arianna, you only have to ask. Politely."

He dumped the drink and nachos in a trash can and went inside. Arianna followed him, wondering again how she had been saddled with brat duty, and why she was going along with it.

⁂

Senator Dillard took a breath before beginning his wrap-up. "My friends, we are at a pivotal time in our state's history. On the road ahead, I see two different visions of the great state of Franklin."

At the side of the stage, Arianna watched the crowd, gauging how they were taking it: what points landed, what didn't. Minor trims to the speech could be the difference between someone going away satisfied and going away inspired.

"In one vision, this is a fallen state in a fallen country," the senator continued. "Where our children's schools are unsafe from the predation of madmen."

Arianna scanned people's faces. Lines like this could easily go wrong: a kid had brought a rifle to school in Parkersburg six months ago, stopped only by a security guard. This was a hot button, and if Jim pushed it too hard then bad things could happen.

She spotted Seth at the back of the room, also watching the crowd. She still didn't know what the senator paid his "good luck charm" for. He was smart, but not brilliant. He barely contributed at staff meetings. Jim didn't even give him specific duties like he did to the other aides and interns. He just needed Seth at every speech. As Arianna watched, Seth made a small gesture with the index finger of his left hand.

The senator leaned forward. "Our people distrust each other. They see a neighbourhood kid running a lemonade stand and they call the cops. There's no fellow feeling in our towns any more. That's what happens when our leaders pay more attention to their pocketbooks than protecting the vulnerable."

When the senator hit the line about lemonade stands, an African-American couple turned to look at each other with concern. Good. Jim's numbers in the AA community had been soft. Lines like this distinguished him from Lloyd Conville's law-and-order bullshit.

Seth was watching the same couple. He saw her looking and smiled, like this was a shared secret.

"There would be nobody in the state house protecting the people's rights: women's rights, worker's rights, LGBT rights. I see the safety net that protects our families, that protects all families, being taken down because millionaires refuse to pay their fair share for its upkeep. I see doctors who don't say 'How are you?' They say, 'How are you paying?'"

Arianna felt the satisfaction as the line she had written landed. At each talking point, she sought out her bellwethers in the diverse crowd. And each time, she found Seth had beaten her to it. At one point he gave her a little wave.

No, not a wave. A graceful dip of the hand, like he was conducting music.

The senator looked down. "I hate to say it, but this is what I see if Lloyd Conville wins this November and becomes senator for Franklin."

At the back of the room, Seth brought both hands down dramatically.

Arianna found herself thinking about what Lloyd Conville winning would mean for her. The party machine usually rehoused displaced staffers, but Jim Dillard was an ageing outsider unlikely to run again. His cast-offs were low value. If Arianna couldn't get another job, she'd lose her house. Her rat bastard ex would petition for custody of Eloise. Everything that mattered in her life would go away if Jim Dillard weren't returned to Washington.

The senator smiled. "But that's not the future I see for us. I see a better world. You can go to the doctor without a wallet biopsy. Your kids play in the schoolyard instead of running lockdown drills. I see a world where government raises up the *people*, instead of raising money for outside interests. I've spent eighteen years in the Senate fighting for a better world, and I'm still swinging. For you."

As the dark mood passed, Arianna felt uplifted. In the audience's faces she saw rapt attention and something she recognised from herself: the euphoria at the end of fear.

Seth was on his phone, bored with the proceedings, waiting for the senator's pause. He put the phone away and turned his attention back to the crowd.

"Lloyd Conville won't represent you," the senator declared. "He sells his voice to the highest bidder and the people of Franklin have been outbid. In November when you get to the ballot box, ask yourself this: what will Lloyd Conville do for your children? Your healthcare? Your schools? Will you walk with him to a world run by the guy who can write the biggest check?"

Seth focused on the transfixed, nervous audience, hand gestures bigger than before. Then he lowered his hands.

Senator Dillard smiled out at the crowd. "Or will you walk with me to a better world?"

"A better world!" Seth called out from the back of the room. The chant caught quickly, becoming first applause, then ovation. As it caught, Seth slunk out the back of the room.

Arianna had never felt such joy from a campaign crowd. Except... it wasn't *quite* joy. It was the relief of salvation, the doom averted.

Arianna intercepted Seth in the lobby. "What the hell was that? What are you doing?"

"Going to Waffle House," Seth replied. "Want to come? I'll split a pecan waffle with you."

Arianna sighed. "What were you doing back there?"

"My job. And now I'm done and hungry. I didn't get my nachos earlier."

"You were doing something to the audience," Arianna insisted.

"Was I?" Seth asked. "What was I doing?"

"I…" Arianna trailed off. It felt stupid to say out loud, and would hardly do her any favours in the campaign. The auditorium doors opened, and an excited crowd flooded into the lobby.

Seth smiled. "If you come up with anything, let me know. Meantime, I have hash browns waiting."

He walked out, leaving Arianna alone in a full room.

{

"We need to push the jobs issue," Mike Stockton said. "Conville wants to let FState and First Franklin Mutual merge, losing half their admin staff."

Arianna shook her head. "If you bring up jobs he'll mention the John Deere plant he's pushing for in Elizabethton. Manufacturing jobs have more emotional heft than finance ones."

They were meeting in the senator's offices in Greeneville instead of a hotel or a strip mall. Technically this violated some campaign finance law or other, but one of the joys of living in Franklin was that people were a little more relaxed about these things. The picture-stuffed boardroom was a natural location for campaign meetings, even if Mike Stockton and Ted Mignola kept getting lost in campaign nostalgia. The three of them sat around the table with the senator. Seth sprawled on a couch at the back of the room, playing a handheld video game, ears covered with massive headphones.

"There isn't a clear through line on jobs," Ted said. "We should focus on issues where you don't get bogged down in nuance. Healthcare, for example. How much money has Conville's campaign taken from Caduceus this year?"

"If we push too hard on healthcare I'll get pressure from the Left to sign on to Medicare For All," the senator replied.

"That's why this is such a good issue," Ted insisted. "You can clobber Conville on contributions from the insurance industry without taking a position on Medicare."

The senator thought for a moment, then turned towards the couch. "Seth?"

The young man on the couch put down the game and moved back a headphone. Arianna recognised the game from Eloise's collection: a slash-em-up with titans and minotaurs. "You're talking about healthcare?"

"Nice of you to join us," Mike answered. "We're trying to decide if—"

"Go after Holston Valley Medical Center. While Conville was mayor of Kingsport, six patients died at Holston Valley after Caduceus refused to honour their policies. Six patients who should have had coverage."

Arianna shook her head. "We're not using dead bodies as campaign props."

"You don't have to," Seth replied. "Just ask how safe people are in medical systems Lloyd Conville oversees."

The senator looked uncertain. "I don't know. It's pretty dark."

"Yeah? Conville's going onstage in Elizabethton tonight with a woman whose husband was killed by an illegal immigrant driving drunk. He's saying you're complicit in an immigrant crime wave. Does this still sound dark?"

Seth put his headphones back on and returned to his game. There was a long silence. Normally Arianna would have asked Seth how the hell he knew this, but something stopped her. She knew what Seth had said was true, she just didn't know how.

"Go with Holston Valley," the senator said eventually. "Mike, Ted, research the hell out of it so I don't put a foot wrong, but this works. Thanks, everyone."

They left the boardroom, Mike and Ted heading to their laptops, Arianna following Jim back to his office. She knocked on the door frame.

The senator turned from a photo on his wall. "You guys getting into it in the boardroom reminded me of the Fraser campaign. We used to argue policy until four AM, then get Matt Fraser prepped for morning TV."

Arianna smiled. "Before my time. Got a minute?"

The senator settled into his chair. "I have some Appropriations committee papers to read, but I can spare five minutes. What's up?"

Arianna closed the door behind her and sat opposite. "This will sound paranoid."

"You're my chief of staff. It's your job to sound paranoid."

"*Was* your chief of staff," she replied. "I stepped down to run your campaign, remember?"

"Well, your seat's being kept warm. What's on your mind?"

"I'm worried about Seth."

The senator looked up. "Worried how?"

"I didn't vet him. I don't know where he came from. I don't trust him."

"Don't hold back, Arianna," the senator said with a half-laugh. "Tell me how you really feel."

Arianna sighed. "Halfway through September, this kid turns up in the middle of my campaign. A month later he has your ear more than I do. He comes and goes as he pleases, but if he's not there for your speeches your staff catch hell. Who is he?"

Jim Dillard stared at her and Arianna could see a steel and anger in his eyes she hadn't seen before. "First of all, this is *my* campaign. And I will run it how I like. That includes decisions on who I hire and who I fire. Is that clear?"

The force behind the words almost made her recoil. "I wasn't suggesting—"

"Secondly, he's a good kid who gives good advice. I don't know what you're insinuating but I know I don't like it. Arianna, I ask for your candour so I can see when I'm making a mistake, not so you can bring me every piece of paranoia you think up. I expect better if you're hoping to be my chief of staff again."

The threat was clear, cold and abrupt. There wasn't a way to continue this conversation and keep working for Jim Dillard. "I understand."

"Good," the senator answered. "Now, I've got some reading to do, and we need to prep for the rally at the performing arts center tonight. Don't let me keep you."

Arianna stood up to leave. As she did so, she realised that she'd been mistaken earlier. The look in the senator's eyes wasn't anger.

It was fear.

❧

"Family is the most important thing in the world to me, my friends," the senator said, stepping away from the podium, microphone in hand. "Looking round this room, I know how important it is to you too. You wouldn't let your Mom buy a car with a bad accident history, would you? When your son goes to college, you research the school first before he applies. The same goes when a loved one goes to the hospital. The same goes when you send a man to Washington."

Arianna half-watched the audience, knowing what she would see there. The same fear and excitement she had seen in Johnson City. The same unease that ate at the pit of her stomach.

The senator paced the stage. "We can only go by the facts, and the facts tell us six people died at Holston Valley while Lloyd Conville was mayor of Kingsport. Not for medical reasons, but financial ones. They died because of complications from a too—light wallet."

The tension grew. At the back, Seth's hands danced: he was entirely engaged this time. Arianna worked out where she knew his gestures from. They were something like a conductor's, but even more like one of the DJs that Eloise was currently obsessed with, letting a piece of music build towards maximum tension before the drop.

Sensing her looking, Seth turned and locked eyes with her for a moment. He winked, then gestured towards the stage. She shuddered, sensing the people pressed around her and feeling suddenly claustrophobic.

"I don't know how much Lloyd Conville knew," Jim continued on stage, "but I know how long he's spent not answering these questions. Do you want a man in Washington who dodges questions like this, or do you want a better world?"

Still looking at Arianna, Seth gestured to the crowd, who chorused "A better world!"

The senator cupped a hand around his ear. "I can't hear you, what do you want?"

"A better world!" the crowd shouted, the tension releasing as frenzy.

"And in November, what are you going to vote for?"

"A better world!"

Seth broke eye contact and walked away. Arianna looked around the crowd and didn't recognise them. She had run town halls for Jim Dillard for years and they were sedate affairs that ended with polite applause. This was something else entirely.

The senator was right. This wasn't her campaign.

‡

Arianna knew she should be asleep in her own king-sized bed, with Egyptian cotton sheets in an air conditioned room. Instead she was going through campaign documents in her Greeneville office at four AM because a voice in her head kept saying something wasn't right.

Seth Hall had almost no digital footprint, in the campaign or outside of it. He wasn't officially on staff: instead there was a stipend in "misc. expenses" to a company called AH Consulting, paying out for the last two months. All that this listed was "Asaph Hall services". The name rang a bell deep in her memory.

All of a sudden she wondered what she was doing here. It was the middle of the night and she was snooping on campaign records, looking into the backgrounds of coworkers. If she had a problem with Seth she should speak to him about it. Or to Jim directly. Except she knew if she did that she'd be leaving the campaign with only the tatters of her reputation. Maybe she should let this lie.

She clenched a fist. No. This was crap. There was something wrong with Seth, something wrong in the campaign, and she either had to fix it, or get the hell out of there. She wouldn't give in to irrational fear.

Except... she had. They all had. She had been constantly afraid for the last month, a fear that was infecting the campaign and their audience. And each time she'd felt it, Seth had been there.

Arianna got up to get a bottle of water, wandering down the half-lit corridor. She stopped for a moment by a picture from the Fraser campaign: an impossibly young Jim Dillard in a group of congressional staffers. And in the background...

She blinked, sure she was losing it, having a waking dream.

At the back of the twenty-five-year-old photo, giving the same insolent, lazy grin, stood Seth Hall.

‽

Arianna didn't see Seth for a couple of days. He wasn't around for TV spots, or for the grip-and-grin sessions in Jonesborough and Fayetteville. However, she was pretty sure he'd be there for the town hall meeting in Gatlinburg. She'd spent the days in between researching, digging things up, trying and failing to convince herself that she was wrong. She turned up at the Gatlinburg venue early and spotted Seth getting out of a beaten up Nissan Stanza in the parking lot.

"Want to split that pecan waffle?" she asked, walking over to his car.

He looked up. "You know what you're accusing me of this time?"

"More than I did before. There's a coffee shop in the lobby. I'm buying, if that helps."

The coffee shop was more a grab and go place than a diner, but there were tables, and loud enough music that they wouldn't be overheard. Once they had ordered, Arianna nabbed a booth and gestured to Seth to sit opposite.

"How long have you been with the campaign, Seth?" she asked.

He shrugged. "A month? Two? I thought you guys kept track of that sort of thing."

She ignored the last part. "Well, every moment you've been with the campaign I've been afraid."

He raised an eyebrow. "Am I that intimidating?"

"No," she replied. "You're a punk kid with a big mouth. You say obvious things and think they're profound, just like all of us did when we were greenhorns. So why does talking to you give me a panic attack?"

"If you think you have a crush on me—"

"Cut the shit," Arianna snapped. "You're not that cute and neither's your act. I've watched you with staffers and audiences. If I didn't know better, I'd say you could control people's fear."

Seth sighed. "You know, Jim's worried about you. He thinks you're overworked. After hearing this I think he might be right."

"Does overwork explain this?" She reached into her bag and slid a photo across the table. "Staffers from Matthew Fraser's 1994 congressional campaign. You wouldn't have been born when this picture was taken. Except you're in it. In a photo that was taken right when the Fraser campaign started to go negative hard."

Seth didn't say anything. He studied the photo with his perpetual half-smile.

To fill the silence, Arianna kept talking. "And then there's your name. I couldn't find anything on Seth Hall. Asaph Hall, on the other hand..."

Seth held his hands up. "You've got me. I'm a nineteenth century astronomer. Don't call the cops, I'll come quietly."

Arianna kept his gaze. "Asaph Hall was most famous for discovering the moons of Mars. Phobos and Deimos. The Greek gods of fear and terror. Funny thing to name a couple of moons after."

There was a long pause after this. On Arianna's side, the pause was because the next thing she would have to say was entirely insane.

As the silence lengthened the grin slowly melted off Seth's face, until his expression was cold and neutral. "What do you want?"

"I want to know what you are."

"You really don't." He paused. "Let's just pretend you're right for a minute. I scare people. It's something I can do."

Arianna closed her eyes. "You're not trying to tell me you're —"

"I'm not trying anything. I've got a particular skill set and I'm trying to apply it outside my field. How does that sound?"

"It sounds like bullshit."

Seth nodded. "Is it bullshit you can accept? For now?"

Arianna thought for a moment. "Why are you working for the senator? Why were you working for Fraser?"

He took a sip of his coffee. "Because it's easy. Because it keeps me under the radar. Because people are simple."

"Simple?"

"I used to be a salesman. It was easy work and stopped me getting noticed."

"Noticed by whom?"

He ignored her. "Nothing sells better than fear. You buy a wonder mop because you're afraid of the neighbours seeing your dirty floor. You buy a tailored suit because you're afraid the promotion will go to someone who doesn't dress like a slob. You buy a house in the suburbs because you're afraid of your kids walking home in the inner city."

Arianna snorted. "That's a very old-fashioned attitude."

"Is it?" Seth asked. "I lose track. In any case, fear sells. And in politics you sell to rooms at a time."

Arianna clenched her fists. "Not here, you don't."

"Why not?"

"Because what fear sells is fear," Arianna replied. "If that was you in the photo, then you won Matt Fraser his congressional seat, but you changed who he was. The man you put in office in 1994 was terrified of losing. He stopped working to make a difference and started working to keep his job, which is why he was out on his ass in 1996."

Seth looked down at his coffee. "I don't follow politics."

"You don't..." Arianna stopped herself. "The point is that I can see you doing the same to Jim. I won't let you ruin another man for fun."

"Fun?" Seth looked at her. "You think any of this is fun to me? I was a primal force: the horror of war. Anywhere a man drew a blade against another, I was there. Anywhere a daughter shed tears on hearing her father's fate, I was there. I was the whisper in the market, the lie in the newspaper, the shadow in the trenches: now I'm..." he checked himself. "I admire your guts, but a word from me and Senator Dillard would leave you in the dirt."

"He would," Arianna agreed. "And then I'd go to the press. With the photos from the Fraser campaign. With every secret I've stored away for a rainy day. The papers wouldn't touch it, but you bet your ass the news sites would. Four weeks out from election day. Your picture everywhere from Five Thirty Eight to the Drudge Report. That would suck for someone trying not to get noticed."

Seth looked at her appraisingly. She stared back, daring him to do his worst.

Finally, he looked away. "As fun as that sounds, I'm going to have to say no to your war. I've had a better offer."

"What kind of offer?"

Seth shook his head. "Nothing for you to worry about. Something closer to my original field. I was going to finish the campaign before I went, but you're right: Jim Dillard is a better man under your guidance than mine." He stood up.

"Where are you going?" Arianna asked.

"Away. I don't do notice periods. If you want to take control of the campaign, tell the senator you fired me." He walked towards the door.

"Wait," Arianna called after him. "You worked on the Fraser campaign with Jim. Why didn't he recognise you?"

Seth shrugged. "My people sit lightly in the memory. It'll be the same this time, too. After a while I'll be little more than a myth."

With that, he was gone, leaving nothing but a fading memory.

≀

"How's the crowd?" Senator Dillard asked as Arianna walked into his dressing room.

She handed the senator a bottle of water. "Bustling. Positive. There's a guy in the line who I'm fairly sure is a cop: he's got his arms folded like he won't believe a word you're saying, but your extra officers pledge will turn him round."

"Good, ah..." he scratched his chin. "Have you seen Seth yet tonight?"

Arianna sighed and closed the door. "Seth won't be here. I fired him."

The senator was out of his chair in a second. "You did *what*?"

She stood her ground. "I saw him using a staff laptop in Greeneville. When I logged onto it after him there was... compromising material on there."

The senator's anger was joined by confusion. "What kind of —"

"The kind of things that might sink a campaign if a journalist found an unlocked staff laptop. I don't think Seth was looking at this stuff, I think he was planting it there. Trust me: you're better off not knowing more than that. All you need to know is that it's handled. All records of him working here are gone, and him with them."

"Do you know who he was working for?" the senator asked.

Arianna shook her head. "He wouldn't say. If we'd handed over him and the laptop to the police they might have found something, but their findings would be the lead story just before the election. I had enough to make him disappear. Once he was gone I destroyed the hard drive."

"Oh," Jim Dillard said, looking shaken. "Thank you."

"It's what I'm here for. That, and giving you your revised stump speech."

"Revised?"

"Minor retooling," Arianna assured him, handing over a thin sheaf of paper. "Keeping us on the sunny side. We could keep the version Seth worked on, but..."

The senator looked worried. "No, I'm happy to look over your revisions. I'll let you know what I think."

"You do that. You're on in thirty."

Arianna stepped out of the dressing room, overcome with relief. Jim had bought it. The campaign was back on track.

As she walked back to her desk, a thought struck her:

*Of course he bought it. Nothing sells better than fear.*

On a warm October evening in Franklin State, Arianna suddenly felt cold.

---

## Fear

Despair         Detachment         Awe

Trepidation                              Lust

# Coda

# 18. The Bureau of
# Sinful and Emotional Gods

## David A. Gray

You can tell a lot about a person by the way they knock on a god's door. The fact that they knock at *all* says they need something real bad. After that, it's a question of how much they can pay, and whether it's worth the trouble for The Bureau of Sinful and Emotional Gods to take the case.

The person responsible for the persistent rat-tat-tat-tat on the other side of the frosted panel must have seen the words "The God of Awe" stenciled large in gold foil, so was either in great need, or possessed of a remarkable lack of caution. And clearly wasn't nursing a vicious ambrosia hangover like me.

"Enough!" I mumbled. "Stop that damnable noise and come in!"

I surveyed my office through gummy eyes that had only been open for ten seconds. Judging by the drool, I'd been sleeping facedown on my desk. Add the footprints on the desktop, and the fact that the items usually arranged there to give a calculated impression of smarts, success and godliness were scattered around the floor, and it was clear someone had been dancing on the furniture.

I gathered myself, remembering that a god has a reputation to uphold and, with difficulty, summoned some awe around me as the door opened. I needn't have bothered.

The kid was a shambling mess of dirt, decomposing clothes and gently writhing tendrils. A thumb-thick root trailed from the back of his neck, out the door, and down the hallway. A Gaia junkie. The host got a bio-narcotic buzz, and a shared consciousness, while the mother plant was granted sentience, a nice source of nutrients, and in the end, a new tree. They didn't usually come out of their groves. And they were pretty resistant to divine powers.

The kid shuffled to a halt and stared at me out of the eye not filmed over with threadlike wriggling roots.

"You're an awe god?" he burbled.

"I'm not *an* Awe god; I'm *the* Awe God. My proper title is The God of Awe. Emphasis on the *The*."

Pedantic, I know, but when you have a pestilence of new gods running around, it's important to keep your brand clear.

"We wish to engage you," he said mushily, in formal tones that suggested it was Gaia herself speaking through him. I sat up a little, and despite my headache, dialed up my awe, just in case. Gaia was a deity of a kind, and had access to a load of buried treasures, so would be a welcome client. And we always needed paying cases.

"Well, let's discuss the details before..."

"When you solve the Magic Eightball case, you must use this wish..."

There was some clumsy rooting around, and a grubby slip of folded paper was handed over.

"I don't have a Magic Eightball case," I said smoothly, and dishonestly.

"Don't lie to us, Mister Awe. You will continue working on the case, but when you find the Eightball, you will substitute this wish for the one your client gives you."

"Like I said, I don't ..."

The plasticky jingle of a large bag landing on my desk got my attention.

I raised an eyebrow.

"250 terabytes. A down payment. The same will come your way again once the job is complete."

I lowered my eyebrow, taking care not to appear impressed. 500T was a respectable fortune in flash memory cards. Not that anyone used the cards for their original purpose anymore: the Undoing put an end to computers, along with cellphones, electric motors, internal combustion engines, and almost everything else tech-related. And most laws of physics. But in a world where it rains miracles and hails curses, folks need a currency that's finite, and impossible to replicate in these post-industrial times. So there I was, a new deity being paid in obsolete memory chips by a sentient plant.

I was weighing up how to refuse Gaia without getting a 500T bounty on my head, when the kid tottered backwards through the door, tugged by the obscenely twitching root cable.

"Do not let us down, Mister Awe. You have accepted payment and we take deal breaking very seriously."

"That's The God of Awe. And I didn't officially ..."

The door shut with a bang.

I decided to go see Lizzie. She's my business partner, and the brains of the outfit. To be accurate there are a dozen business partners – us new gods are smarter than the old ones, and banded together pretty fast. But me and Lizzie, our powers work well together, so we usually double up. I'm Awe, Lizzie is Lust. I'm an Emotion God and she's a Sin God, and one of the most powerful of that lot too. Once Lizzie has turned the lust amplifier up to 11, there's not a living man, woman or near-hume that can resist. And damn few supernaturals, either.

Lizzie had bailed on the party early last night, saying we needed to work in the morning. I recalled laughing at her. I wasn't laughing now.

I stepped into the wood-paneled reception. Marge was perched on her clanky old manual typewriter, and shot me a bored glance. I knew the logic behind hiring a harpy as office manager: no mortal could stand the wash of a dozen different godlike powers wafting from the offices around the reception. Not if you wanted bills to be sent, accounts to add up, and lunch expenses to be managed. And harpies are so caustic that even us gods tread warily around them. But I wasn't convinced she needed to be quite so scornful *all* of the time.

"You let a Gaia junkie in?" I demanded.

"If I stopped every weirdo at the door, you'd never see a client," the aged harpy crowed. I glowered but stayed quiet.

"Lizzie was here. She left a message," Marge added, shedding an oily feather as she hit the carriage return on the antique.

"She said, when you woke up and scraped your face off your desk, to tell you to go meet The Monkey King on his pleasure barge at south seaport. He wants your update on the Magic Eightball case. In person."

"The update is there's no update."

Marge cackled: "Who's the one who boasted he was an old hand at Eightball cases? That this would be – and I quote – 'a piece of cake'? Maybe you can take your trophy Eightball with you and tell him the story of how you defeated a High Angel in hand to hand combat to win it. Again."

There's no point getting in an insult contest with a harpy. It's what they live for. Also, she had a point. It was my big mouth that got us into this case. Magic Eightballs appeared once a decade or ten. You remember the pre-Undoing toy, the black sphere you shook and asked a question to? It's like that, but the answer is always "It is certain". No matter *what* you ask for, so long as your question is six words exactly. They only work once, then vanish. Wars have been fought over them. And yeah, I have one on my desk, that I hit the angel over the head with, denting the heavy ball, and busting it in the process. Which was good news all round, as angels are nuts. Its only use now was as a valuable conversation piece. And it was currently rolled under the furniture somewhere thanks to my drunken dancing.

We were on a retainer from The Monkey King, whose sources had told him the next Eightball would appear in the New Manhattan area some time soon. The King – Louey the 15th, he likes to be called, but nobody does unless he's within earshot – came out of the Undoing as a proper animal deity, with the power to perform minor miracles and hurl lightning. But he also became a tiny wizened ape. And he did well, recruiting thousands of newly sentient simians and non-ape hairy things to do his dirty work, and getting his nimble digits into every pie for a hundred leagues. Deep down though, he was still vinegary about being a minuscule monkey. And he thought an Eightball would be the solution. Louey doesn't take failure well, and I wasn't in the mood to be tenderized by a brace of silverbacks.

"Is that it?" I asked Marge gloomily.

"No, that's not it, lunkhead. When she found you lying on your big fat face, she was none too pleased."

Lizzie wasn't much taller than where my belly button used to be before I woke up a god and found it missing, replaced by an extra foot of height, 200lbs more muscle and shoulders you could seat a dozen people at for dinner. But there's not a deity in the agency who'd be dumb enough to cross her. Such as by lying drooling on their desk when they were meant to be working.

"Did she say where she was headed?"

"She made a point of not saying, but I know it wasn't Old Times Square: she was cursing about being there early this morning."

I sighed and fetched my greatcoat from my office. It's an impressive piece of tailoring, and looks impressive when my awe is up and a gust of wind billows it. Also, it has lots of pockets to keep useful stuff in. I hefted it, felt a dozen useful tools and weapons clink or rattle, and slipped it on like armor. I reached down both sides and felt the smooth heavy butts of Plan B and Plan C. Plan A is my godly awe. Backup plans are a pair of monstrous silver-chased steel and mahogany blackpowder pistols that take an eternity to load, but fire vintage ball bearings as big as plums. They represent the maximum tech that mostly works, now, and I love them dearly. I squared my shoulders and smiled.

Now I could face the day, and kick its ass. Hell, I was even in awe of myself, a little, though not literally: us emotion gods have the weird quirk of not being able to experience the very emotion that we exude. So I was pretty hard to impress.

Marge waited until I was almost out the door before shouting.

"She said you better bring her some real chocolate!"

"That stuff's rarer than even Magic Eightballs!"

"Not to a big-shot god like you, surely?"

I was washed out the door by Marge's evil guffaws.

It was true, though. For all the world is awash in gods and miracles, there's an absence of people actually *making* things. You get a toothache, you go see a Tooth Fairy, who will remove it and give you a 50kb as payment. But a tube of genuine pre-U toothpaste? Those go for around 10megs for the sample size. And real chocolate? Forget about it.

I took the stairs down to street level, to collect my thoughts before I stepped outside into the usual madness. Lizzie wasn't usually an early riser, and I happened to know she hated Old Times Square. And yet she'd been there. And not told me.

"This day's turning out to be a real piece of..." I started to say as I stepped out of our building into the bustling madness of a typical post-Undoing lunchtime. Humes, post-humes, demi-humes, pre-humes and hume-hybrids rubbed shoulders with bio-cyborgs, deities and fantastical creatures, without so much as a shrug.

"Not for me. For me it's a piece of shinola," a voice grated in my ear, and something hard poked into my ribs. There was an overpowering smell of lavender, with a low note of something sickly sweet. I made a calculated guess.

"The undead-ish are into muggings now? Wait 'til the boss hears: you'll be on ghoul duty in the cemetery."

"Shut your yap, you big tub o' lard! Walk ahead of me, and don't try anything cute, like reaching for your museum piece pistols."

I didn't move, but neither did I try anything. Minor gods like me are hard to kill, but a gut stab would still hurt for a while, and I didn't want to find out what a follow-up to the head would feel like. I couldn't awe him much, either: where there's little life, there's little capacity for feeling.

Anyways, I was curious. The undead-ish are an insular lot, and don't hassle the living unless there are orders from the top. They have waste disposal and pest control contracts with the city, which covers almost everything from catching and releasing feral devils and exterminating rat king nests, through to running thousands of gallons of waste over to the hellmouth in The Bronx. And boy, do they hate the z word.

"So why would a nice well-behaved zombie like you be dumb enough to mess with a god?" I asked reasonably.

That did it. He stepped back, furious, and I got a look at the blade. That turned out to be a gun. The pistol was one of those magnetic slug throwers the dwarves made, and the wizards laid some magic on, to encourage the anti-tech laws of physics to look the other way for a second. Nasty. And expensive. The character holding it was typical undead-ish: gray around the extremities, with a variety of band-aids applied to try and stave off the inevitable. Rheumy eyes, thin lips, and a suit that must have been sharp 100 years and 100lbs ago.

This was all wasting my time. I chopped his wrist with the heel of my hand. It made a noise like breaking twigs and the gun clattered across the pavement. Before he could retrieve it, I slapped him across the face, openhanded both times, and medium hard. The kind of slap that would rattle a man's teeth and bring tears to his eyes. If he had tear ducts. Which he didn't. But a few yellow molars flew out.

A crowd started to gather, and I exuded some medium-level awe, that encouraged profound admiration. The effect radiated out in circles, widening eyes and making mouths into O shapes. This would be an "and then the God of Awe did ..." anecdote that would do my rep no harm at all.

"Start talking, Crumbles," I grated, grabbing the undead-ish by his lapels and shaking him like a dog with a desiccated rat.

"I was just delivering a message, I swear!" he burbled. "From Mr. Formaldehyde!"

"And the cherub mail isn't good enough for Mr. Formaldehyde? A moldering two-bit hitman is better?"

I stopped shaking the bozo, as bits of him were coming loose. Mr Formaldehyde was the undead-ish boss, and a big deal in non-living *and* living circles. I kinda liked him and his crypt-dry sense of humor.

"He said I was to make sure you got the importance of the message. Seeing as how it involves your partner."

I reached for him again, intending to shake his head off his shoulders, but he chattered fast.

"We have her. She's safe, and unharmed, but if you want her to stay that way, you best do as the boss wants."

When I spoke, it was with the kind of voice that promises awe followed soon after by pain.

"Which is...?"

"You just have to make sure the boss's wish is the one the Magic Eightball grants. Say it first, and he'll let your partner go and pay 1000T! I'm coming with you to make sure you don't welch on the deal."

"What is it with everybody thinking I know where the damned Eightball is?"

My moldering friend shrugged with a crackling noise.

"Your partner told everybody you would find it before anyone else..."

I thought fast, which in honesty isn't all that quick. After a pause long enough that the creep started edging away, I had a plan. Not a good one, or even a complete one, but it was still a plan.

"You're coming with me, Crumbles."

"That was *my* plan," he groused. "You didn't need to slap me around."

"I totally did. And I'll do it again if you point that peashooter at me."

I ambled over to his fallen gun, picked it up, and handed it right back to him.

Magnanimous, right? The folks watching thought so. But Crumbles here was like all the undead-ish: *very* keen not to become properly posthumous, and so long as he was with me I had a connection to his outfit, and could keep an eye on him. And people say I'm not so smart.

"So where have you got Lizzie stashed? Where did you *think* you were taking me?"

"Dunno," Crumbles muttered huffily.

I raised a hand and he drew back.

"Stop with the hitting! They're up at the park, waiting."

I wanted to go there fast, but if Crumbles had been expecting to take me, it seemed dumb to go without an advantage. And I needed to know what Lizzie had been after up in Midtown.

"We're going there *after* Old Times Square."

Crumbles looked distraught: "But she's in the park..."

"You want another slap?"

"You sure you're not the god of bullying?"

He was right, but right now I'd have slapped my way through every zombie in town to get to Lizzie. Only, they wanted me to go running to save her, and that meant a trap. If I'd had time I'd have gone back up and seen who was around to give me a hand: Misery liked a rumble, and Hatred and Tension were also handy to have around. Crap.

We caught a cab, and I paid the driver in awe, winding it up tight around her so it would last a few days, ensuring great rides and monumental tips. And that she was my biggest and most vocal fan all the while. Cabbies are newbs: folks that for whatever reason pop into existence whole, adult, and confused. They mostly claim to be from the past, but within a few minutes, forget all that and just want a job and a place to sleep. The cabs are wind-up: big coiled copper springs in the back are tightened by a hulking team of trolls, and a flywheel keeps it all moving. Weird, but fast. We got to Old Times Square with only one near-death(ish) experience with a camel train.

There's no place like Old Times Square. The nostalgics that flock there sustain a showy kind of magic that keeps the huge signs strobing. Folks shop, trade, argue and pretend the world is all right for a little while. I didn't know what I was looking for, and I'm not the biggest thinker, so decided to play to my strengths. I told Crumbles to keep quiet, and focused hard, feeling the awe stir and seethe and finally bubble up like a volcano.

"I am The God of Awe!" I roared into the perpetual night that reigned here. I have a voice a parade sergeant major would have died for, and people stopped, stared, and wept. Real awe will buckle your knees, tremble your chest, and loosen your bladder. I went up to six out of ten.

"Who among you saw The God of Lust early today?"

When you're full of awe, you can't lie or hide stuff. I saw hundreds of faces, eager to please me, and distraught at the notion they might let me down.

I laid it on thicker still, and an antiques stallholder raised a trembling hand.

"Sir... I did... she was here at dawn looking to buy something..."

This was good. I stepped forwards, building up the awe on the old lady, when something hard rattled off the back of my head.

A cacophony of angry voices reached me.

"False god!" "Begone!" "Back to Hell, you fiend!"

I turned with a sigh. Jesuses. A score of them. Great.

The tattered mob swept around me like a dirty linen tide, trying to cast me out.

"Beat it," I growled, sweeping back my coat to show Plans B and C. Plan A was still in full flow, but making these bearded loons even more in awe of me would have stir up self-hate in them, which combined with the permanent crowns of thorns that grew from and out of their heads, kinda canceled the effect. I wasn't about to actually shoot one of these madmen: a god has standards, but I was resigned to a comedy fistfight, when I caught sight of a big Buddha half a block away. He was drunk as a skunk, and so I lashed out with my power, whipping up a storm of awe around fatty like none he'd ever seen before. People turned in their hundreds, and he glowed with surprised, tipsy delight. The Jesuses noticed, too, and turned on the hapless Buddha. In the rush to set upon him, they pushed over the stallholder and her wares, and started a small riot.

I pushed through the brawling crowd, Crumbles following me like a thin, decomposing shadow. I thought Buddha would be all right: these big guys look fat but it's mostly muscle under it. I picked my way carefully over the wrecked stall. There was some good stuff: wind-up Rolex watches, Polaroid cameras, an old-style gangster machine gun that looked cool but would only work in a few hi-tech zones, and more. Random junk from before. Worth a fair amount now. I wanted to ask the stallholder what Lizzie was after, but she was gone in the press.

I nearly turned my ankle on a black sphere, and grunted, picking it up.

"Whaddya know, Crumbles? A Magic Eightball!"

It was in good condition: black, shiny, a pre-Undoing gem. Probably worth a meg or two. Shame that it was utterly useless and unconvincing to someone like me, who's seen the real thing close up. Still, I could have some fun with it.

"Make Crumbles into a real boy," I grated, and shook it.

Crumbles stopped dead, and hope and suspicion chased each other across his sharp cheekbones.

I looked in the little window and showed it to my zombie hitman.

*Very doubtful.*

He hissed in embarrassment and loathing, and I saw his hand twitch to his little gun.

"Try it and I'll be asking the Eightball whether you should be fish food or a sewer gator's amuse-bouche."

I threw the cheap plastic novelty into the knot of Jesuses. Hard. And laughed when it took one down.

"How did a shit like you get to be a god?" Crumbles muttered. Fair question, I thought. But the Undoing had been as capricious as it was sudden.

We took the subway up to the edge of the park. Not my first choice, but a diamond rain was starting, and though I'm pretty thick skinned, I didn't want to mess up my coat.

The nightbreed have got the subway working again, in parts, and those bloodsuckers owed me one. They grudgingly let Crumbles come with me: vamps and zombies aren't really good mixers.

The ride was short and uneventful, and I entertained the car full of assorted weirdos with a dose of awe that made me appear positively heroic, and even rubbed off on Crumbles a little. He looked uneasy at being looked at with anything other than disgust, for a change, but I think he liked it.

The park. If the new world is an asylum, and cities like N-NYC are the dangerous lunatics' wards, places like Central Park are the padded cells where the straitjacket cases are hidden away. Except greener. It's a mélange of the best and worst of human nature, a nature lover's wet dream, a dystopian nightmare and a hundred other things shaped by millions of people's twisted dreams and nightmares. I like the place, because anything freaky can seem believable, and that applies extra to us minor gods: it's like an energy boost. But it's a dangerous place, because it attracts all kinds of unsavory deities and supernaturals, and the humes who follow them.

And I was worried about Lizzie going there, though: she's a Sin, and a big deal, but that's less effective where there are lots of things so far removed from hume that she doesn't even have anything to work with. Same goes for me, for sure, but I'm 300lbs with three plans.

"Where to?" I prodded Crumbles with a forefinger and he stumbled a little and shot me a look of pure hate.

"The reservoir," he mumbled. "Your partner said that's where it is."

Something came to me that I should have thought of earlier, if I hadn't been so focused on rescuing Lizzie. And had been a little smarter.

"So why do you need *me*? What can I do that the God of Lust and a legion of your coffin-dodgers can't handle?"

Crumbles just shrugged. "I was told to bring you, is all I know."

Clearly I wasn't about to get anything more from my sullen companion, so worked on a new plan. So far as I figured it, the Eightball was maybe somewhere hard to get, that only a tough god like me could retrieve it. I felt for Plans B and C, and did some mental calculations as to how I should shoot Mr. Formaldehyde first, then me and Lizzie could skedaddle, and lose his legion of zombies. I shouldn't have wasted my brain cells planning.

I let Crumbles lead the way, with a casual mention that if this was an ambush, he'd be whistling through a head-sized hole in his sternum. I made sure to check all around, as the park was tricksy in the extreme. By the time we were close to the reservoir we'd faced down a troupe of thin-lipped wood elves, a clockwork robot and a soul-stealing phantom that made the mistake of drifting through Crumbles, and fled, howling. The sky was blueish, with a floating island way up, and a school of slowly drifting men o'war passing with the gentle breeze, alert for loud noise below that might signal prey.

We crested a low rise and were looking into a natural amphitheater whose backdrop was the roiling water of the reservoir. The topmost turret of Camelot stuck crookedly out of the waves; a raised middle finger to the world.

Down in the middle, on the mossy raised stage area, was Lizzie. And Mr. Formaldehyde. Plus a score and more of undead-ish, armed with everything from stout sticks to swords and a few bolt-throwers.

"Quick march, Crumbles," I grated.

To my surprise, the only person pleased to see me was Mr. Formaldehyde. The zombies looked agitated, and Lizzie looked apoplectic, as far as someone with their wrists tied behind their backs and a grubby looking gag in their mouth could. She looked otherwise well, though I suddenly had the feeling my plan had come to an end. I did what I always do when out of ideas: I walked right into the middle of the action.

"Just in time, Awlly," the chief zombie rasped.

I pointed at Lizzie but was looking at Formaldehyde.

"You've all of one second to remove that gag."

"Of course, of course. It was merely to deter the impressive lust god here from shouting. She has been most uncooperative."

He nodded and a lackey pulled the gag off, nearly losing a finger.

"You idiot!" Lizzie yelled at me. "What are you doing here?"

"You see what I mean? If it helps, we can replace the gag," Formaldehyde whispered.

"You do, and you'll be getting Plan B up your dry ass," I whispered back.

I turned to Lizzie again, whose attempt to kick me was thankfully thwarted by two undead-ish minders.

Formaldehyde raised his hands.

"I believe Mizz Lust is worried about what we must ask of you today, Awlly."

"Which is?"

"We need you to retrieve the Magic Eightball, if you please."

He gestured across the lake, pointing to the turret 100 yards away.

"We are not, ahem, well suited to swimming. And we do not trust Mizz Lust to retrieve it and give it to us."

"You moldering son of a ..." Lizzie muttered. At the same time, she gave me a Look. The capital is because Lizzie and me have a kind of shorthand: when I'm slow to get whatever she's up to, which is always, she looks at me in a pointed manner, and I go along with whatever she says, until such time as I do catch up.

"Look, Awlly will go get it, ok? Untie me, though: we need to talk. Or no deal."

Formaldehyde motioned, and a moment later Lizzie was free, and rubbing her wrists as she leaned in and talked in a low voice.

"Okay, so these assholes ..."

"Bear in mind, Mizz Lust, that we possess good hearing."

"...so these assholes who happen to be clients, need the Eightball retrieved from Arthur."

I frowned. "And that's it?"

The Look. Meant no questions. I sighed.

"Yes, that's it. So strip, big man. Hand me your clothes to look after."

I reluctantly handed over my coat (and plans B and C), which Lizzie carefully folded and placed on the grass, then my shirt, pants and socks boots, which she kicked into a heap. I kept on my underwear, of course: some kinds of awe are private. I couple of the lady undead-ish and one gentleman zombie stared with open admiration, as well they might. Imagine pre-Undoing bodybuilding sensation Arnold Schwarzenegger. But hairier. All I'd taken from my coat was a mesh bag (used for grocery shopping) and a knife that I gripped between my teeth like a pirate of old. Without another word, I jumped in.

The reservoir is home to all kinds of things you don't want to think about. I wrapped myself in awe, to deal with the sentient ones, and struck out with great speed. Something groped at my leg about halfway, and I grabbed the knife and plunged it deep. The water gouted hot and purple, and whatever it was didn't trouble me again. I think I heard a muted dusty cheer when I hauled myself out and through a tilted window ledge into Camelot.

Camelot was once a big deal: back in the day, King Arthur collected an impressive bunch of knights and dreamers, and had a plan to unite all of New New York City. I rode with him for a bit, when it looked like he might actually usher in an era of peace and plenty and all that. Man, the times we had, back then. He even offered to make me a knight. But he got betrayed: not by that sap Lancelot, but by Merlin. Because real post-Undoing wizards are always real asshats. Merlin got what was coming to him, but sank the whole castle in the lake, taking the round table and all of its fellows down with him.

Except Arthur. Who since then has sat alone in the tilted tower, remembering. Why had an Eightball appeared there of all places? Was someone trying to help him out? If so, he'd have used it already. And if I knew Arthur, it would have been for something dramatic and obvious. Most likely it just appeared there because life is cruel.

The tilted staircase wound around and up, and I navigated it like a drunk, knife in hand, awe wound tight around me. Ahead, the door to the last dry chamber. What would I find in there?

"You're too late, Awlly."

The voice was melancholy, and low. Arthur was seated on a once-grand oak throne that was propped under one side to make it almost level. It — and he — was coated in green moss. Here and there, glimpses of tarnished silver armor plate peeked through. Last time I saw Arthur, he was a handsome fellow. Now he looked old and done. I felt guilty about not having visited more. Or ever.

"I used it up," he elaborated, pointing to a black sphere in the lowest corner. My heart skipped a beat.

I crab-walked over to it.

"What did you ask for, sire?"

"To die," he replied simply. "Just a few minutes ago. It hasn't happened yet, but I think I feel something."

I picked up the Eightball, imagining how Formaldehyde would take this. Not to mention Gaia or the Monkey King, though that pair could wait until way later. The little window was blank, so Arthur had been telling the truth. I felt the weight in my hand, the smooth casing, the large dent in one side. And I froze.

"Sire, has anyone been over here before me?"

"ALL of them! Emperors, gods, unicorns, demons... Merlin ..."

"No, sire. I mean today..."

"Only that irresistible little god of something I forget. She made quite an impression, I don't mind telling you. Quite distracted me from making my wish."

Pieces notched together in my head like a large-cut jigsaw puzzle for slow kids.

"About yea big, cute, pixie-cut hair...?"

"That's the one! She was quite the charmer. Got me all dizzy, then left... if you see her can you say I'm asking for her, Awlly?"

"Oh I'll ask, that's certain," I rumbled. Me and Lizzie were going to have words. But what did she do with the *real* Eightball when she swapped it for my genuine used-up one? She'd had no intention of waking me this morning: she'd come in for the Eightball. And if she'd made a wish, we'd all know about it. So where had she stashed the fresh one?

"Can I take this? As a souvenir, sire?"

Arthur waved distractedly. "Yes, yes ... with a bit of luck I'll be gone, soon anyway. How do I look?"

"You look like you're slipping away, sire. Any minute now, I think."

I hoped the mad, sad old king would die just because he believed he was going to. I turned, and trudged down the stairs, heart heavy for all kinds of reasons.

Nothing was dumb enough to take me on during the return swim, and by the time I clambered ashore, I had a sort-of plan. I ignored the trembling Formaldehyde, slinging the shopping bag over a shoulder as I forced my wet feet into socks, making an equally ungainly struggle with my pants, shirt and boots. Lizzie helped at the end, carefully holding my greatcoat out like a squire of old. She was never this solicitous. I was beginning to get a very bad feeling.

Once back in my armor, I fished the Eightball out, and held it aloft in one hand.

"Behold!" I said in a stage voice. "The Magic Eightball of..."

"But hold the beholds!" Lizzie yelled at impressive volume, stalling my speech. She continued: "It is clearly used up! Mad Arthur used it in a futile wish, because you fools prevented me from swimming across earlier and stopping him!"

I shot Lizzie my own Look, that I hoped conveyed 'this is your plan? *This?*'.

I glanced around and could see this would lead to all kinds of violence. I needed to buy us time to split. I prepared to throw it. High.

"No! Behold me again!" I roared. "This is indeed an unused Magic Eightball! See as..."

"Not so fast, fats!" a raging, squeaking voice yelled from the crest of the bowl. "Hand it over!"

A wave of hairy vagabonds came sweeping down the slope, led by the leaping, tiny figure of Louey. Oh great. I shot Lizzie a look and she motioned a kind of "get on with it" thing with her hands.

"I will leave this for you two gents to discuss!" I declared.

It nearly worked, too: Formaldehyde and Louey paused, eyes on the upraised Eightball, consumed by greed. Then Louey's little eyes scrunched up.

"Ya big fraud! That's the same dud Eightball you brag about every time I come to your office! I recognize the big bash in the side. I knew you was holding out on ole Louey!"

Everything stopped. I concentrated like never before and whipped up some industrial level of awe round myself. A hundred armed apes and undead-ish were staring at me, and I knew that whatever I said next had to keep the momentum going, or yours truly would be back in the lake with rocks in his pockets. Or not rocks: my coat was well heavy enough to drown me as was. And I thought I knew where some of the excess weight was coming from.

Lizzie spoke up, voice cutting through the silence. That was fine by me, as all I had was an "um" ready.

"Yes! Arthur did NOT have the genuine Eightball! My brilliant and awesome colleague here knew that would be confirmed when he swam across! He came here to bring us the real thing! Let's hear it for The God of Awe!"

The ragged cheers drowned out Crumbles, who was trying to say that I had had no intention of coming here.

I dropped my conversation-piece Eightball, dug around in my coat's many pockets and with a feeling of sick dread, came up with another, pristine Eightball, whose little window was glowing softly. That silenced them. Then one of the apes howled, and a zombie yelped, as dozens of thick roots erupted out of the grass around the stage. One – thicker than me and white as a corpse – split, to disgorge a Gaia junkie. The woman was wrapped so tight in white hairlike tendrils she looked to be in couture silk.

"The wish must be ours, Mister Awe," she breathed. "You accepted payment."

All around, roots were birthing more of the plant's shock troops, who brandished arm-long wicked thorns with sticky droplets at their tips.

I shot Lizzie a look. She gave a nod, indicating rapid flight. But Crumbles was in the way, pointing his little gun at my head.

I muttered under my breath and he smirked.

"Not so smart now, are you? Thought you could..."

"Are you planning on talking me to death?"

His blue lips twitched in anger and he pulled the trigger. There was a little click and his rheumy eyes widened, and he looked down. I dug my free hand in an outside pocket and held up the little slug I'd taken from the pistol when I palmed it earlier. Then I slapped him across the face, very hard, twice.

"Again?" he squealed, as went down.

There was a moment of supercharged silent tension, and just as everyone, ape, zombie, and plant-junkie made to attack me, two things happened.

First, a tangible wave of pure sexual attraction exploded out through the bowl, sending apes mad, staggering the plant-guys, and even widening the eyes of the zombies. Like I said, when Lizzie lets loose, watch out. Even I felt it, and gods are mostly immune to one another.

Then, about a second later, I lofted the Eightball high. It soared high, landing 30 feet out in the water with a ker-plunk noise. About a third of the crowd ran, shambled or were propelled to the shoreline. Another third leapt on one another in a lustful frenzy. And the last third started hacking and shooting everyone else. Except Louey: he raised both hands at me, and blue fire crackled. That's when I had my single good idea. I pulled out Plan B and Plan C.

"Your puny pistols won't even scratch me!" he crowed. Which may or may not have been true. It didn't matter. I fired. Into the sky.

The twin booms shook the leaves on the trees, and made even my ears ring. One by one, the smarter combatants and copulators looked up. A purplish rope unrolled almost all the way down to the grass close to me. And another landed on a chimp, sticking tight. Then dozens. The men 'o war, attracted by my pistols, were feeding.

Lizzie gave me a grin and we ran for it. All around, figures were being caught up in the sticky tendrils, and lifted into the air: some, in couples, didn't even notice. Lightning flashed up, and one of the jellyfish airbags exploded, sending flaming fragments to earth. We punched, kicked, ducked, rolled, and jumped to the top of the bowl. I didn't look back, and we didn't stop running for about a mile.

I was trying to be casual, but she knew I was still hacked off. We'd been sitting in tense silence on a big rock in a wooded part of the park, watching a herd of white horses bridled in silver, stream past. This was close to a fairy mound, and saner mortals gave it a wide berth, for fear of kidnapping and enslavement. The wee folk ignored us gods, though, if we didn't trouble them.

"How did you know Arthur had it?"

"You know Eightballs: of *course* it would appear close to the craziest person in the park. So I paid him a visit before he got a chance to think of his wish. Didn't think he'd want to kill himself. Did you ... you know... help him do it?"

"I did not! Why would you even ask that?"

She shrugged. "You have a big heart, Awlly."

I took the backhanded compliment in silence.

"So when were you gonna fill me in, Lizzie?"

"When I came and met you downtown, was the plan."

"And what were we meant to do with Arthur's Eightball? We were already being paid enough to retire on, for just handing it over."

"For The God of Awe you sure think small, Awlly. Any one of those lunatics could have ended everything with a wish. Can you imagine the good *we* could have done?"

"Never did hear of an Eightball making the world a better place, Lizzie. What were you gonna wish for anyways?"

She shrugged: "I hadn't worked that out. I was hoping we'd have figured it out together."

I very much doubted that was true, but I was smart enough to not say.

"Wish you'd told me the plan, though."

"You were never a good liar, Awlly: I had to hide the real Eightball in your coat so when we met we could skip town with all the payments we'd raked in, after you met Louey with a straight face. Nobody thinks The God of Awe is sneaky. With Lust, they kind of assume."

"Well, they're not wrong."

She laughed, and something in me unclenched.

"I didn't want to sneak around, Awlly: I only took the one from your office when the vintage one I had in mind turned out to look cheap. Formaldehyde would have worked that out fast."

"And you thought the zombies would be all right with the idea that Arthur used it up?"

She shrugged. "It would have been true, if I hadn't gotten there first."

"They still woulda pounded your head, lady."

Lizzie scoffed: "I can take a legion of zombies before you wake in the morning and peel your face off your desk."

"And how about a troupe of theocidal apes, and a horde of plant junkies?"

"I'd have managed." Then she frowned.

"We need to go back, Awlly, stop any of them from retrieving it."

"No rush, Lizzie."

"There might be an ape in a diving suit down there right now..."

"Probably is."

"So we need..."

I cut her off by rifling through my pockets and pulling out a brown and silver package no wider than her palm and no thicker than a finger. I held it out.

"Is this .... no ...." She took it reverently, and ran a fingernail over the shiny wrapper, that split in a silver-backed curl. I could smell real chocolate.

"Awlly ... where did you get a genuine Hershey's? No-one has them anymore. Oh...you didn't ..."

I'd never seen Lizzie truly astonished before.

I shrugged: "I'm just lucky the Eightball accepted Hershey's as a noun. The word 'bar' woulda taken me over the limit."

She was staring at me, eyes wide and shining. It wasn't astonishment. It was awe.

---

*Awe*

*Fear*     *Lust*     *Curiosity*

*Detachment*     *Love*

# 19. The Silence of Mother

## Gerald Warfield

Bodies floated in the reservoir like tiny islands of gray. Squinting against the morning sun, Moss 17 gripped the back of the bench where he stood and looked out over the water. It was the uniforms that were gray, of course, not the bodies.

This was his customary spot on the far embankment, though he usually came in the evening after his shift at the laundry. Always, he came to this bench. It was weathered and needed paint, and he thought no one else would want to sit there.

Nine. He counted nine bodies, and it had been only three days since Mother had stopped speaking. Couldn't they have held out longer?

ℰ

On the first day, when Mother didn't wake him, he thought he was being punished. He had committed self-sex for the second time this month, and it was permitted only once. Guilt-stricken, he cowered in his cell until late morning, alternately apologizing and begging forgiveness, but she did not respond. Deciding that he must appear at the laundry or risk further punishment, he put on a fresh uniform, cap, and boots and entered shamefacedly onto the open walkway. At once, he saw something was wrong. In the far lane, two Moss women pulled on opposite sides of a wicker basket. The contents of the basket, tiny breadfruits, lay on the ground. The women, their expressions blank, simply pulled the basket back and forth between them. Already late, he sprinted past them and onto the lane to the laundry.

Breathing heavily, he leapt onto the porch of the squat building and pulled the door open. Great puffs of steam, thick with the smell of soap and disinfectant, engulfed him. Inside, workers bent to their tasks, all except his best friend, Pine 4, whose station was empty.

No one looked up to acknowledge Moss's arrival. Even the supervisor bustled about on her platform without a glance in his direction. Grateful to be ignored, he slipped to his table, took up his hook and basket, and went to fish uniforms from one of the rinse vats.

At his table, he pulled wet uniforms through the wringer while avoiding eye contact with Laurel 9 who worked the same task at the table next to him, and Moss 30 who worked on the other side. Without Mother to relay their words, he could neither greet nor respond. But guarded peeks at the other workers revealed the same wary frowns and darting glances. No one he could see was communicating.

Violette IV dropped her load on the floor. The supervisor, who normally would have scolded her, quickly turned and busied herself with racks of detergent jugs. Wasn't Mother talking to the supervisor?

Moss 17 stopped and straightened. He looked left and right, taking in the whole room. Was it possible Mother was talking to no one? A wave of nausea washed over him, and he leaned on his table. He thought he would vomit.

For the remainder of the day, he worked in a trance. No one stopped for lunch; no one knew when it was. The supervisor glanced repeatedly at a shaft of sunlight streaming from a high window. When it reached the sorting table, she made a show of walking to the door and leaving. Everyone looked at one another and then, without further eye contact, they filed out, separate, solitary figures each to their own cells.

Pine 4 was not at the laundry the next day either. Two Birches were also absent. Gray uniforms went from the rinse vats to the sorting racks, but no one took them to the outside lines. The supervisor arranged and rearranged detergent jugs on her high platform, ignoring everyone on the lower floor. By noon, when there was no more room on the sorting racks, he piled wet uniforms on his table.

That evening, the walk to his cell was interminable. He staggered, not having eaten in two days. A food cart lay parked on the lane near his cell, and he took enough to eat for that night. It felt wrong to eat alone but the confused and furtive faces in the dinner room would be worse.

On the third morning, Pine 4 still had not returned. Other workers were missing, too, even the supervisor. Carts lined the walls and uniforms were being washed in cold water because no fires had been lit beneath the vats. Pine 4's work table in the far corner had completely vanished. Moss pushed his way through the backed-up carts to find it buried beneath a soggy mountain of gray. Appalled, he shoved the pile of uniforms off the table and onto the floor. They landed with a loud slosh. When he looked up, the other workers were staring at him. Ashamed of his display, he fled the laundry.

Pine 4 was special, his best friend assigned to him by Mother when they were still children. Never a day passed that they didn't communicate—until now. He had to know what had happened.

≀

He arrived outside Pine 4's single-cell dwelling breathless, not from the walk, but from the anxiety of leaving work without approval from Mother. It felt wrong, except that *everything* in the last two days felt wrong.

Pine 4's cell, one in a long row of Pine chambers, opened directly onto Pine Lane Two. All the doors were aligned, numbered, and closed save his friend's, which stood ajar. That singularity— although the door was open only a crack—so contrasted with the meticulous conformity of the rest of the lane that it bordered on indecency.

He didn't have permission to enter, but what if Pine lay inside sick or hurt? Without Mother he couldn't call for help. Surely she would understand. Surely Pine would understand. He raised his cap, brushed a quick hand across his smooth scalp, and bit his lip. Then he pushed the door the rest of the way open.

The room lay in shadows, and in the middle, Pine hung by his neck from a rope looped over a lamp hook in the ceiling, his face discolored, his eyes wide.

Moss cried out—inside his head, of course—but Mother didn't hear, and because Mother didn't hear, no one heard.

His pulse throbbed, he couldn't breathe. He wanted to pull the door closed and make the horror go away, but it was too late.

Reluctantly, he crept into the room, stepping around an overturned chair. Pine's cot, neatly made, rested against the far wall. His excretion chair sat on the left, its lid down; the uniform closet on the right stood open. He reached out to Pine's body, felt the coarse material of his trouser leg and the solid flesh beneath. The body swayed in response. He'd not been told to touch Pine, and it seemed a strangely intimate thing to do now, almost erotic.

He dropped his hand, brushing against one of Pine's scuffed, black boots. *Why didn't you wait?* He wiped tears with the palm of his hand. *You always got depressed so easily.* His throat ached. They had shared one another's thoughts, even fantasies since childhood.

Looking up once again at Pine's face, the thought came to him that he should show others that his friend was dead. He glanced about for Pine's green cap, so they would know who he was. It lay against the wall on the other side of the chair. He righted the chair, placed it in front of Pine, and set the cap in the middle of the seat, the "4" facing the door.

For a few moments, he stood before Pine. *Go with Mother,* he thought, and then wondered about the ritual phrase that he had always taken for granted. What did it mean, now that Mother had turned her back on them?

Stepping into the walkway, he blinked and shaded his eyes. Other Pines passed, their numbered green hats bobbing in the morning sun. Standing squarely in the walkway, he looked at the two nearest and raised his hand, extending his fingers toward the door. The first Pine looked into his eyes, slack jawed, and went around him. Moss moved his arm up and down, waving again to the door. The second Pine stopped. Her glance followed his arm out to his hand and then to the cell door. She started toward the door but looked back at him, her brow furrowed, and then she entered the cell. Two other Pines brushed past him from behind and through the doorway. One sank to her knees and hugged herself.

The first Pine stepped back onto the walkway and looked directly at Moss. She extended her arm and waved her hand toward the north, the direction of the reservoir.

⁂

He suspected what he might find before he arrived. Those cut off from Mother, and thus from everyone, didn't last long. Once, an Oak had killed a Moss in the field with a hoe. He didn't know why. Only Mother knew, and her punishment was swift. No one could send their thoughts to him; he could send his thoughts to no one. After three days, the man vanished into the woods, probably soon dead.

But now it was different. How could everyone in the village have committed the same crime? And what if some of them didn't know what the crime was? Questions circled and re-circled in his mind. What had happened?

Every day, Mother summoned an individual to attend to her for her nourishment and cleaning. Perhaps the last person called to duty might have seen something or at least know when it happened. But who that person might be, he had no idea. The last time he had been summoned was several months ago, and the memory was dark. Mother was not nice to look upon.

When he reached the reservoir, he could do nothing but stand there, grip the back of the bench and count the bodies. Never had he needed a command from Mother more than now. When animals drowned in the reservoir—anything from a rat to a farm animal—someone was sent to remove them lest they make the water bad. If he could report these bodies to Mother, he was sure that she would tell him the same. The mere thought of her instruction was enough to start his feet toward the muddy bank.

But he stopped before reaching the water. Iris 9 was approaching the reservoir. Surely, she had not come to drown herself, too. He looked away, hoping not to attract her attention. In the corner of his eye he saw her sit down on the next bench, which relieved him, and he ventured another glance. Her eyes were closed; her brow was knit. Was she in pain?

Oddly, she did not have on her purple cap—another sign of their collective descent into chaos—but he recognized her without it. Did she remember? She was even sitting at the same bench as before. But perhaps, like others, she had no thoughts at all in the absence of Mother.

The incident had occurred more than a year ago. One of Mother's mistakes, yet his cheeks burned to think about it. In the evening, after work, he had sat by the reservoir on this same bench, and a woman had sat at the other end. He couldn't see the number on the front of her cap, but it was purple, so he knew she was an Iris. She faced forward, watching a pair of ducks on the shore, but in a sidelong glance he saw her smooth neck and the subtle blush of her cheek. *May I touch you?* he asked. Mother did not relay the Iris's answer, but then Mother was sometimes slow. *And if Mother is willing, may I kiss you?*

The Iris still showed no visible response, but he heard the voice that Mother conveyed back to him. *I would touch you, too. Kiss me.*

He took a deep breath and faced her. Reaching out, he took her shoulders and leaned forward to kiss her lips. The young woman twisted away violently and leapt up striking his nose with her elbow and tumbling him to the ground. Her eyes were wide, and her mouth gaped open as she looked down at him.

Moss was too confused to call for Mother. He felt blood trickle from his nose and reached into his uniform for a cloth. Just then a man, another Moss, walked stiffly from the lake. Beyond him, on the next bench, sat another Iris, a 9 on her purple cap. Moss and the other Iris looked at one another, Moss now holding the cloth to his nose to stanch the blood. She put her hand to her mouth, and they fled in opposite directions.

¿

He turned back to the water and took a tentative step. Mud squished beneath his boot. Surely she was watching. A few more steps and cold water poured over the tops of his boots, chilling his feet. She probably thought he had decided to drown himself like the others.

The nearest body floated facedown. It seemed to be male. From the green of the cap, still on his head, it was another Pine. Wading until he was waist deep, Moss could not bring himself to touch the body, so he reached around and gripped the back of its collar.

He towed the body until it touched the mud in the shallows, and then it was harder to pull. Another pair of hands reached down and grasped a trouser leg. Shocked at the intimacy, Moss's reaction was to look away. But the hands pulled with him, and together they dragged the limp body to the edge of the water and through the mud, leaving long ruts up to the dry bank.

When he straightened and dared to glance at her, he saw that her right arm was injured. Four long gashes, recent wounds, had scabbed over. They had not been treated, no salves, no bandage, and there was a bit of red along the perimeter of each. The sleeve of her uniform was also ripped. It was as if an animal had clawed her. Moss turned his head so as not to intrude. He wanted to ask her for help with the rest of the bodies, but of course, Mother wasn't listening.

When he entered the water again, he was gratified that she followed. Together they dragged the remaining bodies onto the bank, lining them along the edge of the grass. To give them a more orderly appearance, they straightened the arms and legs. It helped, making them tidy.

Winded, he sloshed in his wet boots and uniform to his bench and sat, shuddering from the cold. Iris followed and sat at the other end, which pleased him, although it also made him anxious. Was she following commands? Did she hear Mother's voice? He emptied his boots of water. Was he supposed to do something? Finally, he became so self-conscious that he stood to leave, but when he stepped forward his boot caught the bottom edge of the bench and he fell, pitching forward onto the grass. Stunned, he lay facedown, little flashes of light wiggling before his eyes.

Hands gripped his shoulder and turned him over. Iris knelt next to him, and he looked up into her face. She had touched him. Should they mate now? But in her eyes he saw the same haunted look as he had seen on the faces of others. No, this had nothing to do with mating. She struggled with the absence of Mother, just as he did, perhaps more so. He got up and clumsily tried to brush off the front of his uniform.

He didn't want to leave Iris looking so troubled. On her own, she had helped him pull the bodies from the reservoir, and she had touched him. Emboldened, he stepped closer and took her hand. She did not respond.

From habit he cried for Mother. How was he to know what to do? People were dying around him, and now he held Iris's hand.

§

Cold despair curled in Moss's gut. He could not talk to Iris, and she could not talk to him. They simply stood, holding hands.

His original idea, to find out Mother's caregiver of three days ago, seemed hopeless. There was nothing to do except—perhaps—maybe—*to go see* Mother. The thought made his knees weak. Yet the hand he held gave him courage.

He motioned with his arm and fingers like he had done before, but Iris did not respond. He started forward, and her hand slipped out of his. No, he couldn't do it alone. Reaching down and taking her hand once more, he gently tugged, and this time she moved forward to walk with him.

On Central Lane, they passed ominous signs: the jacket of a uniform crumpled on the ground, a single shoe resting in a doorway. Near Pine's street, a vulture tore at something unidentifiable beneath a tree. Moss grimaced, and they both hurried forward. He had never before seen a vulture in the village. Just the fact that Iris walked in the open without her numbered hat signaled a growing disorder. How could people communicate with her if they didn't know her number and that she was an Iris?

Coming to Lane One, they rounded the corner, and ahead of them a wide roof of thatch spread above the round house that sheltered Mother. Iris jerked to a stop as if only now realizing where they were going.

What should he do? Should he try to pull Iris along with him? Should he leave her and see Mother by himself? Moss looked back at the imposing house of Mother and then at the sky, searching for answers. Mounds of clouds stacked overhead, pressing down like enormous rolls of fat. A cold wind had sprung up, and he shivered.

His uniform was still wet from the waist down. He saw that Iris shivered, too.

Urgently, he pulled on Iris's hand again. She looked wild-eyed but allowed him to lead her toward the structure. He smiled, trying to convey that he understood. The presence of Mother could be—difficult. There were cases where people had fainted upon seeing her for the first time.

The House of Mother was different from any other house in the village. It was round and covered by a vast thatch roof. A central portal framed in heavy wooden beams led to two access passages, one left and one right, both of which circled to the far side of the structure and to the entrance of Mother's chamber.

As they entered the portal, Iris slumped as if she might sink to the floor, clearly overwhelmed by the sheer peril of entering into the Presence without a summons. Moss supported her with an arm around her waist, but his own heart beat wildly, too. He resolved then to protect her from any punishment. He would tell Mother that it was not Iris's fault, that she was merely weak and had allowed him to lead her into this perilous breach of protocol.

Inside the hallways of Mother's house, ceramic lanterns always burned on high shelves, even during the day. It was each caregiver's duty to fill the lamps and trim the wicks. But now only a single lantern sputtered to the left of the doorway, its open flame casting a fitful light into the perimeter passageway. Moss squeezed Iris's hand and called out in his mind one last time asking permission to enter into Mother's presence—to no response.

Moss released Iris's hand and reached up to take the remaining lantern from the shelf. Together, they started down the left passageway, their footsteps rustling the straw on the floor. As they got closer, a buzzing could be heard from the interior. Iris squeezed her eyes shut so that Moss had to lead her. They rounded the edge of the passageway and entered into Mother's chamber.

Moss raised the lantern. Additional light streamed from a circular opening above. In the middle of the room the mountain of flesh that was Mother rested on a circular platform of wood raised the height of a man. Great swaths of cloth draped the massive mounds and hung limply off long rolls of fat. Her head at the top, dwarfed by the gargantuan body, lay back and faced upward. Her mouth gaped open. Diminutive arms hung limp, seemingly from beneath her massive jowls. The hands, more like claws, terminated in pointed nails.

Below the heavy platform that supported Mother, a thick layer of straw had been stacked to catch the waste that fell from her massive body. Clotted and thick with flies, it clearly had not been changed.

Paralyzed at first, Moss gaped. As shocking as the great, ruined body was, the presence of vultures was worse. Perched on ledges of fat, they had torn through the cloth to gouge out chunks of flesh with their hooked beaks. A long strip of flesh dangled from the beak of one. Some of the birds spread their wings and squawked at the intrusion of Moss and Iris, but others simply continued their feast. To the right, a wooden stairway and a long plank extended out over Mother so her feeders could reach her mouth. Feeding bowls were stacked at the bottom of the stairs, some of them still full.

Moss let out a cry. Crouching, he placed the lantern on the floor and then bounded upright and ran to the stairs, leaping them three at a time. Reckless, he charged out onto the runway above Mother, waving his arms and crying out again.

The vultures squawked and flapped into the air. Two circled the room beneath the roof; the rest exited through the opening in the center. Moss stopped at the end of the plank, suddenly frightened at what he had done. He had cried aloud, and that was shocking enough, but now he looked directly down into Mother's face. The end of a feeding stick rose from her mouth, but not far enough. Now it was clear what had happened. He knew how long the stick was. It had been crammed down Mother's throat.

He could not read an expression on her face. Flies covered her eyes, and her mouth was filled with squirming, white maggots. The gorge rose from his stomach, and he swallowed to keep from throwing up. Sinking to his knees on the plank, he gripped its edges, suddenly fearful of losing his balance and falling onto the great, decaying body.

The humming of flies filled his ears. The odor, pungent and rotten, threatened to choke him. And then he saw that she held things in her delicate, clawed hands. In one, a torn piece of gray cloth was stuck in her claws. In the other she held a cap, a purple cap.

Who had done this thing? Frightened, yet determined to find out, he lay prostrate on the plank and reached down. Leaning perilously over the side of the runway, he could barely reach the cap. Careful not the touch the flesh, he lifted it from Mother's limp fingers. But, already, he knew what it said. Kneeling on the runway, he turned the cap right-side up. The number "9" was embroidered on the front.

His eyes clouded, and he dropped the hat. He hadn't meant to. It hit the plank with a little thud and then bounced off to fall into one of the gaping holes the vultures had excavated, too far down for him to reach.

Trembling, he looked back at Iris, so small, standing just inside the doorway. She stooped, picked up the lantern by its handle and held it out to him, a lonely, desperate gesture. She tried to smile, but it came out a grimace.

Moss looked back and forth between Iris, holding the flickering light, and the massive, putrefied body below. How could she have done this?

He turned on the narrow runway and attempted the hazardous walk back to the stairs. Certain he would fall, he spread his arms for balance. The stench had grown in power, threatening to knock him from the narrow gangplank. Would he lose his balance and fall into the mountain of rotting flesh? He did not fall. He reached the steps, gasped for breath, and descended the stairs to the dirt floor.

Iris had remained in the same spot and followed his progress with a somber face. Again, she extended the lantern, tears streaming from her eyes.

When he reached her, he didn't know what to do. This woman, alone, had done the unthinkable, causing a profound turmoil from which there would be no recovery. She deserved his wrath, but it was a different emotion that rose within him, something he had no name for: admiration perhaps, though far stronger, more like yearning to be with her, to keep her close to him.

Iris weakened further as she endeavored to hold the lantern. Lips trembling, she struggled, opened her mouth, and abruptly made a sound. "Ka."

It meant something. Yet whatever it was, she continued to diminish like a distant light fading out. She lowered the lantern further. She was giving up. Moss could feel it.

He, too, struggled to make his mouth work. "Ka." The sound was similar to hers. Then he reached out and clasped the lantern. Their hands touched. He would help her. It was a desire that overrode all others. He wanted it more than he feared Mother or the village.

Moss looked back at the monstrous body resting on its framework of timbers. Iris's great work was unfinished. One final thing remained to end the era of Mother, and he would do it. Iris would see him do it.

With the lamp, he went to the edge of the heavy platform that supported Mother and to the mounds of hay and detritus that lay beneath. Kneeling, he took off his hat and placed it on the top of the mass of dry stems and leaves. Then, he raised some of the brittle tangle from the floor and placed the lantern beneath it. The hay sucked the fire into its dry thicket with a crackling sound. Moss rose and turned away. He did not want to see the flames take his hat.

When they reached the outer doorway, Moss hesitated before stepping into the sunlight. Iris moved close, so close their shoulders touched. He looked down to see the four deep scratches on her arm where her uniform was torn. They seemed to be healing. He wanted them to heal. Glancing about the edge of the village, no one was in sight. They must leave this place before the flames were noticed. "Ka," he said.

They walked quickly and without holding hands, so as to attract little attention. When they passed the last row of cell houses on the west side of the village, they came to the fields where crop plants were tall and bread pods ripe. Several villagers harvested amongst the furrows, picking the pods and placing them in long sacks. They could not have been told to do so. It was a good sign.

At the far end of the field on a low rise stood one of the huts where they had been instructed to keep tools with which to work the crops. The hut drew them, and they followed one of the long furrows between the tall breadfruit plants toward the isolated structure.

A few wooden diggers and a basket were propped against the outside wall. The thatch was in good repair, and the inside, full of tools, could be emptied. There would be room enough for two cots. Moss had never heard of two villagers living together in the same cell. Mother had never commanded it, but the thought entered his mind. It was part of a bigger thought that he hadn't put together yet of the two of them together.

He made the sound "Ka." She came to his side and put her arm around his waist. Looking out through the doorway, they saw a white column of smoke rising from the village. It pointed into the sky—a sky where the clouds had broken and begun to drift away.

—

*Curiosity*

*Awe*        *Love*        *Hope*

*Lust*        *Joy*

# 20.    Potential

### Felicity Drake

Aspasia leaned over the railing of the research vessel and looked out at the vast kelp field for the last time. The water was an impossibly lucid turquoise; beneath the surface, ribbons of dark kelp fluttered peacefully.

In the distance, dry, bone-white limestone pinnacles peeked out from the surface of the ocean, the remnants of Nauru's phosphate strip mines. Once there had been an island there, home to thousands. Then the sea rose and they scattered, and only the Cook family remained. It was their kelp farm that encircled what was left of Nauru.

For the last night of their expedition, Aspasia's grad students had taken it upon themselves to finish up their remaining bottles of wine, and she could hear them below deck, playing music and laughing. Even if she had wanted to join them, it wouldn't have been quite appropriate for her to get wasted with her students. Besides, she had more or less outgrown that sort of thing.

Instead, she lay out on the deck of the ship, unfolded her screen, and dipped back into the database of genetic donors.

She'd known she wanted a baby ever since she was a baby, had been the sort of child who loved to toddle around with a baby doll and mimic all her parents' caretaking. She'd earned pizza money babysitting in college, and had even thought about becoming a preschool teacher until archaeology stole her heart.

But practical concerns had prevailed: her dissertation first, and then tenure, and then this once-in-a-lifetime excavation...

Before she left for Nauru, she had promised herself this would be the last delay, and had visited a fertility clinic to get the ball rolling. She ooh-ed and aah-ed at the wall of faintly glowing amniotic bubbles, filled with everything from pinprick-sized embryos to alien-looking fetuses to great big healthy babies just about ready to pop. All she had to do was pick a donor, have a few ova extracted, and the clinic could incubate her baby right there.

Since then, Aspasia had barely done anything else in her free time but scroll through the donors. The only entrance requirement was an absence of serious genetic defects; otherwise, it was a delightful rainbow of human biological diversity. Male and female, with every possible variation of phenotype: tall and short, big and small-bellied, bulbous and pointy-nosed, freckled and birth marked.

The associated biographical information on the donors was even more varied. As she scrolled through their profiles, she imagined the child each one might produce. Would the chess champion's baby grow up to be particularly brilliant? Would the opera singer have a baby with perfect pitch, in spite of Aspasia's own musical deficiencies? Would this minor-league baseball player produce a future Little League star? At each new profile, she felt a moment's flash of recognition and thrill—*this is the one!*—until she remembered the thousands of other, equally promising vials of genetic material tucked away inside the clinic's refrigerators, just waiting for her to choose.

As long as she didn't decide, the baby was a creature of infinite possibility. Simultaneously tall and short, willowy and sturdy, shy and boisterous. In its imagined state, the baby was perfect. She felt like the moment she made a decision, the moment she foreclosed all other possibilities, she would be doing the child a terrible injury.

Aspasia folded up her screen and set it aside. Her next appointment at the fertility clinic was in exactly one week. Closing her eyes, she listened to the hypnotic, amniotic thrum of the waves against the ship. She only had a few days left to decide.

≀

Aspasia inhaled the rich scent of coffee and shivered in pleasure. The coffee aboard the research vessel had been truly dismal.

It had taken a few days to sweep the cobwebs out of her apartment, supervise the transfer of their research materials, and make sure her grad students were all set up in the lab, but now she had an afternoon free to meet an old friend in the glass-walled cafe on the top floor of the library. Joining the line for a frothy cappuccino, she admired the view: Washington Square Park far below and the graceful curve of the Wall Street Seawall in the distance.

"Aspasia!" Octava exclaimed, rising from their usual corner table and opening her arms for a hug. She was grayer than she had been just six months before, and when she wrapped her arms around Aspasia, her hug was as wonderfully squishy as ever.

Octava was a primatologist, specialized in species lost in the Anthropocene extinction. She and Aspasia were in different departments, but they shared a love of all the people and creatures who had disappeared in the twentieth through twenty-second centuries. They had found themselves attending the same talks often enough that they became friends.

"I know you were in the Pacific," Octava began, "but, remind me what you were doing out there in the watery depths?" It was understandable that she had forgotten; Octava didn't keep up with new developments in archaeology. (Aspasia flattered herself to think that any archaeologist of note would, naturally, be aware of her project.)

"Well—do you remember a country called Nauru?" Aspasia asked.

"I can't say that I do."

"It was one of those Pacific islands wiped out by rising sea levels in the early twenty-second century. Maybe eighty percent of its population got resettled, but the other twenty percent slipped through the cracks and became climate refugees. Some stayed on the island until the end; others tried to survive on the sea.

"It's been hard to do any research on this population, just because of the nature of maritime archaeology: artifacts scattered over a wide area, sea-water dissolving human remains. This project is special because the Cook family built themselves a small but seaworthy submarine—so they could go underwater to weather hurricanes and storms—which has survived with its pressure hull intact. Meaning that the inside of the submarine remained dry, preserving not only the family themselves but also their belongings, even their electronics.

"A kelp farmer stumbled across the submarine a few years ago, and since then I've been just aching to go. It took some time getting permission from the Council of Displaced Nauruans and the Pacific Islands Memory Institute and the university and everyone. But we made it, and it was incredible—probably the most thorough evidence we'll ever see of this lost population. We've just gotten things back to the lab, and it'll be a long while yet before we're ready to publish, but I'll be telling you all about it as the results come in. Whether you like it or not, probably."

"Don't be silly—it sounds fascinating. You said the submarine was intact, not flooded? Then what happened to it? How did they—

you know." Octava was not as accustomed to dealing with human death as an archaeologist.

"How did they die? Plain old entropy—a series of valves failed in the main ballast tank blowing system, and they weren't able to get enough air in to resurface."

"They couldn't repair broken valves?"

"This wasn't a government or military project. It was a handmade submarine cobbled together by an amateur welder with nothing more than spare parts and hope. John Cook—that's the father—must have been trying to repair it to the very last. The mother and daughter were together in the sleeping quarters when they died, but we found his remains alone in the pump room."

"It's a remarkable story. That poor family."

Aspasia slipped her hand into her pocket and felt the polyethylene sample bag there, the tiny chunk of bone inside it. She was eager to get back to the lab.

"I'd better go, Octava," she said, "and make sure my grad students aren't getting themselves into any trouble."

"Of course. Would you like to stop by my lab sometime? It's been too long since you've seen the gorillas."

"I'd love to. Besides, I want to talk to you about the baby."

≀

Aspasia took one last, longing look at the still image of Donor 3492, with his prominent cheekbones and laughing eyes and Ph.D. in microbiology. Then she hurried to fold up her screen and stuff it in her pocket. She didn't want any of her grad students to catch her mooning over the donor database.

"I've just finished the child's facial reconstruction. Would you like to see?" Stella asked, greeting Aspasia at the door.

"Her name is Nina," Aspasia corrected. She was strict with her lab on this point alone: if they handled human remains, they had to call them by name. If the specimen's name was unknown, they could give it a nickname, but she couldn't tolerate referring to people with numbers or designations. It was never 'the femur' or 'the sample'; it was Nina's femur and Nina's sample.

"Oh, yes—Nina." Stella brought up the facial reconstruction program and showed off her progress.

Aspasia watched the animation onscreen: the three-dimensional scan of the familiar skull, the layers of muscle, skin, and then the finishing touches. A chubby-cheeked, nut-colored face with dark eyes and hair stared back at her. Reconstructed,

Nina was posed just like a donor in the database: a sample of humanity.

Next, Aspasia visited Minnie in her corner, surrounded by monitors and rattling boxes of antique hardware. "Any progress on the electronics?" she asked.

"I'm trying to connect Nina's computer to our system. I had worked out a whole plan on the boat, but now that I'm actually trying it..." Minnie groaned and buried her head in her arms.

"It's no small undertaking," Aspasia reassured her. "Don't be hard on yourself. You'll get it."

As the submarine deteriorated, the Cook family had scavenged their belongings to patch and repair. They used and reused everything; Aspasia had discovered a few patches made out of cans of processed meat, emptied, shaped, and hammered by hand. Minnie, who was becoming something of an expert in twenty-second-century technology, marveled that everything nonessential had been picked clean of parts. The parents' computers, handheld devices, and even the submarine's radio communications console had been cannibalized; they had no way of communicating with the outside world.

And yet Nina had a primitive but functioning computer loaded with educational software that would have been cutting-edge back in the early twenty-second century, and an engineering set and a chemistry kit and a digital piano. All of which were dusty and rusty and ancient by the time Aspasia's lab got to them, but Minnie assured her they were damaged only by age.

What were Alice and John educating their daughter for? She would never meet a French speaker. She would never get a job where chemistry or algebra might come in handy. No one would ever read her eccentrically punctuated short stories about mermaids in space.

"So," Stella began tentatively, interrupting Aspasia's thoughts. "Can I ask about the baby?" She was the most senior member of the lab, and it was natural she would be the boldest. Once she raised the subject, the other grad students clustered around.

They'd spent six months living on a boat together. Whatever gravitas she'd once had as their professor was long gone—and to be honest, it had never been much. They had cut each others' hair and applied sunblock to each others' backs; on one memorable occasion, she'd had to lance a boil on an unfortunate grad student's thigh.

She knew much more about her students' personal lives than she had ever intended to, and naturally, she had told them about her plans for a baby. It was what she was looking forward to after the excavation, after all. And she'd had so much downtime on the boat, away from civilization, plenty of time to brainstorm ideas for a mural to paint on the nursery wall (either charismatic megafauna or the Pyramids) or to make lists of names for boys and girls (Clarence and Wilma were her current frontrunners, but the lists were long).

"There's no baby yet," Aspasia sighed. "I haven't been able to make up my mind about the donor."

"Do you have a shortlist?" Stella asked.

A reasonable question. She hadn't made a list of candidates, hadn't even come up with a list of desirable criteria. Every profile she saw, she found herself imagining the baby that donor could produce.

This donor was a ballet dancer; their daughter would grow up willowy and strong, and Aspasia would make sure to let her try out whatever sports she liked, and maybe she'd end up being a dancer like her father, or maybe she'd be a scientist like her mother, or maybe both. That donor had the most devastating dimples she'd ever seen; their baby would have her wrapped around its little finger with every smile and would grow up charming and just a touch spoiled. And the next donor was a world traveler, never settled down in one spot for long; their son would love to accompany Aspasia on her archaeological expeditions, and she'd show him the world, and maybe once his wanderlust drove him as far as he could go, she'd be visiting her son on the lunar colony.

"I've gotten nowhere," she admitted. "I'm no closer than I was six months ago."

"We could help!" Minnie chirped, hopping up on the lab bench so she could see Aspasia's screen over her shoulder.

"We could choose the ideal donor for you," Stella agreed.

"How are we defining ideal, exactly?" Aspasia laughed.

Stella tapped her fingertip against her nose, thinking. "No family history of major health problems. Tall. Athletic. Attractive. Intelligent. That sounds fairly universal, doesn't it?" She lifted the screen from Aspasia's hands and started scrolling through. "Too short. Too tall. Funny nose. BRCA mutation carrier."

"No, but look," Aspasia protested, wrestling her screen back. "The short one's a theoretical physicist. The tall one's a professional cellist. The one with the nose was an Olympic silver medalist in curling. And the BRCA carrier—no, you're right, I ought to be careful about that."

"There are thousands of donors here. There have to be a couple who check all the boxes."

"It's not about checking boxes." Aspasia folded up her screen and smiled at her lab—who, although she might not agree with their strategy, had only the very sweetest intentions. "Come on, now, back to work; we shouldn't keep the past waiting."

❡

"I brought you some kelp," Aspasia explained, handing Octava the bundle. "Fresh from our dig site."

"Wonderful—I'll fry it up with some scrambled eggs tomorrow morning. Jim will love it." Octava ushered Aspasia into her lab. "Would you like to visit the gorillas?" she offered.

"I'd love to!"

Octava scanned her ID and pushed open the door to the gorilla habitat. It was a great big dome with a translucent cover almost like a greenhouse; inside, it was warm and humid, full of plants that could never have grown in Manhattan's climate. The groundcover was lush and green, but the trees were all still saplings; the habitat itself was only a few years old.

Inside, the gorillas raised their heads as they approached: massive, stocky animals, with intelligent eyes staring out of their wizened faces. There were just five of them, the first phase of Octava's attempt to restore a small population of eastern lowland gorillas, which had gone extinct in the late twenty-first century.

"They've gotten so big!" Aspasia marveled. She hadn't seen them in six months, and the male, in particular, was noticeably larger. "There's just the one male, right?"

"It's how they lived in the wild—at least according to twenty-first-century observers. We're afraid that if we introduced another male, Charlie would chase him off, and there'd be nowhere for him to go. I've got a request in with the city to expand the habitat whenever there's more reclaimed land available, but..." Octava shrugged. "The gorilla lobby isn't exactly high on the mayor's priority list."

A female lumbered over on her feet and knuckles, approaching Octava and her guest without apparent fear.

"This is Mary—our first successful clone," Octava explained. "She's the grande dame of the troop."

Aspasia didn't know what to do. For a moment she had the ridiculous impulse to shake the gorilla's hand.

"She's beautiful."

"Isn't she?" Octava gazed at the gorilla with evident maternal pride. "Once our next round of clones is born, we'll try giving the babies to the females, instead of hand-raising them ourselves. There's no guarantee it'll work, but we can hope."

"You're going to make more?"

"Let me show you."

Aspasia followed Octava through the thick plastic door leading out of the enclosure and back into the climate-controlled lab. A transparent wall at the rear of Octava's office showed a dimly lit room with a wall of amniotic bubbles, all empty.

"Our gestation chamber," Octava explained. "We'll start the new batch next week. I don't even want to *talk* about how long it took to get approval—people can be touchy about primate cloning." She poured a cup of herbal tea for Aspasia and one for herself. Then, sitting across from her, she leaned in with a sparkle in her eye. "Speaking of gestation... You mentioned you wanted to talk about the baby."

"I'm stuck, Octava," she admitted. "My lab offered to help me choose the right donor to grow a superbaby, but that's not really what I had in mind."

"What do you have in mind?"

Aspasia bit her lip, hesitating. How could she explain it out loud, even to Octava? That when she thought about the baby, she could see reality splitting apart into threads. Her future with Baby A, fussy and high-needs and waking up ten times a night, growing up into a sensitive and clingy and delightful child. Her future with Baby B, a good eater, always at the top of the growth charts, towering over her by the time he was twelve, teasing her by using her head as an armrest once he grew up to be a big healthy giant. Baby C, who would start talking early and never stop, who would play rhyming games, and make up knock-knock jokes, and drive her half-crazy with love and frustration.

"I don't know. There are so many options," she managed lamely.

"You can't optimize a baby, Aspasia."

"That's not what I'm trying to do." She shook her head. "I don't want the perfect baby. I just want the perfect baby *for me*."

"You're experiencing analysis paralysis," Octava diagnosed. "Like trying to order dinner off the world's longest restaurant menu."

"It's more important than dinner!"

"I know, which makes it worse." Octava shook her head fondly. "Historically, you know, humans didn't get to make these kinds of choices. They had to accept the roll of the dice with whatever genetic material they had on hand."

"I'm aware of how human reproduction works. Worked."

"I know. But sometimes it's worth reminding ourselves of the way things used to be. Human females lived and thrived even when they couldn't choose which baby they had, or even if they had a baby."

"You think I'm overthinking it?"

"No—just that maybe we aren't perfectly equipped to make choices like this. Mary, our gorilla, couldn't make a decision like this, and we're not so different from her."

"You and Jim—did you ever consider using donor material?"

"No, not seriously. You know, not that we're anything to brag about, genetically. I'm short and fat, and he's bald and flat-footed, and our family medical histories are a real mess. But I figure the genes from our short, fat, bald, flat-footed, asthmatic, diabetic ancestors made it this far. They can probably hold out for at least one more generation."

Octava's son, now eight, was indeed short and chubby and asthmatic. Aspasia liked to play cards with him at his parents' dinner parties. He was certainly never going to be a star athlete, but he was also the only eight-year-old she knew with an ammonite fossil collection.

"Do you mind if I lecture you a little?" Octava asked gently.

"Please, go ahead. I need all the wisdom I can get."

"It doesn't matter what donor you choose. It absolutely doesn't matter. Whatever child you get, you're going to love."

Aspasia frowned into her teacup. That much was true, at least; she'd lived with hundreds of imaginary babies, and had never questioned for an instant that she'd love each one of them. It didn't seem to obviate the need to choose, though.

"If you want someone to make the decision *for* you," Octava continued, "I can do that. I'll filter the database by any constraints you have, and then I'll write a little script to choose randomly. Once the decision is made, you'll feel better."

It was a generous offer. And a good idea, really. Octava had good judgment, and she and the clinic could ensure they chose a donor without any incompatibilities. She could even do it without showing Aspasia the chosen donor's profile so that the baby would continue to be a surprise as it grew.

So why was she still hesitating?

"I—that's very kind, but I'm not ready to decide yet."

"When's your appointment?" Octava asked, ever practical.

Aspasia didn't want to admit that it was in three days. She could postpone, of course; her own ova were time-sensitive, but she could always use donor ova in a year or five years or ten. But then, she had to consider that if she couldn't make up her mind after six months of agonizing, perhaps more time wasn't the answer.

"You'll figure it out," Octava murmured. She wasn't the type to mouth insincere platitudes, so it was almost heartening to hear that from her. She would figure it out.

⁂

Aspasia paced up and down the clinic's waiting room, which looked in on its gestation chambers: all glowing and full, with embryos floating around inside them like egg yolks. It was advertisement of a sort, she guessed, proof that their clinic really produced life.

She reached into her pocket and felt the polyethylene sample bag, the perfect cylinder of bone extracted from Nina's femur.

Her number was going to be called next.

She slipped out of the clinic and headed downtown to Octava's lab.

"I've made a decision," she announced, placing the polyethylene sample bag in the center of Octava's desk.

"What is that?" Octava asked, looking up from her screen and blinking.

"My child. An arbitrarily chosen child, out of the nearly infinite possible children available in the past and future."

Octava squinted. "...that's a bone sample. Twenty-first century, if I'm not mistaken?"

"Her name was Nina."

"Maybe you should clarify exactly what you're asking me here."

"I would like you to gestate a child using this genetic material. You're starting a new round of gorillas in just a few days, aren't you?"

"Are you kidding? This material is a hundred years old!"

"She was alive at the same time your gorillas were."

"Right, and my gorillas were the subject of a primitive but organized attempt at genetic preservation. We have dozens of tissue samples for each of our subjects, taken while the animals were alive, preserved in multiple ways. You have... a skeleton sample, a century old, no marrow or non-skeletal tissue left, no deliberate attempts at preservation. It'll be a miracle if this thing has enough intact DNA to work with, and—what am I talking about?" Octava shook her head. "The tissue preservation isn't the issue. Sorry, professional instinct. You're talking about *human cloning*."

"No—not in the general sense. I'm talking about choosing a genetic donor for my child."

"Don't play semantics with me, please. You're asking me to clone a human being. You do understand that's explicitly illegal *everywhere*?"

"For good reasons that don't apply in this case," Aspasia insisted. "I'm not attempting eugenics. I'm not experimenting on humans. I'm not doing anything that could affect society. I'm just... having a baby with the genetic material of my choice."

Octava shook her head, her lips pursed in wordless disapproval.

"Octava, how many human beings are currently alive?" Aspasia asked.

"Three billion, give or take a few hundred million. But you know that."

"Yeah. And how many are dead?"

"What, how many people have lived and died, throughout all history? Sorry, I don't know that off the top of my head. Do you?"

"Of course I do. I mean, estimated, because there's no good premodern data. About one hundred and twenty-five billion. Stunning, isn't it? The humans living today are less than three percent of the humans who have ever lived—a tiny, tiny minority. Why is our voice so much louder?"

Octava, her chin in hand, tilted her head slightly.

"It's strange to think of creating new life when so much life has already been lost—do you ever feel that way?" Aspasia pressed.

"Those are the rules of the game, Aspasia. You're talking about denying the very nature of biological life."

"Yeah. Isn't that your job?" Aspasia leaned in. "Eastern lowland gorillas ought to be extinct. But they're not. Those five animals in there died a hundred years ago, and they're also alive today."

"Excuse me. It's not as if I'm tampering with nature. Eastern lowland gorillas were an anthropogenic extinction. They died because of human activity."

"*So did Nina*," Aspasia insisted. "Why do people from the future deserve to live more than people from the past?"

"People from the past already had their chance to live."

"Not all of them." She was aware that she was losing her ability to debate this rationally, if she'd ever had it. Her approach to this was fundamentally unreasoned. It was just an understanding, all through her body, that Nina's death had been wrong, and that she was in a position now to give life to one person, and why shouldn't that person be Nina? "How is it fair that her island is underwater? Why, because our island had the money to build a seawall and hers didn't?"

"Are you going to clone *all* the twenty-second-century climate refugees?"

"I would if I could! Wouldn't you?"

"Aspasia," Octava sighed, rubbing her furrowed forehead. "You take things awfully literally." She was silent for a long time, and then she picked up the polyethylene bag. "You really want me to grow you a daughter in my lab?"

"Yes."

"You understand that she won't be exactly what she was, don't you? Even if the cloning process is successful, the epigenetic and developmental factors alone, not to mention her entire environment..."

"Of course I understand. I don't expect her to be what she was. I just want..."

How could she explain it? That the moment she'd considered it, the superposed futures had collapsed into themselves. The infinite array of babies with their infinite possibilities—Nina had infinite possibility too. If she hadn't been born where and when she had been born, she could have been a chemist, or a musician, or a writer, or an environmental engineer, or a welder, or an artist, or any number of things. Aspasia had seen it all in her schoolwork, her toys, her tiny skull.

Octava bit her lip, frowned at the desk, and then pocketed the polyethylene sample bag. "I'll see what I can do."

⁊

Early in the morning, just before dawn, Aspasia let herself into Octava's office. Octava had kindly added her university ID to the electronic lock so Aspasia could come and go freely; she was in the primate lab so often that she could identify all the grad students and gorillas by name.

Inside their habitat, the gorillas were snoring. Aspasia tiptoed past and entered the gestation chamber.

Six of the amniotic bubbles on the wall were full. As the sun rose, the bubbles began to glow, simulating the faint light that would penetrate a mother's uterus during the day. The fetuses inside were visible as dim shadows.

Although gorillas and humans had similar gestation periods, the human fetus was already a bit larger than the gorilla fetuses around her. The details of her conception were private, of course, but the whole lab knew they were expecting five gorillas and one human; Octava had explained to her graduate students that Aspasia wanted to gestate her child right there in the university, where she could visit her freely, not in a formal clinic restricted by business hours.

At twenty weeks, halfway through her planned gestation, Nina was about the size of a bell pepper. Aspasia could imagine holding her in her cupped palms.

Aspasia carefully flattened her hand against the flexible side of the amniotic bubble as it glowed brighter and brighter. Nina was visible in clear outline now: her curled legs, her perfect eyelids, the nubs of her ears. She had been moving around in the amniotic bubble for a few weeks already, and on that morning, Aspasia noticed for the first time that she had discovered her thumb.

She was going to be so curious, such a little explorer, Aspasia thought, and then she corrected herself. She had been; she already was; she was going to be—all at once.

*Hope*

*Curiosity*

*Joy*

*Love*

# *About the score*

Writing from emotion is one thing. Getting almost a score of authors to agree on what those emotions are is another. I went through half a dozen formulations before settling on what became the final score. Most were simply too complex – attempting to dictate what emotions would peak where, for example. Others relied too heavily on continuity of emotion from one story to the next. Later versions had too many gradations. On a spectrum from hope to despair, what's three quarters of hope? Half of despair? What's exactly in between the two? Even if we name it, will it mean the same thing to different people?

The final score, while still complex, is much simplified from early versions, and rightly so. It's built from six emotional groups, with four gradations of each – primary positive (e.g., Hope), secondary positive (Longing), secondary negative (Tension), primary negative (Despair).

- Hope/Longing/Tension/Despair
- Curiosity/Interest/Trepidation/Fear
- Awe/Respect/Detachment/Boredom
- Joy/Serenity/Sorrow/Misery
- Love/Friendship/Dislike/Hatred
- Lust/Fun/Disgust/Loathing

The stories are further gathered into two set – the Hope set (Hope, Curiosity, Awe) and the Joy set (Joy, Love, Lust).

Each story has just two core emotions – a major emotion, meant to be the emotional centerpiece of the story, and a minor emotion, as a 'harmony' or 'counterpoint' to the main emotion.

Writers were shown the full score, but were given just these two cues for their own story. A.C. Worth's "Homecoming" for example, was built on Joy (the positive end of the Joy-Misery range) and Longing (the mid-positive of the Hope-Despair range). That was it; authors could choose for themselves the theme, context, plot, setting, characters, etc. - so long as they evoked the key emotions.

The result was as varied as I hoped. The stories range from epic fantasy to hard SF to contemporary contemplative fiction. Taken together, though, they form a coherent, cohesive emotional theme.

There's a firm logic to the sequence of emotions in the anthology. There's an overall theme, which is Hope and Joy – the anthology starts with those notes (Joy+Longing and Hope+Serenity) and finishes with them (Hope+Joy) – and there are clear movements – sections of positive emotions, sections of negative.

To borrow and misuse musical terminology, the book is structured as follows:

**Overture** – Hope and Joy

**Hope triad** – Hope, Curiosity, and Awe

**Joy triad** – Joy, Love, and Lust

**Bridge** – a mix of positive and negative secondary emotions

**Joy triad (inversion)** – Loathing, Misery, and Hatred

**Hope triad (inversion)** – Boredom, Despair, and Fear

**Coda** – All the positive emotions, ending with Hope+Joy

As noted, there's a logic that defines the structure, but it's not rigid.

- **Overture** – each story has the primary positive emotion of Hope or Joy, and the secondary positive of the other.
- **Hope triad** – each story has the primary positive emotion of one of the Hope set, and the secondary positive emotion of the next in line. For example: Hope (primary positive of Hope) + Interest (secondary positive of Curiosity)
- **Joy triad** – similar for the Joy set, but the last story substitutes the secondary negative of Joy (Sorrow) for the secondary positive (Serenity)
- **Bridge** – all the secondary emotions: positive from the Hope set, negative from the Joy set.
- **Joy triad (inversion)** – each story has the primary negative emotion of one of the Joy set, and the secondary negative emotion of the next in line. For example: Loathing (primary negative of Lust) + Sorrow (secondary negative of Joy). However, the last story substitutes the secondary positive of Lust (Fun) for the secondary negative (Disgust).
- **Hope triad (inversion)** – similar for the Hope set, but with only negative emotions.
- **Coda** – all the primary positive emotions; one from each set per story.

In graphic form, it looks somewhat like this (where darker colors signify darker emotions):

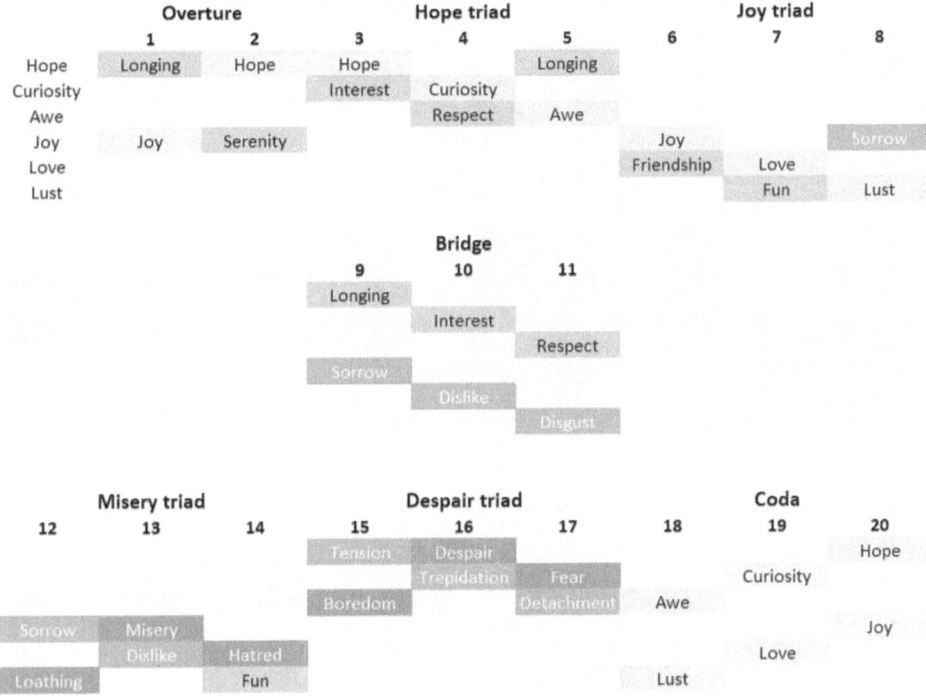

That all sounds fairly technical, and there was certainly technique to it, but the overriding goal throughout was an interesting read. I admit to it being fun to construct, but the main thing was to make it fun to read, and I hope we've succeeded there.

Morris Allen

# Copyright

Authors also retain copyrights to all other material in the anthology.

## Metaphorosis Publishing

Metaphorosis offers beautifully written science fiction and fantasy. Our projects include:

### Metaphorosis Magazine

*Metaphorosis* is a weekly magazine of SFF short stories, including work from all the authors in this anthology. Find out more at magazine.metaphorosis.com, and sign up to be notified of new stories weekly.

# Metaphorosis Books

Recent books from Metaphorosis can be found at books.metaphorosis.com, and include:

### Score

*an SFF symphony*

What if stories were written like music? *Score* is an anthology of varied stories arranged to follow an emotional score from the heights of joy to the depths of despair – but always with a little hope shining through.

### Best Vegan SFF of 2018

The best vegan science fiction and fantasy stories of 2018!

### Metaphorosis 2018

*All* the stories from *Metaphorosis* magazine's third year. Fifty-two great SFF stories.

### Metaphorosis: Best of 2018

The best science fiction and fantasy stories from *Metaphorosis* magazine's third year.

### Metaphorosis 2017

*All* the stories from *Metaphorosis* magazine's second year. Fifty-three great SFF stories.

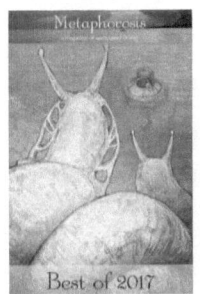

### Metaphorosis: Best of 2017

The best science fiction and fantasy stories from *Metaphorosis* magazine's *second* year.

### Metaphorosis 2016

*Almost* all the stories from *Metaphorosis* magazine's first year.

### Metaphorosis: Best of 2016

The best science fiction and fantasy stories from *Metaphorosis* magazine's first year.

**Reading 5X5**

*Five stories, five times*

Twenty-five SFF authors, five base stories, five versions of each – see how different writers take on the same material, with stories in contemporary and high fantasy, soft and hard SF, and a mysterious 'other' category.

**Reading 5X5**

*Writers' Edition*

All the stories from the regular, readers' edition, plus two extra stories, the story seed, and authors' notes on writing. Over 100 pages of additional material specifically aimed at writers.

**Best Vegan SFF of 2017**

The best vegan science fiction and fantasy stories of 2017!

**Best Vegan SFF of 2016**

The best vegan science fiction and fantasy stories of 2016!

**Susurrus**

A darkly romantic story of magic, love, and suffering.

www.ingramcontent.com/pod-product-compliance
Lightning Source LLC
Chambersburg PA
CBHW031619100726
47898CB00006B/1856